THE
PHANTOM
PATROL

THE PHANTOM PATROL

A Billy Boyle World War II Mystery

James R. Benn

Published by Soho Press, Inc.
227 W 17th Street
New York, NY 10011

Library of Congress Cataloging-in-Publication Data

Names: Benn, James R., author.
Title: The phantom patrol / James R. Benn.
Description: New York, NY : Soho Crime, 2024. | Series: The Billy Boyle
WWII mysteries ; 19
Identifiers: LCCN 2024003784

ISBN 978-1-64129-543-7
eISBN 978-1-64129-544-4

Subjects: LCSH: Boyle, Billy (Fictitious character)—Fiction. | LCGFT:
Detective and mystery fiction. | War fiction. | Novels.
Classification: LCC PS3602.E6644 P43 2024 | DDC 813/.6—dc23/eng/20240202
LC record available at https://lccn.loc.gov/2024003784

Map 70 of Northwestern Europe, 1944 courtesy of
the US Army Center for Military History

Printed in the United States of America

10 9 8 7 6 5 4 3 2 1

For Debbie

A heaven on earth I have won by wooing thee.
—William Shakespeare, *All's Well That Ends Well*, act 4, scene 2

Don't let any civilian leave you, when the story's over, with any comfortable lies. Shoot down all the lies. Don't let Vincent's girl think that Vincent asked for a cigarette before he died. Don't let her think he grinned gamely, or said a few choice last words. These things didn't happen.

—J. D. Salinger, "The Stranger," 1945

THE
PHANTOM
PATROL

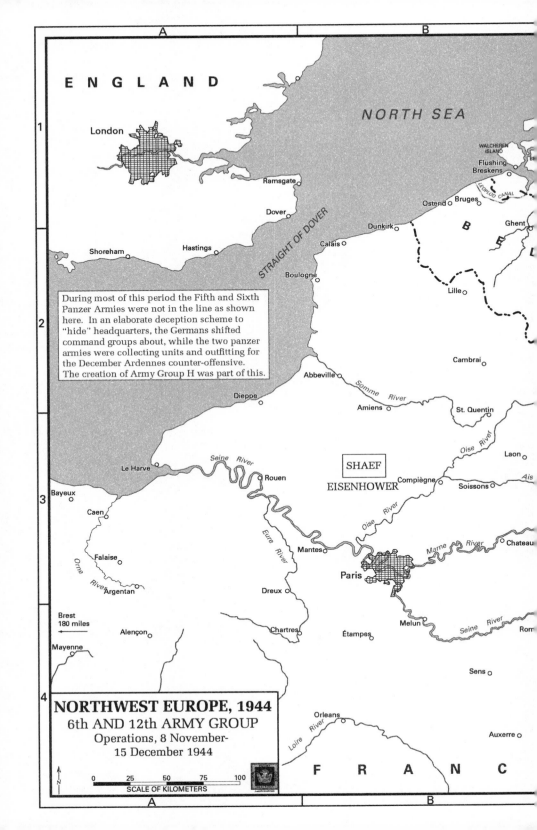

ENGLAND

NORTH SEA

London

Ramsgate

Dover

Shoreham   Hastings

WALCHEREN
ISLAND

Flushing
Breskens

LEOPOLD CANAL

Ostend   Bruges

Ghent

Dunkirk   B

Calais

Boulogne   Lille

During most of this period the Fifth and Sixth
Panzer Armies were not in the line as shown
here. In an elaborate deception scheme to
"hide" headquarters, the Germans shifted
command groups about, while the two panzer
armies were collecting units and outfitting for
the December Ardennes counter-offensive.
The creation of Army Group H was part of this.

Cambrai

Abbeville   Somme   River

Dieppe   Amiens   St. Quentin

Oise   River

Laon

Ais

Le Harve   Seine   River

SHAEF
EISENHOWER

Rouen   Compiègne   Soissons

Bayeux   Oise   River

Caen   Marne   River   Chateau

Falaise   Eure River   Mantes

Orne   Paris

River Argentan   Dreux

Brest
180 miles

Alençon   Chartres   Melun   Seine   River

Mayenne   Étampes   Rom

Sens

NORTHWEST EUROPE, 1944
6th AND 12th ARMY GROUP
Operations, 8 November-
15 December 1944

Orleans

Loire   River   Auxerre

0   25   50   75   100
SCALE OF KILOMETERS

F R A N C

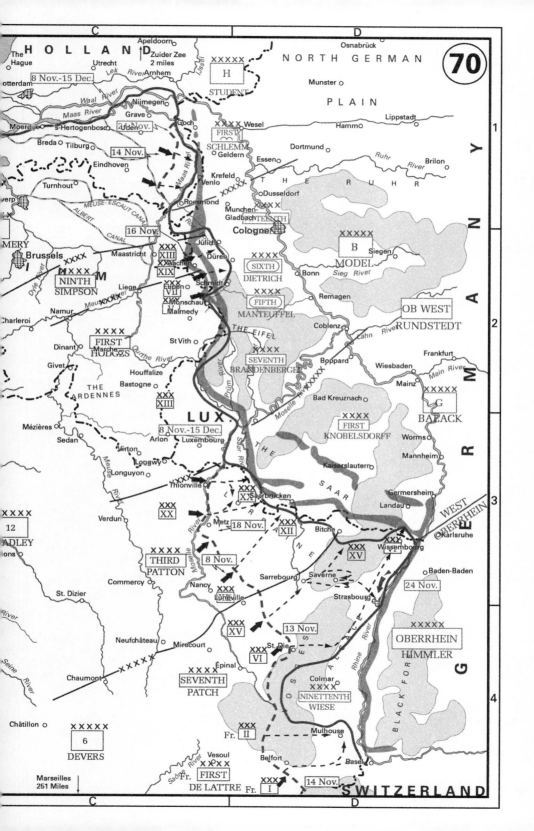

CHAPTER ONE

Paris, December 13, 1944

THE NIGHT WAS cold, cloaked in a deep darkness brought on by a bank of clouds sailing in on the winds and vanquishing the moonlight. Dead leaves, crisp and brittle, swirled in man-sized cyclones on the cobblestones, one so dense that I mistook it for someone sauntering through the graveyard.

But no one was strolling through the Père Lachaise at this hour. I knew that for a fact, having been here lying in wait for the last five hours. Standing in wait, as a matter of fact, with only Marcel Proust for company. He didn't have much to say, being six feet under. I had a small cemetery chapel to lean against. But that didn't stop my legs from cramping up, and not for the first time, I sat on Marcel's cold tombstone, offering up my apologies for the disrespect.

I heard a scrunching sound, maybe leaves being crushed underfoot. Or the wind, sending leaves skittering against a wall.

Scritttch. The sound drew nearer.

I squinted, trying to locate where the noise came from. Somewhere along the path, close to where Kaz was hiding. I couldn't see him, but we'd been through enough that I trusted he was right where he needed to be.

I spotted it. A large leaf, its curled lobes arched downward, its stem pointed upward like the tail of some gruesome insect dancing down the cobblestones. I almost laughed. Spooked by a dead leaf. I checked the luminous dial on my watch. A little past four in the morning. We'd expected them at one o'clock, or oh-one-hundred, the way the army liked to say it. I began to think about giving the whole thing up. Blame it on bad intelligence, but it seemed to me that the Syndicat du Renard was not coming out tonight.

I thought about slinking back through the tombstones and monuments to where Kaz was hidden near the grave of Oscar Wilde. The Père Lachaise Cemetery, all eighty acres of it, was a ritzy final resting place for the rich and famous, as well as regular Parisians who were lucky enough to get in. We were here with a team of Counter Intelligence Corps agents, waiting for a gang that aimed to do a little grave robbing. Or so we'd been told.

I stretched, trying not to stiffen up. I moved around the tiny chapel, watching for any sign of movement before I headed in Kaz's direction.

Then I heard the footsteps. The fall of a bootheel on gravel. Silence.

A sliver of light, quickly extinguished.

I froze, listening for another sound. It was impossible to see any distance through the crowded grave markers, crypts, and mausoleums, but from what I could make out, the light and sound had come from behind me, deep within the cemetery.

Had they already gotten in? We had the entrances covered. Two CIC agents were at the rue des Rondeaux gate, thirty yards in the other direction. Our source had said they'd use that entrance, but I guess his dope didn't extend to their arrival time.

I took off a glove and unholstered my Colt, stepping over graves and catching the slightest of sounds, probably much like the noise I was making. I stopped beside a tree, about halfway to Kaz's location. I edged around the trunk and saw a mausoleum, not six feet in front of me. The thick wooden door was open.

They'd been inside the cemetery all night. Before we got here.

Patient bastards.

I heard the clink of metal on wood. The sound of tools being carried.

I followed the sound, which was headed for Kaz's position. There was no way our guys outside or even the two agents at the gate had heard, and I could only hope Kaz had picked up on the clatter.

The wind kicked up, swirling leaves again and making enough noise for me to barrel around a couple of tombs and make my way to the path. That's when I saw them, four guys gathered around a flat gravestone. They were blurs, the darkness too complete to make an identification. Which was why we had CIC special agent Jerome Salinger with us. He'd interrogated a few men who were suspected of black market activities but had been let go for lack of evidence. Later they were found to have links to a syndicate run by an unknown character known only as the Fox.

We were hoping the Fox would turn out to be one of the men Salinger had interrogated, or that one of his men could be convinced to turn against him. We wanted an identification badly. The Fox had been responsible for the assassination of a CIC agent who'd gotten too close. Which is why we'd laid this trap. The syndicate might think they'd outwaited us, but we still had the place surrounded.

I heard the brush of fabric against stone.

A hand gripped my shoulder.

"Billy," came the whisper. It was Kaz, light on his feet and his Webley revolver at the ready.

"They've been inside all along," I said softly, leaning close.

"Yes. They failed to extinguish their light when they opened the mausoleum. I saw it out of the corner of my eye. What shall we do?"

I knew Kaz would be up for a fight. The only question was, how to make sure we won it.

"Let's take them," I said.

The scrape of stone on stone told us they'd gotten to work with a pry bar.

"We could wait for them to remove whatever they are after," Kaz said.

"Or grab them while they're busy with the stone," I said.

"Good," he whispered. "Let us announce ourselves with a gunshot. That will bring the others running."

I nodded and squeezed his arm. We stepped onto the path, each of us automatically keeping to one side, maximizing the space between us. The figures ahead and to the right hadn't noticed us yet, which told me they'd expected us to be gone.

Or, that waiting for hours was their regular routine. A routine of extraordinary patience and caution. I didn't like it.

But it was too late for second thoughts. Kaz raised his pistol as I leveled my automatic at the men clustered together over the grave.

"Halt!" I shouted. Kaz fired, the discharge shattering the still night.

Two shots came at us, and we each dove for the cover of the nearest stonework. It looked like only one man had fired, probably a lookout who was at the ready. But the burst from a Sten gun announced they'd come loaded for bear.

Or for us.

I fired at the afterimage of the muzzle flash, then ducked as another burst slammed into the mausoleum. Kaz let off two more shots and I backed up, taking cover behind a tree as a gunman fired into the position I'd just vacated. I didn't have a clear shot at him, but as I scrambled between the graves, I realized these guys must be soldiers. Deserters, probably, but they knew to outflank an opponent after keeping him pinned down. I got behind them and heard frantic shouts in French coming from farther down the path.

More of them? Maybe. But I didn't have time to count. I rose from behind a tomb and fired once, twice, aiming for the moving bodies coming my way. One guy grunted and went down. I instinctively ducked, expecting return fire. There was one shot, then nothing.

"They're running," Kaz shouted. "Get clear!"

Now I really had a bad feeling.

I went back the way I'd come and saw two figures moving down the path. Our CIC agents.

"Take cover!" I shouted. I heard Kaz yelling at the reinforcements coming from the other direction, sending them after the retreating gunmen.

Then the explosion. It came from just over the wall, a blast followed by the *whomp* of exploding fuel. A truckload of it, by the size of the fireball.

The next explosion was different. A sharp *crack* and a small, bright flash came out of the open grave. Not enough to do a lot of damage, unless you were standing over it. Which is what I would have been doing if Kaz hadn't given the warning.

I walked up to the smoldering tomb as flashlight beams and the tread of boots drew closer.

"Did they get away?" Special Agent Salinger asked, skidding to a halt and playing his flashlight over the grave. It was empty, except for drifting smoke, shreds of burnt canvas, and scorch marks.

"One of them didn't," I said, pointing to where I knew one man went down. Salinger went to inspect the corpse as Kaz returned, shaking his head.

"They're gone," he said. "Up and over the wall, I suspect. The burning truck drew everyone's attention."

"Obviously part of the plan," I said.

"Hey, Captain Boyle," Salinger said. "I wish you hadn't plugged that guy. We could have interrogated him."

"There was a lot of shooting," I said. "I thought asking nicely wouldn't be very effective."

"What do you mean?" Kaz asked Salinger as he eyed the corpse.

"He'd taken a slug in the side," Salinger said. "A bad wound, but not fatal. So why the bullet to the head?"

"I did fire twice," I said. "But I think I only hit him once. I heard him grunt when he went down."

"It was up close, right between the eyes," Salinger said. "There's a tattoo of unburned powder. Looks like a small caliber weapon. That wasn't you?"

"Nope. I wasn't that close, and my .45 doesn't qualify as small caliber. But I did hear another shot. I thought it was aimed at me," I said.

"Excellent planning and a ruthless approach," Kaz said. "Who are we dealing with here?"

"And what the hell was in that grave?" I asked.

CHAPTER TWO

MILITARY POLICE AND more CIC agents swarmed into the cemetery from their posts by the entrances, drawn by the explosions and curiosity now that something had finally happened.

"No one was hurt when the truck went up," Colonel Harding said, shining his flashlight into the empty grave. Sam Harding was my boss at Supreme Headquarters, Allied Expeditionary Force. He headed up the Office of Special Investigations and the brass had decided we were the right outfit to tackle the Syndicat du Renard, a criminal gang headed by a mysterious character nicknamed the Fox.

They might have been wrong.

"Stop!" I shouted to the gathering GIs. "This is a crime scene. Get out onto the streets and find out if anyone saw these guys go over the wall."

"And be careful," Kaz said. "They killed one of their own rather than leave him wounded. Search any vehicle you see. Go!"

Kaz—Lieutenant Piotr Augustus Kazimierz—was small and wiry, but he spoke with enough authority to get everyone's attention. The fact that he still held his Webley in one hand and bore a scar that split his face from cheek to jaw granted him a certain power that went beyond his lieutenant's bars and British Army uniform with the POLAND shoulder flash. We'd been together since I arrived in England back in '42. My first impression had been one of a bespectacled academic, and it didn't take long to discover there was a whole lot more to the man. People who didn't get beyond that first impression usually came to regret it. We'd had a bit of leave in England, and this was our first assignment after what was supposed to have been a rest in a quiet little village.

"Come on, let's get organized," Sergeant Salinger said to his fellow agents. They each grabbed a few MPs and headed to the various exits. It was a long shot, but I knew it was better than letting them trample over any clues that might have been left.

"Show me where they were hidden," Harding said.

"You're going to love this," I said, leading Harding to the mausoleum. One of the CIC agents had left the door open and a lantern inside. A soft yellow light glowed from within. Harding went first, ducking as he entered. The narrow space was empty. The rough image of a sitting fox adorned one wall. A few lines of charcoal on stone. An upswept tail around its paws, the head in profile with sharply pointed ears.

"Looks like Renard is taunting us," Harding said. "Nothing else?"

"The place is clean, Colonel," I said, sweeping my flashlight over the floor. The space was tiny. "Just a bench."

"Where's the coffin?" Harding asked.

"This is a cenotaph, Colonel," Kaz said. "An empty tomb. A memorial to three brothers killed in the last war."

Harding sighed, then went silent. He'd been in the Great War and knew that so many of those killed were lost forever to artillery explosions in the muddy trenches.

"Get someone to scrub that wall clean," Harding said, pointing to the charcoal sketch. "Then meet me at the Trianon. This is getting out of hand."

THE SUN WAS hardly up by the time we made the ten-mile drive to Versailles, west of Paris. It was almost winter, and in these last weeks of autumn the days had grown shorter. The sun arrived reluctantly and departed in the afternoon like a barfly skipping out on his tab. The streets were empty of civilian traffic. Resources such as fuel, electricity, and food were in short supply and buildings were still pockmarked from gunfire exchanged during the Liberation, but this was Paris, and even in the gloom the city held the golden promise of light and joy.

Salinger was in the back seat of the jeep, leaning forward to chat with Kaz in what sounded like fluent French. I was too tired to pick up anything. Besides, the little French I knew came from collaring French Canadians for weekend bar fights back in Boston, and that sounded nothing like what these two were spouting. I'd been a young cop back then, but now I was a few years older, wearing khaki instead of blue, and still unable to parlez-vous the français.

We stopped at the ornate gate to the Palace of Versailles, where I flashed my ID at the MP. He waved us through, and we entered the great cobblestoned courtyard, then headed to the Trianon Palace Hotel. That's where Colonel Harding had his office, as did General Eisenhower and a whole boatload of SHAEF staff. The Trianon was a long, narrow five-story building of gleaming white stonework, usually with a few staff cars flying generals' pennants lined up in the drive. But it was too early for visiting brass. Right about now they were being roused out of bed in any of the dozens of hotels SHAEF had requisitioned throughout Paris and served hot coffee in porcelain cups. Two hundred and fifty miles to the east, GIs were waking up in foxholes and mixing instant java in their mess kits and praying for a change of socks, so I wasn't about to complain about duty in the City of Light.

"Billy," Kaz said, as I parked the jeep. "Sergeant Salinger is friends with Ernest Hemingway, did you know that?"

"Small world," I said, catching a glimpse of playfulness in Kaz's eyes. "How do you know Hemingway, Sergeant?"

"I looked him up when I was stationed here, after the Liberation," Salinger said. "We had a few drinks and talked about writing."

"You must write fiction if you're saying you had a *few* drinks with Hemingway," I said as we walked inside. "A few bottles is more his style."

"I've had one of my short stories published," Salinger said, looking away as if he was embarrassed to admit it. "And I almost made it into *The New Yorker* in 1941. But after Pearl Harbor, the editor said the story didn't fit the times. It was about a disaffected kid worried about the possibility of war."

"They probably wanted something more heroic," I said. Never having read *The New Yorker*, I had no idea, but it seemed a safe bet.

"I'll try again when the war's over," Salinger said. "But at least I got to know Hemingway. He's a terrific writer. You've met him?"

"Yeah, just before the Liberation," I said. "He was running around the countryside with his own private army at the time. Bigger than life." It seemed Salinger thought a lot of Hemingway, and I saw no reason to say anything bad about the guy. "Did he help you out?"

"Yes, he read some of my stuff," Salinger said. "I try to work on a few things when it gets quiet."

"Where're you stationed now?" I asked as we took to the stairs off the main lobby.

"With the 4th Division. Stuck in the Hürtgen Forest," he said.

"You must not mind a trip to Paris, then," Kaz said. The Hürtgen was a meat grinder. Dense forest in rough terrain, it had chewed up thousands of soldiers over the last few weeks.

"Well, Ernie is up there too, covering the fight for *Collier's*. I wouldn't mind getting back to see him," Salinger said.

"That must have been some damn good advice he doled out, Sergeant," I said as I opened the door to Harding's office at the end of the hall. "Most guys would prefer Paris to a foxhole, even one with Ernest Hemingway in it."

"If I live through this war, I aim on making it as a writer," Salinger said. "It wouldn't hurt to have Ernest Hemingway in my corner."

"Well?" Harding snapped as soon as the door shut behind us. He was seated at his desk, leafing through papers and looking none too pleased with the reading material.

"The search didn't turn up anything, Colonel," Salinger said. "The truck was an old prewar job, probably stolen. Might be worth asking the French police to look into it, but I doubt they'd find anything useful."

Harding told us to take a seat at the conference table while he made a call to have coffee brought in. Both things were the highlight of my day so far. A map of Paris was laid out on the table, marked with all the positions we'd taken to watch the cemetery. Salinger shed his jacket and leaned against the table, studying the map while slowly shaking his head. His khaki uniform was notable for the absence of any rank or unit markings.

"We planned for everything," Kaz said. "Except for the Fox to be waiting before we got there."

"We should check into the truck, and also the guy who tipped you off," Harding said, sitting at the head of the table. "You got a line on him?"

"I have his last known address," Salinger said. "He was an informant for Agent Phil Williamson. My guess is he didn't like his paymaster getting bumped off and took his revenge by ratting out this operation."

Williamson was the CIC agent who'd been killed, rubbed out by the Syndicat du Renard. The hit was both brazen and professional. Two shots from a silenced pistol, on the street in broad daylight. No one saw a thing, which was probably the healthiest approach.

"These men are disciplined," Kaz said. "They don't act like common thieves."

"I think we might be dealing with a combination of military

men and organized crime," Harding said. I yawned, nodding my head to keep from dozing off. The door opened and a GI rolled in a cart with a big pot of coffee. We all focused on the stimulating sips of hot joe for a few minutes until Salinger set down his mug.

"It could be the Traction Avant gang," he said. "That's who we were investigating when I was here, and it's possible they're behind the Syndicat du Renard."

"A gang named after a car?" Harding asked.

"Their preferred getaway vehicle," Salinger said. "The front-wheel drive Citroën Traction Avant. They organized themselves after the Liberation. Mostly professional criminals who'd fought with the Resistance, fascist militiamen now gone underground, and policemen who've been kicked off the force."

"Sounds like they'd fit the bill," Harding said. "You get anywhere with your investigation?"

"There was damn little cooperation, Colonel," Salinger said. "The police in Paris don't like talking about their corrupt brethren, and no one wants to suggest that a criminal element comprised part of the Resistance. Or worse, that they've now made common cause with ex-Vichy fascists."

"It makes sense that the French authorities would not want to cooperate if it meant revealing such an embarrassment," Kaz said, the warm cup cradled in his hands. "It does not fit with the image General de Gaulle is cultivating for his provisional government. Corrupt police, crooked partisans, and former fascists cannot exist in his vision of a revitalized France."

"I can understand that," I said as the caffeine jolted me awake. "I bet the Paris police would take the desecration of the Père Lachaise Cemetery as an affront to their national honor. The place is a monument to French culture."

I noticed Kaz raise an eyebrow. It took a lot to impress him, but it looked like my notion had.

"That's an excellent approach, Boyle," Harding said, with more surprise in his voice than was necessary. I was glad Salinger didn't know me well enough to join in. "Get over to the Paris police and see Commissaire Marcel Rochet. He's the guy who refused to cooperate with the investigation in the first place. I got the sense his hands were tied, but maybe the bomb changes things. Rochet is with the Police Judiciaire Criminal Brigade."

"La Crim, as the locals call it," Kaz told us.

"I can check on the snitch," Salinger said. "Jacques Delair. Last known address was a room above a bar in Montmartre."

"Okay," Harding said. "Why don't the three of you meet up this afternoon and drive out to the 203rd General Hospital. It's in Saint-Cloud, just west of Paris. That's where they're performing the autopsy. Ask for Captain David Jacobs, Medical Corps, and see if the body has anything to say."

"Anything else, Colonel?" Salinger asked.

"Yes. Grab a couple of hours' sleep and then think about what could have been hidden in that grave," Harding said, struggling mightily to keep a yawn in check. "We'll meet back here at eighteen hundred hours."

Six o'clock. I was so tired I had to count on my fingers to be sure.

CHAPTER THREE

SLEEP SOUNDED SWELL, but food was foremost. Kaz, Salinger, and I feasted on scrambled eggs and hot rolls in the Trianon dining room. The eggs were fresh, a rarity even at an army headquarters. Of course, this HQ was right next door to Marie Antoinette's Versailles playground, so we were in the high-rent district.

"Where are you quartered?" I asked Salinger as I finished another cup of joe.

"Here in Versailles," he said. "A pension on the rue de Provence. A drab little rooming house. I was hoping for something in Paris."

"General Eisenhower has been working to keep Paris from being overrun by headquarters men," Kaz said, dabbing at his lips with a linen napkin. "Parisians are already complaining that the Americans outnumber the previous occupiers and are requisitioning all the best buildings."

"When I was here right after the Liberation, everyone loved the Yanks," Salinger said. "But some of the rear area guys had a notion to get rich by pilfering supplies and selling them for top dollar. It was all small-time stuff at first, nothing like the Syndicat, but it soured a lot of Parisians on us."

"The general declared Paris off-limits except for official business and GIs on leave," I said. "It helped some."

"What he hasn't managed to stop is the influx of SHAEF

personnel," Kaz said. "It's a huge operation—so large that the French have decided the initials really stand for *la Société des Hôteliers Américains en France.*"

"I haven't heard that one," Salinger said, laughing as he rubbed the dark stubble on his chin. He had a long face, heavy dark eyebrows, and a bit of a mustache that almost worked to make him look older. I guessed he was in his midtwenties.

"How do you get on with senior officers when you're running an investigation?" I asked, curious about how a younger guy with no visible rank could get older officers to pay attention, much less answer his questions.

"It's easier not displaying rank. All we have are these," Salinger said, tapping his US brass collar insignia. "We're mainly noncommissioned officers, and keeping people in the dark about our rank makes things easier. We operate in plain clothes as well, but not near the front."

"What do you say when a colonel or a general tells you to beat it?" I asked.

"I inform him that while I can't divulge my rank, at that moment the investigation places me one grade above his," Salinger said. "That gets their attention."

"Parfait," Kaz said, and the two of them went back to chatting in French. I liked the CIC approach, and it was nice to know we had a Get Out of Jail Free card if we needed to play it.

We all ran out of steam at the same time. Outside the Trianon, the sky was a crisp blue, the sun brightening above the eastern horizon. Kaz and I were staying at the Hotel Royale, and everyone planned to rendezvous there at one o'clock for a spot of lunch before heading off for the autopsy.

A light lunch, that is.

The Hotel Royale was a small hotel on a busy street, surrounded by shops and apartment buildings. Nothing fancy, but we had a room with two soft beds overlooking a small park. The trees were bare, the only vehicles were military, and the sidewalk cafés were closed for the winter, but as soon as my head hit the pillow none of that mattered.

A few hours later, I'd ditched my fatigues, washed up, and put on my Class A uniform for a visit to the 36 quai des Orfèvres, home of the Police Judiciaire Criminal Brigade. In the open jeep, the wind whipped my face, slapping away any further thoughts of sleep. La Crim. Kaz had managed to wake before me, appearing clean-shaven, refreshed, and alert in his sharply creased British Army uniform. Times like this, I thought he had a butler stashed away somewhere.

"How do you want to play it with Rochet?" I asked as we crossed into Paris on the boulevard Saint-Michel. "Harding thinks he might be sympathetic now."

"He must know of the damage to the cemetery," Kaz said. "I'd say we appeal for assistance in bringing the perpetrators to justice."

"Maybe focus on Americans in the Syndicat du Renard? Drop a hint that the ringleader is a Yank?" I said as we passed the Luxembourg Gardens, some of the trees shattered from the heavy fighting back in August.

"That could backfire," Kaz said. "We should assume Commissaire Marcel Rochet knows more than he admits. Certainly, he is aware of the various factions in the Syndicat. Possibly the leader."

"A straight-out plea for help, then," I said.

"One policeman to another," Kaz said. "We also have an interesting puzzle to present him."

"What was in the grave, and why was it worth killing one of their own?"

"Any decent detective would be intrigued," Kaz said. "Let us hope Rochet is possessed of both curiosity and decency."

Those were open questions. I had no idea about Rochet's background or how he'd spent the Occupation. Was he one of the enthusiastic planners of the 1942 roundup of Jews? The

French police had done the Nazis' dirty work for them, taking
thousands of Jewish people from their homes in a citywide raid.
Some cops had carried out their orders reluctantly, while a few
managed to look the other way and give people a chance to
escape. Then there were those who were enthusiastic, even going
so far as to bring in fascist militiamen to help.

I had no idea which group Rochet belonged to.

We crossed a bridge to the Île de la Cité, a small island in the
Seine, famous for the Notre Dame Cathedral and a host of fancy
government buildings, including the Prefecture of Police, and
one block away, the headquarters of the Police Judiciaire. Both
had riverfront views worth a million bucks. It was nothing like
my old Boston PD headquarters, a good half mile from the
Charles River and nowhere near as ornate.

"You ever read any of the Inspector Maigret novels?" I asked
as I parked the jeep.

"No, I have not," Kaz said. "Although Georges Simenon seems
to be quite prolific. It should be an easy matter to pick one up.
Do you enjoy them?"

"I do," I said, opening the door for Kaz. "This is where he
works."

"In the novels," Kaz said, a half-smile flitting across his face.
I'd gotten used to Kaz's smiles looking slightly crooked. His scar
had the habit of getting in the way of a good grin.

"I'll try to remember," I said, giving Kaz a gentle nudge with
my elbow. "Just don't tell me Hercule Poirot isn't real. Think we'll
run into him?"

"He is Belgian," Kaz said as we neared the desk in the lobby.

"So is Simenon," I said. "I wonder if they know each other?"
It must have been the lack of sleep, but I thought that was
hilarious. Kaz said nothing, but the desk sergeant must've heard
mention of Simenon and rolled his eyes, perhaps thinking we
were literary tourists. The French cop had about ten years on me,
not to mention thirty pounds.

"Commissaire Marcel Rochet," I said. "S'il vous plaît."

"Pourquoi?" He sighed, puffing out his chubby cheeks and looking at me with tired, dark eyes. I understood he wanted to know why, but I looked to Kaz for a coherent answer. He snapped off a few forceful lines that included mention of the cemetery. Kaz's fluency and commanding tone got the sergeant's full attention. He made a telephone call and directed us to Rochet's office, two flights up.

"We may see Inspector Fayard, the commissaire's assistant," Kaz said as we hustled up the marble stairs. "Rochet has been called out to a murder scene."

"Maybe Fayard can give us some sense of Rochet's interest in the investigation," I said. The hallway was thick with officers in dark blue uniforms and plainclothesmen, along with a smattering of secretaries weighed down with stacks of files. The third door down had Rochet's name above it. Kaz gave a sharp knock on the polished woodwork and opened it.

The room was small, four desks crammed together in the middle. File cabinets lined two walls, and another was filled with a detailed street map of Paris. A door led to what I guessed was Rochet's private office. A classic layout for a team of detectives, right down to the one guy left to mind the fort while the others took the homicide call.

"Inspector Louis Fayard," Fayard said, standing to greet us. "How may I help you?"

I introduced Kaz and myself, and complimented Fayard on his English.

"The commissaire is often assigned cases involving English and American soldiers," Fayard said. "He wants his men to have the necessary language skills. Please sit and tell me what brings you here."

We arranged ourselves at the vacant desks as Fayard took a pack of Gauloises from his pocket, offered them around, then lit up. I put his age at thirty or so. Thick brown hair and piercing hazel eyes contrasted with a nose that had been broken, maybe twice, giving him a distinctive profile.

"You are aware of the events at the Père Lachaise Cemetery last night," Kaz said.

"I am," Fayard said, offering nothing but blue smoke.

"My superior officer had requested assistance from the commissaire but was turned down," I said. "In light of the desecration of this shrine to French culture, we wondered if he might reconsider."

"The Syndicat du Renard does not exist," Fayard said.

"Counter Intelligence Corps agent Williamson would beg to differ," I said. "If he could. I wounded one of the Syndicat's men last night. They put a bullet in his head rather than leave him alive, and he was one of their own. The Fox is real."

"Of course. I am only relaying what the men upstairs have informed us of," Fayard said, jabbing at the ceiling with his cigarette. Ashes fell onto his sleeve, and he shook them off. "You have heard me say this, yes?"

"Yes, and we understand," Kaz said. I nodded my agreement.

"We are hunting the Syndicat as well," Fayard said. "Our orders are to eliminate them as a threat."

"As a criminal and a political threat," I said.

"Exactly, my friend. The politicians do not wish it to be known that these factions are now working together. Fascists, disgraced flics, resistants, and deserters," Fayard said. "Deserters from all sides."

"Germans?" Kaz asked.

"Yes. The Boche are brutal but not all are stupid. Some stayed behind to save themselves. I know many feared being sent to the Russian front. With money, they hope to disappear before the reckoning comes," Fayard said. "We can share information, but we cannot be seen to cooperate. The Syndicat is an embarrassment to the bosses above my bosses."

"I wish we had something to share," I said. "We had an

informant tell us about a pickup at the cemetery, but we had no idea what it was."

"Or that they were there before us," Kaz said. "Long before."

"We also have no idea what they had hidden there," Fayard said. "People have begun to hear stories about the Fox, and they know to keep their mouths shut."

"We're going to the autopsy of the gang member who was killed," I said. "We'll let you know if we learn anything."

"You can leave a message for us at the Trianon Palace Hotel," Kaz said, writing down Colonel Harding's name and telephone extension. "I assume Commissaire Rochet feels as you do?"

"I trust he does, and I shall inform him of our meeting as soon as he returns from Montmartre," Fayard said, pocketing the note.

"American, British, or French?" I asked.

"The victim is French," Fayard said. "The suspect is American. He was discovered by a flic who was told of a struggle upstairs by a bar owner. He found the soldier searching the room with the corpse still warm."

Kaz and I exchanged a look.

"A room above a bar in Montmartre," I said. "Was the victim Jacques Delair by any chance?"

Fayard checked a sheet of paper on his desk. His eyes went wide.

"How did you know?"

"Inspector, I think we have had cooperation thrust upon us," I said.

CHAPTER FOUR

FAYARD REACTED QUICKLY, joining us as we clambered down the steps and bolted for the jeep. He jumped in the back and directed us to the Pont Notre-Dame.

"Now tell me how you knew of this," Fayard said, grasping the back of my seat as I sped across the river, glad of the light traffic.

"Jacques Delair was the informant who tipped us off about the cemetery," I said, glancing back at Fayard.

"Turn left, there!" he shouted.

"Billy, focus on the road," Kaz said, and filled Fayard in on Delair's motivation to snitch on the Syndicat and Salinger's plan to speak with him.

"The Fox must have known of Delair's betrayal," Fayard said. "Or perhaps your agent was too enthusiastic in his questioning."

"No," Kaz said. "Delair was not thought to be hostile. He had a grudge against the Syndicat. Likely, that is what got him killed, not a visit from our colleague."

"Very well," Fayard said, tapping me on the shoulder and pointing out the next turn. It took us up, into Montmartre, a Parisian neighborhood perched on a hilltop with a white-domed basilica at its back. The last time I was here, I'd been on foot and running for my life. I much preferred being behind the wheel.

"The next left takes us to the place du Tertre. The Café Cadet is on a side street," Fayard said. I slowed down as I entered the

square, but not enough to avoid a disapproving look from a guy
sweeping the sidewalk in front of his restaurant. I took a hard
right onto rue Saint-Rustique, which was well named. A narrow
cobblestoned lane with three-story buildings that nearly blocked
out the sun, it looked like the perfect place for a hideout.

The Café Cadet was a sad-looking joint with wooden shutters
and a low door. Sometime in the last century, in what must have
been its heyday, it had been painted green. The uniformed flics
standing outside were probably the biggest crowd it had seen in
a while. One of them held up his hand to stop us as I parked next
to a Citroën that had to be Rochet's. Then he spotted Fayard,
who ushered us inside as the cop saluted.

The bar had that dingy look a late-night place took on in the
light of day. Not that the small windows let in that much light,
but it was enough to see Salinger and Rochet seated at a table
in the corner. A detective leaned against the wall behind Salinger,
which told me Rochet didn't trust the CIC man enough to be
alone with him.

"Captain Boyle," Salinger said the second he spotted me. The
cop behind him put a hand on his shoulder, keeping him in his
seat.

"We just heard," I said and smiled at the cop while Fayard
spoke to his boss, as Kaz listened in. "Delair's dead?"

"He'd make a doornail look lively," Salinger said. "The commissaire thinks I did it."

"No, no, Agent Salinger," Rochet said, wagging his finger. "You
are merely being questioned. Not charged." Rochet smiled, as if
this was no more than a pleasant misunderstanding. He had high
cheekbones on a thin face, with dark eyes set slightly too close
together. Not a bad-looking guy for all that, even with his
receding hair, wavy, but thick with gray.

Fayard introduced us, explaining our presence here. Rochet
leaned back in his chair, not rising or offering a hand as he
studied Kaz and me.

"Ah, the persistent Colonel Harding," Rochet said, as if he'd just remembered a pesky detail. "The matter at the cemetery might have convinced me of the need to work with you, but finding your compatriot searching the room of a recently murdered man—well, that is a problem."

"He was carrying out the task assigned to him, sir," Kaz said. "Without the assistance of your team, we have to follow every lead, no matter how minor."

"Commissaire, I was a policeman in America before the war," I said, taking a seat at the table next to Salinger. "I know that this gives us an opportunity. Both of us."

"My opportunity here is to take a suspect into custody," Rochet said. "It would please my superiors. If you were a policeman, you can understand the demands put upon us. What opportunity do you offer?"

"Delair was killed for what he knew," I said. "He'd known about the cemetery hiding place, but he was obviously not aware of the details. If we find who killed him, it brings us closer to the Syndicat."

"*If.* Such a wonderful word," Rochet said. He pushed back his chair and stood. "Nearly as helpful as *maybe* or *perhaps* in that it conjures a host of possibilities. Make the possible a certainty and I will have no further need of Special Agent Salinger. Until then, I will take him back to the Trente-Six where we can continue our discussion." That was what the local cops called their police headquarters, after its street address. Rochet nodded to his man, who took Salinger by the arm. "Be at my office at nine o'clock tomorrow morning. Bring me evidence and you may take your friend with you."

"When I said I wanted to stay in Paris, this isn't what I had in mind," Salinger said. "I hope you can pull this off, Captain."

"One moment, Commissaire," I said. I stood with my hand on Salinger's arm. "May I ask a few questions?"

"Be quick about it," Rochet said. "Fayard, go upstairs and see if they've found anything, then report back to me." Fayard darted up the narrow, dark stairs at the back of the bar and Rochet nodded for me to proceed.

"Did you see anybody leaving the premises?" I asked Salinger.

"No," he said, shrugging off the grip Rochet's man had on him. "The barkeep was cleaning and let me go upstairs. I knocked and got no answer. The door was unlocked, so I went in. That's when I found Delair. Already dead."

"The owner said he heard a struggle," Rochet said, clasping his hands behind his back and rocking slightly. A man sure of himself. "That is why he alerted a police officer on patrol."

"How was he killed?" I asked.

"A knife to the heart," Rochet said. "The weapon was on the floor near him."

"Agent Salinger's hands aren't bloody," I said.

"No, but his sleeve is," Rochet said, motioning with his hand for Salinger to raise his.

"I checked his pulse," Salinger said as he showed the blood-stains on his sleeve. "That's when I brushed against his wound."

"Or did it happen when you fought with him?" Rochet asked. "Perhaps he drew the blade and you had to defend yourself?"

"No, and there was no fight," Salinger said. "I began a search of the room. That's what the barman must have heard."

"Interfering with a murder scene is a serious offense," Rochet said. "But one that can be overlooked if circumstances warrant. Be sure they do."

Fayard clomped downstairs, followed by two detectives. By their frowns and shrugs, I understood they'd found nothing of interest.

"May we search the room?" I asked.

"It is at your disposal," Rochet said, nodding in the direction of the stairs. "Now you must excuse us."

"I will join you, Billy, after I speak with the officer first on the scene," Kaz said. He left ahead of the knot of policemen as they led Salinger away.

Fayard detached himself from the others long enough to lean in close. "I am sorry, Captain. This situation changed everything. The commissaire had to act as he did. I hope you find something. Soon."

With that, Fayard disappeared, leaving me alone in the gloomy bar and wondering what the hell I could come up with that would spring Salinger. Searching Delair's room after two pros had just struck out seemed to be a waste of time, but it had to be done. I took the stairs, feeling hemmed in by the narrow steps flanked by grimy, peeling wallpaper. The Café Cadet looked like a decent hideout, but if this was where Jacques Delair called home, he wasn't a very successful thief.

There were three rooms upstairs. Delair's was easy to pick out. The door was open and there was blood on the floor. Given the looks of this joint, I wouldn't have been surprised to find another corpse or two.

I could see where Delair had fallen, near the window set into the sloping roof. Maybe on his way to call for help? Blood had pooled under the bed, following the course of the uneven floor. The sheets and mattress had been pulled off. A small nightstand had been tossed on the bed and emptied of nightclothes and a box of cigars. An empty box, which meant the cops had swiped them or Delair had finished smoking the last one recently.

An armoire had been searched, Delair's clothes in a pile at the bottom. One decent suit, a few shirts, and two pairs of trousers. A wooden chair was tipped against a small table with a stool shoved underneath. Newspapers and a couple of magazines had been gone through, and two pictures had been removed from their frames and tossed on top of the pile. There was little to show that this was home to anyone. A transient's hideout at best.

"Have you found anything?" Kaz asked, standing in the doorway.

"Nothing, except this must have been Delair's place of business," I said. "Good for planning a heist and not much else." I moved to a chest of drawers and found nothing but rumpled linens. "What did the cop say?"

"According to him, things happened exactly as Rochet described," Kaz said, shuffling debris on the floor with his foot. "The barkeep agreed with him. Most enthusiastically."

"You think they're lying?" I asked, looking up from the empty frames.

"They looked to each other several times, as if seeking confirmation," Kaz said. "It could be nothing, but clearly they were both eager to be done. The most innocent explanation is that the officer came in for a drink while on duty, and they both heard Salinger's noises upstairs. So they concocted a white lie about the flic being called for."

"Or the barkeep saw an opportunity to pin the murder on Salinger and went looking for a witness. But why would the cop lie about that?" I wondered out loud.

"Delair is connected to the Syndicat. That would give any man pause," Kaz said, picking up one of the pictures. "Especially given what happened to poor Jacques."

"Yeah, ending up in a dump like this is added insult to deadly injury," I said.

"Jacques seems to have had excellent taste in artwork," Kaz said, moving closer to a window and holding up one of the pictures. "One frame only held a cheap reproduction on flimsy paper. But the other contained this."

He held the thick sheet of paper by its edges. It showed a seated woman in medieval dress. It was dated 1520 with a large capital *A* and a smaller *D* beneath it.

"Is it real?" I asked.

"If I am not mistaken, a chalk and charcoal drawing by Albrecht Dürer, a High Renaissance painter and engraver," Kaz said. "Hidden in plain sight."

"Whoever killed Delair wasn't much of an art expert," I said. Good thing Kaz was no slouch in that department.

"Luckily, neither were Rochet's detectives," Kaz said. "This may give us the advantage we need." I stared at the drawing. Once you knew it was the real deal, it was hard to miss. Stuck up on that wall in a dusty frame, it was simply part of the dismal furnishings. It reminded me of something, but I couldn't put my finger on it.

"You mean trade this for Salinger?" I asked.

"Let us not be hasty," Kaz said. "He is safe enough for now, which gives us time."

"To do what?"

"To visit a museum, my friend, and to meet a remarkable woman," Kaz said, grabbing a magazine and placing the drawing carefully between the pages. "Which will be much more pleasant than an autopsy."

I couldn't argue with that.

CHAPTER FIVE

"'THE PURLOINED LETTER,'" I said, banging my palm against the steering wheel. "That's what this reminded me of."

"Ah, the Edgar Allan Poe story," Kaz said from the passenger seat, arms wrapped around his chest, holding Albrecht's artwork snug under his trench coat. "I know this one. The police suspect a stolen document is hidden in some fellow's house. They search everywhere, to no avail."

"Right," I said, passing a stream of bicyclists on the rue Rodier. With gasoline still scarce, Parisians were out in force on their bikes. "The guy hid it in plain sight, like a normal piece of mail."

"The story was set in Paris," Kaz said. "A French detective this time. C. Auguste Dupin."

"Yes, and he made a fool out of the police detective," I said. "We could use his help right now."

We passed the Ritz Hotel, where Hemingway liked to do his drinking. If he was holed up in the Hürtgen Forest, he'd need a few stiff drinks just to stay warm. I hoped he was writing about what the GIs were going through. People needed to know what this war was like now that the Germans were defending their own border. The sprint across France was over.

"There ahead, the Jardin des Tuileries," Kaz said. "The Jeu de Paume is at the corner."

I pulled over by a long rectangular building, surrounded by trees and the gardens ready for their winter's rest.

"You think this lady will know anything about where this drawing came from?" I asked Kaz as we walked into the museum.

"If anyone does, it will be Rose Valland," Kaz said. "She worked here during the Occupation and kept track of all the artwork the Nazis were stealing. A spy, hidden in plain sight, to continue the theme of our conversation."

"Dangerous work," I said. We entered and found ourselves in a grand hallway with a wide, gleaming white marble staircase on the right.

"Albrecht, I think you will like your new home," Kaz said, opening his trench coat and daintily holding the magazine by its corners.

"Hey, it is an improvement, but are we going to let it go that easily?" I asked.

"It is the surest path to information and Salinger's release," Kaz said, walking over to a stack of wooden crates leaning against a wall. Farther down the hall other boxes had been opened and paintings were in the process of being removed. "I read about Mademoiselle Valland in *Le Monde* just yesterday. She's been appointed to the Commission for Artistic Recovery and is working to bring stolen art back to France."

"Or finding it within France," a woman said, appearing from behind the crates, clipboard in hand. "That article was overly enthusiastic, but thank you for reading it. What can I do for you, gentlemen?"

"Rose Valland?" Kaz asked. She nodded, and Kaz went on to introduce us. This was one of those occasions where Kaz threw in his title. Baron Kazimierz, of the Augustus clan. He mostly used it with maître d's to get the best tables, but this time it seemed to fit the situation.

"We need your help," I said. "And we have something for you."

Kaz opened the magazine, carefully displaying the chalk drawing. Mademoiselle Valland leaned forward to look, adjusting her tortoiseshell glasses as she did. In her midforties, she had a round face, thin lips, and dark hair pulled tightly back. She wore no jewelry or rings. Her eyes fluttered across the drawing, and she touched the edges with her fingers.

"Authentic," she declared. "Come with me."

We followed her down the long hallway, passing blue-coated men unpacking works of art.

"It looks like you've recovered a good number of paintings," I said.

"A few. Too few compared to the treasures taken by the Boche," she said, opening a door at the rear of the hall and gesturing for us to sit. Her office was small. One tall window let in what light there was on this gray day, and Rose pushed aside the pile of papers on her desk to make room for the Dürer. She adjusted a gooseneck lamp, illuminating the sheet.

"Magnifique," Kaz said, his voice hushed. The lighting brought the chalk and charcoal lines to life. Five centuries old and it was still stunning.

"How did you come by this?" She gave each of us a hard stare of suspicion.

"We found it in a bar in Montmarte, Mademoiselle Valland," Kaz said. "Hanging in an upstairs room in a cheap frame."

"Was there anything else?" she asked, her eyes returning to the medieval lady.

"No," I said. "Except for a corpse, which had been removed by the time we arrived."

"Tell me, gentlemen, how did you come to be in a dead man's room in Montmarte, and how did you know to look for this drawing?" she asked.

"We are with SHAEF," I said.

"Yes, I can tell by your shoulder patches," she said. Kaz and I both wore the flaming-sword patch that was the symbol of Allied headquarters. "Now, tell me more."

Kaz gave her the basic facts, starting with our stakeout at the cemetery and ending up with our trip to the Café Cadet with

Inspector Fayard. He left out the part about Salinger. Best not to complicate things by telling her our partner was a murder suspect.

"I know Louis Fayard," Rose said. "He has assisted us in the past. What did he think of this?" Her hand swept above the drawing.

"We found it after he left," I said. "Do you know his boss, Commissaire Rochet?"

"He is well-known," Rose said, a wariness creeping into her tone. "What are you after?"

"Have you heard anything of the events at the Père Lachaise Cemetery last night?" I asked.

"It has not been reported in the newspapers, but yes, I know there was an explosion, and American soldiers asking many questions," she said. "That was your doing?"

"It was the Syndicat du Renard," I said. "They took something from a grave and left a bomb in its place."

"You know of them?" Kaz asked.

"I do. I know that they have deserters from all sides within their ranks," Rose said, placing her hands on either side of the drawing. "British as well as American. Thank you for returning the Dürer. Good day."

"Madame," I said, "please call Inspector Fayard. He'll vouch for us. We are not deserters."

"Mademoiselle," she corrected me, coldly.

"We have not been entirely honest," Kaz said. He stood and motioned for me to do the same. "Our colleague had gone to the café to question a man in connection with the Syndicat. He found the body, but when the police were summoned, they took him into custody."

"Your friend is a suspect in a killing? This does not give me confidence."

"Which is why we didn't bring it up right away," I said. "We thought the drawing might provide some clue as to who the real killer is." I didn't like the way this was going. If Rose Valland was an expert on stolen art, we needed her on our side, not suspicious of our motives.

"Wait outside," she said, one hand on her telephone.

"I hope Fayard speaks well of us," Kaz said as he shut the door behind him. "Otherwise, we have lost the drawing and any advantage it provided." A few yards away, we could hear pry bars opening wooden crates and the sound of workmen setting heavy frames against the wall.

"I think we have learned something," I said, and I could tell by Kaz's look that he had the same thought.

"A tomb is the perfect place to hide stolen art," he said. "Like the dead, graves are patient and hold their secrets. Rose is suspicious of us, but perhaps she has reason to be."

"Her suspicions probably kept her alive during the Occupation," I said. "Some things are hard to shake off."

"Entrez." Rose's voice boomed from behind the door. We entered, and the first thing I noticed was that the Dürer was safely out of sight. The second thing was that Rose Valland was smiling.

"Louis Fayard is a good judge of character," she said. "He is also intelligent and checked on your identities with French officers at SHAEF. They say you may be trusted."

"Did he mention our partner?" I asked.

"Only that his release is up to the commissaire. But he did have new information to share with me," she said. "It may involve the Syndicat."

"What exactly is your interest in this gang?" Kaz asked.

"I am interested in recovering artworks stolen from France," she said. "Some of those thefts were aided by the Carlingue."

"The French Gestapo," Kaz said.

"Correct. They helped to confiscate art from private citizens, often a forced purchase for a fraction of the true value," she said. "If you were a Jew, there was not even a pretense of payment.

After the Liberation, many Carlingue went into hiding, or joined criminal gangs such as the Syndicat."

"Or Traction Avant," Kaz said.

"Exactly. Fayard has been watching a small warehouse in Boulogne-Billancourt, purchased a year ago by a member of the Carlingue, in hopes that the owner would show himself. It was a garment factory, but with the rationing and shortages after the Germans came, it went out of business," she said. "He knows I am searching for artworks that never made it out of Paris. I think the Carlingue may have hidden some there, including the other five Dürer pieces. The one you brought me is part of a set of six."

"Why do you think it's in this warehouse?" I asked.

"Captain Boyle, I made it my business to keep track of every piece of art the Nazis brought here. This was their clearinghouse. They shipped over two thousand crates stuffed with magnificent pieces out of this very building. I know what was taken and where. The delivery here of six Dürer pieces was recorded. But they were never listed as being taken to Germany. If nothing else, the Nazis are excellent record keepers. There is no outgoing bill of lading for the drawings, but they are not here," she said, tapping her finger on the desktop, her voice sharp and angry.

"Someone looted the looters," I said.

"That is my theory," Rose said. "I want them all returned. This warehouse may be nothing, but we must check. The fact that you discovered one tells me the others must be close by."

"Could be. Whatever they took away from the cemetery, they had to stash it somewhere. It would make sense to let the dust settle before moving anything valuable," I said. "Wait a minute, did you say *we* must check?"

"Of course, Captain Boyle," she said. "If there are paintings there, they must be secured. Will you drive? Inspector Fayard is expecting us."

"Enchanté," Kaz said. He offered Mademoiselle Valland his arm and they left, chattering in French like two old friends.

CHAPTER SIX

WE DROVE ALONG the Seine toward Boulogne-Billancourt, an industrial neighborhood on the west side of the Paris city limits. The Allies had targeted the Renault automobile factory several times, and evidence of the bomb damage was still obvious. Strong, stout buildings and warehouses gave way to a field of rubble, blackened brick walls standing amid wrecked machinery.

This was the city of darkness.

"It could have been so much worse," Rose said. She gripped her hat with one hand and the passenger seat with the other. "The Germans had all the monuments and bridges wired with explosives. What the Germans could not steal, they would destroy. Thank God the Allies came quickly."

"Mademoiselle, you spoke of recovering stolen art," Kaz said, as he leaned forward from the back seat. "I understood it was all taken to Germany. Except for what might have been pilfered, of course."

"The Resistance managed to stop some of the transports. But we're still finding trains that the Germans abandoned. The last days of the Occupation were total chaos. We are still discovering batches of artwork, as you saw at the museum. Hidden in the countryside by Nazis who expected to return, no doubt. There, turn left, Captain," Rose said, tapping my arm.

The road took us past single-story brick buildings, most with broken windows and debris scattered out front. This was once a manufacturing area, but four years of war and depravation had put an end to that. There were shortages of everything. Nothing was being produced for civilian consumption, as testified by the worn clothes of even the most fashionable Parisians. I spotted two police cars tucked between buildings and pulled over next to them. Fayard was leaning against one and flicked away a cigarette as Kaz vaulted out of the jeep to offer Rose his hand as she stepped out.

"Mademoiselle Valland," Fayard said, coming to shake her hand. "I hope we find something today. Too often we have not."

"I know you wanted to wait and catch the owner," Rose said. "One less fascist on the loose would be a good thing. So, I am in your debt."

"If we find the rest of the drawings, it will be worth it," Fayard said. "The set was from a private collection, you told me?"

"Yes. A Jewish family. But I doubt they will return from the East. The Germans made sure all those trains got through, the beasts," Rose said. "Now, shall we look inside?"

"Please wait with this officer," Fayard said. He snapped his finger at one of the uniformed policemen. "I will call when it is safe."

Fayard motioned for us to follow him and two other cops. He drew his pistol, and Kaz and I followed suit. He explained the building had been under surveillance and appeared to be deserted.

"We don't know what we will find inside," Fayard said. "The windows have been painted over, and we did not wish to reveal our interest." He nodded in the direction of a building across the street. A large garage door faced the road. The wide windows above it were darkened. Around the side, a sign that read *propriété privée* was nailed above a wooden door with peeling black paint. I figured we weren't all that worried about violating the property rights of a French Gestapo turncoat.

"Do you have a key?" Kaz asked, eyeing the sturdy padlock.

"No, I have Bernard," Fayard said. Another snap of the fingers and a burly cop took a running start and barreled into the entryway. The wood gave out a sharp crack and Bernard put his shoulder into it again, shattering the door and stepping back as if to admire his work. The hinges still hung on, as did the padlock, but the entire center of the door collapsed into the warehouse. It fell against the concrete floor with a thump, like a boxer taking a mean right hook to the chin.

Fayard told us to wait and went through the door, pistol at the ready. One cop followed him in, and Bernard went around front to cover the garage door. Fayard barked some orders from inside. Kaz stood at my back, watching for any movement from the adjacent building as I gazed into the darkness. Overhead lights flashed on, shadows cast in sharp relief.

"Entrez," Fayard shouted, then called out to Bernard.

I squeezed through the narrow opening, Kaz right behind me. Fayard, his face set in a tight grimace, pulled on the chains that opened the main doors. More light flooded in. At first, I couldn't make out what I was seeing. Then it came into focus.

Furniture.

Couches, dressers, end tables, chairs, bed frames, dining tables, and desks were stacked at least five feet high and ran along the length of the warehouse. Tables were set along the walls with all manner of delicate objects on them. Everything from violins to vases, stretched from front to back.

"What is this place?" I asked.

"A Möbel-Aktion warehouse," Valland said, standing in the entry, studying the enormous stack of goods.

"Furniture action?" Kaz asked. For once, even he was stumped.

"The Germans are a thorough people," Valland said. "They took our art. They took the Jews of Paris. Then they stole everything those Jews left behind. That was the job of M-Aktion. Thieves."

"They were unable to transport all of the looted belongings," Fayard said. "We've found a few of these smaller collection points, furniture that they could not transport back to the Reich. They had used a department store in central Paris for storage, but when that was full, they took over warehouses, often with the help of willing Frenchmen, to house the remainder."

"They took so much they couldn't find space on the last trains out of Paris," Valland said.

"But they took every Jew they could find," Fayard added. "And to my shame, we helped them."

"The roundup of Jews in 1942, you mean?" I asked.

"Yes. That is why I joined the Resistance soon after," Fayard said. "And why I help Mademoiselle Valland whenever I can. She is a very brave woman."

"Pfft. Enough of that, Inspector," Valland said, waving a hand in Fayard's direction, as if swatting away a fly. "What will you do with all this?"

"I am glad it is not my problem," Fayard said. "The government moves it all to another warehouse, I suppose. Then we wait and see who returns after the war."

"Returns from the East?" Kaz said. "You must know there is no return from those camps."

"That I cannot believe," Fayard said, shaking his head. He turned away, unwilling to meet Kaz's gaze. "We know the Nazis went through thousands of apartments to take their valuables. Surely some will return. We must safeguard their possessions for them. They cannot all have been killed, can they?"

"Come, Louis," Valland said. "There is nothing for us here. It would be better to burn it to the ground. The owners will not be coming back, and who else has a right to it?"

Fayard didn't respond. He walked away; his shoulders hunched as he searched the pile of possessions as if looking for something he might recognize. Far as I could tell, all he saw was his own failure. He hadn't kept the Jews of Paris safe, so now he wanted to save something, anything, of their past, some object he could hold for a future that would never be. But there was nothing here with enough value to buy back the honor of a French policeman who sent citizens of his own city to the death camps.

"Is there any chance of artwork being hidden here?" Kaz asked, after moments of heavy silence.

"No. Möbel-Aktion was a separate department of the ERR," Valland said. "The Einsatzstab Reichsleiter Rosenberg, that is. The ERR oversaw the looting of artwork, using the Jeu de Paume as their headquarters. M-Aktion had the job of acquiring possessions from Jewish homes and sending them to Germany. They often worked at odds with each other, competing for transport."

"I will have my men check everything as it is removed," Fayard said, returning to the conversation. He'd composed himself; only a twitching muscle in his jaw betrayed any emotion beneath the surface. "But there is a thick layer of dust everywhere. These things have been undisturbed for some time."

"Good," Valland said. Then she turned to us. "I am sorry to have wasted your time, gentlemen. I thought there was some slight chance of a connection with the drawing, but no luck."

"How did you find this Dürer?" Fayard said.

"It was in Delair's room," Kaz said. "Your men searched the frame but neglected to check the drawing itself."

"This drawing should have been brought to me straightaway," Fayard said, glowering.

"We only sought to authenticate it, Inspector," Kaz said. "There was no reason to waste your time until we knew."

"Absolutely correct, Inspector," Valland said. "Did I not call you immediately? And did it not lead to the discovery of this abominable place?"

"I defer to your interpretation, Mademoiselle," Fayard said, with a small bow in her direction. "As for you, Captain, I wish you could have discovered something that would have helped free your partner. But you still have time."

"Not much," I said. "Any advice as to what would convince Rochet to release Agent Salinger?"

"Anything that would remove this case from his jurisdiction," Fayard said. "He does not wish to be involved, since it may reflect badly on the Police Judiciaire."

"And himself," Valland said. "That is what he fears the most. He barely managed to keep his post after Liberation."

"There was no evidence of active collaboration," Fayard whispered. "But he never looked the other way when it came to helping the Resistance or any of the many unfortunates hunted by the Gestapo."

"We have to come up with something," I said. I had no idea what that might be.

"We must get to the autopsy," Kaz said, glancing at his watch. "Perhaps that will reveal a clue."

"I hope the dead are of more help than the living," Fayard said.

I agreed. The dead know many things. Getting them to share their secrets with the living was the tough part.

CHAPTER SEVEN

I WAS HUNGRY, but I wasn't going to admit it. Not after viewing the remnants of so many lost lives in that dark, depressing warehouse. Prized possessions stacked like cordwood; heirlooms reduced to forgotten booty. Besides, we were late to the autopsy, and lunch at a French bistro would be a mistake, for a number of reasons.

"It is strange," Kaz said, his voice a soft murmur. We'd both been quiet since leaving Rose Valland and Fayard at the warehouse.

"What is?" I asked as I drove over a bridge spanning the Seine.

"This war is devasting. Thousands die every day. Cities are bombed and families destroyed or made homeless. We have almost come to accept it," Kaz said. "But to see those furnishings intact, knowing the owners are likely dead, is somehow more depressing than seeing an entire ruined city. It is quite melancholy, don't you think?"

"Yeah," I said. I glanced at Kaz as I took the turn for Saint-Cloud and the 203rd General Hospital. He had a faraway look in his eyes, and I still worried about his moods. When I'd first met him, he thought he had little to live for. Everyone he loved had been killed, and he was careless of his life. Kaz was a crack shot with his Webley revolver, and there were times I wondered if one night he'd turn it on himself. Things had changed, but I still watched for the signs. This was not a good sign.

"I'd be glad to find the bastards responsible, wouldn't you?" I asked. I figured it might help to give Kaz something to look forward to. Like revenge.

"There is a whole nation of them waiting for us," he said.

"Well, right now we've got a date with a corpse," I said. It seemed like focusing on the present might be the healthier approach. "Nazi Germany will have to wait, okay?"

"There will be an accounting," Kaz agreed. "It is only a matter of time."

"And lives," I said, following the signs for the 203rd Hospital. I joined a line of slow-moving traffic, mostly ambulances, as it wound along a curved drive. The vehicles halted at the entrance and began unloading their stretcher cases. The bandages were clean and white, the GIs having already been patched up at a forward hospital and sent here for further treatment. Meaning more surgeries and a chance to recover if they lived through them.

"Some claim that the war is almost over, and that the Germans are about to collapse," Kaz said. "I have a feeling these men do not share that same enthusiasm."

"Optimism increases in direct proportion to the distance from the front," I said, driving to where I knew the morgue would be. Live patients come in the front. The dead are brought out the back.

Inside, we followed the signs for the basement. As we drew closer, the antiseptic smell of liberally applied carbolic soap wafted up. I swung open the double doors to the morgue. Kaz crinkled his nose. As clean as they kept it, the odor of death hung in the air—a putrid, metallic smell tinged with a whiff of vomit. Three empty tables stood in the middle of the room, the floor still wet from a thorough cleaning. An orderly rinsed a mop in a deep sink, his white gown wet and streaked with pink. He hefted a full bucket and headed our way.

I asked him where I could find Dr. Jacobs while avoiding a

glance at the contents of his pail. He crooked a thumb in the direction of a side door and told us we'd missed the fun part as he passed us with the sloshing bucketful.

"You're late," said the man standing over the single well-lit table near a half dozen body drawers. He'd tossed his white smock on a chair and was pulling a smoke out of his shirt pocket. "Some colonel called and said you'd be here an hour ago. Boyle and Kazimierz, right?"

"Yes. Our apologies, Doctor," Kaz said. "The investigation delayed us."

"Ah, don't worry about it," Jacobs said, lighting up with his Zippo. "I was late too. My last operation took longer than expected. I just don't like desk jockeys at headquarters telling me to hurry up when my dance card is filled with wounded boys." Jacobs wore the caduceus insignia of the Army Medical Corps along with his captain's bars on his rumpled khaki uniform, yet he still managed to look like a civilian. His dark, wavy hair needed a trim, but he kept his mustache neatly shaped.

"I don't blame you, Doc," I said. "You work on the living and the dead?"

"Because I did a stint as a county coroner back home, I inherited this duty when I got here. Not a big demand for autopsies at the 203rd. Main cause of death around here is shrapnel, slugs, and Adolf Hitler," Jacobs said, blowing blue smoke. He drew back the sheet covering our corpse. "So, a criminal case is a change of pace. What do you want to know about this guy?"

The stiff had two bullet wounds, pale, graying skin, and dull brown eyes. He was on the tall side with close-cropped hair and an old scar on his calf. Maybe thirty or so, lean and muscular. He looked like the kind of guy you wouldn't want to encounter in a dark cemetery. Too bad for him I did.

"Cause of death looks obvious," I said as I leaned over the corpse to study the entry wound in his forehead. "Small caliber, dead center."

"Up close and personal," Jacobs said. "The abrasive tattooing from the gunpowder residue makes that obvious. I took a .32-caliber round out of his skull. Death was instantaneous. The wound on his side came first. A larger caliber weapon that sent the bullet right through him, puncturing his lung."

"The fatal round matches a shell casing we found nearby," Kaz said. "A small pistol, easy to conceal. Maybe a Beretta, Walther PPK, or Remington. All common enough automatics."

"Would that have been fatal?" I asked, looking at the unpleasant hole my larger .45-caliber slug had made.

"Not if he'd received medical attention, no," Jacobs said. He eyed the holster on my belt. "Is this your work, Captain?"

"I hit him, yes," I said. "But someone else finished him off."

"Could he have walked on his own, Doctor, after that first wound?" Kaz asked.

"No way. He'd be in serious shock," Jacobs said. "Sounds to me like a case of dead men telling no tales."

"That's what we think," Kaz said. "Did the autopsy tell you anything else?"

"He had a meal that included mussels a good twelve hours before he died," Jacobs said. "There wasn't a lot in his stomach. His clothes are on the desk. You can look, but there was nothing to identify him. No wallet or papers."

"Not even a clothing tag," Kaz said, rifling through the bloodied garments. I stared at the dead man, wondering what secrets he'd held in that now scrambled brain of his. I also marveled at the split-second decision his partner in crime had made. No hesitation at all.

Just twelve hours ago, this guy was alive. He was likely no angel, but he was part of this world. The world in which I dwelled. Now that connection had been severed, and as in so many cases, it haunted me. Not my role in his death—that was the chance he took. It was the transition from life to death. When he'd last shaved, did he think about it being his final strokes with the razor? When he left his bedroom, did he have any sense that it was the last time he'd see it?

No, of course not. But still, here he was, naked and cold on a metal table. Pretty soon he'd be a line in a report. Buried and forgotten. But until then, in my mind, he wavered between life and death, this investigation keeping his memory alive, even though anyone who cared about him might never hear how he ended up.

"There is one thing you may find of interest," Jacobs said, loud enough to shake me out of my thoughts. Or had I been falling asleep on my feet? The doctor smiled and lifted the body's left arm. On the underside of the arm, above the elbow, a small black ink tattoo read AB.

"A blood type tattoo," Kaz said. "This man is SS."

"Waffen-SS, to be precise," Jacobs said. "Your corpse is a Kraut."

"What? Doesn't anyone else do those?" I asked, trying to take in the implications of a Waffen-SS man as part of the Syndicat du Renard.

"No," Kaz said. "Dog tags are standard for that information, but the Waffen-SS added the tattoo in case a soldier was missing theirs. It is a unique approach." The Waffen-SS comprised the combat branch of the SS and were known for their brutality and penchant for war crimes.

"This'll come in handy once these bastards try to hide after the war," Jacobs said. He dropped the arm like the piece of dead meat it was. "I had photographs taken of his face and the tattoo. It's in the file with my report. Hope it helps."

"Indeed it might," Kaz said. He took the paperwork and studied the photograph. "The SS on the loose in liberated Paris. That ought to get Commissaire Rochet's attention."

"We'll make sure it does," I said. For the first time, I began to see a way out of this, for Salinger, at least.

"If there are SS behind our lines, I hope the rest of them end up like this one, and fast," Jacobs said. He pulled the sheet over the dead man's face. "I've got family in Czechoslovakia, and I don't like their chances."

"He's more likely to be a deserter," I said. "We're tracking down a gang of criminals and they aren't fussy about who they work with."

"If a crook takes a Nazi into his gang, know what you've got?" Jacobs asked. I shook my head.

"A gang of Nazis."

CHAPTER EIGHT

JACOBS TOOK US to the switchboard room where we made a call to Colonel Harding. I gave him a rundown on the situation and asked if he could arrange for an officer to meet us at the Police Judiciaire at 36 quai des Orfèvres.

I had a very specific French officer in mind. Harding agreed with my choice and told us to hotfoot it back to Paris and spring Salinger. That sounded great, except for the part that left us no time to grab a meal, so Kaz broke out a couple of Hershey's bars from the supply we kept stashed in the jeep. Chocolate and cigarettes came in handy for opening doors and loosening lips as well as staving off hunger.

We crossed the Seine once again, taking the Pont Mirabeau, and drove through the busy Montparnasse neighborhood while munching on our chocolate bars.

"I am looking forward to this," Kaz said, cleaning his fingers with a white handkerchief. "I did not take a liking to Commissaire Rochet. Colonel Baril was an inspired choice."

"I don't think he'll like Rochet much either," I said. "Especially if he was able to dig up anything about his activities during the Occupation." Colonel Jean Baril was a buddy of Sam Harding's from the First World War. I'd last seen Baril in North Africa when he was working to bring the Vichy French forces over to the side of General de Gaulle's Free French. Baril and a group of officers had planned a coup to coincide with the Allied invasion of Algeria, but things went to hell in a handbasket once the Vichy government found out about it. Colonel Baril was arrested and tortured by the Garde Mobile, the fascist paramilitary police. He barely survived and spent months recovering in the hospital. Sam had kept tabs on his old pal and was delighted when Baril showed up as part of de Gaulle's military delegation to SHAEF. His assignment was to define what areas came under the jurisdiction of the French government and what military decisions were best left to General Eisenhower and SHAEF.

It wasn't an easy job.

Colonel Baril's anti-Fascist credentials were excellent, having endured terrible abuses at the hands of Vichy police forces. Which made him just the right candidate to confront Rochet and pry Salinger out of his grasp.

"The French can be touchy about their sovereignty when it comes to Allied forces on their territory," Kaz said as I parked the jeep near the Trente-Six. "Colonel Baril represents his government's interests enthusiastically. But there is one thing de Gaulle's people are even more sensitive about."

"Collaborators," I said as we took to the sidewalk.

"Yes. Collaborators who are still in their positions of power," Kaz said. "Let us hope that Baril knows of Rochet's background. I sense there is something there the commissaire wishes to keep hidden." Ferreting out pro-Vichy officials was another part of Colonel Baril's job, something he did quietly, but effectively. There were plenty of officials who'd served in the Vichy regime still in place. They weren't all fascists, after all. Someone had to keep the lights on and telephones working. Baril was interested in those who worked far too willingly with the Milice, those French right-wingers who fought the Resistance and did the Nazi's dirtiest work for them.

Baril was waiting for us at the entrance. He was tall and lean, exactly as I remembered him, except for the snow-white hair beneath the rim of his cap and a cane gripped tightly in his left hand.

"Colonel Baril," I said, coming to attention and saluting, as did Kaz. It had been more than two years since I'd seen him, but he looked much older. Thinner. Pained.

"It is good to see you again, Captain, under much more agreeable circumstances," Baril said, returning the salute. "You as well, Baron."

"My pleasure, Colonel," Kaz said. "You must be pleased to see Paris again."

"I find it preferable to a Vichy prison, a hospital ward, or a desk in Algiers," Baril said, mustering a smile. "It is good to be back in France. Now, I understand you have information about a German deserter, and you wish to use this to convince Commissaire Rochet to release an American counterintelligence agent. Correct?"

"Yes, Colonel," Kaz said. "We have photographs of the dead German and his Waffen-SS blood group tattoo."

"Let me see," Baril said. He stepped away from the entrance and the steady flow of police. It was obvious his cane wasn't for show. Whatever had happened to him in that Vichy prison, he still carried the wounds.

"There was no other identification on the body," I said, and gave Baril a quick briefing on the cemetery raid and the Syndicat du Renard.

"Yes, I know of the Fox and his men. Traitors, cutthroats, and deserters from any army accepted with open arms," Baril said as he studied the photographs. "They would not make the mistake of carrying identity papers. The only Germans we know of in his employ are men from the Alsace."

The Alsace was a contested region on the border of France and Germany. Thousands of former French citizens found themselves serving in the Nazi army after their region was made German territory.

"Useful men," Kaz said. "Many Alsatians speak French and German. Perfect for stay-behind agents."

"Agreed," Baril said, handing the folder back to Kaz. "Rochet is vulnerable to criticism in this regard. Leave it to me, gentlemen."

"Colonel Baril?" It was Inspector Fayard, standing in the open doorway. "Commissaire Rochet asked me to escort you upstairs."

"Lead on, young man," Baril said as he leaned heavily on his cane. "We have much to discuss with your superior."

Now it felt like we were getting somewhere. Like dinner after we got Salinger out of here. Baril took the steps slowly but showed no pain. The only clue was the white-knuckle grip on his walking stick. When the colonel reached the commissaire's office, Rochet rose from his desk, extending his hand. Obviously Baril was seen as a special guest.

"BIENVENUE, COLONEL. VOTRE présence nous honore," Rochet said, his eyes riveted on Baril.

"We all speak English well enough," Baril said. "Let us do so, unless there are things you do not wish our Allied friends to hear?"

"No, of course not. Merely the force of habit. Please sit, Colonel," Rochet said, smiling while he ignored Kaz and me. "It is an honor to have a representative from General de Gaulle visit us. How may I assist you?" He was laying it on real thick.

"Commissaire Rochet," Baril said, "I do recall the name. From reports." He sat, easing himself into the chair and extending his leg. He tossed his kepi onto Rochet's desk, revealing that shock of white hair and leaving unsaid what was in the reports. "I understand you are holding an American counterintelligence agent."

"I am honored you have heard of me," Rochet said. He sat behind his desk, arms extended as if he were manning the ramparts. He looked at me, but his gaze quickly returned to Baril. "Yes, we do have an American sergeant here for questioning in a matter involving a gang. We are trying to determine if he is involved with them." His voice was even, wary about what this representative of de Gaulle's might be after.

"A gang? Common criminals?" Baril asked.

"Perhaps not so common as bold," Rochet said. "But criminals, certainly."

"We have a photograph. Do you recognize this man?" Kaz gave the photo of the dead man's face to Fayard, who laid it in front of Rochet.

"The man who was killed at the cemetery?" Rochet asked. "No, it is not familiar. Inspector Fayard?" The inspector agreed, and Baril nodded as he took the photo and returned it to Kaz. Rochet relaxed, folding his arms on the desk and leaning forward.

"Rochet. Yes, I do recall the name," Baril said, as if it had just come to him. "You were involved in putting down the revolt at La Santé Prison in Montparnasse, yes? Bastille Day, wasn't it, a month before la Libération?"

"We were called in to assist, yes," Rochet said as he leaned back and arched his eyebrows in Baril's direction. "We wanted to control the situation before the Germans became involved. They would have only made matters worse. For everyone."

"Indeed, the Boche made many things worse," Baril said. "But so did the Milice, did they not?"

"A renegade group," Rochet said. "They operated without control of any kind. I agree, it is quite sad that any of our countrymen sided with the occupiers. But things are different now, n'est-ce pas?" He tilted his head, inviting agreement. Hoping for it.

"I would hope so," Baril said. "Tell me, are you familiar with the name Brossard?"

"Brossard?" Rochet said. As he rubbed his chin, making show of trying to remember, he looked to Fayard, who stood by his desk. "I can't quite place the name. Can you, Inspector?"

"Yes, Commissaire. He was the chef de centaine of the Milice detachment that responded to the La Santé Prison uprising," Fayard said. His face was stoic, delivering the information while giving no impression as to his opinion.

"A renegade group, Rochet?" Baril asked. "An entire company brought in to put down a prison revolt? Who would have approved such a thing?" I watched Rochet's mouth drop as he tried to form an answer. He was smart enough to close it and say nothing. Instead, he folded his arms across his chest.

"Thirty-four prisoners were killed," Baril said, glancing in my direction. "Many of them resistants. Brossard and his Milice were quite brutal about it from all accounts. And we do have accounts of that day."

"It was necessary," Rochet said. "Sadly. We did not have the manpower, and the Germans threatened to bring in tanks. Many more would have lost their lives."

"In North Africa they were the Garde Mobile. They changed their name to the Milice, but I know what they are capable of," Baril said, tapping his bad leg. "All too well."

"Things happened," Rochet said, the pitiful excuse coming out in a slow exhale.

"Yes, things happen," Baril said, nodding energetically. "Sometimes they can be understood. Perhaps. But there is something I do not understand, Commissaire. How is it you had an agent of the SS roaming the streets of Paris?"

That was Kaz's cue. He took the photograph of the dead man's arm and slid it across Rochet's desk.

"This is the corpse from the cemetery?" Fayard asked, leaning over his boss's shoulder. Rochet had gone rigid.

"Yes, the same man," I said, my eyes on Rochet. "That's his Waffen-SS blood group tattoo. He was part of the gang Agent Salinger tried to stop in an operation the Police Judiciaire declined to be part of."

"This is unfortunate, Commissaire Rochet," Baril said. "You

participated in an action against the Resistance with one of the worst of the Milice leaders, and instead of hunting the SS loose in your city, you imprison an American counterintelligence agent. This may require an investigation. Is there anything else we might find out about you?"

"No, nothing," Rochet said. Beads of sweat appeared at his temples. "The matter at the prison was a difficult decision, but we had little choice. And we've had no indication of German agents in the city. A deserter, most likely. Right, Fayard?" He looked to his inspector, desperation in his eyes.

"It is likely, sir," Fayard said. "I assume you will wish me to look into the matter? Perhaps Agent Salinger could assist me."

"Of course, this must be investigated," Rochet said, slamming his hand on the desk. "Release the American at once."

"Immédiatement, Commissaire," Fayard said, stone-faced. But as he left the room, he tossed a quick wink in my direction.

CHAPTER NINE

"THE MATTER OF Rochet and the prison has already been investigated," Colonel Baril told us as we waited outside for Fayard to bring Salinger up from the cells. "The truth is much as he claims. While it is true the Boche would have been far more vicious, he is still tainted by his association with Brossard and the Milice."

"There will be no repercussions for him?" Kaz asked.

"It has been discussed. For now, no further advancement is allowed," Baril said. "Since he knows it has not been decided, we can pressure him if need be. I would like to see the Syndicat du Renard destroyed, so let me know if I can help, and keep me informed, if you will."

"Certainly, Colonel," I said. "Can we give you a lift back to Versailles?"

"No, my driver is here," Baril said, pointing with his cane as a Citroën Traction Avant pulled to the curb. A lieutenant jumped out and opened the door for his boss.

"Lieutenant Adrien Moreau," he said, standing at attention. He was a small guy, barely twenty and working on a pencil-thin mustache in hopes of looking older.

"Contact the lieutenant when you learn more," Baril said. He winced as he bent his frame to slide into the passenger seat, a hand gripping his bad leg. "Or if you need assistance."

"That is a man in a permanent state of pain," I said as the car drove off.

"He looks much older than when we last saw him," Kaz said. "But we are lucky he is still in uniform. We may well need his help."

At that point Fayard delivered Salinger, apologizing for jailing him.

"Not your fault, Inspector," Salinger said. "Besides, I needed to catch up on my sleep after that all-night stakeout."

"I have been authorized to review our files on the Syndicat and the Traction Avant gang with Agent Salinger," Fayard told us. "We start tomorrow morning. Bonne soirée."

"Suddenly everyone wants to help," I said as I yawned. My eyes felt gritty and heavy with fatigue. "Where were they last night?"

"Fayard told me you brought in a big gun connected to de Gaulle," Salinger said. "That got Rochet's attention. Thanks. You guys look beat, by the way."

Since Salinger had caught up on his sleep, lounging in a cell while we'd been following leads all around Paris, I told him to take the wheel and tried to stay awake while we gave him what little news we had.

I went over Kaz's discovery of the drawing by Albrecht Dürer in Jacques Delair's room and our trip to the Jeu de Paume to see Rose Valland. I shared her suspicions about the involvement of the French Gestapo known as the Carlingue, and our trip to the dreary warehouse stacked floor to ceiling with household possessions looted from Jewish homes.

"I didn't even take notice of what was on the wall at Delair's," Salinger said. "It was just a place he used to lay low. I didn't expect to find him dead, but it made sense if the Syndicat knew he tipped us off."

"There is more," Kaz said, explaining about the autopsy and the SS blood group tattoo.

"No wonder Rochet was so cooperative," Salinger said. "Doesn't make him look on top of things, does it?"

"We're not doing that well ourselves," I said, glad of the cold breeze on my face. It helped keep my eyes open. The cloud cover was thick, masking the light of the sun which was already nearing the horizon.

"Albrecht Dürer makes sense if the Krauts are involved," Salinger said as he slowed for the gate by the Trianon Palace Hotel. "He's German. Ever seen his self-portrait?"

"Right," Kaz said from the back seat. "Strong, good-looking fellow with long blond curls."

"An Aryan poster boy," Salinger said. "The Nazis use some of his artwork in their propaganda. Knights on horseback, that sort of thing."

"Interesting," Kaz said. But then, so was the notion of a soft bed.

Salinger pulled up in front of the Trianon to let us out. We agreed to get in touch tomorrow after he went over the files with Fayard. I didn't have a plan and I was too bushed to think of one. But I did remember to show Salinger the photograph of the stiff from the morgue.

"I know you didn't recognize him last night, but it was dark," I said. "Give this a gander."

"He's got the look," Salinger said, holding up the photograph to study it in the graying light. "The same look as all the other crooks and thieves we questioned. A hard face, with sharp edges and no sign of softness. But not one I ever saw. I don't know how much more help I can be."

"Rochet authorized Fayard to cooperate with you just to cover up the fact that he threw you in the slammer," I said. "That's progress, so see what you can dig up. We'll be in touch through Fayard's office. Go get some rest."

Good advice, I thought as Salinger departed and we headed upstairs to Colonel Harding's office. My mind was on hot food and sleep as I struggled to form a succinct report that would satisfy Harding and let us get back pronto to the Hotel Royale and those clean white sheets.

"Tell me everything about the drawing you found," Harding said before we even sat down. He didn't look tired at all, but then he hadn't been driving all over town and running on two hours of sleep. Maybe he'd napped, or maybe it was that spit-shined West Point posture that kept him looking alert.

"It was hung on the wall in plain sight," I said. "Kaz spotted it right away, but the Paris cops missed it."

"We took it to Rose Valland at the Jeu de Paume museum," Kaz said. "She told us it was from a set of six drawings by Dürer. The other five are still missing, removed by the Nazis."

"Good work, Lieutenant," Harding said. "Do you suspect Delair was killed for stealing it from the Syndicat?"

"No, not really," I said. I glanced at Kaz who sent back a slight shrug. "We figured it was because he snitched. Why would they leave it in his room if he was knifed for stealing it?"

"Not every Parisian assassin is an art expert," Harding said. "The killer might not have known why Delair had to die."

"From what we understand of the Syndicat, they are ruthless," Kaz said. "They may care less about recovering the drawing than making an example of Delair."

"That makes sense," Harding said. "After today's events, what do you think was taken from that grave last night?"

"Artwork?" I said, wondering why Harding was suddenly interested in the arts. Or had my thinking been dulled by lack of sleep? "So, is the Syndicat going high-class and trafficking in stolen art? I thought drugs, booze, and cigarettes were more their speed."

"Don't forget murder," Harding said. "Killing a CIC agent isn't a move they'd make unless they had to. Agent Williamson must have gotten close."

"Which all points back to Jacques Delair," Kaz said. "They are covering their tracks, that much is for certain. Perhaps we should warn Salinger and Inspector Fayard. The Syndicat may have informers among the police."

"What's your take on Fayard?" Harding asked.

"Decent guy," I said. "Can't say the same about his boss Rochet. He's only cooperating because Colonel Baril put the squeeze on him. I don't think Fayard or Salinger are under any illusions about what the Syndicat will do if threatened. But they're only going through files tomorrow. I think they can take care of themselves." Harding nodded his agreement.

"Colonel Baril suffered considerably at the hands of the Garde Mobile in North Africa," Kaz said. "I am surprised he is still in uniform."

"What he endured would have broken other men," Harding said. "But Jean Baril is not other men. He wasn't happy being left with the Free French in Algiers after he was finally released from the hospital. Pushing paper in a backwater theater isn't his speed. Getting this post did him a world of good. But, I have to say, I was shocked by his appearance when I first saw him."

"He still has a presence," I said. "Rochet didn't stand a chance."

"Good. I knew he'd chew Rochet up once he found his connection to the Milice," Harding said. "He asked to be kept abreast of any developments. We'll keep him informed."

"Anything else for now, Colonel?" I asked.

"Be here oh nine hundred," Harding said. "I'll brief you on a related matter."

"Related how?" I asked.

"Tomorrow," Harding said. "And watch yourselves."

WE MADE IT to the Hotel Royale dining room without falling asleep. Kaz consulted with the waiter, and a bottle of chenin blanc and plates of chicken parisienne with mushrooms and rice quickly appeared.

"Santé," Kaz said, raising his glass. I returned the toast and clinked. The cool white wine was dry and crisp, the food steaming hot. But hungry as I was, I wasn't quite ready to dig in.

"What's with the artwork angle and the secrecy about tomorrow morning? Something's up, and it's more than this Parisian gang, bad as they are. Why do you think he warned us to watch out?" Then I gave in and took a mouthful of food. It was heaven on a fork.

"It may be that between what the Germans took and what the Jeu de Paume saved, there is a gap," Kaz said. He paused to sip his wine. "As we saw with the Dürer. The Syndicat is taking advantage, as criminals are wont to do."

"They've got Krauts in their ranks who might know a few things about where stuff is stashed," I said. "Still, it seems there must be more to it."

"A complication that can wait until tomorrow," Kaz said. "The same cannot be said of this food."

A wise man, my friend Kaz.

CHAPTER TEN

FOG SHROUDED THE gardens and statues of Versailles. It had rained during the night and the roads were slick. I couldn't see more than ten feet in front of me as I drove down the avenue de Trianon, barely getting out of second gear.

"This is such miserable weather," Kaz said. He tucked his gloved hands into his raincoat pockets and shivered. "I know I should not complain given that men at the front are living in holes in the ground, but the cold and damp conspire against me."

"Sam told me that things are pretty quiet right now," I said. "A lot of guys have houses or bunkers to sleep in, but they still have to man their positions. It could be worse. The Germans could be shooting at them around the clock."

"Which they will do, once we advance into Germany proper," Kaz said. "Still, it is good that the fighting has lessened. Perhaps it will last through Christmas."

One thing I knew for certain was that nothing lasts in this war. If things are calm today, chaos can't be far behind. But we ended with the optimistic thought about Christmas and headed inside, where we found a surprise waiting for us in Harding's office.

"Big Mike!" Kaz said as he tossed his coat onto a chair. "I thought you were in London."

"Same here," I said. "I heard you were getting your leg checked out. What brings you to Paris?"

"Aw, Sam can explain," Big Mike said as he stood to greet us. First Sergeant Mike Miecznikowski was part of Sam Harding's Office of Special Investigations. He'd been with our team since Sicily, and a while back he'd injured his leg. According to Colonel Harding, he'd been sent back to a hospital for another dose of physical therapy.

Big Mike wasn't one for the niceties of military protocol, as evidenced by his use of Harding's first name. He was as friendly as he was broad at the shoulders, and his easy, informal style won him friends of every rank. Plus, he was an expert scrounger, which any sensible officer appreciated in a noncom.

"Big Mike's leg is fine," Colonel Harding said, moving from his desk to the conference table. "He had a job to do, and it had to be on the q.t."

"Sorry, guys," Big Mike said with a grin as he returned to his seat. In front of him was a tube about a yard long, covered in waterproof fabric.

"It must have been sensitive if we were kept in the dark," Kaz said, sitting across from Big Mike and eyeing the container. "But also, not without danger, Colonel. You could have sent any courier to transport this object. But you chose Big Mike. Which means you wanted someone with an imposing presence."

"To scare the bad guys," Big Mike said. "Like I used to do back in Detroit." Like me, Big Mike was an ex-cop. He was still part bluecoat and would break out his Detroit PD badge now and then to prove it.

"I figure there must be a piece of artwork in that case," I said. "But why are you bringing it back from England? If that's where you went."

"It is," Harding said, gesturing for Big Mike to open the tube. "Another reason I sent Big Mike was that I thought a sergeant, even one this size, would attract less attention than an officer. This is a highly delicate situation."

Big Mike gently extracted a roll of paper. I judged it about thirty inches by three feet once it was laid out.

"Meet *Nudes Reclining to the Right*," Big Mike announced. It was a drawing in red pencil, a sketch of two women with flowing hair, who looked like they were swimming upstream.

"Gustav Klimt," Kaz said. "His style is unmistakable. This looks like a study for a larger piece."

"It is," Harding said. "The painting is called *Water Serpents*. It's currently missing, appropriated from a Jewish family in Vienna. The Germans took this piece from an art dealer here in Paris."

"You recovered it," I said. "So what's the big secret?"

"We found it in England," Harding said. "At an estate in Upper Slaughter, somewhere in the Cotswolds."

"Real pretty country," Big Mike said. "Too bad I had to hotfoot it back here."

"Wait," I said, trying to take in the implications. My mind was still a bit fuzzy from yesterday. "More artwork? Is this connected to the Syndicat?"

"I didn't see any connection until you found that Dürer print," Harding said. "And all I know now is that we have art theft happening in Paris and artwork showing up in England. I want to know how it got there, and if it leads back to the Syndicat."

I leaned over to study the drawing. I didn't know anything about Gustav Klimt except that he liked naked ladies. These two women leaned languidly against each other, one of them gazing directly at the viewer, hair swirling over breasts and buttocks.

"This would definitely be banned in Boston," I said. I sat back in my chair, not wanting to appear overly interested in what the artist had so vividly accomplished with a few pencil strokes.

"The Nazis were not fans themselves," Kaz said. "I believe Klimt is on their list of degenerate painters."

"This is fascinating, Colonel, but what does it have to do with us? I thought we were after whoever killed our CIC agent," I said, trying to figure out Harding's angle. The army frowned on looting, but there was no way we were going to put a dent in that particular racket. "Why all the cloak-and-dagger with Big Mike's trip to England? It's not adding up."

"Let me lay it out for you," Harding said, but he was interrupted as his office door swung open.

"Good morning," General Eisenhower said. We all stood to attention, but he waved it off as he leaned against Harding's desk, hands in his pockets. "Have you finished briefing them, Colonel?"

"We were just getting to the crux of the matter, General," Harding said. He did sit down, but he did it at attention. "It may help if they hear from you how important this is."

"Important enough for me to order you to send Big Mike to fetch that thing," General Eisenhower said, nodding at the sketch on the table. "Everything go okay?"

"Smooth as silk, General," Big Mike said.

"General, I look forward to hearing how this sketch attracted your interest," Kaz said. "Militarily, I mean."

"Lieutenant Kazimierz, even a fella from Abilene can appreciate fine artwork," the general said. "But it isn't Mr. Klimt's technique we're concerned about. It's a matter relating to intelligence. Intelligence at the highest levels."

"There's some link between the estate in Upper Slaughter and an intelligence service, General?" I asked, trying to see how this might have implications for the war effort. Was the Syndicat trading artwork for military secrets?

"To be precise, the family in question is linked not to one intelligence service, but to the dissemination and distribution of intelligence throughout the European Theater of Operations," Eisenhower said. "Which means this will have to be handled with discretion, William."

In settings like this, he often called me by my first name, as long as I hadn't done anything to get him mad at me. In private, I called him Uncle Ike.

Not that he was an actual uncle. He was related to my

mother's family, and he was an older cousin of some sort. On the few occasions I'd met him as a kid I'd called him Uncle Ike, and it stuck. I'd ended up attached to his staff after I barely managed not to flunk out of Officer Candidate School. It was supposed to be a cushy job in Washington, DC, but it turned out my Uncle Ike was being sent to head up American forces in Europe, and he wanted a detective on his staff to handle delicate—and some dangerous—assignments.

This one seemed more delicate than most.

"You can count on us, General," I said. Not because we were all that diplomatic, but on account of this sounding like a trip back to England. "I hear the Cotswolds are beautiful, even this time of year."

"Sorry, William," he said. "You're going somewhere closer and even soggier. Colonel Harding, why don't we use the map room? I've got a few minutes before the intelligence briefing."

When the Supreme Commander has a suggestion, everyone agrees. We left Harding's office for the map room down the hall.

"How are your folks, William?" Uncle Ike asked on the way.

"Well, sir. I got a letter from my mother a few days ago," I said.

"Please give her my best," he said. "You are writing home regularly, aren't you?"

"Yes, sir," I said, making a mental note to get a letter off soon.

We entered a large room with maps laid out on tables and map boards set up around the perimeter. General Eisenhower stood by a map showing the front lines from Switzerland up to Holland.

"General Montgomery has his 21st Army Group on our left flank, mainly in Belgium," Uncle Ike began. "That's made up of the British Second Army and the First Canadian Army, each with nine divisions, plus other attached units."

"Just south of Montgomery we have General Bradley's 12th Army Group, covering southern Belgium, Luxembourg, and much of the French border with Germany," Harding said. "The

12th Army is even larger than Monty's, and much more spread
out." Bradley's army group included George Patton's Third Army,
and south of him, the 6th Army Group held the line all the way
to Switzerland and the Italian border.

"Intelligence is a two-way street, gentlemen," the general said.
"It needs to be gathered at the front lines, and it must also be
delivered to the front securely. General Montgomery has devel-
oped an excellent method for both. Colonel Harding will provide
the details, but that network is now potentially at risk. I need you
to find out for certain. Straighten this out, quickly. And no international incidents while you're at it. Good luck." He gave me a
smile and a pat on the shoulder as he left.

"Belgium?" I said. "Monty?" Not that I had anything against
Belgium, but General Bernard Law Montgomery had a reputation for disliking Yanks and placing his headquarters in field
tents and trailers when perfectly good chateaus stood empty.

"That's where you need to start," Harding said, and went on
to detail the intelligence network we were going to investigate.

The British had created a unit called the GHQ Liaison
Regiment. Its role was to patrol the front lines and send reports
directly to headquarters. These were small units in radio-equipped
jeeps, motorcycles, and scout cars. The patrols had been code-
named Phantom, and that was what they were commonly called.
They operated up and down the line, observing and radioing
reports to higher headquarters. There was one patrol for each
division, and the technique had been replicated for General
Omar Bradley's army group. That made for dozens of Phantom
patrols with unrestricted access to not only combat areas but rear
area headquarters. There were also Special Liaison Units, officers
who delivered high-level intelligence from secure sites in Great
Britain to commanders in the field.

"It all adds up to a lot of people with security clearances running around between the Continent and England," Harding said.
"They can come and go as they please."

"It was one of them who smuggled the Klimt sketch out of France?" Kaz asked.

"Yes. Captain Malcolm Rawson," Harding said. "An intelligence officer who works with the Special Liaison Unit. He's based at the 21st Army Group main headquarters and provides top secret briefings at Monty's tactical HQ. He keeps in touch with the Phantom patrols in person. He has complete freedom of movement."

"Not to mention a pal who carried the drawing back to England for him," Big Mike said. "A friend of his who had a week's leave. Rawson told him it was a Christmas gift for his mother, and he wanted to be sure it got there in time. His friend got suspicious and opened it. He realized Rawson had used him, and that if things went south he'd be an accomplice."

"What did he do? I can't imagine he picked up a telephone and called SHAEF," Kaz said. He studied the map, his finger tracing the route between Montgomery's tactical HQ near the Albert Canal and the main HQ farther to the rear, outside of Brussels.

"No, he called Scotland Yard," Harding said. "They decided it was a hot potato and sent it our way, courtesy of Chief Inspector Scutt." We'd worked with Scutt a couple of times. He was beyond retirement age and still doing his bit, staying at his post until the war was over. The Yard was shorthanded, and he was likely glad to get a tricky case off his desk.

"Who took Rawson into custody?" I asked, wondering if Big Mike had cuffed him once he had the evidence.

"No one," Harding said. "We're watching him in hopes his supplier contacts him again."

"You'll never guess who's doing the watching," Big Mike said, barely suppressing a grin. "Peter Seaton."

"Diana told me he'd been transferred out of the Med," I said. That was when we'd gathered at her father's place, Seaton Manor, for a bit of leave. Diana's father, Sir Richard, held some shadowy post with the British intelligence services. He might even have been the guy who pulled whatever strings got his son, Peter, onto Monty's staff.

Diana Seaton and I were close. Closer than an Irish kid from Boston and a British aristocrat had a right to be. I fell for her hard when I first ran into her in '42. I'd spent the last few years worrying about her making it back alive from each of her missions with the Special Operations Executive. Agents behind enemy lines in occupied Europe weren't known for their longevity.

"Peter is quite an intelligent chap," Kaz said. "A good choice for our inside man." Kaz had known Peter long before I did. Kaz and Diana's sister, Daphne, had been in love. The kind of love that withstood the Blitz and grew even deeper as London burned. A killer had put an end to Daphne and gave Kaz the scar that would always remind him of what he'd lost. Even now, he'd often trace that line of sorrow on his cheek, a faint imitation of a lover's caress.

"Captain Seaton will provide you with whatever information he can," Harding said. "You'll look him up as a friend and no one will be the wiser."

"We should get going. It's a long drive into Belgium," I said, glancing at the map.

"First thing tomorrow," Harding said. "Today you deliver this drawing to our Civil Affairs people."

"Why not to Rose Valland?" Kaz asked. "After all, it was taken from a French art dealer."

"That's part of the problem," Harding said, ushering us out of the map room as the brass filed in, glancing in our unauthorized direction. One British officer wearing horn-rimmed glasses looked particularly aggrieved at our presence. Harding kept quiet until we were back in his office with the door firmly shut. "We don't want any political or diplomatic issues. We can't afford any potential discord between allies."

"Ah, I see," Kaz said, tapping his finger against his jaw. "The Klimt was stolen by the British and spirited out of France. It is not bad enough that they were plundered by the Germans, but to have it repeated at the hands of the English would be an insult."

"Exactly. General de Gaulle is very sensitive on matters of sovereignty," Harding said. "That's why you're going to return this to a collection center outside of Paris. It's run by the Monuments, Fine Arts, and Archives section of SHAEF Civil Affairs. They'll add it to their stash of recovered artwork, and it will then be returned to the French authorities."

"As if it never left the country," Big Mike said. "It's important that the French think it was simply misplaced and never left their borders."

"We have a Monuments section? Never heard of them," I said.

"It's a small group spread out among all the advancing armies," Harding said. "They do what they can to safeguard cultural monuments and works of art from unnecessary war damage. General Eisenhower himself approved it before the invasion."

"They call themselves the Monuments Men," Kaz said. "A unique formation in the history of warfare, dedicated to protecting culture in the midst of carnage. It will be fascinating to meet them."

I didn't disagree. I just hoped they knew how to keep a secret.

CHAPTER ELEVEN

"WE'LL WORK BOTH ends against the middle," Harding told us as he handed over our official orders and travel documents. "Big Mike will stay here and coordinate with Agent Salinger and Inspector Fayard to see if we can nail anyone from the Syndicat and get them to talk. After you deliver the drawing to the Monuments Men, work on finding out where Captain Rawson picked up that Klimt."

Harding confirmed he'd arranged for us to take the train from Paris to Brussels in the morning. Given all the military traffic on the roads, that would save time and hard driving.

"Do we have a cover story, Colonel?" Kaz asked. "We will need a reason to hang about General Montgomery's headquarters."

"It's all in your orders," Harding said. "You've been detailed to study how the British operate their Phantom units so we can improve our own operations in General Patton's Third Army."

"The Brits will love that," Big Mike said. "Telling Georgie Patton how to run things will go over big with them."

"If there's a trail to follow, you'll have carte blanche to go wherever you want," Harding said, taking a moment to aim a warning glance at Big Mike. At SHAEF, even the slightest swipe at our allies was quickly discouraged. "Let's hope Captain Seaton has a lead by the time you get there. And yes, there is an appeal to vanity in mentioning General Patton. The rivalry between him and Monty is well-known. But you will both refrain from any criticism, no matter the provocation. Understood?" The rivalry between Monty and Patton was common knowledge ever since their race to capture Messina during the invasion of Sicily.

"No problem, Colonel," I said. "I know General Eisenhower values Anglo-American cooperation." Before D-Day, he'd sent an American officer back to the States for calling another officer on his staff a "British son of a bitch." When the British officer told Uncle Ike that he didn't bear a grudge and hoped he'd reconsider, the general told him that he wouldn't have cared if he'd been called a son of a bitch, but a British son of a bitch was unacceptable. The American went home.

"Have no worries, Colonel," Kaz said. "We shall be the very model of Anglo-American harmony."

"You'd better be," Harding said. "Now get going."

Kaz and I made plans to meet Big Mike at Inspector Fayard's office after we delivered the Klimt and see if Salinger had come up with anything in the police files. We headed for Lognes, a town about twenty miles east of Paris. The Monuments guys had a collection center for wayward artworks in a building next to an army hospital.

The fog had cleared, but now a chill, thin mist drifted across the roadway. We took a route south of Paris, crossed the Seine again, and followed the road signs east to Lognes. It didn't take long to leave the city behind. Soon we were driving through fields and woodlands, military traffic heading in both directions.

Vehicles filled with supplies and GIs headed for the front ground, their gears grinding on the winding road as the wind picked up and blew away the mist. Ambulances and empty trucks filled the opposite westbound lane—a stark display of the expenditure of lives, blood, and treasure this war demanded.

"It is a good thing the Luftwaffe is no longer a threat," Kaz said, pulling back the canvas enclosure and gazing at the sky. "This road would be a prime target."

"Nobody's flying in this weather," I said. "At least not low enough to strafe a convoy." High above us, the sky was a solid, flat gray. Ahead, on the horizon, a series of ridgelines and treetops merged into a dull smudge of white and brown.

In another mile we passed the wreckage of two trucks that had slid off the road. Accidents in heavy military traffic were common, especially when vehicles ran at night with limited lights. Ice coated the sagging canvas tarp and shattered crates that had been emptied of Spam, beans, or whatever the quartermaster was serving up.

We slowed to take a right at an intersection marked by a sign for Lognes and the 7th Convalescent Hospital. Convalescent hospitals were for guys lucky enough to be able to recover from their wounds within weeks or perhaps months. Which, in the contorted logic of the combat soldier, was unlucky since it meant a return-trip ticket to the front lines.

Ambulances coming from the west took the turn as well, and soon we were in a line of vehicles making for the hospital. We pulled away as they halted in front of the three-story stone building that still bore the marks of shelling. Orderlies spilled out and unloaded stretcher cases, hustling them through the open doors and into the warmth.

"Over there," Kaz said, spotting a cluster of signs. One of them read CIVIL AFFAIRS MFAA. An arrow pointed down the road to a squat wooden building. Behind it were four large hospital tents, marked with a bright red cross and surrounded by jeeps and more ambulances. Across the way, three smaller wooden buildings were marked as administrative offices and a motor pool. A single jeep sat in front of the MFAA.

"Busy place," I said. I parked and got out just as a truck backed into the spot next to me.

"You the guys from SHAEF?" asked a GI who jumped out of the cab.

"Yeah, we're those guys, soldier," I said. I'm not concerned with a lot of army spit and polish, but I don't mind returning a salute

now and then. I fixed him with a stare that I'd often seen Colonel
Harding toss in my direction, and that did the trick.

"Sorry, Captain," he said, straightening himself and offering
a salute. "Lieutenant Rick Hansen. I was told to expect you."
Hansen was tall and thin in a Midwestern clean-cut kind of way.
He wore a knit cap and a field jacket buttoned up tight, allowing
no sign of his rank. His eyes flitted about, as if he was expecting
trouble right around the corner. "May I see your identification,
please?"

I was a bit surprised by his sudden switch to proper procedures, but I showed him our orders detailing the return of the
artwork and what was expected of him. I introduced Kaz, who
kept a tight grip on the tube holding the Klimt.

"Everything okay here, Hansen?" I asked when he returned
the papers.

"Sure, Captain. Nothing's wrong. Let's go inside," Hansen
said. He glanced at the corporal who'd been driving the three-
quarter-ton Dodge truck. "Corporal Pascale, you know what to
do." I thought he was telling the corporal to unload the truck,
but I could see it was empty. Probably because the identification
marking on the bumper—9A 35M—showed it was from the
Ninth Army's 35th Evacuation Hospital, one of the many
vehicles delivering wounded here.

Pascale saluted as we passed by. It was a lazy effort, but it was
nice to be noticed. The corporal was short with dark, curly hair
and an old scar under one eye. He didn't look like he was from
the Midwest. Unless it was Midwest of Scollay Square, one of
Boston's more colorful, and dangerous, neighborhoods. I nudged
Kaz and shot a glance in Pascale's direction. A brief nod in return
told me Kaz got the message to watch the corporal.

"You know what's expected of you, Lieutenant Hansen?" I
asked while I surveyed the room. It was a large open space, with
workbenches on two sides and stacks of crated artwork. The smell
of sawdust hung in the air, and fresh-cut planks were stacked

against one wall. About a dozen framed paintings leaned against the other wall. Duffels and sleeping bags sat by the door.

"I was told to cooperate, that's all," Hansen said. "What do you need, Captain?"

"For this to be returned to the proper French authorities," Kaz said, handing him the tube. "Along with the other artwork."

"What is it, and where'd you get it?" Hansen asked.

"It is a drawing by Gustav Klimt, *Nudes Reclining to the Right*," Kaz said. "A study for *Water Serpents*. How we came by it is unimportant."

"What you need to do is return it," I said. "It looks like you're getting a shipment ready."

"We are," Hansen said. He opened the tube and gently drew out the paper. He set it on a table and his eyes went wide. "I never thought I'd see so much art up close. This is beautiful."

"So you understand what you need to do?" I asked, trying to bring him out of his artistic trance.

"Captain, this piece hasn't been cataloged. There's no paperwork," Hansen said.

"This is the army; paperwork gets lost all the time. No questions, just do it, okay?" I said.

"Sure, Captain. We'll just stick it in one of the crates. As long as it's going to the rightful owner, right?"

"It is. The Krauts took it from an art dealer in Paris, and that's where it's being returned. Rose Valland at the Jeu de Paume will take care of it," I said.

"You know Mademoiselle Valland?" Hansen asked. He seemed impressed.

"Yes, and she will be pleased to find the Klimt returned," Kaz said, appearing to answer the question. "But keep this to yourself, please. It is a very delicate matter."

"I don't get it, but orders are orders," Hansen said. "I am really looking forward to meeting her. We should have everything boxed up and loaded by this afternoon. You were just in time."

"It looks like you're packing to leave for good," I said, crooking a thumb in the direction of the personal gear. Kaz wandered around the room, studying the paintings being readied for shipment.

"We have to," Hansen said. "Someone tried to break in last night. Never happened before."

"What was taken?" I asked. Now Hansen's jumpiness made sense.

"A Modigliani," he said. "*Seated Man with a Cane.* A very nice work looted from a Jewish art dealer by the Nazis after he fled France. We'd found it in an abandoned German truck outside Sedan, along with a load of furniture and rugs."

"How do you manage to come upon such treasures?" Kaz asked. He held up a painting of some lady in an old-fashioned gown, making a show of studying it, but looking out the window as he did.

"We put out the word in our area to watch for any kind of artwork the Germans left behind," Hansen said. "The Krauts liked to decorate their headquarters with anything they could get their hands on. A lot of trains and truck convoys were abandoned when they hightailed it out of Paris, and we go through those. Most soldiers are glad to let us know what they've found, except for booze."

"But someone decided to help themselves to what you have here," I said. "Don't you have any security?"

"We keep the place locked up, but it's only the two of us," Hansen said. "We bunk in a room out back with a small stove, so we keep an eye on the place as best we can. Hardly anyone knows we're here or what we do."

"Someone does," I said. "Why'd they take just one painting?"

"They were spotted breaking in," Hansen said. "A couple of doctors were walking back from those tents and noticed a flashlight at the back door. They yelled and got the attention of a few GIs who came running. The thieves bolted, but they grabbed the

Modigliani. It was the nearest painting to the door. Some local thieves who got lucky, I guess. Lord knows where they'll try to sell it."

"You are eager to leave?" Kaz said, as he kept watch at the window.

"I don't want to take a chance on them coming back," Hansen said. "We need to move closer to the front anyway. We'll bring this load into Paris and then relocate."

"You've reported the theft?" I asked.

"Certainly. To my superiors at Monuments, Fine Arts, and Archives," Hansen said. "Listen, I'll take care of the drawing, but we have a lot of work to do. Pascale and I have to do it all, from cataloging to packing, loading, and delivery."

"Delivery?" Kaz asked. He turned from his post by the window and leaned against the wall. I could see by his slight smirk that he was up to something. "Really?"

"Of course," Hansen said. "It's why we have to get a move on. This is a big load."

"There's something else, isn't there?" I asked him. Kaz was waiting to see if the lieutenant would come clean, and I thought I'd push him a bit.

"No, why do you say that, Captain?" Hansen said. I nodded to Kaz.

"Because you stole that truck," Kaz said. "Corporal Pascale is busy painting over the identification number right now."

"Hey, we can't steal something from the army," Hansen said. "We're army too. It'll still be an army truck. We just need to get this stuff out of here."

"You don't do your own deliveries, do you?" I said. I took a step forward and tried to look intimidating. Hansen was holding back, and I wanted to know what had spooked him.

"No, the quartermaster arranges all that," Hansen said. He let out a puff of air as if he'd been holding his breath. He looked relieved, which was a good sign he was telling the truth. "Bills of lading, the whole nine yards. But we can't stay here. We need that truck."

"So do the wounded, Lieutenant Hansen," I said.

"Listen, there's no shortage of trucks, not for the hospitals. They come through here by the dozens every day. But we're the poor relations as far as the army's concerned. All we have is one jeep, no other transport," Hansen said. He rubbed his hands together, lacing and unlacing his fingers. He had a case of the nerves, and I wondered if it was from me or an even greater threat. "I wouldn't do anything to endanger our guys. But if we don't leave with the paintings, the thieves will be back."

"How do you know that?" I asked, taking another step forward, hands on my hips. A provocative display to jar some sense into him.

"Because they told me," Hansen gasped, the truth escaping like air from a burst balloon.

"Jesus, Mary, and Joseph," I muttered as I brushed past the skinny second louie and went out the door, coming face-to-face with Corporal Pascale.

"Sir?" he asked, his eyebrows raised in all innocence. He went to salute and then seemed to notice the paintbrush in his hand.

"Get inside," I said. "And put the paint down."

"Captain, the lieutenant told me to finish this now," Pascale said. He shrugged at the apparent unsolvable contradiction.

"Move, you mug," I said, my frustration mounting. I grabbed Pascale like I would any two-bit bum back in Boston. By the neck, and none too gentle. White paint splattered on the ground as he dropped the brush and paint can. "You gotta let the first coat dry. What kind of car thief are you, anyway?"

"Hey, Captain, take it easy," Pascale squawked as I powered him into the room. Hansen looked miserable. Kaz was idly inspecting paintings as if he were browsing in an uptown art gallery.

"All right, I expect you two to come clean," I said. "We're

investigating the murder of a CIC agent at the hands of a gang
that is moving into stolen artwork. Picking right up where the
Nazis left off, for fun and profit. So spill, or I'll take you into
custody right now, and misuse of army equipment will be the
least of the charges."

"It's just like I told you, Captain Boyle," Hansen said. He
wrung his hands and paced the room as he detailed what had
happened. He and Pascale heard the shouts of the two doctors
who had given the alarm as they walked back from the mess tent.
The corporal bobbed his head in agreement, sweat beading on
his forehead. They'd run to the rear of their building, where
Hansen spotted the thieves escaping. He made a point of telling
us he was a sprinter on his college track team, and that he decided
to run the pair down, hoping that the guy carrying the framed
painting would drop it in favor of a sure getaway.

He didn't. Even so, Hansen outpaced the other pursuers and
began to close in on the thieves. Although it was dark, he kept
his eye on the light-colored frame and stayed with it. Which
meant he hadn't noticed the other bad guy hiding behind a stack
of crates, who burst out from his hiding place, barreled into
Hansen, knocked him down, and pushed the business end of a
pistol into his face.

"He told me they'd be back," Hansen said. "Through the front
door, in broad daylight, and they'd kill both of us if we resisted.
Then he was gone."

"That's why we gotta get outta here, Captain," Pascale said.
"These guys mean business."

"He's right," Hansen said. "There's no one here to protect us.
No MPs, and we're not part of the hospital unit. We're high and
dry here, Captain."

"What did he look like?" I asked Hansen, feeling some sympathy for the guy. The only reason he hadn't gotten his head
blown off was his assailant didn't want to give away his position.

"A big guy. Thick eyebrows, thin lips. But that's all I remember.

It all happened so fast I couldn't think straight. But he didn't sound American. He spoke English fine, but I think he was French."

"He had an accent?" Kaz asked.

"Very slight. But he said something in French as he left. *Craignez le renard*," Hansen said. "It means *be afraid of the fox*. Any idea what that's all about?"

CHAPTER TWELVE

"OVER HERE," HANSEN said as he showed us the route he'd taken in pursuit of the runaway thieves. The alley ran between three large medical tents on one side and supply tents near the road on the other. Taut guylines left a path no more than five yards wide.

"They had scouted the area," Kaz said as he stood next to a stack of crates draped in canvas. "They had their escape well planned."

"Where'd they go from here?" I asked Hansen.

"Down to that road, then they took a left," he said. "I was too shook up to follow. Frightened, really."

"Don't worry about it, Lieutenant," I said. "It took guts to give chase. We'll look around some more, but why don't you go start loading up. But don't leave until we get back."

"You're not going to report me?" Hansen asked.

"For scrounging up a truck? You're not going to get a medal for it, but I applaud your creativity. Make sure Pascale doesn't smudge the paint job," I said. Hansen grinned and gave an enthusiastic salute before he ran back, showing off his track skills.

"He's lucky to be alive," Kaz said. "The Syndicat apparently has a long reach."

"But how did they know about this place, and how vulnerable it was? They must be getting the inside dope on these Monuments guys," I said. We followed the path Hansen had seen the thieves take, which led to a side road that formed the border of the medical unit. The last structure was a large supply tent surrounded by crates covered by camouflage netting. A sergeant walked out, lit up a cigarette, and came to attention when he noticed us.

"Can I help you, sir?"

"Were you around for the excitement last night, Sarge?" I asked.

"Not much excitement around here, so I guess you're talking about the fellows who pinched that painting," he said. "You catch 'em yet?"

"Not yet. You see anything?"

"Just them driving away," he said. "I heard all the hoot and holler, so I came outside for a look. Then a jeep started up and I saw this guy lugging a painting. He jumped in and they took off down that road. Didn't get a look at either of them if that's what you're after."

"A jeep?" Kaz asked.

"Definitely," the noncom said, taking a drag. "Don't much like looters. I got a hard enough time keeping these medical supplies from walking off. Hope you find 'em."

"Thanks, Sarge," I said. We turned back to the collection center, both of us eyeing every vehicle on the road.

"A jeep," Kaz repeated.

"Yeah. They weren't after a truckload," I said. "They knew what they wanted."

We found Hansen and Pascale hammering together packing crates to hold the larger paintings. I got right to the point.

"What's the most valuable painting here?" I asked.

"That's difficult to say, Captain. It's hard to put a price on great art," Hansen said.

"Think like a thief. Which would get the biggest paycheck?"

"Forget about provenance and any legal issues," Kaz said. "There are wealthy people who will pay any amount to own a rare piece."

"Well, this one qualifies," Hansen said, lifting an oil painting onto the table. "*Portrait of an Old Man*, attributed to Rembrandt. It's from his workshop, definitely. It might even be a portrait of him. If it had his signature, the value would be inestimable."

The framed painting was about four feet tall, with a dark background and an elderly, brooding man. It wasn't exactly cheery, but it drew your eye and kept it riveted. I explained about the jeep and our guess that a single painting had been targeted.

"Where'd you find it?" I asked.

"A chateau outside of Soissons," he said. "It had been a regimental headquarters, but the Germans cleared out and left their loot behind. They had paintings and furniture stacked up in the foyer, but our flyboys plastered their trucks before they could load up."

"Fortunate timing," Kaz said. "But I imagine other treasures were lost during the Nazi retreat. The roads were littered with destroyed German vehicles."

"We were lucky to find it. But how did the thieves know it was here?" Hansen asked. "We get a lot of middling artwork. The place could have been full of it."

"They must have an inside line," I said. "Who knew you had this?"

"I sent a report in a few days ago," he said. "I asked for a pickup and listed the most important pieces we had, along with the total number. This one was right on top."

"To Civil Affairs in Paris?" Kaz asked.

"Yeah. MFAA is spread out everywhere. There're teams on the front lines and collection points like this one, always on the move. Civil Affairs is our only contact," Hansen explained.

"Okay, hustle up. We'll escort you back to Paris," I said. "Pascale, you got the new ID painted?"

"We are now ZC Q MT," he said proudly. "Part of a maintenance unit with the quartermaster in the Zone of Communications."

"Congratulations on your new vehicle," I said. "I'm going to organize some help loading up. How much longer?"

"We have about an hour's work to knock these crates together," Hansen said. "No more."

I headed to the administration building across the street. Armed with my SHAEF orders, I managed to wrangle a detail of six GIs to help. I hoped none of them recognized their truck. Pascale had chosen his identification well. The Zone of Communications, otherwise known as COMZ, covered all those areas behind the front. It was a huge territory with quartermaster trucks spread out across France. One more would easily go unnoticed.

The GIs helped with building the crates, and with ten of us at work, the truck was packed with its precious cargo in no time. I detailed Kaz to scrounge sandwiches at the mess hall. I didn't want any stops on the drive to Paris. Pascale offered to go, but I told him he was needed to check that the load was secured. It wasn't that I saw any reason to mistrust him, but on the other hand, this could have been an inside job. I preferred to keep both Monuments Men under close watch until we rolled up at the Jeu de Paume. Just in case anyone was paying attention, we said our destination was Reims, in the opposite direction.

We hit the road, taking the lead with Hansen and Pascale close behind. Kaz unwrapped a corned beef sandwich, and we each chowed a half. Traffic was light once we cleared the hospital. Well ahead of us, a motorcycle courier on a Harley-Davidson sped up, the low, deep-throated sound of the engine bringing back memories of street patrols in Boston. The sky was still gray, but the wind had died down and the road was dry. Not a bad day for a drive.

"The army gets a lot of things wrong," I said around a mouthful of food. "But fresh-baked bread isn't one of them." How GI cooks managed it still amazed me.

"Much better than bully beef and biscuits," Kaz said. "Although I do look forward to dining in Paris tonight."

I agreed wholeheartedly as I slowed to navigate the road as it curved through a small village. Traffic threaded in at an intersection, and I wanted to be sure we weren't separated. I glanced to the rear; Pascale was at the wheel right behind us.

A blur. Flapping canvas on a truck bed. Everything slow, everything fast.

Harsh smash and rending metal.

Kaz thrown against me as the jeep spun from the impact.

We were nose up on the narrow sidewalk. I tried to think, to puzzle out what had happened.

"Truck," Kaz gasped. His Webley was already in his hand.

Not an accident, I told myself as I followed suit and drew my automatic, tumbling out of the jeep and holding the weapon with two hands to steady my aim. A big, six-wheeled deuce-and-a-half truck had clipped us and smashed into the smaller truck Pascale was driving.

A khaki-clad man stepped down from the cab and aimed a pistol right at me. Kaz and I both fired, and he went down, slumped against the front wheel. I saw other GIs coming down the street, probably drivers drawn by the accident. This was going to get confusing real fast.

We skirted the rear of the big truck, with Kaz sticking his Webley inside as I kept watch.

"Nothing," he said, his breath ragged.

"You okay?" I whispered. I didn't feel great myself. I felt the shock creeping up and tamped it down best I could. Kaz nodded. He motioned for us to move, and we peered around the corner of the truck bed to the wreckage of Pascale's vehicle.

"Drop them," demanded a large guy. He had Hansen by the neck, an automatic pressed against his skull. Blood dripped from the lieutenant's forehead and his legs looked wobbly.

"No," I said. "Take what you came for. But we're not going to let you kill us all."

"Not both of you," he said. "A standoff, yes? But only one."

"Okay," I said. I dropped my pistol. Kaz was a much better shot. "How's the corporal?"

"Hurt," Hansen said. "Unconscious."

"Enough!" barked his captor. "Kick the gun far away."

I complied. He sounded exactly as Hansen described. Good English with a slight accent. French? Maybe.

"Now I know why you didn't shoot him last night," I said, taking a step forward. "You needed him today."

"Stop and follow me." He backed up to the rear of the truck, dragging Hansen by the collar. "Stay between me and your friend with the pistol."

We found ourselves by the tailgate. A small crowd of onlookers began to melt away, the drawn guns trumping any curiosity about the crash. I couldn't blame them. Any observer would have a hard time telling the good guys from bad. Kaz was ordered to drop the tailgate, which he did one-handed, keeping his barrel trained on our opponent.

"The Fox couldn't have been too happy about your botched raid last night," I said, trying to get him talking to buy time. I needed to figure out what came next.

"Shut up and get in there," he said. His only other response was to dig his pistol farther into Hansen's cheek. "Tell him where it is."

"Where what is?" Hansen said. He squirmed under the choke-hold on his neck.

"The Rembrandt. That's all I want. Tell him where it is."

"Attributed to Rembrandt," Hansen said. That earned him a whack against his head.

"It's not worth dying for," I told him. "It's in back, right?"

"Yeah," Hansen said, sagging in the grip of the much stronger man. "Back right. Marked RVR, *Portrait of an Old Man*."

I went into the truck, inching my way down the narrow space. Crated paintings leaned against each other, but the one marked as a Rembrandt van Rijn was at the front of the stack. I dragged it out, stood on the tailgate, and gently lowered it to the ground.

"What now?" Kaz asked.

"Now we all act very carefully," the thief said. "No bullet holes in Rembrandt." He instructed Hansen to pick it up, holding him by his collar. He backed away, keeping hold of Hansen and using the painting as a shield. As soon as he was at the center of the intersection, a jeep rolled up, followed by a motorcycle. He had Hansen place the crate in the jeep, and then told him to run. He fired one shot into the air, which was enough to send any remaining gawkers running. He got into the jeep, holding on to the crate. The motorcyclist gunned his engine, and the jeep with the Rembrandt followed.

Hansen made for the truck's cab and checked on Pascale. He was softly groaning. His cheek was bruised and bloody, but there weren't any other obvious injuries.

"We need to get him to the hospital," Hansen said. "How about the other fellow?"

"Dead. We'll check him for clues, but I doubt we'll find any. Was the guy who grabbed you the same one who tackled you last night?"

"Yeah. I thought he was going to kill me," Hansen said.

"He had no reason to," Kaz said. "But it would not have troubled him one bit."

"Jesus," Hansen murmured, as he discovered the blood dripping from his forehead. He leaned against the truck and pressed a handkerchief against the cut. Vehicles maneuvered around the wreck and traffic began to flow.

"There's an ambulance," Kaz said, pointing across the intersection. It was headed for the hospital. He waved it down and we got Pascale loaded onto a stretcher. Hansen told him he'd be back to check on him tomorrow.

"The truck," Pascale said, wincing in pain.

"It's wrecked, don't worry about it," Hansen said.

"I know, Lieutenant. But that big deuce-and-a-half ain't got a scratch on it."

I told Pascale he was a damn good car thief and to rest up. We went back to inspect the vehicles. The jeep's rear axle was busted.

The three-quarter-ton truck had a smashed radiator and who knows what else. But the huge six-wheeler, capable of carrying two and a half tons of cargo, didn't even have a ding on its big steel bumper.

"Looks like we need to move the artwork again," I said. "You okay, Lieutenant Hansen?"

"Happy to be alive," he said. "Let's get going. I want to be long gone when that bastard opens the crate and finds Pascale's artwork inside."

The crate marked RVR was a decoy. It had been Pascale's idea, our insurance policy against an ambush. The corporal had fit a wood plank into an empty frame and painted the familiar picture of a bald man with a long nose peering over a wall.

KILROY WAS HERE.

CHAPTER THIRTEEN

I DRAGOONED A squad of GIs to do the heavy lifting under Hansen's supervision. Captain's bars come in handy, especially when there's no one around who outranks you. While they moved the artwork, Kaz and I dragged the body off the street and went through the dead guy's pockets without too many curious eyes watching us.

"Empty," Kaz said.

"Yeah, not even dog tags," I said. "Let's take a look at his arm." We pulled off his jacket and unbuttoned his shirt. The only thing harder than undressing a corpse is dressing one, but at least we didn't have to worry about that. He had one bullet hole in his chest, and another bullet had grazed his jacket. I had squeezed off two rounds, but I'd bet it was Kaz who hit him dead center.

"No blood group tattoo," Kaz pronounced after he pulled the sleeve off. I grabbed the web belt, holster, and pistol, not wanting to leave loose weapons lying around. He was similar in age to his partner. Midtwenties. He had what looked like a shrapnel scar on his shoulder and a weathered look on his face. A man who had endured the elements. Fairly muscular. Close-cropped, fair hair.

"A soldier," I said. "What side is an open question."

Kaz draped the guy's jacket over his face, which displayed open-eyed surprise at meeting his fate despite such a well-laid trap. Perhaps he'd counted on smashing into art experts instead of two veteran gunmen. Which told me the Syndicat either got careless or they didn't know we were on their trail. A slight edge, either way.

We grabbed the jerry cans secured to the rear of the jeep and emptied the fuel into the deuce-and-a-half. As soon as the big rig was loaded, we took off before the MPs showed up, leaving two wrecked vehicles and an unidentified corpse behind. I didn't want to have to answer a lot of questions about any of that, much less the fortune in artwork we were transporting. We stopped at a rail crossing as a train rumbled by, and then took off on the empty road.

Kaz found a first aid kit in the truck and bandaged Hansen's cut, which had finally stopped bleeding. There was just enough room in the cab for the three of us, as long as Kaz kept his legs clear of the gearshift.

"Will this get me a Purple Heart?" Hansen asked as I got used to the feel of the truck, which was nowhere as nimble as a jeep. I was glad we had a lightweight load as opposed to a ton of ammo at our backs.

"A wound has to be from enemy action to get a Purple Heart," I said. "The jury's still out on that one."

"How do you feel?" Kaz asked the lieutenant.

"Like I've been hit by a truck," Hansen said. He smiled, but he wasn't joking.

"How'd you get into the art business?" I asked him. I was curious, but mostly I wanted him to stay awake and alert in case he had a concussion, or worse.

"I studied art at the University of Chicago," he said. "That got me a job restoring antiquities at the Baltimore Museum of Art until I joined the army in '42. I was pushing papers at a base in Louisiana when I saw the notice calling for art professionals to join a unit to protect cultural artifacts in Europe. That was right up my alley, so here I am. Never thought it would get this personal."

"The Nazis take plundering very seriously," Kaz said. "So does the Syndicat du Renard."

"Do you have any idea who at Civil Affairs might be tipping off the Syndicat?" I asked as I pressed the accelerator on the wide, straight road. We skirted the Bois de Vincennes, a huge wooded park on the east side of Paris. Not a motorcycle or ambush in sight.

"No, but I don't know the staff there well," Hansen said. "They employ a lot of French experts, so the information could come from anyone who's worked with them."

"Have there been any other attempted thefts?" Kaz asked.

"None that I know of. No one even thought about being robbed, not after we recovered so much of what the Nazis stole," Hansen said. "Maybe it's the Germans taking it back?"

"I think they have more to worry about right now," I said. "Like keeping us out of the Fatherland."

"There is much money to be made here," Kaz said. "And right now, things are fluid, which is the perfect time to strike. I imagine issues of provenance are greatly confused, which will only help the thieves."

"The Krauts forced Jewish owners to sell their art at rock-bottom prices," Hansen said. "That got them a legal bill of sale. But it's still theft. I don't know how things are going to get back to their original possessors after the war if they're still alive. But our job is to save as much artwork as we can and sort it all out later."

"You can chalk up today as a small victory," I said as we barreled across an arch bridge spanning the Seine. I threaded through the narrow streets of the city, all of us on alert for any signs of trouble. There was nothing but the usual Parisian traffic, and soon we found ourselves at the Tuileries Garden and the long, rectangular Jeu de Paume museum.

"We were not expecting a delivery," Rose Valland said, coming out to inspect the truck at her door. "But it is good to see you, Captain Boyle. Baron Kazimierz, have you brought me ce gros camion filled with paintings?"

"It is much larger than we required, Mademoiselle, but it was all that was at hand," Kaz said. "Allow me to introduce Lieutenant Rick Hansen, who sustained his injury fending off an attack on this very cargo."

Hansen about fainted at being in the presence of the famous Rose Valland, the savior of so much precious art. I filled her in on what had happened, leaving out the corpse but definitely including Kilroy.

"Absolutely brilliant," she said, clapping her hands in admiration. "Please, come inside while we have the truck unloaded. There are forms to fill out, as always. We will have coffee. *Real* coffee. I still cannot believe it."

Hansen chatted away with Valland, telling her about the discovery of the potential Rembrandt found in a German headquarters.

"We must take a look as soon as it is uncrated," she said, after telling an assistant to bring coffee to her office. "And we must ask Monsieur Narbonne. He is here today reviewing some pieces. He possesses a good eye."

"Who is Narbonne?" I asked.

"Stephan Narbonne is an art dealer," she said. "He closed his Paris gallery when the war began. He was worried about bombings, although things collapsed before it came to that. Still, it was fortunate. He sold some of his collection and moved to the country in southern France, where he hid the best of his paintings in an attic."

"Smart guy," Hansen said as we entered Valland's office. "The Germans never discovered him?"

"No. Being in Vichy France provided some protection. He kept to himself and waited things out. When the Germans crossed the demarcation line, they never came to his area," she said. "His village, Valence, was too small to be noticed, perhaps. He returned to Paris a month ago to open a new gallery."

"A resourceful man to have kept his collection intact," Kaz

said. "You said he was reviewing paintings. Is he buying from the museum?"

"Oh, no. Monsieur Narbonne has several clients who employ him to search out artwork that was taken from them by the Nazis, by outright theft or forced sales far below market value," Valland said. "We have rooms of orphaned pieces, I am sad to say. Stephan has been able to reunite some with their rightful owners."

The coffee arrived and Valland asked her assistant to find Narbonne.

"I wonder if Narbonne has heard about the Syndicat?" Hansen said as he accepted a cup of coffee from Valland.

"Everyone has heard about the incident in the cemetery," Valland said. She poured Kaz a cup and then one for me. "Everyone in the art world, I mean. It is a small community and word travels quickly. As it will with this latest incident, I am sure."

"Who else knows?" Hansen asked.

"Well, all the thieves in Paris," she said, and took a sip. "The appearance of an unscheduled delivery today is unusual, and the staff will gossip, of course."

"The Syndicat is getting more brazen. Perhaps you should ask Inspector Fayard for police protection," I said. I tasted the coffee. It was welcome, even with the hint of chicory. After four years of occupation and shortages, Parisians were still stretching their supply of java by adding ground chicory root, and Rose Valland was no exception. Times continued to be tough for civilians, and I couldn't blame them for hedging their bets. Hey, back in 1940 I doubt many thought the Germans would crush their massive army in less than two months and march into Paris unopposed. I'm sure some worried it could happen again.

"We do have our own guards, but perhaps such a precaution would be worthwhile," Valland said. There was a knock at the door and a man entered. Tall, with dark, curly hair and a thick mustache. Solidly built, he looked to be in his early fifties, maybe older.

"Monsieur Narbonne, entrez," Valland said. She introduced the three of us.

"Enchanté," he said, shaking hands with each of us. He wore a blue double-breasted suit that fit him well. Most Frenchmen these days wore clothes that fit loosely, the result of a poor diet and rationed clothing under the Germans. Life must have been easier in the hills of southern France. "Forgive me, please. My English is little."

"As is my French," I said. Valland offered him coffee, which he declined. His face reflected the curiosity he must have felt at being called into an office with three soldiers. Experience would have demonstrated nothing good comes of such a summons. We wore khaki, but his response was to field gray.

Valland began to explain the situation. I heard Rembrandt's name and saw Narbonne's eyes light up. She gestured to Hansen, who threw in a few halting French phrases.

"Je comprends," Narbonne said, nodding his agreement. We all filed out of the room, coffee forgotten. Valland led us down a hallway to where workers had pried open the crate and were admiring the canvas set on a table against the wall.

"Magnifique," Narbonne said, one hand covering his mouth in a gesture of awe and surprise. He leaned in close, examining every inch of the painting. He stepped back, this time with his hand on his chin in contemplation. "Hmmm."

"What do you think?" Hansen blurted out.

"Rembrandt? Perhaps," Narbonne said, then spoke with Valland.

"From his workshop, certainly, he tells me," Valland said. "But it is impossible for him to say more. It could be an authentic Rembrandt, but other experts should be consulted."

"Il existe de nombreux autoportraits de Rembrandt," Narbonne said, shaking his head.

"Yes, forty self-portraits, many of him as an older man," Hansen offered. "It could be."

"I agree," Valland said. "But this is an important painting, even if it is only attributed to Rembrandt's workshop. You did well to save it, Lieutenant."

"Bravo. Bien fait," Narbonne told Hansen.

"It's valuable, right?" I asked, cutting to the chase. "What could you sell it for?"

"Dix mille dollars américains. Peut-être plus," Narbonne said, snapping his fingers to show how easy it would be. Ten thousand bucks, maybe more. A savvy businessman, he'd had no problem understanding my question.

Hansen whistled. Too bad he wouldn't get a finder's fee.

"Do you have any clients missing a Rembrandt?" I asked him. Kaz pitched in to translate. The answer was no. His clientele had been forced to sell many kinds of artwork, but no paintings by the Dutch master. Narbonne's job was to search through collection points and museums to track down which had been returned and begin the lengthy process of restitution.

"He says the paperwork is terrible, since many were forced to sell, and in the eyes of the law, are no longer the rightful owners," Kaz explained.

"Thank you both for your help," I said. "Perhaps there will be something of your clients' in the rest of the shipment."

Narbonne nodded politely and asked Kaz a question. "Êtes-vous des hommes de Monuments?"

"He's the Monuments man," I said, pointing to Lieutenant Hansen. Narbonne embraced him and laid on the double-cheek-kiss routine.

"Héros!" Narbonne exclaimed, grasping Hansen by the shoulders and hugging him again. I backed away, not that any of his enthusiasm was directed my way. I wanted to get moving before someone opened the crate with the Klimt stored inside and started asking questions.

We managed to disentangle ourselves only after Narbonne gave Hansen his card and invited him to visit his gallery on the avenue Matignon. Rose Valland asked Hansen to return to the museum for a tour when he was next in Paris. The bump on his noggin and the Purple Heart forgotten, Hansen had his head in the artistic firmament.

"Where to, hero?" I asked as we clambered into the truck.

"I'd love to celebrate with a bottle of wine and dinner, but I better report to Civil Affairs and let them know about Corporal Pascale," Hansen said. "And get a bunk for the night. But I've never been there. You have any idea how to get to SHAEF head-quarters?"

"That we can manage," I said, starting up the rig. "Maybe you should drive and get used to this thing. It's yours until the army realizes otherwise."

"I can handle it, Captain," Hansen said. "I grew up driving a tractor on the farm. Where are we going, exactly?"

"Versailles," Kaz said.

"The palace?" Hansen gasped.

"Not the big joint, just the Trianon Palace Hotel," I said. "It's where we work when we're not out rescuing Rembrandts."

"You better stay at the wheel, Captain. I'll be busy gawking at the architecture."

CHAPTER FOURTEEN

THE AFTERNOON LIGHT was already fading, and it was only four o'clock. As we crossed the Seine one more time, the air turned colder, and a slight mist turned things damp. The wipers on the deuce-and-a-half worked better than the jeep's, meaning you didn't have to operate them by hand and drive at the same time.

We eased up at the main gate and the guard, who gave me a nod of recognition, waved us through. Hansen gazed out the window, slack-jawed.

"It is even more impressive in daylight," Kaz said as I pulled up in front of the Trianon.

"Hard to imagine," Hansen said, jumping down from the cab and taking in the five-story Trianon Palace. It was only then that I noticed the identification number on the truck.

"You're in luck," I said, pointing to the marking; GHQ G-5 HQ 2.

"How's that, Captain?"

"The Syndicat knows how the army works. GHQ stands for SHAEF, and Civil Affairs is G-5. No one would question this truck being loaded with artwork," I said.

"Damn. They had all the angles figured, didn't they?" Hansen said.

"Except for Kilroy," Kaz said as we walked to the entrance. The American, British, and French flags out front were being lowered by their respective soldiers. Their day was done, but we still had plenty to do.

Inside, the sergeant on desk duty told us Civil Affairs, G-5, was on the third floor. We took Hansen up, showing him our Office of Special Investigations on the second floor.

"Sounds pretty vague," Hansen said. "What's it mean?"

"We'll explain later," I said. "We'll talk to Civil Affairs with you, since it might take some explaining. Then we have a report of our own to make."

We entered the G-5 office, which was a large, open room with signs listing all functions of a civil affairs command: medical, judicial, refugees, war crimes, and fine arts. We made for the fine arts desk, manned by a Captain Willoughby. He was nearly bald, wore thick glasses, and definitely had a few years on the rest of us. He looked surprised to see Hansen with his bloodied bandage.

"There's been a development at the Lognes collection point, Captain. Lieutenant Hansen helped us to thwart a major theft," I said. I sat in front of his desk and motioned for Kaz and Hansen to do the same.

"I know of Lieutenant Hansen and Corporal Pascale," Willoughby said. "But who are you?"

I gave him a rundown of our involvement, leaving out the Klimt and explaining we'd been sent to assess the possible threat. I praised Hansen for his quick response to the attempted theft, his role in thwarting the ambush, and his initiative in getting the delivery to Rose Valland.

"This is all unexpected," Willoughby said, trying to catch up. "We didn't have a delivery scheduled."

"Which demonstrates the lieutenant's resourcefulness," Kaz said. "Do you not agree?"

"But what does this Office of Special Investigations do, exactly?" Willoughby asked.

"We investigate things," I said. "Special things, as ordered by General Eisenhower."

"I see. Yes. Well done, Lieutenant. Let me see about setting up a new collection point for you, someplace with better security," Willoughby said. "But how did you transport everything? You only have a jeep."

"This MFAA team now has a new deuce-and-a-half truck, Captain," I said. "Official army issue."

"But how?"

"Courtesy of the Office of Special Investigations," Kaz said, with a smile.

"I wish all our officers were as resourceful," Willoughby said, sensing he shouldn't press the point. "Return in the morning, and I'll have your new orders drawn up."

"I'd like to get back and check on my corporal, sir," Hansen said. "He was injured in the ambush."

"I am sorry, but it will have to wait until tomorrow," Willoughby said. "I have an appointment. Ah, here he is now." The captain stood, showing more interest in this visitor than in Hansen. A civilian walked through the office, and by the polite smiles that greeted him, I gathered he was no stranger.

"Captain Willoughby, I will wait outside, yes?" The guy was well-dressed, his unbuttoned wool overcoat displayed his three-piece suit. But what stood out was the slight *vee* sound in his accent. Kaz and I exchanged glances. A German?

"No, no, come in, Monsieur Grau," Willoughby said. "I'd like to introduce you to one of our field officers, Lieutenant Hansen."

"Henri Grau, at your service," he said, shaking hands with Hansen and looking in our direction. He was ruddy faced, with light brown hair and lively eyes. On the short side, with a slight paunch. "I see by your expressions, gentlemen, that you detect my accent. I have seen that look before."

"I shouldn't be too worried," I said, after introducing Kaz and myself. "Not if you've been granted entrance to SHAEF headquarters."

"Swiss, perhaps? Or from Alsace-Lorraine?" Kaz asked.

"I am Swiss, yes. From Basel, where most people are raised speaking German, but without the less desirable traits of our cousins across the border," Grau said. "To be honest, it says Heinrich on my passport, but Henri makes it much easier. First impressions are so important in my profession."

"Henri—Monsieur Grau—is an art dealer," Willoughby explained. "Something of an expert. He's been helping us assess some of the recovered art. I worry about fakes being substituted for the real thing."

"I've looked at a few paintings, that is all," Grau said, waving off the compliment. "But you, Lieutenant Hansen, you do the real work, so close to the fighting. You have my admiration."

"Thank you," Hansen said. The poor guy was in danger of being overloaded with praise today.

"Have you come all this way to simply look at a few paintings?" Kaz asked. I watched his eyes narrow, the way they did when he was trying to understand something. I knew the accent bothered him. As a Pole, he had good reason to be suspicious of anything Germanic.

"No, Lieutenant Kazimierz, I have come here as a businessman," Grau said. "I have an art gallery, and the supply of decent artwork has gotten quite low due to our recent isolation. Now that the American and French armies have opened the border from Geneva to Basel, we Swiss can once more travel and import goods. I introduced myself to Captain Willoughby as a courtesy and to let the proper authorities know I am interested only in art with a legitimate provenance."

"And how is business?" Kaz asked.

"Very good," Grau said. "I've made several purchases already, all at a fair price. Mostly from people who took precautions early and hid their artwork. Now, they need money. It is good business for everyone. That is what we Swiss like. Good business, yes?"

"Excuse us, gentlemen, but we must go," Willoughby said.

"Monsieur Grau has made a reservation for dinner. I'll see you at oh-nine-hundred hours, Lieutenant Hansen."

Grau gave a little Continental bow in our direction as Willoughby ushered us out of his office. The two of them walked quickly down the hall, hurrying to wherever Grau was paying for dinner.

"Monsieur Henri sounds so much better than Herr Heinrich, don't you think?" Kaz asked as we took the stairs.

"Better for business," I said. "He is Swiss, after all." We'd had a previous experience with the supposedly neutral Swiss. Cash was king in their world, for the most part.

"I wonder if he's been to see Rose Valland," Hansen said. "That guy Narbonne is working on reuniting stolen art with the original owners, but I bet he's got his eye out for bargains as well. Grau might be more straightforward about his intentions."

"Perhaps," Kaz said. "I imagine all art dealers are alert to profit. I was startled at the sound of his voice, that is all."

Grau was lucky Kaz didn't pull his Webley on him.

"You want to tell me more about what the sign above the door means?" Hansen asked as we entered Harding's office.

"We investigate low crimes in high places," I said. "Along with anything else General Eisenhower wants done quietly."

"Who's this?" Colonel Harding said by way of greeting. Salinger was just pulling on his coat and Big Mike was on the telephone. "And why are you late?"

"Lieutenant Hansen, sir. I'm with the MFAA collection point, formerly at Lognes. I'm the reason they're late."

"It wouldn't have anything to do with a dead body left at the scene of an accident in Saint-Denis?" Salinger asked.

"If that's on the road a little west of Lognes, I'm afraid so," I said.

"CIC pulled me off this case to investigate," Salinger said. "Apparently it's a GI with no identification."

"I don't know if he's a GI or not, but he was part of an ambush aimed at nabbing a Rembrandt from Lieutenant Hansen's collection," I said.

"Attributed to Rembrandt, or possibly from his workshop," Hansen corrected. "Either way, it's worth a bundle."

"Whoa. Slow down," Harding said. "Start from the beginning and tell me if your assignment was completed."

"Seems like I should hear this before heading out," Salinger said, shrugging off his coat.

"All set, Colonel," Big Mike said as he hung up the telephone. "Fayard is sending a detail to watch the museum. I'll meet him there once I hear what these two have been up to."

We gathered around the conference table and reported what we'd found. I started with the Klimt being secured inside one of the crates and then reviewed the attempted break-in the night before, and our deduction of what the Syndicat was after. How with the lack of security at the Lognes collection point, we'd decided to escort Hansen and Corporal Pascale to the Jeu de Paume, only to run into a carefully staged ambush. I wrapped up with the shootout and the decoy crate that Pascale had created. Everyone liked the Kilroy gag.

"We recommended that Mademoiselle Valland call in additional protection," Kaz added, "since the Syndicat may well know where the shipment ended up. They are brazen enough to raid the museum."

"You all know more about this gang than I do," Hansen said. "But the more publicity an art robbery gets, the fewer the number of potential buyers for the stolen pieces. The price is less, too, since there's more danger of being discovered. A nice, quiet theft allows the buyer to claim they didn't know anything about the robbery and got fooled by phony paperwork."

"Good point, Lieutenant," Harding said. "But we're not taking any chances. Agent Salinger, get out to Saint-Denis and see what you can find. Big Mike, make sure Fayard's got enough men at the museum."

"There's one other thing, Colonel," I said before Big Mike and Salinger left. "So far, we've seen three members of the Syndicat. The stiff at the cemetery, the dead guy at the ambush, and the one who got away. Make that four if you count the motorcyclist, although I never got a good look at him."

"So?" Harding asked.

"They all look like soldiers, Colonel," Kaz said. "We know one was Waffen-SS, and the other two had the same look. Men who were fit, scarred, and the right age."

"SS? That's the first I've heard of them mixed up in this," Hansen said.

"They may not all be SS," Kaz said. "But it is certain we are dealing with men who have been hardened by combat and likely have access to weapons. These aren't your common Parisian criminals."

"Isn't that what we already thought?" Harding said, tapping a pencil on his desk.

"We considered the possibility of a gang of deserters and criminals," Kaz said. "If these three men are any indication, it may be much more serious."

"Both the cemetery action and the ambush were signs of a well-planned operation," I said. "Gangs tend to be sloppy, and the Syndicat has shown no signs that."

"What about the botched break-in? Lieutenant Hansen almost caught one of them," Harding said.

"The only thing he almost caught was a bullet," I said. "Since they were only after one painting, the burglary had a good chance of success."

"All right, we need to keep an open mind about this," Harding said. "I'll watch for any reports of German infiltration. Anything else?"

"Yes," Kaz said. "We encountered two art dealers today. Stephan Narbonne, who spent the war in the village of Valence in southern France. Also, Henri Grau, a Swiss national from

Basel. He goes by the French version, but his first name is actually Heinrich. He was here today visiting Civil Affairs. Could you have both men checked out?"

"If Grau was granted access to SHAEF, that ought to be easy enough. Do you think these two are involved?" Harding asked as Kaz wrote out their names.

"Perhaps not," Kaz said with a shrug. "But they both are in the business of buying and selling art. It may be nothing."

"One more thing you should know," I said to Salinger as he got up to leave. "Our jeep was wrecked as well as Hansen's Dodge truck, which was borrowed from the motor pool."

"Borrowed meaning stolen?" Salinger asked.

"The identification number is creative artistic license," Hansen said. "Just so you don't think it was stolen by this gang."

"That'll save me wasting time," Salinger said. "But how did you get to Paris with all those paintings?"

I told him where to find the deuce-and-a-half we'd liberated from the Syndicat and how vital it was for Hansen to have a truck. Salinger said he'd record the ID number and look into where it was taken, but that probably the gang had changed the number, too, and he saw no reason to keep the vehicle for evidence.

"I'm beginning to think Pretty Boy Floyd would feel right at home with you bunch," Harding muttered. "Now get out before I decide I'm Eliot Ness!"

CHAPTER FIFTEEN

WE SOLVED HANSEN'S housing problem by having him
bunk with us. After Kaz sprang for dinner and some fine wine
in the hotel dining room, Hansen didn't seem to mind his bed-
roll on the hard floor. The next morning, we showed up at Civil
Affairs and found Captain Willoughby ready with orders for
Hansen to proceed to Mourmelon, where the 101st Airborne
was resting and reorganizing after a long fight in the Netherlands.

"A division of paratroopers ought to provide you with suffi-
cient security, Lieutenant," Willoughby said as he gave Hansen
his orders. "If you need a replacement for Corporal Pascale, let
me know."

"I'm sure he'll be fine, Captain," Hansen said. "He was just
banged up."

"Good. You'll need help getting set up at Mourmelon. They're
to provide you with radio communications, fuel, and whatever
else you require," Willoughby said. He gave Hansen a nod and
began to shuffle his papers.

"Did you have a pleasant dinner, Captain?" Kaz asked. "With
Henri?"

"Yes, I did. Henri Grau is a pleasant and knowledgeable
fellow," Willoughby said. "Now if you will excuse me, Lieutenant,
I have work to do."

"Of course. But I am curious. How did you come to meet

Monsieur Grau? I'm sure he couldn't have walked in here unannounced," Kaz said. "Unless someone vouched for him. I think he is the only neutral national I have seen at SHAEF."

"We've had members of the International Red Cross in this very office," Willoughby said. "Swiss, Irish, and Swedish. It's not unusual at all."

"On official business, as was Grau?" Kaz asked.

"Henri Grau has assisted the Fine Arts section," Willoughby said, his lips compressed as if trying to keep his irritation bottled up. "He is also a pleasant dinner companion and quite knowledgeable when it comes to Vermeer and other Dutch painters of his era, which is an area of interest for me."

"Did you mention Mourmelon as a new location for Hansen's collection point?" I asked.

"Captain, I resent the implication that I would discuss military matters with a civilian, no matter how helpful he has been to our efforts," Willoughby said.

"Of course you wouldn't share actual military information," I said. "I was just wondering if Grau would be reviewing any of the artwork Lieutenant Hansen gathers."

"I have no plans to utilize Henri in the future, mainly because he's returning to Basel for the holidays. Apparently, he's made some purchases and is looking forward to restocking his gallery. Now, I must finish this report, if you'll excuse me. I'll be briefing General Bradley's staff at his headquarters in Luxembourg City in two days on what to expect when we cross into Germany proper."

"Cathedrals and that sort of thing?" I asked.

"Important cultural structures of course," he said. "As well as depositories of looted art. I've done it before at other HQs. Good day, gentlemen." With that, Captain Willoughby returned to his paperwork and did a convincing job of ignoring us. We took the hint and left since it was obvious that he was focused on his report, as well as saying nothing of any substance about Grau.

"It is early yet, but let us stop and see if Colonel Harding has found anything," Kaz said as we walked down the stairs. "Willoughby seemed nervous, did he not?"

"Hey, I was pretty nervous he was going to pull my orders and put me on KP just for associating with you," Hansen said. "You think there's something phony about Grau?"

"I am the suspicious sort, that is all," Kaz said. "What are Willoughby's qualifications as an art professional?"

"He taught art history at some college in New England," Hansen said. "No museum experience, nothing hands-on. He knows the basics, but that's it. Probably why he's glad to have Grau helping him."

That made sense to me. So did Kaz's intuition. Only one could be right and I had no idea which.

Harding was at his desk going through a mountain of papers. He leaned back in his chair and stretched. "I thought you two would be on a train by now."

"Last night we decided to go back to Lognes with Lieutenant Hansen," I said. "We want to check on Corporal Pascale and see how he's doing. We'll catch the train at the Lognes station."

"The fellow who came up with the Kilroy joke? He ought to get a promotion for that," Harding said. "Okay. Peter Seaton will have someone waiting for you at the Leuven train station, so don't take too long. We had some news last night, by the way. Salinger found the guy he'd originally questioned."

"Great," I said. "Is he talking?"

"No, he's been pretty closemouthed, mainly due to a bullet through the heart," Harding said. "A .38 slug. Nice shooting, Lieutenant Kazimierz."

"I told you to wound him, Kaz," I said, wincing at the bad luck.

"As I recall, you did an excellent job wounding his jacket sleeve," Kaz said. "A pity, Colonel."

"It is," Harding agreed. He was either scowling or smiling. It was hard to tell sometimes. "CIC has Salinger hunting down leads on stolen trucks, but between accidents and enemy action, there are so many lost vehicles it'll be hard to find where it came from."

"Colonel, have you been able to look into the art dealers?" Kaz asked. He was rocking backward on his feet, a sign of his eagerness to pursue the mystery of Monsieur Grau.

"Grau seems legitimate. He presented his Swiss passport when he first visited SHAEF," Harding said. "It passed muster, and he was invited here by Civil Affairs, courtesy of Captain Willoughby. Security did check out his identity, and there is an art gallery in Basel under his name."

"And Stephan Narbonne?" Kaz asked.

"Lieutenant, am I your superior officer or your personal concierge?" Harding said. "Do you have any reason to suspect Narbonne?"

"No sir, no reason," Kaz said, taking half a step back. "I thought it worthwhile since they both have connections in the art world."

"Big Mike is with Fayard and they're going to the Jeu de Paume. I told him to have Fayard check the man out. I think that's satisfactory, don't you?" Harding said.

"Excellent idea, Colonel," I said, hustling Kaz out before he had a chance to ask Harding to pick up his dry cleaning.

ONCE WE CLEARED the wonders of Versailles and after a stop to fill the tank at a fuel depot, Hansen took the wheel. We passed through familiar countryside, a rare sliver of blue sky to the east.

"How about filling me in on that Klimt?" Hansen asked as he downshifted to take a tight curve. "We have been through a few things together in the last thirty-six hours. You ought to trust me with the story by now."

From the middle seat, Kaz gave me one of his raised-eyebrow looks and I nodded, agreeing it was okay to fill in Hansen.

"It had been sold on the black market, likely by the Syndicat du Renard," Kaz began. "A name with which you are now familiar. The officer who purchased it had it smuggled back to England, where it was quickly discovered. Bad form to steal art from your French ally after all they've endured at the hands of the Nazis."

"Bad publicity, too, if General de Gaulle ever found out," Hansen said. "Which is why you wanted it returned without any documentation."

"Exactly," Kaz said. "It would simply be chalked up to sloppy paperwork, rather than generating discord between allies. This should go no further, of course. Rumors can be more damaging than the truth."

"It never happened," Hansen said. "I'll be sure to tell Pascale to keep mum."

"Any idea what the Klimt drawing would go for?" I asked.

"I'm not an appraiser," Hansen said. "The painting itself would be worth thousands. Tens of thousands, maybe. A collector specializing in Klimt would be very interested in a pencil study, but I have no idea how much they'd pay. You must know what your buyer paid, right?"

"That's what we are going to find out," Kaz said. He wisely avoided saying the officer had not yet been arrested. We weren't going to be anywhere near Hansen's new collecting point at Mourmelon, but there was no way of knowing who in the army's art world he'd be chatting with and what he might let slip.

We drove through Saint-Denis, where the wreckage at the intersection had been cleaned up. Civilians made their way between shops, hurrying in the damp air. Except for yesterday's incident, the war had passed them by. Lucky them.

Things were quiet at the Convalescent Hospital, a far cry from yesterday's convoy of wounded. Hansen's collection point had already been turned into a supply room with GIs off-loading crates of rations from another deuce-and-a-half.

"I hope Pascale won't be here too long," Hansen said as we went in search of his ward. "I'd hate to have to break in a new man."

We found a clerk at a desk in the center of the main hallway, surrounded by stacks of paper and clipboards. An orderly delivered more papers, adding to the pile.

"I'm looking for Corporal Victor Pascale," Hansen said. "He was brought in yesterday after a traffic accident in Saint-Denis."

"Hang on, Lieutenant," the clerk said, thumbing through sheets on a clipboard. "Pascale, you said? I got no one here by that name."

"Check again," Hansen said. "It was yesterday afternoon."

"Okay, okay, but we haven't had any new admissions since noon yesterday. His name would be on this list, sir."

"It wasn't scheduled," Hansen said. "Maybe someone forgot the paperwork. Who can I check with?"

"This place runs on paperwork, sir. But you can ask Dr. Graham; he's the tall guy right over there." The clerk pointed to two doctors in white coats walking down the hall. One of them stopped to light up a smoke as Hansen approached.

"Dr. Graham? I'm looking for someone. My corporal. Vic Pascale," Hansen said.

"You're the art guy, right? Heard you two pulled out," Graham said. "I don't know where your corporal is, sorry."

"He was brought in yesterday. We had an accident on the road and a passing ambulance brought him here," Hansen said. Graham shrugged and looked toward the other doctor.

"I'm sorry, Lieutenant," the doctor said. "I was on duty when he came in. He didn't make it."

"What? He was fine, except for a bump on the head. He was talking, awake, and everything," Hansen said, trying to make sense of what he had been told.

"Internal injuries. His pressure was dangerously low when we got him on the table. The cut on his head was superficial, but he was bleeding internally. There was nothing we could do. He was gone in minutes."

The doctors left, Pascale's death part of their daily routine. Hansen stood rooted to the spot, watching them as if one might turn around and say he was wrong.

"He was fine," Hansen said. "He told me to take the truck."

"Let's go get a cup of coffee," I said.

There was a small mess downstairs for doctors and staff to grab a quick bite. The three of us sat at a table, hands held around our coffee cups as if in prayer.

"I'm sorry about this," I said. "Had you and Pascale served together long?"

"No, not really. Three, four months now," Hansen said. He looked at his coffee, then away, and spoke softly, "No one I know has ever died. Not even my grandparents. Pascale and I weren't even close, but we were together every day. I never imagined . . ."

His voice trailed off, and at that moment, Hansen looked nothing like an arts professional and US Army officer. He was a kid, blushing embarrassment and coming to grips with sudden death.

"It was an accident, basically," he went on. "They probably didn't intend to kill anyone. They just wanted the painting. A second's difference and he would have been alive. What am I supposed to tell his folks? That's up to me, isn't it?"

"Writing is your responsibility," I said, "but his death wasn't, and you shouldn't discount it as an accident. It's the war. If we weren't fighting the Nazis, Pascale would have been living his life back home. Everybody who dies, whether it's in a car crash or at the front, is a casualty of this slaughter."

"There are no accidents in war," Kaz said. "Only the living and the dead, and the sadness we carry."

CHAPTER SIXTEEN

WE WERE LATE getting to the Lognes railroad station, but so was the train. We watched Hansen depart for Mourmelon as the locomotive chugged out of the station, spewing coal smoke. There were three passenger cars with a dozen forty-and-eights at the rear. The boxcars had been designed by the French army to carry either forty men or eight horses, and the name had stuck. Now they hauled supplies to the front. Not too long ago the cargo had been artwork and whatever else the Germans could loot before they retreated.

Before that, these very boxcars might also have transported Jews, members of the Resistance, and others to their death, cramming a lot more than forty people in each. Suffering trailed us like a bad dream that stays with you even after awakening.

We found seats, stowed our gear, and settled in among the civilians and soldiers making their way to Belgium. It was quiet, probably because we were heading toward the fighting.

"I wager that on the return trip to Paris we shall see a livelier bunch," Kaz said as he crossed his legs and shook out a crease in his trousers.

"Let's hope it's sooner than later," I said.

Kaz made no response, both of us understanding how little control we had over where this investigation might lead. He opened his copy of *Le Monde* and was soon lost in the French newspaper. I stared out the window at the landscape flowing by.

Open fields, some with a few surviving cows grazing, others littered with the wreckage of tanks and the debris of battle. The next village we stopped at was unmarked by war, other than the absence of motorized vehicles and young men. Down the line, the next village was shattered, destroyed by artillery. The war ran its own lottery, depending on terrain, resistance, and impersonal luck.

I was jolted awake as the train pulled into Leuven. The rail yard was busy, and the platform crowded with passengers and luggage. It almost looked normal except for the neatly stacked piles of brick and rubble on the other side of the tracks. We grabbed our bags and waited on the platform, scanning the crowd for our contact.

"Captain Boyle and Lieutenant Kazimierz?" A British Army noncom approached and saluted, his hand palm forward.

"You found us, Sergeant," I said.

"Not hard to spot a Yank and a Pole around here, sir," he said. "Staff Sergeant Berrycloth. Captain Seaton instructed me to deliver you to him at main HQ straightaway." Berrycloth wore his three stripes with a crown atop them and a decent mustache that decorated a long face and tired eyes. He was maybe thirty, but the last few years looked to have been hard-won.

"Captain Seaton is not at the general's tactical headquarters?" Kaz asked as we walked to Berrycloth's jeep.

"No, sir. Monty likes to keep his staff small when he's close to the front," Berrycloth said. "Main HQ is just a few miles north. We're set up in an old school. It keeps the rain out."

"Sounds better than a tent or a foxhole," I said as I got in the back of the jeep with the bags.

"That it is," Berrycloth said in a low voice. He tugged his beret on tight, started the jeep, and we pulled out of the station, merging into the military traffic headed for the front.

"Have you been with 21st Army Group long?" Kaz asked.

"I've only been assigned to headquarters for a couple of

months," Berrycloth said, hitting the accelerator as soon as traffic thinned. "Been in the army since '39. I've already seen this part of the country, except I was going in the opposite direction. Toward Dunkirk. I like it better this way."

"How'd you end up at Monty's HQ?" I asked, hanging on as Berrycloth took a curve with little regard for the pull of gravity.

"Took some shrapnel and ended up in hospital for a month. They sent me to work with Captain Seaton because I'd taken a radio course when I first joined up. Always enjoyed fiddling with 'em. So that's what I do, for the most part. Tell me, is it true what they say? That Jerry's done for and the war's almost over?"

"Sarge, you've been in the army for five years," I said. "What do you think?"

"Ah well, I thought if that one rumor was true, two officers from SHAEF would know. Too bad. At least things are quiet right now," Berrycloth said. He drove us through a small town and turned off onto a long drive with a wide array of military signs, camouflage netting, and antennas. He parked in front of a long three-story brick building.

"A girls' school. None currently in residence, I'm afraid," Berrycloth said with a glimmer of a smile as he killed the engine.

"Welcome to Saint Catherine's School for Wayward Englishmen," Peter Seaton exclaimed as he descended the steps from the main entrance. "Piotr, it's marvelous to see you. It's been too long."

"It has," Kaz said as they shook hands and clasped each other by the arm. "I am glad you are this much closer to home. Might you get leave for Christmas?"

"No, I'm fairly new here so I'm afraid I'll be on duty while other chaps make it across the Channel," he said. "Billy, how are you?"

"Just dandy," I said. The last time I saw Peter was in Algiers, and the tan he'd earned in North Africa was beginning to fade. He had the same high cheekbones and thin nose as Diana, along with sandy-colored hair and lively eyes. "I'm glad you're our host. I'm looking to learn a thing or two about the Phantom patrols." That was for the benefit of Sergeant Berrycloth, and to remind myself about our cover story.

I followed Peter and Kaz in. They walked side by side, speaking softly and catching up the way old friends do. They'd known each other since 1940, when Kaz met Daphne during the Blitz. Now they shared a bond of memory and unspoken grief which had yet to lessen.

"There are dormitory rooms upstairs," Peter said as he stopped in front of what had likely once been a classroom. "Berrycloth will see to your bags while we wait for the intelligence briefing to begin."

"Perhaps we'll have a chance to discuss our mutual friend later," I said. I kept my tone conversational as we shrugged off our coats and settled into the back row.

"At dinner, certainly," Peter said. He caught my eye and then directed his gaze to an officer sitting at a table on a raised dais. Captain Malcolm Rawson was my guess. He unfolded a map and studied it while I studied him. Dark hair, cut short and beginning to recede. Midthirties, soft cheeks, and a Clark Gable mustache. He didn't look like an art thief, but I hadn't made the acquaintance of many. Three, actually, and two were toes up. So what did I know?

A few more officers filtered in, filling up the twenty or so seats. Rawson stood to attention as a senior officer along with a major walked to the front. Everyone rose, but the officer waved off the military courtesy as he stood in front of a large wall map outlining current positions from the Netherlands to Switzerland.

"Brigadier Edgar Williams, Monty's head of intelligence," Peter whispered.

"I saw him at SHAEF," I said, recognizing the Brit in the horn-rimmed glasses who'd been displeased at our presence in the map room.

"How about the other chap?" Peter asked, grinning.

"Is it him?" Kaz whispered to Peter. I shrugged and wondered, *him who?*

"Before we begin the daily brief, I should like to acknowledge our two visitors from SHAEF headquarters," Rawson began. "Captain Boyle and Lieutenant Kazimierz are here to learn from our Phantom chaps. To benefit General Patton as I understand it." Rawson smiled and there was a ripple of laughter across the room.

"Needs the help, does he?" Brigadier Williams said, flashing a disarming grin to show no offense was meant. "Glad to have you here. Now, we are just back from an intelligence briefing at SHAEF ourselves. I'll leave it to the good major to summarize the findings whilst I report them to Monty. But I will share one bit of good news. For those of you who have had leave approved for the holiday, it looks like you may proceed with your plans. But no further leave will be granted, so don't bother asking." This was greeted by groans and applause in equal measure as Williams took his leave. "The floor is yours, Niv."

Niv?

"Major David Niven, late of the silver screen," Peter said. "Now one of our intelligence wizards."

"The last time I saw him he was Raffles," I said.

"With Olivia de Havilland," Kaz said. "Delightful film."

"All right, gentlemen, calm yourselves," Niven said, quieting the chatter that followed Williams's departure. "Here's the gen. The Germans opposite our 21st Army Group front appear to be inactive at the moment. Resting and refitting, preparing defensive positions against our expected offensive, that sort of thing."

"When is the offensive?" asked one officer.

"The date's slipped my mind, old chap, but I'll ask Monty when I see him," Niven said with a grin that he quickly put away as he got down to business. "Now, there are a few points of interest when it comes to our American friends to the south. We know that several SS panzer divisions have been pulled from the line opposite General Bradley's 12th Army Group. There are mentions of a new Sixth Panzer Army being organized somewhere beyond the Rhine, perhaps in the vicinity of Cologne or Bonn. The conclusion seems to be that this force is being prepared to launch a counterattack once the Americans achieve a breakthrough east toward the Rhine or the Ruhr Rivers."

"Seems to be?" Rawson asked. "That's a touch vague, Niv."

"There are some dissenting voices. The head of First Army G-2, Colonel Monk Dickson, is more than a little alarmed at the buildup opposite him," Niven replied. He pointed to the area First Army was responsible for. "Look familiar?"

It was the Ardennes Forest, north of Luxembourg.

"The same area Jerry attacked through in 1940," Peter said.

"Yes, exactly," Niven said. "It would give me pause as well, but we think the Germans are much too weak to pull it off again. It makes more sense that they are building up forces to hit us at our most vulnerable, which will be when we cross those damned wide rivers."

"What do you think, Niv?" asked another officer.

"Dickson is worried enough that he wrote up an official G-2 estimate, warning of an all-out attack. Or counterattack," Niven said. "It's a bit confused, but he does have interrogation reports that cite a high level of morale amongst captured German troops. That's not something we've seen in a while. But no one else is taking up the cause, so I don't know what to make of it. General Patton's head of G-2, Colonel Koch, had some concerns about the transfer of three divisions from Scandinavia to the Western Front, but no one knows where they now are. Desperate men are apt to take desperate measures, so I'd say it bears watching."

"Well, I've got my leave sorted, so I'll leave you to it while I watch from London!" the officer replied, earning a round of chuckles, even though there wasn't much humor in it.

I looked at the map, remembering the news in 1940 of a

sudden, unexpected strike into France through the supposedly impenetrable Ardennes. The Germans wouldn't try that same trick a second time, would they? And in winter to boot?

Impossible.

Which is what they said about Charley Nash and the First National Bank in Charlestown. Charley walked into the bank one morning, gave the teller a bag, and told her to fill it with cash. He showed a pistol for motivation, and she gave him all she had without making a fuss. He walked out, cleared the door before she sounded the alarm, and got clean away.

The next morning, Charley must've figured if it worked so well once, why not twice?

He went back to the bank, pulled the same routine, and got clean away.

CHAPTER SEVENTEEN

AS THE MEETING broke up and people began to filter out of the room, I watched Captain Rawson make his way toward us. He welcomed us to headquarters and offered whatever help he could provide as we studied their Phantom techniques. As nice as could be expected from an art smuggler.

"Later," Peter whispered as he ushered us away from Rawson. "First I'll show you the Phantom Operations Room. Then I'll fill you in on Malcolm."

"At least tell me what a movie star is doing here, if you won't let me tackle Rawson," I said.

"David Niven was in all the newspapers when war broke out," Kaz said. "He flew back to England from Hollywood and enlisted. Reenlisted, actually. He'd been a lieutenant in the army before he went into films. I hadn't heard much more about him."

"Niv trained with the Commandos and led a Phantom patrol," Peter said. "He's been on Monty's intelligence staff since Normandy. Quite competent and very amusing. Ah, here we are."

PHANTOM OPS was painted above the door. Inside, maps covered three walls, all with acetate overlays marked in colored grease pencil. Sergeant Berrycloth stood with a clipboard in hand, directing a corporal as he updated positions. Beneath curtained windows a radio squawked, and more incoming data was recorded.

"All intelligence from our Phantom patrols comes through

here," Peter said, obviously proud in spite of this being a cover story. "Patrols are spread out over the equivalent of twenty divisions under Monty's command."

"You have maps of American units as well," Kaz pointed out.

"The Ninth Army and First Army under General Bradley have adopted the Phantom technique," Peter said. "We take their updates and add them to ours. This is probably the most current map room in northwestern Europe. It's heartening to know your General Patton has seen the light." Peter shot me a wink, reminding me to play along.

"He wants a direct report," I said. "Tell me, how do you get radio messages from First Army? They're about a hundred miles away."

"Berrycloth, fill in our guests, will you?" Peter asked.

"Certainly, sir. It's made possible by a Royal Signals Wireless Station in Spa, Belgium. They've set up a powerful transmitter and seventy-foot masts for aerials. It's a semimobile radio station, capable of broadcasting over a thousand-mile range, code-named Golden Arrow. Once a Phantom patrol gets within twenty miles of Golden Arrow, the Signals lads can relay the message here quite easily."

"I imagine it is used for other communication purposes as well," Kaz said, studying the map and the notation *GA*. "It is near First Army headquarters, is it not?"

"Quite close, sir. The First Army signals detachment uses them every day," Berrycloth said. "They also provide support and security. It's a twenty-two-man detail with a lot of delicate equipment. Those lads can amplify a message to go anywhere in Europe."

"Captain Boyle? I have a message for you from Colonel Samuel Harding at SHAEF," said a noncom at the door. He handed me a note that said I should telephone Harding at his extension at the Trianon.

"Telephone?" I asked Peter.

"Yes, we're hooked into the Belgian telephone network. They can connect a call to Paris," Peter said. "It's fine to use as long as you remember anyone can listen in. It's not a secure line. It could be anyone from a curious operator to a German sympathizer. It's useful for keeping much of our communications off the airwaves. Jerry can learn a lot simply from the volume of traffic, even if it's coded."

"I wonder what this is about," Kaz said as we followed Peter to the main switchboard room. "Perhaps the case has been resolved."

"Telegrams and long-distance calls are seldom good news," I said. "Let's hope this is an exception."

Peter told one of the switchboard operators what we needed and left us to it. We were told to wait at a side table with a heavy black telephone as the operator went to work plugging in electrical switches and making connections. Just as Diana had once done with the First Aid Nursing Yeomanry with the British Expeditionary Force back in 1940. She could have been stationed not far from here, and it was disconcerting to witness this scene, knowing what had happened to her on the retreat from Dunkirk and the voyage across the Channel to England. She'd been evacuated on a destroyer with the wounded, many of them laid out on stretchers on the deck. Then the Stukas came. Her ship was hit and keeled over. Helpless men slid beneath the waves while Diana floated away and was saved by one of the small boats that made the treacherous journey. It changed her life and launched her on a course of revenge with the Special Operations Executive. Maybe revenge was the wrong word. Perhaps she simply needed to know she was saved for a reason.

"Are you thinking about Diana?" Kaz asked, tapping my arm.

"How did you know?" I said, startled out of my thoughts.

"Because it is logical that you would, and also because our operator has been calling your name, quite loudly. Pick up the receiver, Billy."

I did and was rewarded with a series of clicks as the final connection was made. Big Mike answered and put Harding on right away. I listened, watching Kaz's impatience play out as he drummed his fingers on the wooden tabletop. Harding went on at length, and Big Mike came back on the line when the colonel was done. He thanked me for sending him to the art dealer on avenue Matignon that I'd recommended, but said that his writer friend hadn't found anything he liked. After a few pleasantries, we disconnected.

"Let's go outside," I said. We needed to discuss this in private.

"What did the colonel say?" Kaz asked as we exited the building and stood near parked vehicles, our shoulders hunched against the cold.

"Inspector Fayard is now investigating the murder of five men," I said, and gave Kaz the rundown on what Harding had said. He'd disguised it by saying that Fayard had been pulled from the art heist investigation, but the obvious news was the increased body count. Four Frenchmen had been found in a garage in Belleville, in the northeast corner of Paris. One killed execution-style, shot in the back of the head. The others killed by a variety of gunshot wounds, which suggested things had gotten out of hand. A fifth man was found floating in the Seine, hands bound and throat slit.

"The guy in the river was a known crook," I said. "Fayard also identified one of the dead men in the garage as a black marketeer who had been suspected in an art theft before the war. Another of the four was identified as a deserter from the French army, a former Resistance fighter who didn't like the discipline of de Gaulle's army."

"Harding thinks this is connected to the Syndicat due to the brutal style?" Kaz asked.

"That and the fact that a painting was found in the trunk of a car in the Belleville garage," I said as I rubbed my arms to warm up. "*Man with a Guitar*, by Georges Braque. Never heard of him."

"A Cubist painter of some renown," Kaz said. "The Nazis detest Cubism as degenerate art. But that did not stop them from looting and selling it for profit. Perhaps this means the gang is disintegrating. Torn apart by greed."

"Maybe," I said. "But if so, it's the first sign of weakness they've shown. Harding also described them specifically as civilians. He said the floater was thin as a rail."

"Even the deserter would have thought of himself as a civilian," Kaz said. "And most French civilians lost weight during the Occupation, even those operating in the black market, since it makes little sense to eat the profits. It is very cold out here. Do you have anything else?"

"Only that Big Mike and Salinger went to Stephan Narbonne's art gallery and came up with nothing," I reported. "They acted like a couple of GIs looking for a bargain, but Narbonne was on the up-and-up. Salinger acted like a hustler with his bodyguard, but Narbonne didn't bite."

"So he is either honest or too smart to fall for such a routine," Kaz said. "Not very helpful. Now may we please go inside?" I didn't mind at all, glad to feel the door close out the damp chill.

Civilians, Harding had said. As opposed to what? It had to be an oblique reference to the two previous corpses we'd encountered. Men you'd first describe as ex-soldiers. Fit, hardened men.

"I think perhaps the local talent is being aced out," I whispered to Kaz as we walked back to Operations.

"That would make sense if the Syndicat was wrapping things up and leaving with their profits," Kaz said. We stopped in front of the door, standing aside from the flow of soldiers in the hall. "But the presence of the painting by Braque suggests they have not sold off everything. Perhaps the men in the garage shot one of their number who had betrayed them to the Fox himself. Then fell into fighting over the painting and how to split the proceeds."

"Maybe. It's not like the Syndicat to leave money on the table. Now let's try and get Peter alone and find out what's going on with Rawson," I said, opening the door and nearly banging into Captain Malcolm Rawson himself.

"Sorry, old chap," he said stepping aside. "No need to gossip about me out-of-doors. I am ready to tell all."

CHAPTER EIGHTEEN

RAWSON LED US to Peter's office, which looked to once have been a roomy broom closet. We managed to sit around a table after Peter swept off an array of maps and documents, dumping them onto his desk. I had questions for both of them, and even though Peter was a friend, I liked having the two of them on the other side of the table in what had become an unexpected interrogation.

"I know this isn't what you expected, but Malcolm has a good explanation," Peter began. Rawson nodded, eager to agree.

"I thought knowledge of the situation was to be kept secret," Kaz said. "Captain Rawson was to be under surveillance, quietly."

"It was I who brought it up to Peter," Rawson said, leaning forward, in what might be an expression of earnestness or a reasonable imitation. "I was worried when I didn't hear from my family about the drawing. It was to be a gift for my mother. She's rather an art fancier. Never rubbed off on me, but she loves the stuff. Old Klimt in particular."

"Is that true, Peter?" I asked.

"Yes. I didn't know how to respond at first," Peter said. "I was going to contact your Colonel Harding, but when Malcolm said he was going to make inquires to be sure it had been delivered, I decided to give him a listen before he put his foot in it."

"And I'm glad you did," Rawson said. "I had no idea when I bought it from Teddy that it was purloined. He told me he'd purchased it fair and square in Paris with the intention of sending it to his fiancée. But she gave him the heave-ho in what you Yanks call a Dear John letter."

"Wait, who's Teddy?" Sometimes a suspect who talked too much was harder to interrogate than one who kept his lips zipped.

"Teddy Dankworth, of course," Rawson said. He raised his hand to make another point, but Peter pressed it down and told him that was enough for now. Rawson looked disappointed. He was a guy who liked to talk, or at least didn't know when to stop.

"Captain Dankworth commands a Phantom patrol," Peter said. "He's on loan to your First Army right now. Apparently, he bought the drawing in Paris and told Malcolm he was waiting for paperwork from the purchase to show its proper provenance and all that."

"Well, it was a swell deal, and I didn't want to lose out, so I paid and told Teddy to give me the paperwork when he could," Rawson said. "I've had enough of paperwork in the army and don't care much for the civilian variety these days. It's just a gift to mother, not a bequest."

"Have you seen this paperwork?" I asked.

"No, but I haven't seen Teddy either," Rawson said. "General Hodges at First Army has probably seen more of him, don't you think?"

"Captain Rawson, what exactly are your duties at 21st Army Group?" asked Kaz.

"I gather data on the strength of the enemy opposite us and maintain their Order of Battle," he said. "Commanders, strength, organizational structure, that sort of thing."

"An important position," Kaz said. "It must take an intelligent chap to sort all that out. Yet you believed what Teddy Dankworth told you?"

"Well, it was Teddy. He has a way of making you believe him," Rawson said.

"Tell us how you got the Klimt to England," I said.

"Oh, I simply gave it to a lieutenant pal of mine. He was off on leave and happens to live one village over from mother. Made all the sense in the world to me, at least at the time," Rawson said. "He's not in trouble over this, is he?"

"Not at all," Peter assured him. The lieutenant was more likely to get Rawson's job than a reprimand. "Anything else for Malcolm? If not, he has duties to attend to."

"No, that's all," I said, not wanting to unleash another waterfall of words. I stood to let him pass by in the cramped space and gave him my thanks for his cooperation. And silently, for leaving.

"He's really a bright fellow," Peter said. "He's nowhere as naive about enemy intentions as he is concerning his fellow officers."

"There is more to Teddy, I take it?" Kaz said as we shuffled ourselves back into our seats. Outside, the single small window above Peter's desk was already flecked with rain as the sky darkened.

"A good deal more," Peter said, leaning back in his chair. "This entire affair seems more at home in Teddy's lap than Malcolm's. Teddy Dankworth is a gambler, and usually a lucky one. He is also the treasurer of our officer's mess. There's never been an issue before, but he had a recent streak of bad luck at cards that coincided with a fair bit of cash in his care. He floated himself a loan, which turned out to be paid back by Malcolm's purchase. I didn't believe the story about his fiancée for a moment. Teddy isn't thoughtful enough to buy such a present. It went for several hundred pounds, I heard."

"You are sure of all this?" Kaz asked.

"Quite. It positively reeks of Teddy Dankworth's approach to life," Peter said. "He's a fine officer, and he gets better the closer he is to the front. But I wouldn't trust him with my checkbook or my girl."

"Where can we find him?" I asked.

"Roaming the aforesaid front lines," Peter said. "Let's go to Ops and take a look."

We found Berrycloth updating the map board. Peter asked him for the last reported location of Dankworth's patrol.

"He's currently with the American 106th Division, east of St. Vith," Berrycloth said. "They are a fresh unit, just arrived on the line two days ago. The captain is reviewing Phantom procedures with division staff."

"They are flush up against the Schnee Eifel," Peter said. "Some of the highest ground in the Ardennes. Unforgiving terrain."

"We need to talk to Captain Dankworth, and soon," I said. "When is he returning?"

"Not for several days," Berrycloth reported. "His patrol will be with the 106th for another forty-eight hours. Then he'll make his way back to First Army headquarters at Spa."

"Then we need to go to him," I said. I studied the map showing roads between Spa and St. Vith and tapped on a small town. "Maybe he could meet us here, halfway between the 106th and First Army HQ."

"Malmedy," Peter said. "That should work. We'll sort that out, won't we, Berrycloth? For now, I suggest dinner as the next item on our agenda. I've invited Niv. You'll like him, I'm sure."

Dinner with a movie star, commando, and intelligence wizard sounded like a nice break from dead Parisian crooks and pilfered artwork. Kaz and I went to our room, which contained two cots, one table, a crucifix, and a window with a view of the rainswept courtyard.

"I hope the food will be an improvement over the accommodations," Kaz said, throwing his coat on the table.

"I thought an army group headquarters would be a fancier joint," I said.

"General Montgomery favors the austere," Kaz said. "He has a penchant for schools. Did you know that in England he used his old boarding school as his headquarters? A trifle bizarre, in my opinion. But one that I will keep to myself within these four walls. Monty walks on water for many of his men."

"My school was run by nuns, and one time around was enough for me," I said. We freshened up and headed down to the mess, located in the east wing. It was a long, rectangular room sporting tall windows with the occasional breeze wafting through the curtains. Peter was at a table at the back, speaking with a white-jacketed orderly who stepped aside as we approached.

"We have duck tonight. And a decent Bordeaux," Peter said as we took our seats. Austerity did not reign in the officer's mess, apparently. "That should take the sting out of Malcolm not being your criminal mastermind."

"It is a beginning," Kaz said. "Tell me, how freely can we speak around Major Niven?"

"Listen, Niv comes off as quite lighthearted, but don't let that fool you," Peter said. "He's made of stern stuff. The only English actor to hightail it back to Old Blighty and sign up when war was declared."

"Oh, not that stuff again," Niven said, sidling up silently and depositing himself in his seat. He moved with a languid grace, his pencil mustache and sharp, clipped vowels marking him as one of the upper crust. "Don't listen to Peter. The British embassy wanted actors to stay put in Hollywood and encourage support for the war effort. I was simply too excitable to obey orders. Now, remind me what you chaps are up to?"

Peter introduced us, careful to note that Kaz was a baron of the Augustus clan, which elicited one raised eyebrow from Niven. He leaned back in his chair as he appraised Kaz for a few seconds. "And what of you, Captain Boyle?"

"We're here to learn about your Phantom patrols," I said. "And recommend improvements to General Patton."

"Like hell you are. Ah, here's the wine," Niven said. We waited while it was poured, Kaz and I exchanging glances.

"A toast," Niven said. "To the truth, however elusive she may be." We raised our glasses, clinked rims, and drank.

"The perfect sentiment for an intelligence officer," I said, avoiding his challenge.

"There's truth in that, Captain Boyle," Niven said. "A good intelligence officer does his research on what doesn't feel right. Which is how I know you work in General Eisenhower's Office of Special Investigations. And by the way, the bit about Patton was a little too on the nose, gave me the feeling I was being manipulated right off the bat."

"We thought it was clever," Kaz said, acknowledging that Niven had made us. "Your fellow officers found it amusing."

"Oh, it was. But I am cursed with a cynic's mind," Niven said. "It only took a quick telephone call to a friend at SHAEF. He says you are well regarded but known to be devious. Both of you."

"We shall take that as a compliment," Kaz said, with a subtle bow of his head.

"Niv, Billy and the baron are friends of the family," Peter said. "I'd trust them with my life."

"Well, you won't be the one to put his life into their hands, will you?" Niven said. His gaze slowly turned from Peter to me. "Peter asked me to take you to rendezvous with Captain Dankworth. I must travel to First Army at Spa for an intelligence gathering, so it makes sense, and I am somewhat willing to accommodate his request. But I wish to know the purpose."

"Okay," I said, taking a gulp of wine. "It all started at a cemetery in Paris."

"Well, that's got my attention," Niven said. "Do go on."

I described the stakeout and how it was linked to the investigation of the murdered CIC agent. I detailed what we knew about the Syndicat du Renard and their recent move into art thefts, and how our informant had been murdered. Then I covered the raid on the Monuments Men collection point. Kaz took over and told the story of the ambush and our theory that the Syndicat was made up of deserters in league with the Parisian underworld. He reviewed the latest news about the five dead criminals. Peter chimed in about the Klimt that Rawson had sent home.

"Wait, where's Dankworth in all this?" Niven asked, draining his glass.

"He sold the drawing to Rawson," Peter explained. "They need to find out where Dankworth purchased it and from whom."

"Listen, Teddy Dankworth can be a tad careless in his personal affairs," Niven said. "But he's hardly a thief. He may flirt with the notion from time to time, but no more."

"That may be what happened," Kaz said. "He is likely only at the edge of this affair, but he may have valuable information. We have no plans other than to speak with him."

"This all fits what we know of Teddy," Niven finally said. "All right, it's just fantastical enough to be true. I'll take you and be glad of the company. Ah, here's the duck."

We feasted on roast duck served with rice, mushrooms, and carrots. One bottle of Bordeaux led to another, and the conversation rolled around to the movies.

"Do you miss Hollywood?" Kaz asked after a while.

"It's all a bit silly, you know," Niven said. "Playing children's dress-up games in front of grown-ups. I try not to take it too seriously, which comes easily when I recall my first screen test. It was at Metro-Goldwyn-Mayer, and my nerves were jangled. I thought they'd give me something to read, but instead they turned the camera on and told me to recite something. All I could remember was a limerick, so out it came:

There once was a young man from Leeds,
Who swallowed a packet of seeds.
Great tufts of grass
Shot out of his ass,
And—"

"Niv, how are you?" said an officer, who came up from behind, slapped his shoulder, and ruined the last line.

"Jakie, I'm still alive," Niven said. "Glad to see you are. Care to join us?"

"No, no, I'm knackered. Just got in. You'll have my report in the morning, Peter. I'll leave you to your guests," he said, then stared at Kaz. "We've met, haven't we?"

"Yes, at Royal Ascot in '39," Kaz said, rising to shake hands. "Baron Piotr Kazimierz."

"Of course! We both lost a bundle on the nags and drank too much champagne, didn't we?"

"It would have been more if we'd won!" Kaz said. "It's grand to see you again."

"The pleasure is mine," Jakie said. "Sorry that I can't stay and catch up, but I'm about to fall over. Good night, gentlemen."

"Jakie's patrol was a rough one," Peter said after he'd left. "One man was badly wounded."

"Phantom?" I asked.

Peter nodded. "Jakie Astor is one of the best."

"Astor? As in *the* Astors?"

"Yes," Kaz said. "As in one of the Astors you would encounter in the Royal Enclosure at the Ascot racecourse."

"Oh yes, that's our Jakie," Niven said. "His pocket change could buy us all out. Fine chap. What say you to a nightcap?"

CHAPTER NINETEEN

"REPORTS OF ARTILLERY fire coming in from Dankworth's patrol," Sergeant Berrycloth said the next morning in the Ops room. "Nothing unusual, just another day on the Siegfried Line." That was what the Germans called the line of bunkers, tank traps, and fortifications on their border. Artillery duels were commonplace, each side looking to spot the other's gun emplacements.

I drained my third cup of coffee, waiting for the jolt of caffeine to overcome the effects of too little shut-eye and too many nightcaps. Niven showed no signs of wear and tear as he reviewed incoming reports and the weather forecast.

"We'll have a touch of fog to contend with," Niven said. "And the usual drizzle. Seems to be standard issue these days."

"There's something else," Berrycloth said, pressing a headphone closer to his ear. "One of our other patrols says the Germans were aiming searchlights at the clouds. It lit the area up like a full moon."

"Probably creating light to move units off the line and bring in replacements," Peter said. "Someone ought to wake up the artillery and put a stop to that. Are you chaps all set? Have enough cold-weather gear?"

"It's never enough," Kaz said, shrugging into his camouflage windproof smock. Niven wore the same over his wool battledress, and they both finished off with a thick leather jerkin. I wore my wool mackinaw jacket over as many layers as I could put on and still manage to move.

"I've sent a coded signal to your Colonel Harding," Peter said. "He has your route and assigned radio frequency should he need to be in touch."

"You have a radio?" I asked Niven.

"My boy, we are riding in style," he said. "My personal M3A1 scout car, outfitted with a powerful receiver and the latest wireless set. Armored sides, four-wheel drive, and a fifty-caliber mounted machine gun should we stick our nose where it doesn't belong. Quite roomy, and there's an ample supply of brandy aboard. What else could one desire?"

"Armored top and bottom?" I offered.

"Well, there's only a canvas top, and if we hit a land mine, I'm afraid the brandy will have been wasted," Niven said. "But far better than a jeep, I dare say. Are we ready?"

"As ever," Kaz said, pulling on his lined gloves. Niv had given us woolen balaclavas to wear under our helmets.

"Call in before you're out of range," Peter said. "I'll give you the latest. Good luck."

We said farewell to Peter, who promised to get off a letter to his father, Sir Richard, telling him of our fortunate meeting. Diana was still in residence at Seaton Manor, so she'd hear the news as well. Last I knew, she was awaiting her next assignment with the Special Operations Executive, and I hoped the wait would be a long one. Everyone said the war was almost over, so why should she risk her neck now?

The scout car had a white *P* emblazoned on the hood, marking it as a Phantom vehicle, and giving it priority on the roadways and at fuel depots. The canvas top didn't do much against the cold, but it was a lot roomier than a jeep.

About an hour out, as we approached Liège, Niven pulled

onto a side road and clambered into the back of the armored car to radio headquarters. He donned a headset, sat on a ration crate, and fiddled with the dials.

"Damn and blast!" Niven shouted. He lifted the headset from his ears as the tinny sound of music and static filled the air. "Jerry is flooding our frequencies with music. Worst of all, it's that ridiculous stuff with tubas and accordions. Should be against the Geneva Convention."

"Is that typical?" Kaz asked.

"It's not unheard of," Niven said, turning the dial slowly. "Sometimes it's Wagner."

After a couple of minutes, he found a clear channel and gave Peter his location. He listened, then winced as the music began again.

"Dankworth is in St. Vith at the headquarters of the 106th Division," he said. "He reported heavy artillery fire."

"In St. Vith? Isn't that about twenty miles behind the front line?" I asked. "The Krauts must be targeting it with their heavy stuff."

"That, or the front line isn't where we thought it was," Niven said. "Or maybe I misheard. There was a lot of static. I can't raise Dankworth, so we'll just continue and see what we find."

"Sounds like that might be shrapnel and tree bursts," I said.

"You signed up for the tour, Billy," Niven said. "No turning back now. Odds are Jerry moved up some of his big guns to keep the new arrivals on their toes. That might account for the search-light trick."

We drove on through Liège and then to Spa, where road signs pointed to First Army headquarters. The ground was covered by a thin layer of snow that drifted across the road and hid patches of ice. Just before the city, Niven pointed out several tall aerials sticking out of the trees.

"That's the Golden Arrow wireless unit," he said. "As powerful as anything they have at SHAEF."

Spa was Niven's destination, but he wanted to find Dankworth and see for himself what the situation was, so we drove right by the elegant Hotel Britannique and headed for St. Vith. There had been no sign of frantic activity at the hotel, only the usual flow of officers and couriers headed in and out.

"The Britannique has an excellent restaurant," Niven said. "Perhaps we can dine there tonight."

On the road to St. Vith, I began to have my doubts about making dinner reservations. Ambulances came down the road, headed for Spa. A scattering of jeeps and trucks, driving at high speed and oblivious to the icy road conditions, passed us. The canvas top on the last truck was unsecured, flapping in the wind. Inside, half a dozen GIs huddled together.

When the next jeep came along, Niven slowed to a stop and waved his hand to get them to do the same. Six men were crammed into the vehicle, which didn't stop. One of them pointed down the road, jabbing his finger to the east.

"This doesn't bode well," Niven said. "Perhaps we'll find someone who will sit still for us up ahead in Malmedy."

There was nobody in Malmedy. No GIs, no civilians.

"This is where the script reads, *It's quiet, too quiet,*" Niven said. "In a bad movie, at any rate."

"Many of the civilians in this area speak German," Kaz said. "They may know of an attack. Or they saw those men in flight and are taking no chances."

We kept going. The next village was Baugnez, at the intersection of three roads. A gentle hill rose up between farmers' fields covered by winter stubble, and Niven gunned the scout car over the frozen ground to the top. He killed the engine, and we got out. The distant echo of artillery rolled over the countryside. A light snow swirled in the air as heavy clouds loomed above us.

"There," Niven said, pointing as he scanned the hills through binoculars. Smoke smudged the horizon in several places. "Either they hit us, or we hit them. I'll try Teddy again."

It was no good. Even from this high point we couldn't raise Dankworth, Peter, or even the Golden Arrow wireless section through the static and blare of Germanic melodies. We kept going, forested hills rising on either side of the road and the temperature turning colder.

"No more retreating vehicles," Kaz said after fifteen minutes on the road. "Perhaps it was a local attack and those men panicked."

"The 106th is a green unit," I said. "Maybe that's all it was. We'll find out soon enough."

"Sooner," Niven said. "It looks like these fellows are standing their ground." Ahead, where the road divided, two jeeps were parked around a road sign. Eight MPs in their distinctive white helmets stood by as one of them held up his hand for us to stop. Those helmets had earned them the nickname "snowdrops," a moniker they didn't much appreciate.

"What's going on, Sergeant?" Niv asked, tipping back the rim of his British helmet. "Seems to be a bit of a fuss ahead. We saw a number of vehicles making for the rear."

"The Krauts put on a harassing attack, sir. Some of the boys decided to skedaddle a mite soon," he said, in a soft Texas drawl. "They'll catch hell for sure."

"What's the situation now?" Niv asked.

"Germans have cut the road to Amel, but they've been stopped there," he said. "Last I heard, anyway. Long as you stay on the road to St. Vith, you should be fine. Don't take any side roads. You could find yourself face-to-face with a Tiger."

"Has St. Vith been shelled?" I asked from the rear seat.

"Can't say, sir. I haven't been there. Hope to be soon, though, it's damn cold out here," he said, adjusting the blue scarf around his neck.

"Thank you, Sergeant," Niven said.

"No problem, sir," he said, stepping back and directing us to the turn for St. Vith. The other signpost pointed to Amel, apparently in German hands. "Remember, stay on the main road."

"Harassing attack?" Kaz said, glancing back at the roadblock. "What is that, exactly?"

"A strike designed not to gain ground but to keep the enemy off-balance," I said. "Maybe a commando attack on a supply depot or a headquarters, or a raid to test defenses."

"Searchlights, heavy artillery, it seems like a lot went into this," Kaz said.

"Just as we do, the Jerries need to keep their troops sharp, especially in this weather," Niven said. "Sort of a large-scale exercise to keep them on their toes, and to keep us guessing." The curving road dipped into a valley and ran straight between two ridges, keeping to the right of a flowing stream. Niven gave it the gas and we picked up speed.

"Maybe there is a depot at Amel," Kaz said, unfolding a map.

"That's an old map," Niven said. "It won't show any new installations."

Kaz grunted, studying the map. He turned it one way, then the other.

"It may be an old map," he said. "But it still shows towns where they should be. This is not the road to St. Vith. We are headed for Amel."

"Are you sure?" Niven asked, glancing at the map. When his eyes returned to the road, he gasped. Ahead, off the embankment, was the smoldering hulk of a deuce-and-a-half truck, bodies of GIs scattered around it.

A flash of fire and a sharp crack.

An explosion off the side of the road shattered a tree and pinged shrapnel and splinters against the scout car.

"Hang on!" Niven shouted and spun the wheel, sending the vehicle into a field. He downshifted to gain traction. Another crack and I swear I saw the shell pass just in front of our windscreen. The scout car swerved and spat snow from the tires. An explosion close by, then another, showered us with dirt and swirling smoke.

I heard rifle fire and stuck my Thompson out the rear window, sending bursts in the general direction of the enemy. I didn't expect to hit anything but maybe they'd keep their damn heads down.

Niven swerved again, then drove straight between two trees and came out onto a rutted lane that ran between the field and a wooded hilltop. The lane was lower than the border of trees and rocks. The armored car thudded as the rear wheels dropped, throwing us side to side in a bone-jarring crash. Niven kept control as the four-wheel drive chewed up the loose stone and gravel, putting distance between us and the ambush.

No one spoke as Niven drove on, over the crest of the hill, then following the contour of the lane, which was no more than a farmer's track. He found a clearing in the woods, halted, and backed the scout car in.

"That, Baron, is a very good example of a harassing attack," he said. "Any further questions?"

"It felt more like bloody murder to me," Kaz said. "Are you both all right? Am I all right?" He felt around for injuries and seemed surprised to find none.

"They sent us into a trap," I said.

"The MPs?" Niven said. "Perhaps the signpost was turned around by the Germans."

"Genuine MPs would know which direction divisional headquarters was," I said. "They changed the sign and have been sending reinforcements to be captured or killed. I should have known. They were four to a jeep."

"You are right," Kaz said. "Two jeeps, eight MPs. The American army always assigns three men, maximum, to a jeep. It could take more in a pinch, but the standard for any mission is three men."

"Their English—I mean their American English—was spot-on," Niven said.

"We only heard one guy. And there are plenty of Germans

who came to work in the states, particularly in the Texas oil fields," I said.

"I suggest we make our way back to them," Kaz said. "I volunteer to man the .50-caliber machine gun."

"Excellent notion, but we can't afford to take that chance," Niven said. "If we get taken out, no one will know about this masquerade. We'll find a way to St. Vith from here and make our report. Agreed?"

"Reluctantly," Kaz said. I nodded my head, which was still vibrating from the wild ride.

"I should have known as well," Niven said, easing out of our hiding place and taking the downhill track.

"How's that?" I asked.

"The chap never asked for an autograph."

CHAPTER TWENTY

WE THREADED OUR way through fields and across a small stream until we hit a road. Kaz checked the map and was sure we'd gained the route to St. Vith, south of where the ersatz MPs had stopped us.

Fairly sure, anyway.

The road was empty, which meant they were still diverting traffic to Amel. But the fact that no one was fleeing from St. Vith was a good sign. Whatever had panicked the guys we'd passed must've come from the direction of Amel. If the ambush that hit us was any sign, there were panzers and infantry in that direction.

"I have not heard of German infiltrators wearing American uniforms before," Kaz said. "It is surprising they have not done so."

"Or British uniforms," Niven said, as he carefully braked to take an icy curve. "Plenty of our Teutonic friends learned their English at school in Britain, or from British teachers in Germany. English-accented speakers would be easier to recruit. If we can get this damned radio to work, I'll send word to Peter to be on the lookout."

Kaz spotted a signpost ahead. St. Vith was five kilometers away. All we had to do was trust it pointed us in the right direction. After passing through another small village closed for business, the road twisted around a hill with a wooded crest. As we reached the summit, we were greeted with a view of the low-lying land ahead.

Smoke rose from the crossroad town of St. Vith. One house on the outskirts was in flames, and shell craters stood out as dark stains against the white snow. An explosion erupted just short of the town, followed by two more that struck near the rail line that ran through it.

"Incredible," Niven said. He pointed to more columns of smoke in the distance as the rattle of small arms fire echoed across the hills. "This is no small-scale raid. I'll try the radio again."

For once, the channel was clear. But Dankworth wasn't answering, and that could be bad news. The Golden Arrow wireless station was on air, and Niven gave them a top-priority message for Peter Seaton at 21st Army Group. I asked for the same message to be sent to Colonel Harding at SHAEF. It was short and sweet. Widespread attack in the area of St. Vith. Heavy shelling and armored breakthrough at Amel. English-speaking Germans posing as MPs.

"They said every message this morning is top priority," Niven said as he threw down the headphones in frustration. "Let's find Teddy. All his transgressions will be forgiven if he's managed to get word to headquarters."

We drove on down the hill as the shelling let up. Vehicles were speeding in and out of the town center, and GIs ran to cross the streets, hoping to reach shelter before the next rounds fell.

"Back in Spa they have no idea," I said. "It's business as usual."

"Artillery's probably cut the phone lines from St. Vith, and Jerry's musical interludes have done the rest," Niven said, turning onto the main street where a crudely painted sign proclaimed a small hotel to be the divisional command post. He slewed the scout car to a halt, and we made for the CP as another salvo of shells screamed overhead.

"What the hell! Has Monty sent reinforcements?" asked a GI taking cover in the doorway.

"For this little dustup? I doubt you need our help, Private," Niven said. "How long has it been going on?"

"Since dawn, sir," he said. "Say, ain't you . . . ?"

"Yes, I am. Basil Rathbone, at your service. Now, where can I find your intelligence section?"

"G-2 is right down the hall, can't miss it. Hey, I love those Sherlock Holmes movies. How d'ya have time to make 'em and serve up here?"

"The magic of Hollywood, my good man," Niven said. "Don't forget to duck."

"Hell, I ain't stood up straight in days." With that, he was off.

"You don't like being recognized?" Kaz asked, removing his steel helmet.

"Every now and then it gets tiresome, and I trot out Basil to stand in for me," Niven said. "I gave him permission to do the same, but he's yet to have been bored by accolades."

The CP was busy—men scurrying in and out, radios blaring static, and shouts from an upstairs room. G-2 was in a large office with the usual maps pinned to the wall. A noncom was shouting into a walkie-talkie, but no one seemed to be answering.

"Who are you and what can I do for you?" asked an officer clutching a sheaf of papers. "I'm Major Walter Stout, and I don't have a lot of time."

"Major Niven of 12th Army Group," said Niv, giving our names as well. "We're looking for Captain Dankworth, one of my men. He heads a Phantom patrol and came here to brief you chaps. But first, you need to know there are Germans disguised as American MPs on the road north of here. They've got the road signs turned around and sent us to Amel, saying it was the way to St. Vith."

"Amel's in German hands," Stout said, his brow wrinkled as he tried to assess what Niven was telling him.

"Which is why they sent us there, Major," Kaz said slowly.

"We ran into armor and infantry and barely escaped. Others haven't been so lucky."

"Damn," Stout said, none too happy about more bad news. "How many?" I gave him the rundown and he bolted from the office, returning a minute later. He'd sent a platoon along with a detachment of MPs to identify any genuine snowdrops.

"Now, tell me again what you want?" Stout said, rubbing his temple. He looked like a guy with too much on his mind.

"Captain Dankworth and his men," Niven said, reminding him. "A Phantom patrol."

"Right, right. Good man," Stout said, leaning against his desk. "I sent him to my cavalry reconnaissance squadron this morning. He was supposed to train them, but I'm afraid he ran into a chainsaw instead."

"Where is the squadron?" I asked.

"Krewinkel, a little town about ten miles northeast of here," Stout said. "They got hit hard early this morning but they're holding. Having Captain Dankworth and twenty extra men was a big help."

"Are you in touch with them?" Kaz asked.

"I was by telephone line until an hour ago," Stout said. "The Germans must have cut the wires and we lost radio contact."

"We need to speak with Dankworth, Major," I said.

"Be my guest. I just hope he's in one piece," Stout said. "Do you have any news about the rest of the front?"

"We were hoping you would," I said. "When we drove through Spa there was no sign of anything brewing. As we got closer to you, we saw signs of panic. Vehicles on the road hell-bent on getting to the rear. Then the artillery, not to mention the phony MPs."

"We've been sending reports to First Army, but they just keep asking questions," Stout said. "They insist we're facing minimal forces on our front. The Krauts are supposed to have nothing but horse-drawn artillery and only a pair of horses to pull them. I'll tell you what, though, they sure as hell are working those two horses to death."

"Major, I will have to withdraw Dankworth and his men," Niven said. "Their orders are to avoid direct contact. Won't do to have them captured and let Jerry rummage through their maps and notes."

"Understood," Stout said. "But take a load of ammo, willya? My guys need it."

We removed the canvas top and stacked cans of belted .30-caliber ammo for the machine guns, along with bandoliers of M1 rounds and boxes of grenades, inside the scout car.

"Tell Lieutenant Mills to pull out if he's about to be surrounded," Stout said as we were ready to leave. "And good luck."

Luck seemed to be in short supply as we headed for Krewinkel. Sporadic shelling fell around us, and although we drove by one gun emplacement, all the other movement was away from the front. And it wasn't organized. Small groups of dispirited GIs, some without weapons, others looking over their shoulders as if Tiger tanks were on their tail.

Maybe they were.

"Do Phantom patrols routinely carry documents that should not fall into enemy hands?" Kaz asked as Niven steered around a shell hole in the middle of the road.

"No. I was rather dancing around the subject of a man being captured and talking after torture," Niven said. "I have no indication that the enemy knows of our patrols or techniques, but I'm sure their curiosity would be piqued given the amount of radio equipment and the large letter *P* splashed on every vehicle. Things will get dicey if they stumble onto our real purpose."

As the scout car crested a ridge, the sound of battle slammed us, the acoustic wave rolling up from the bowl-shaped depression below. Machine guns, grenades, and rifle fire snapped and exploded throughout the small village below. White-clad figures ran out of the forested hill opposite the clustered buildings. From our vantage point we could see half-tracks and jeeps hidden behind structures, and rapid fire taking down the attackers as one after another wave came on.

I grabbed ahold of the .50-caliber machine gun mounted on a swivel above the front seat, and braced myself as Niven took off. I squeezed off a few bursts, watching where the tracer rounds hit. The road curved, houses blocking my view of the advancing Germans. Then the road straightened, and there was nothing but open ground between us and the Krauts. I screamed for Niven to stop, and he hit the brakes as I swiveled the machine gun and fired into the flank of the enemy, sending up geysers of snow, mud, and blood. The big .50-caliber slugs didn't leave a pretty picture.

The Germans retreated, falling back into the cover of the woods and behind the hill. Niven gunned the car and pulled up behind a stone schoolhouse.

"Hey, Lieutenant, more limeys!" a GI shouted from his post by a window. "No offense meant, sir. Thanks for chewing them bastards up."

"That was your countryman's work," Niven said. "Who's in charge?"

"That would be me. Mills," a lieutenant said, coming downstairs and taking in the three of us. "What's the story?"

"First thing is we brought ammo," I said, crooking my thumb in the direction of the door. "Courtesy of Captain Stout. He said you should pull out if you're about to be surrounded." Mills barked orders for a couple of GIs to unload and distribute ammo.

"If you got in okay then we're not surrounded," he said. "We've got our flanks well covered, and these stone farmhouses are solid. There's a good field of fire on all sides and we strung barbed wire where we could. Are you here to join Captain Dankworth?"

"I'm afraid I've come to take him away," Niven said. "Security concerns. I'm sure you understand."

"I get it," Mills said. "But I'm sorry to lose his firepower. We may need to pull up stakes sooner than later. Say, you look familiar."

"It's that guy," a GI weighed down with bandoliers said. "From the movies."

"Major David Niven, at your service," Niv said. "Also from 21st Army Group, more to the point. Where is Dankworth?"

"He's in the church across the street with half his men," Mills said. "The other half are on the top floor here."

"How long can you hold out once he leaves?" Kaz asked.

"As long as the Krauts don't see him pull out, we should be able to take one more attack," Mills said. "But then they'll notice. I only have two platoons, and it won't be enough to hold all the buildings. Once they get into the town, it's all over."

"All right," Niven said. "We need to speak to Dankworth and then we'll make a plan. No luck with the radio, I take it?"

"No, reception is terrible. These villages sit in depressions with ridges all around them. Plus, all the phone lines are cut," Mills said. "Hey, is this happening all over?"

"Not sure," I said. "But whatever's happening, you're at the sharp end." I told him about the phony MPs, then the three of us darted across the street to the church.

"Good afternoon, Teddy," Niven said as we strolled into the nave.

"By God, Niv, what are you doing here?" Dankworth said from his position at one of the narrow windows. A few other Brits greeted Niven, then turned to the GIs to explain the presence of a movie star in their midst.

"I didn't know the USO was doin' shows this close to the line," one of the Yanks said. "Any dames with ya?" He winked to show Niv he was kidding.

"No, but we brought ammunition. And I'll dance with you later if you let me lead," Niven said to a round of laughs. "Teddy, I've come to take you away from all this. Better all around, I'm sure you'll agree."

"Niv, you didn't come down here just to tell me that," Dankworth said. He kept his eye on the ground out in front of the church but couldn't help glancing back at Niv. Confusion swept across his face. He wore a dark mustache under an elegant nose and dark eyes beady enough to make you wary of them. A scar gracing one cheekbone went a long way to forgiving those dangerous eyes.

"Looks like they're getting ready for another go," one of Teddy's men said. "On the hill to the left."

"We could use another man in the belfry with the machine gun," Dankworth said.

"I shall go," Kaz said, his Sten gun slung over his shoulder. Dankworth stared at him, perhaps wondering why a Polish officer was here, or in awe of what a facial scar could really look like.

"Let's have a chat once we send this next batch of Jerries to hell," Dankworth said. "I thought German parachute troops would be more sensible than this. They keep charging headlong into our guns and barbed wire."

"Here they come!" yelled one of the men in the belfry. Rifle fire spat rounds against the stonework, and the rapid fire of a German MG 42 machine gun raked the village. Everyone held their fire. I eased the barrel of my Thompson out the shattered stained glass window and waited.

The paratroopers in their white camouflage smocks ran down the hill, their screams shrill in the cold air. They reached the first line of their own dead, jumped over corpses, and made for the barbed wire strung between trees and walls.

"Now!" Dankworth ordered, and everyone pulled the trigger. Some of the Germans went to their knees and aimed fire in our direction. Others slumped dead as slugs ripped through them.

Mortar rounds exploded to our front, flinging shrapnel against the granite wall. I flinched, moving away from the window, which was probably the intent. I stuck my Thompson out and squeezed off several bursts, trying to send the message that we were still on the job.

The .30 caliber upstairs was chattering, but the smoke from the explosions made it hard to pick out targets. More rounds zinged through the windows, sending what little glass was left flying.

"Grenade!" a GI shouted. He grabbed the potato masher and flipped it out the window where it exploded in midair.

"Left flank!" Dankworth yelled. I took a grenade from my pocket, pulled the pin, and waited three seconds to be sure it wouldn't come back at me. I leaned out and threw it to the left, then ducked back in. After the explosion, I emptied the rest of my clip in the direction of the threat.

"They're getting close," one of the Brits shouted. A GI stepped back from his firing position, his eyes wide with fear.

"Look, go ahead and shoot one of the bastards," Niven said, dropping an empty clip from his Sten gun and reloading. "You'll feel better, I guarantee it." That elicited a smile from the fearful private, who returned to his post, M1 blazing.

The fire coming at us lessened, until all that was left was a field of white and red.

"Hold your fire," Dankworth said.

"They've pulled back," Niven said.

"Third time today," Dankworth said. "You'd think they'd learn."

"Amis!" came the shout from the hill above. Then in perfectly clear English, "Take a ten-minute break. We'll be back!"

"And we'll be right here, you son of a bitch!" responded the private, to the cheers of his mates.

"Well done, all," Dankworth said, slumping against the wall and sliding down to rest. "Before they return, Niv, do tell. Why are you here?"

"After all this," Niven said, gesturing to take in the room, the village, the struggle, "I doubt you'll believe it. I hardly do."

CHAPTER TWENTY-ONE

"ARE YOU INSANE?" Dankworth demanded as he gathered up his gear. "You came all this way to ask me about a painting?"

"A drawing," Kaz said as he came down from the belfry. "By Gustav Klimt."

"Who exactly are these people, Niv?" Dankworth inquired. He looked over at Kaz and me, then glanced out the window, where long shadows crept like fingers to claim the dead.

"Get ready to move out, lads," Niven said. "Teddy, let's adjourn to the sacristy, and I'll explain."

Dankworth nodded to his men and told one of them to inform the others in the schoolhouse it was time to withdraw. We walked behind the altar into the small sacristy, where the priest's vestments hung on hooks and shelves held candles and prayer books. Niven introduced us, stressing that we'd been sent by SHAEF.

"I know this may sound strange in the midst of battle, but we're investigating a criminal gang in Paris that's responsible for the murder of two American soldiers," I said. "The Klimt drawing you sold to Captain Rawson has been linked to them. It's artwork that the Nazis looted."

"It was then stolen by the Syndicat du Renard," Kaz said. "We need to know how it came to be in your hands."

"Niv, this has to be a joke," Dankworth said.

"Don't treat it as one," Niven said. "For once in your life use your common sense and answer their questions."

"We're not here to bring charges," I said, letting the notion of that possibility hang in the air. "We just need to know where you got the drawing."

"All right," Dankworth said, pulling out a pack of Woodbine cigarettes and lighting up. He took his time, probably deciding how much of the truth to tell. "I won it in a card game, last time I was on leave in Paris."

"Teddy," Niven said, shaking his head.

"No, really, I did. I never heard of this gang, and I certainly wouldn't traffic in art stolen by these Nazi swine," Dankworth said. He gave a slight nod in the direction of the enemy, living and dead. In the field, a lone German, undoubtably wounded, crawled slowly up the hill, pulling himself along with one arm.

"From whom?" I asked, waiting for him to spin the rest of this tale.

"A fellow named Jacques," he said. "I don't recall his last name, if he ever gave it."

"A card game. In Paris. Where you won a valuable drawing from a man named Jacques," Kaz summarized. "You insult us with such a simplistic story."

"Where did this card game take place?" I asked, if only to see what he came up with next. I looked outside again. The German was still moving. None of his pals came to help, but no one shot at him either.

"That I remember," Dankworth said, blowing smoke to the ceiling. "A dump on the place du Tertre called the Café Cadet."

"Jacques Delair?" I asked after a stunned silence. It had taken me a moment to realize he was telling the truth.

"That's him," Dankworth said, jabbing the air with his ciga-rette. "Wiry little fellow, terrible at cards. We played faro in the bar until Delair lost more than he had. Things got a bit tense, until he offered the drawing."

"How did you meet him?" I asked, moving to the edge of another window and staring out through the broken glass. There wasn't much light left in this day, but there was enough to see that the German had stopped dead, only a few yards from the top of the hill.

"I was with Henri Alain, one of our French liaison officers," Dankworth said. "We were drinking at a bar in Montmartre and Henri asked around about a card game. That led us to Delair at the Café Cadet."

"I know Alain," Niven said. "He likes the horses and is rather deft at cards. He can verify this?"

"Of course he can," Dankworth said. "Delair showed us the drawing up in his room. He wanted five thousand francs for it, claiming the difference in its real value would cover his debt. We settled on two thousand, and I thought it was fair. I'm familiar with Klimt's work and knew it would bring twice that, if not more."

"Teddy, you never cease to amaze," Niven said. "You did sell it to Rawson to cover an existing debt, then?"

"Yes, yes. But let's not go into all that. The officer's mess accounts are perfectly balanced, and I've resigned as treasurer. If anyone's going to get in trouble over this brew-up, it should be the chap who entrusted me with a tin box of cash."

"Gentlemen, are you satisfied with this story?" Niven asked.

"Delair is dead," I said. "Found in that same room."

"This brings us full circle," Kaz said. "Which means we know nothing except that Captain Dankworth is telling the truth."

"Well, that's an accolade I don't hear very often. So, if I'm ever going to hear it again, we should leave before Fritz gives it another go," Dankworth said.

No one disagreed, including Lieutenant Mills once we discussed plans with him. He'd sent a patrol to check the flanks, and they'd spotted Germans working their way through the woods on one side. In a few hours, the noose could be too tight to withdraw.

Dankworth's men stealthily got into their vehicles and made

ready to go, as we did. As soon as Mills had his machine guns open up, the small convoy made its way out of the village. With any luck, the Germans might mistake the sounds for reinforcements or not hear the engines over the chatter of the .30 calibers. I manned the .50 caliber as Dankworth's small column of jeeps and trucks drove by, drivers laboring to stay on the icy road while keeping engine noise down.

I looked back as tracers raked the tree line, hopefully driving the Krauts to cover. Smoke grenades blossomed swirling clouds, turning the fading light into a murky, gray haze. That signaled Mills was about to pull out. Niven shifted into first and drove gingerly, leaving distance between Dankworth's rear vehicle and the scout car. Getting caught in shellfire or an ambush while bunched up on a roadway was a good way to get killed. Or captured.

"I'm losing sight of them," Kaz said from the passenger's seat.

"I can't see a thing," I said from my standing position. "And I'm freezing."

"Damn wind is blowing snow across the road," Niven said, his hands tight on the wheel. "At least that means the Jerries will have the same problem."

I stayed upright, figuring it was worth being whipped by the wind and snow if it meant I could spot movement coming up on our sides. Or hear the clank of tank treads. We had about ten miles to travel and couldn't be sure the Germans hadn't broken through and cut the road to St. Vith.

I flexed my fingers to keep them from going numb. If I had to work the big .50 caliber, they needed to be limber. The balaclava kept my face warm, but my eyes stung from the cold. Trees bent in the wind, twisted into strange shapes, then re-formed into pines swooshing back and forth, casting broken branches across our path.

The narrow road curved around a hill. It seemed that the Ardennes was made up of nothing but hills with a few roads following the path of least resistance. Somewhere, artillery was fired in one direction or the other. Shells screeched overhead and dull *crumps* signaled their distant hits just as the wind picked up and howled at us. Ahead, a pine tree swayed, and I waited for the others lining the road to do the same.

It wasn't the wind. It was a German tank smashing all in its path.

No, it wasn't a tank. It was an armored half-track, only marginally better news.

Niv slowed to a halt. I trained the machine gun on the half-track, which skidded as its front tires turned to take the road to St. Vith. Then another came through and did the same, as if they owned the place.

"They haven't seen us," I said as I leaned down. The Kraut half-tracks were open, with a mounted machine gun and a squad inside. My bet was they were all huddled together for warmth instead of watching for retreating Yanks.

"Just the two?" Niven asked. I told him that was all I could see.

"We can't let them catch up with Teddy," he said. "Or continue on to St. Vith."

"Well then," Kaz said, "we should dissuade them."

"Well said, Baron. Help Billy change ammunition. There's a case marked API at his feet. Ought to rip right through that light armor and set off their fuel tank."

Kaz and I got to work with the armor-piercing incendiary ammo, setting up the steel case and feeding the ammo belt into the receiver.

"Ready!" I yelled.

"You've got to take out the closest one fast," Niven shouted. "Before the chaps ahead stop and deploy."

I didn't say anything, just nodded. It was pretty obvious we didn't want a squad of Krauts tossing grenades at us. I gripped the machine gun and braced myself, waiting to get close. In the darkness, the armored half-track was a blur of gray amid blowing snow. The blur slowed and two helmeted forms rose from the rear. Bright flashes sparked, and small arms fire pinged against our armor as Niven sped up.

I fired. The bright white incendiaries turned into explosive bursts as they hit the half-track square on. The driver tried to pull off the road, either to escape the hail of bullets or to bring their forward-facing machine gun to bear. I fired again, a longer burst this time, riddling the thin armor and sending men spinning as they attempted a vault over the side to evade the white-hot slugs. I poured it on until the half-track smashed into a tree, came to a jolting halt, and burst into a ball of flame.

The light was searing, but I could make out figures in white smocks spreading out on either side of the road to flank us. They'd reacted fast, and Niv did the same. He may have yelled something, but with Kaz's Sten gun chattering and my .50 mowing down Fritzes, I didn't hear a thing. It only took a second to grasp his plan.

Niv gunned the scout car and rammed the burning half-track, pushing it with our heavy steel bumper into the second German vehicle. The flames licked at us, but Niven put our vehicle in reverse and drew back, giving Kaz and me a chance to fire at advancing troops who stood out like actors on a floodlit stage. A grenade thumped against the side of the scout car, bounced into a ditch, and exploded harmlessly.

Niven hit the accelerator again, leaving an empty spot of roadway where two more grenades exploded. Moving around the burning half-track, I concentrated my fire on the lead vehicle, which had started to move forward, away from the inferno. The Kraut machine gunner fired at something ahead of us, but stopped as the incendiary slugs shredded the front driver's position, and he slumped down into the smoking interior. As we passed, Kaz popped up and tossed a grenade inside, the muffled explosion and screams signaling the end to that threat.

"Damn! There's another," Niven yelled. Muzzle flashes lit the scene fifty yards ahead. The lead vehicle must have already been on the road when we'd spotted the other two, and it looked like it had caught up with Teddy's bunch. In the darkness, German units making the breakthrough were probably colliding with retreating Americans all across the front.

Niven sped up and I targeted the half-track. Its machine gun had been aiming at a target to its left, so I kept my bursts centered on the vehicle. I saw the rounds hit and spark as they drilled through the armor. The driver tried to leap out, but he fell head-forward to the ground as explosions sounded from within the half-track. Ammo and grenades were cooking off, the devil's own fireworks erupting from the belly of the steel beast.

Rifle and small arms fire died down. I didn't dare fire any more for fear of hitting Dankworth's men. Niven advanced slowly as I swiveled the .50 caliber, looking for any remaining white-smocked threats. There was no sound other than the crackle of flames and my own beating heart.

"All clear," a voice announced as a British soldier stepped into the opening, waving his rifle.

"Teddy?" Niven shouted. I told Niv that Kaz and I would check the rear for Germans. We made a circuit of the area, encountering nothing but corpses and the terrible smell of burning flesh. Light from the flames illuminated the trees lining the road, casting weird dancing shadows over twisted metal and ruined bodies.

"These are SS," Kaz said, checking the body of an officer. Fortunately, except for the top part of his skull—which was nowhere to be seen—he was nearly intact, which made for a less messy search. "This fellow is a Sturmbannführer. A major, prob-ably in command of this unit." Kaz carefully removed the map case that was slung across his chest.

"We may have something," I announced to Niven and the group of men gathered around him. I stopped when I saw the bodies on the ground. One was a soldier with a leg wound being tended to. The other was Teddy Dankworth, and he was beyond care.

"He went after that half-track with grenades," a trooper said as he knelt in the snow, grasping Teddy's limp hand. "A proper bloody fool thing to do. Saved our lives, he did."

"Sergeant, we need to see to the wounded," Niven said, laying a hand on his shoulder. "And get Teddy in the truck. We can't hang about here."

"Aye," the sergeant said. Still, he didn't move. Niven organized the men and got the wounded into their vehicles before he asked the sergeant to help him carry Teddy. That drew the noncom out of his shock and grief. He rubbed his hand across his face, banishing tears, and got on with the job.

CHAPTER TWENTY-TWO

NIVEN ORDERED DANKWORTH'S men to find quarters for the night in St. Vith. They had two wounded men who needed medical care. In the morning they could return with them, and Teddy's body, to 21st Army Group. He left them with three bottles of brandy from his stash and orders to make their report on the attack as soon as possible.

"We're too close to things here to know if it's a local attack or something larger," Niven said as we drove on to Spa and First Army headquarters. "I can't believe the Germans have enough divisions to launch a large-scale offensive. Can you make anything out of those papers, Baron?"

"The light is too poor," Kaz said. He had a blanket draped over his head and was using a red-filtered flashlight to go over the captured documents. The ride was rough as well. Niven was driving with headlights blacked out, and we didn't want to make ourselves a well-lit target. "On the map it appears St. Vith is a German objective, but that is rather obvious given it is a crossroads. It provides access to several good routes west."

"We'll give this to Colonel Koch at First Army G-2," Niven said. "You can help speed things up with the translation."

"There's something about Einheit Stielau," Kaz said. "A special SS unit. Stielau is the commander. It says strict security is to be maintained at all costs."

"Well, they did a poor job of that," Niven said, carefully

steering the scout car around an icy bend. "What's their assignment?"

"They're the Germans in American uniforms," Kaz said, his voice raised in excitement. "The MPs on the road to Amel were part of Einheit Stielau. It says here there are eight teams being sent out in jeeps. One soldier in each will wear a blue scarf to aid in recognition in case they come into contact with German units."

"The MP we spoke with wore a blue scarf," I said. "Is that their mission? To send GIs in the wrong direction?"

"Wait, wait," Kaz said as the scout car hit a shell hole and gave us all a bounce. "These orders are quite verbose. And the ride is unsteady."

"Sorry, chaps," Niven said. "But count yourselves lucky we arrived after the artillery barrage and not during. The driving's a bit tricky." Two overturned trucks flanked the roadway, a sign the Germans had this stretch under observation, at least during daylight hours.

"Hurry in any case," Kaz said. He switched off the light and came out from under the blanket. "Einheit Stielau has three specific priorities. We must get this information to headquarters."

"What are they?" I asked, holding on as we bumped across another shell hole.

"The first is demolition of ammunition and supply dumps. The second is to sow confusion by altering road signs and removing minefield warnings," he said. "The third is to disrupt the chain of command."

"By doing what, exactly?" I had a bad feeling that I knew the answer.

"By cutting telephone lines, which is simple enough," Kaz said. "Then by attacking radio stations and headquarters units."

"Good God," Niven said, coming down heavy on the accelerator. "They could be halfway to Paris by now."

"Or pulling up to the Golden Arrow wireless unit," Kaz said.

"Imagine what four German commandos disguised as Americans could do against a twenty-man signals unit. They'd be wiped out in an instant."

"I've got to radio them," Niven said. He drove to the crest of the next hill, hoping for good reception. He halted at the crossroads sign for Amel, the intersection where we ran into the phony MPs. Kaz and I got out to watch the road for unwelcome visitors as Niv fiddled with the radio dials. New-fallen snow scrunched under our boots, a few lazy flakes swirling in the air.

"At least the sign is pointed in the right direction," Kaz replied. "I wonder what they are up to now."

"There were two jeep teams," I said. "They've probably split up. I bet they'd just come up the road from Amel when we got there." At the mention of the town, I strained my eyes to catch any sign of movement from our right flank. Nothing. But farther off to the north, thudding explosions rippled across the hills, bright flashes of light sparking in the darkness.

"Is that not where we are going?" Kaz asked as the barrage let up.

"No, it most definitely isn't," Niven said. "The damned radio won't work."

"Can you fix it?" I asked, knowing it might already be too late for the Golden Arrow boys.

"Of course not. I'm an actor by trade, not an electrician," Niven said. "It gave out one blast of static and then died. Either of you handy with wires and whatnot?"

"Did you give it a whack?" I asked.

"Yes, and to no avail," Niv answered. More explosions lit the night sky, far enough away to bring back memories of festive fireworks. For anyone closer, steel shrapnel and tree bursts would spoil the effect. "The only good news is we don't have to drive toward that. Let's get back to St. Vith."

We turned around, leaving behind a dark road leading to an enemy-held village and a landscape ripped by high explosive shells. I had the distinct feeling of a noose tightening around my neck.

"There's one other thing," Kaz said, patting the leather case. "Einheit Stielau operates under the overall command of Otto Skorzeny."

"He's the guy who rescued Mussolini back in '43, isn't he?" I said.

"Yes. He's an SS colonel and Hitler's favorite commando," Kaz said. "Which means there must be a larger component to this plan. Something more than eight jeeps."

"Skorzeny is the man responsible for keeping Hungary in the war," Niven said. "Back in October, the Hungarians tried to surrender to the Soviets before they were overrun. Skorzeny kidnapped the son of the Hungarian regent Miklós Horthy and forced Horthy to resign in favor of a pro-German government to save his son. The baron is right. Skorzeny is a headliner, not a bit player."

"You're thinking Eisenhower?" I asked.

"Or perhaps his immediate subordinates," Kaz suggested. "Bradley or Montgomery?"

"I don't think Monty considers himself anybody's subordinate," Niv said, cracking a debonair smile. "But whoever Skorzeny is after, it will have strategic implications, you can count on that."

I tried to think through the chances of German agents making it all the way to Paris. Now that we knew about their dirty tricks, it was going to be a lot harder for them to get through roadblocks and checkpoints.

While I thought about Paris, the Germans weren't forgetting St. Vith. A salvo of shells exploded across the train tracks and the main road, shattering the top of a four-story building and sending debris cascading into the street. Niv maneuvered around it and pulled the scout car into an alley next to the command post. Inside, Major Stout looked up from a report, a layer of dust decorating his helmet.

"You find your man okay?" Stout asked, barely registering our presence. "Captain Dankworth?"

"Yes," Niven said. He looked at the map on the wall, leaving so much unsaid. "He was with Lieutenant Mills and his men at Krewinkel. Now, we need to use your radio. Immediately."

"Stand in line," Stout said. "I've got a ream of messages to get out."

"Do you speak German, Major?" Kaz asked, setting the leather map case down on Stout's desk.

"No. We have a couple of men who speak it well enough to question prisoners in case you need them. Why?"

"I am sufficiently fluent to understand the importance of these papers," Kaz said, opening the case. "Maps showing the intended route of the offensive. Operational orders for the disguised MPs."

"What orders?" Stout demanded.

"Sabotage, for starters," I said. "Then attacks on headquarters units and radio stations."

"They're targeting *us*?" Stout said, opening the map.

"Perhaps, Major," Niven said, barely hiding a roll of his eyes. "But my primary concern is the Golden Arrow wireless station outside of Spa. It is a British signals unit, as I'm sure you know. And although a forward headquarters such as this would be a valued target, I would be most concerned about First Army HQ in Spa."

"They are likely not to be as well prepared as you, Major," Kaz said, smoothing the waters. Stout nodded his agreement as he traced the arrows leading to St. Vith on the map.

"Goddamn," he muttered. "We never did find those jeeploads of Kraut MPs. Follow me." Stout might have been a touch slow when it came to assessing new information, but once he worked it through, he wasted no time.

"Priority message for Golden Arrow, goddammit," Stout bellowed as he stormed into the radio room. "Now."

He had the radioman issue an alert for the British wireless unit to take defensive precautions against German saboteurs wearing American uniforms. Then he radioed First Army HQ with the same warning.

"I can't say much more about these papers," Stout said. "Not over the airways. We can try and get a telephone call through." We adjourned to another room with a couple of telephones and wires strung out the window.

"Are the phone lines still working?" I asked.

"On and off," Stout said. "Their artillery cuts the lines, and we fix 'em. Or they tap the lines and try to give phony orders. Have to assume they're listening in." He dialed a number, got the First Army switchboard, and demanded to speak to Colonel Dickson. Dickson was the head of First Army G-2 and was one of the few who'd warned of a German offensive.

"Monk?" Stout yelled into the phone. "Yeah, Stout here. We got some dope. Those snowdrops we reported? Expect more snow. In the higher elevations. Got it? Hey, you like *Fibber McGee and Molly*? Great show, solid gold stuff. Hope to hear more of it, don't you? Okay, good luck."

As Stout hung up the receiver, the screech of incoming artillery shattered the air. Explosions rocked the building, showering us with dust as we hunched over, thankful for our helmets. Stout picked up the telephone and listened.

"Dead air," he said. "We got through just in time."

"I understand about snowdrops meaning the MPs, and higher elevations referring to higher headquarters," Kaz said. "But who is Fibber McGee?"

"An amusing American radio program," Niven said. "Every Yank knows it, and the reference to radio gold should not be lost upon Monk Dickson. He's a smart chap."

"He confirmed he understood," Stout said. "We've been practicing our double-talk the last few hours. Now, Lieutenant, how about we go over the rest of those Kraut orders?"

"I am glad to, Major," Kaz said. "And some food and drink would be most welcome."

Stout ordered up some grub and, in a few minutes, we were eating ham and cheese sandwiches washed down with what Niv and Kaz proclaimed a fairly decent red wine.

"Where'd you pick this stuff up?" Stout asked, downing a healthy gulp.

"Jerries crossed the road in front of us," Niv said. "Three half-tracks. Teddy—Major Dankworth—was ahead of us. That's where he was killed."

"Sorry," Stout said. "Mills told me about the fight. Said Dankworth and his men were a big help. You fellas too."

"They got back okay?" I asked.

"Yeah. I knew we couldn't hold Krewinkel for long," Stout said. "But even a delay of a few hours helps."

"Do you have any idea how widespread this offensive is?" I asked as I polished off a sandwich. I had no idea how hungry I was.

"It's happening all along the First Army front," Stout said. "It's big."

"The Ardennes once again," Niven said. "It seems insane. They must have thrown in all their reserves."

"If you want insane, look at this," Kaz said, placing a sheet in the middle of the table. "It details their final objective. Antwerp."

"All the way to the coast?" I said, looking at the map on the wall. "That would take them through Montgomery's rear area. Do they have the strength to pull it off?"

"We've identified the 9th SS Panzer on our front," Stout said. "And there are plenty more units."

"The armored spearhead is Kampfgruppe Peiper," Kaz said, running his finger along the lines of German. "An SS formation named for their commander. His orders are to cross the Meuse River and advance on Antwerp."

"You better get all this to Monk at First Army HQ first thing in the morning," Stout said. "We've got to stop these bastards before they pull off the impossible."

"I shall include a request for clear skies in my bedtime prayers," Niv said, downing the last of his wine. "A few squadrons of fighter bombers ought to put Herr Peiper off his game."

"His route takes him north of us on his drive to the Meuse," Kaz said. "And the last weather forecast I saw called for several days of low cloud cover. The Germans probably planned on the weather negating our airpower."

"We'll leave at first light," I said. "I'd rather not cross paths with all that firepower."

We grabbed our sleeping bags and unrolled them in a vacant room on the top floor of the hotel that served as the command post. The bed had been taken for a makeshift hospital, but the ancient radiator did its best to keep the room above freezing. Niv had brought along his last bottle of brandy, and we toasted to the memory of Teddy Dankworth.

"To Teddy," he said. "A man who died as he lived, in a desperate gamble. A true rogue of the highest class."

We drank.

"To think this all began with a smuggled drawing," Kaz said. "It seems quaint to have been so concerned by it."

"Compared to being caught in a large-scale enemy offensive, it is," I said. "But all the recovery of looted artwork is important to the French. It's their heritage."

"I don't think Teddy knew it had been stolen," Niv said. "At least not by the Nazis. He did have standards, after all."

"I wonder if Colonel Harding is still after the Syndicat du Renard," I said. "Or have the Germans filled his dance card?"

"I can't imagine there would be time to deal with petty criminals while the Germans are advancing on Antwerp and driving around disguised as MPs," Niven said. "They could be at the gates of Versailles by morning. Imagine what four men armed with tommy guns and grenades could do at the Trianon."

With that cheery thought, Niv knocked back the last of his brandy and burrowed into his sleeping bag. I was left thinking about those petty thieves, a fitting description of low-life guys like Jacques Delair, a snitch and career criminal. But the two members of the Syndicat we'd encountered had a different look. Were they simply well-fed and healthy gangsters and deserters? Ex-soldiers who'd decided to profit from the war instead of dying in it, perhaps?

Or were they something else?

Artillery fire peppered the town, a few rounds every ten minutes or so. Just enough to keep everyone nervous and awake. I dreamed of thunder and savage lightning, unable to escape the barrage of terror even as I lay in a fitful sleep.

CHAPTER TWENTY-THREE

SUNRISE WASN'T UNTIL eight thirty, but we were on the road well before that. A dull predawn light reflected off leaden clouds to the east as we drove out of St. Vith. We'd had eggs and coffee, filled up the fuel tank, stocked up on ammo, and stuffed a thermite grenade into the leather case with the captured German documents. If we ran into trouble, we didn't want the Krauts to discover we'd read their mail.

"No shelling this morning," I said as we stopped, hopefully for the last time, at the turnoff for Amel. I got out and used binoculars to study the ground leading to the village. No sign of movement.

"Nothing this way either," Kaz said, surveying the road to Spa from our vantage point.

"I appreciate not being shelled as much as the next chap," Niv said as we clambered back into the scout car. "But it also means the Jerries may be advancing and holding off for fear of hitting their own."

"It could have been our artillery hitting back last night," I said. I figured by now we would have brought up the reserves.

"Billy, we've been caught with our pants down, good and proper," Niv said. "The generals gambled and left this sector of the front lightly defended, and we're paying the price. Keep an eye peeled, will you?"

The cold nearly peeled my eyelids off. I stood, grasping the machine gun so I could get a good view of the road ahead. We'd done away with the canvas top for better visibility, not that it did much against the frigid winds and blowing snow.

The sun had finally risen above the trees, piercing the cloud cover with a dull yellow light, when I spotted a familiar hilltop.

"Up there," I said, tapping Niven on the shoulder. "Isn't that the high ground we drove up after we passed through Malmedy?"

"Right you are," Niven said. "We tried to get a radio message out. You're thinking of admiring the view from atop that hillock?"

"It might be smart," I said. "Be nice to know half the German army isn't waiting around the next bend in the road." Kaz agreed, so Niv eased the scout car onto a snow-covered field and took a narrow logging trail to the summit. He left the vehicle under the cover of overhanging pines, and we trudged through the snow to the top. Timber was stacked along the route encircling the hill. The top was bare of trees and just high enough to provide a wide view of the terrain below.

"Is that Malmedy straight ahead?" I asked, adjusting my binoculars.

"No, that is Baugnez, a small village. We drove through it yesterday. Not much more than a few farms at a crossroads," Kaz said. "Malmedy is a few miles farther on."

I spotted a puff of smoke off to the right, then it was gone. A plume of exhaust? I scanned the road to the east of the village, trying to find the source.

"Do you hear that?" asked Niv.

"Engines," Kaz said. "Where?"

"There," I said, pointing to the road on our right leading into Baugnez. The first thing I saw was an eight-wheeled German reconnaissance vehicle. Then a line of half-tracks came into view, followed by a column of tanks.

"Herr Peiper, I presume," Niven said. "What I wouldn't give for a working radio and clear skies. Damn and blast!"

"At least we can notify First Army once we get there," I said.

"Or if we get there. We won't stand a chance if we cross any part of Peiper's force."

"Oh no," Kaz murmured. He swiveled his binoculars and adjusted them, zeroing in on something in the village.

"More Jerries?" Niven said, keeping his eyes on the German column.

"No, Americans," Kaz said. "Several trucks heading south through Baugnez. I don't think they see the Germans."

"Let's get the scout car up here and fire some warning shots from the .50 caliber," I said.

The Germans beat us to it. Tanks fanned out from the road, jolted to a halt, and opened fire. The first truck went up in a ball of fire, then rounds smashed into the rear vehicle. It was over in seconds. The tightly packed column was trapped, and it didn't take long for GIs to leave their vehicles, hands held high. Focusing my binoculars, I watched as SS troops dismounted from trucks and rushed the men, disarming them and roughly searching each prisoner. It was hard to count, but it looked like sixty or more Yanks.

The armored column continued through Baugnez after the attack, leaving their infantry to deal with the POWs.

"There are more prisoners in the trucks," Kaz said. I watched as the Germans forced about thirty more GIs out into the field to join those who had just given up. Through the powerful binoculars, I could almost make out their faces. I couldn't hear a thing, but I could imagine the fearful questions as the SS lined them up in rows.

Why? A prisoner count? Interrogations?

A machine gun on a half-track fired at the prisoners, at this distance a dull, insistent, ripping sound. Americans fell to the ground as the group pressed into itself, as if there might be refuge at the center. But the machine gun ate into the crowd, sending up showers of snow and blood. The SS men joined in, firing at those who tried to run, making for the safety of the nearby woods.

"Good God," whispered Niven, taking the binoculars from his eyes. I kept watching, seeing men make it to the tree line. Some were cut down, but I could see others had gotten away. The machine gun stopped, leaving it to soldiers with rifles and submachine guns to fire into the writhing remnant of defenseless men.

It finally stopped, the valley below us going quiet.

"No prisoners," Kaz said. He rubbed his eyes as if to vanquish the vision of the violent massacre. "Peiper doesn't wish to be held up on his quest to cross the Meuse River."

"What was that, a hundred men or so?" Niven asked. "They could have been marched back to the German lines. It's cold-blooded murder."

"It is the way of the SS," Kaz said. "They fight and kill without honor."

I was still watching the field. Officers walked among the bodies, pistols drawn. Faint pops echoed as they administered the coup de grâce to anyone left alive. One officer waved his arm, signaling their work was done. As they mounted their vehicles to follow the armored spearhead, it began to snow. By the time the trucks had cleared the village, the bodies of the executed GIs were already covered with a blanket of white. But nature's grace could disguise the brutal atrocity we'd just witnessed for only so long.

"What do we do now?" Kaz asked. "If Billy hadn't suggested the detour up this hill, we could have been right in the middle of all that."

"We could make a run for it," I said. "We just need to clear the village before any more Germans come down that road."

"A bit too late for that," Niv said, pointing. "More armor."

"Yes, Peiper's force is fairly large," Kaz said. "The orders listed artillery and anti-aircraft formations, among others. His lead units are probably bypassing defenses when they can."

I watched as tracked artillery and other heavy stuff rumbled along in the swirling snow. If we could get across the road, we should be okay. Peiper was heading west. We needed to go north, toward Spa.

"Let's head west ourselves, if we can find a road. This ground is too open," I said, gesturing to the fields below us. "We need cover to make a dash across Peiper's line of advance."

"As good a plan as any," Niven said. "Baron, hold tight to that satchel. At the first sign of trouble, pull the pin and toss the thing overboard."

I pulled on my balaclava and tied my scarf snug around my neck. Standing up in the scout car with a face full of blowing snow was unpleasant, but so was the idea of running into a panzer. Niven took the scout car cross-country again, cutting through a frozen field as Kaz clutched the precious satchel of secrets in his lap. Now we had something else to report to Monk Dickson at First Army. Word of the massacre had to get out before any more of our guys surrendered expecting to be treated according to the rules of war.

Which, now that I thought about it, was going to stiffen the resolve of every GI rifleman on the front. They'd be out for revenge. And knowing what to expect at the hands of the SS, there'd be little percentage in giving up. So far, it didn't look like the Germans had made many mistakes in this offensive, but this might have been a big one.

"Ah, an actual road," Niven shouted as he maneuvered through a row of trees. The snow squall had let up, and he slowed to check the surface. "Tank treads and tires. No telling which way they're headed. So, westward."

We came to a fork in the road and went left to Bellevaux, if the sign marker was to be believed. Kaz found it on the map and said a road led north from it to Malmedy. We'd cross the westward path of Peiper's route about a mile north of Bellevaux. All we needed was some cover to watch for the right moment.

"Easy as tea and cakes, gentlemen," Niven said. He slowed as the road curved around a frozen pond and a thicket of trees.

Which put us right in front of a well-camouflaged anti-tank gun. Two GIs stepped out from behind the gun, one of them holding up his hand for us to stop. Niv hit the brakes, and I noticed two more Yanks step out of a foxhole behind us. That made four weapons trained on us, not counting the 57mm cannon.

"What's the password, pal?" came the challenge.

"No idea, sorry," Niven said. "No one's bothered to tell us."

"You!" shouted one of the GIs behind me. "Hands off the Ma Deuce and step down."

"Okay, okay," I said, fairly sure these were real GIs. The Fritzes weren't likely to know that GI nickname for the big .50 caliber. I let go and got out of the vehicle, hands raised. "Hold on to your horses."

"You know the password, buddy?"

"That's Captain buddy to you, and no, we don't. We're trying to get to Spa and had to take the long way around. I've got no idea what your unit's password is," I said, lowering my hands.

"Keep 'em up!" he shouted, his carbine leveled at my belly. He looked nervous, so I complied.

"Sarge, lookit this," another GI said. He'd taken the satchel from Kaz and was leafing through it. "They got Kraut documents."

"We are bringing those to Colonel Monk Dickson at First Army," Kaz said. "It's imperative they get into his hands."

"No password, and you got German papers. I can buy your story about being off course, a lotta guys are today. But there's Krauts driving around in American uniforms. So you," the sergeant said, pointing his tommy gun at Niven's head, "who won the '43 World Series?"

"Haven't the foggiest idea," Niv said, unwrapping the scarf from around his face. "But I did costar with Ginger Rogers in *Bachelor Mother*."

CHAPTER TWENTY-FOUR

"HEY, I SEEN that," another GI said. "That's the guy!"

"Who?" the sergeant asked.

"You know, that actor. Whatshisname."

"Major David Niven, pleased to make your acquaintance," Niv said. I was relieved he didn't blurt out Basil Rathbone this time.

"You're a long way from home, Major, and I don't mean LA," the sergeant said. "You're the first Brit I've seen out here."

"Yes, well, it's rather a long story, and we do need to get these documents to First Army. Are you aware there's a strong German column just north of us, heading west?" Niven said.

"We don't know a damn thing. We had orders to dig in here early this morning," the sergeant said. "Our captain said he'd be back by now, but I have my doubts. He took the truck to Malmedy to get more ammo, but it shouldn't have taken him this long."

"He go by himself, Sarge?"

"Yes, he did, Captain," he replied. "And he ain't come back." The sergeant didn't say it in so many words, but I got the feeling he felt his officer hightailed it for the rear area. Captains didn't usually make ammo runs. Or maybe he'd run into Peiper's column.

"What's your name, Sergeant?" I asked.

"Prentice, Captain."

"Well, Sergeant Prentice, I'd say you've been abandoned. No radio?" I asked. He shook his head.

"It's foolish to stay here," Niven said. "I'm countermanding that order. You've already been outflanked by a superior force, and there are no Germans behind us. The best thing to do is pull out and accompany us to Spa. You may be needed there. Captain Boyle, do you agree?"

I did, and it took the savvy sergeant a full five seconds to think it over before telling his crew of six to mount up. They hitched the towed anti-tank gun to their truck and were ready to roll in ten minutes flat. With that done, I told them what we'd seen at the Baugnez crossroads.

Their faces went dark.

"We're in the shit now, ain't we, Captain?" the movie fan said. "Just mowed them down in cold blood?"

"Yeah. Best bet is the SS have orders to take no prisoners. They're in a damn hurry," I said. "So, if it comes down to it, don't give up."

"We'll make 'em pay," said the sergeant. "We're pretty good with this piece of ours."

"You'll need to be," I said. "I just wanted you guys to know the score."

We pulled out through Bellevaux. A few curtains opened as we passed the houses in the village, the good citizens of this Belgian town certainly thankful not to have a battle brewing in their midst. The tree-lined road sloped up, past a church with a gray slate roof and a crowded graveyard. At least the gravedigger wouldn't be working overtime today.

The road became a narrow lane cut into the side of a hill. The ground was bare, probably good grazing for sheep. Up ahead, a stone farmhouse and barn sat high on the hill, just below the ridgeline. The snow on the curving driveway was recently churned up, and I spotted the cause as we got closer. A German armored reconnaissance vehicle was parked close to the barn, nearly hidden from view.

"Where are they?" Kaz said as he joined me next to the

machine gun. He swung his Sten gun in the direction of the farmhouse. I looked back at the truck and saw Prentice aiming his M1 from the passenger's seat.

"On the hill, maybe," I said. As we had done, they could be seeking a good vantage point. "Keep moving; they might not spot us." I prayed they were busy looking in the opposite direction, but even so, I knew that armored car had a crew of four, and that two men would have stayed with the vehicle.

I signaled to Sergeant Prentice to hold his fire. We were drawing close to a line of pine trees along the roadside that might provide enough cover if those two Krauts were busy taking a smoke break instead of keeping their eyes peeled. I glanced back as we drove past low-hanging branches and saw no movement from the farmhouse.

Which is how I missed what was ahead of us. The first thing I saw was two Germans strolling in the road, one lighting a cigarette, the other waving his hand. I'd been focused on the guys behind us, and they must have thought the sound of our approaching vehicle was their own armored car returning.

I realized all that in the split second it took to squeeze the trigger, catching a glimpse of the open-mouthed shock on their faces. Niv accelerated, surprise our strongest ally. Ahead, hugging the edge of the road and the cover of the pines, was one half-track and a small truck. I sent burst after burst into the half-track, making sure its mounted machine gun wasn't brought into action. Tracers shredded the light armor and the vehicle exploded, sending up a sheet of flame. The truck drove crazily down the road, then rammed a tree. Soldiers spilled out, diving for the ditch.

Niven braked and slewed across the road, giving cover to Prentice and his men in the truck. Small arms fire arose from the Germans to our front, rounds zinging off our armor plate. But they weren't our real worry.

"Can you get that gun into action?" I yelled to Prentice, who was already out of the truck, weapon in hand.

"Not soon enough," he said. "That armored car will be down here in no time. It's got a 20mm automatic fire cannon. It'll chew us up before we get our gun unhitched."

"Kaz, take over," I said, climbing down from the mount.

"Gladly," he said, squeezing off a few bursts to let the Fritzes to our front know we were still in business.

Niven joined me as we moved to take up positions behind Prentice's truck. Niv's Sten gun was slung over his shoulder, and he held the thermite grenade tightly.

"That's our only one, better make it count," I said, gesturing toward the white phosphorus grenade intended to burn the captured documents in case we were taken prisoner.

"Seems a shame to waste on paperwork when the bloody Germans are so close," Niv said.

"There!" Prentice shouted. The revving engine of the reconnaissance vehicle announced its presence as it stuck its nose around the curve and sprayed us with fire from its 20mm cannon. Slugs shattered wood and ripped through the truck's canvas top. "Hold your fire."

"I'll work my way through the trees," Niven said. "I'll come up behind the blighter."

"We're ready for him," Prentice said, nodding to the trees on the other side of the road. Two of his men were prone behind a thick pine with a bazooka.

"You sure about this, Sarge?" asked one of his men. "They've got us surrounded. Maybe we should take off into the trees."

"Look, you chaps only have to do this once," Niv said, his voice carrying over the gunfire. "But I'll have to do it all over again in Hollywood with Errol Flynn!" That got a laugh, even from the GI who'd suggested a wintry walk in the woods.

"Let's hit 'em from both sides," I said. "Okay?" Everyone was in, probably buoyed more by a movie star risking his neck than anything I said. I crawled on my belly, following Niv as he slithered through the snow beneath the heavy overhanging branches.

With no return fire, the Kraut vehicle drew closer, blasting away at the truck. Kaz continued to fight his own battle, his bursts short and well disciplined. Even in this cold, a gun barrel could overheat.

Niv stopped, drew himself up on his knees, and leaned against a trunk. The armored car came on, tires crunching the packed snow. I crawled to a tree closer to the road and gave Niv a nod, just as Prentice's men opened up with small arms fire. I signaled Niv to wait for Prentice's men to fire the bazooka. I saw the flash, then the rocket exploded on the front plate of the armored car.

But it kept coming.

"Go!" I shouted and ran to the next tree, firing my Thompson at the gunner. He was in an open turret, but it was covered by a steel grate to protect against grenades. I saw my rounds ricochet off, but at least it distracted him. The driver stopped as he swiveled his gun to search out the threat to his flank, and that was when Niven tumbled down the embankment, rolled the thermite grenade under the wheels of the armored car, and dove into the ditch on the other side. The explosion was a mix of intense, bright white light and roiling smoke as the phosphorus hit the undercarriage. Hatches popped open as the bazooka fired again, penetrating lower, near the engine, this time sending its explosive force out through the openings as the crew tried to escape.

I stood and trained my Thompson on the burning vehicle, but there was no reason to worry that anyone had survived.

"You okay?" I asked Niv as I helped him out of the ditch.

"Never better," he said, grimacing as the smell of burning rubber and flesh filled the air. "Let's see to the baron."

Prentice ordered the bazooka team to come with us while the others watched the road for any last-minute visitors. The bazooka men stayed hidden in the pines, working their way forward of our position. Kaz sprayed the ditch where the German truck had gone off the road, earning sporadic return fire. Then he targeted a small stone structure, some kind of farm building with one squat window facing us. His tracers struck the masonry, sending shards flying. Automatic fire came back at us, kicking up snow.

"They are the more vigorous defenders," Kaz said. "They have better cover."

"We can take care of that," Prentice said. Using hand signals, he ordered the bazooka team to crawl closer while we covered their approach. At his nod, we cut loose with fire to keep the Krauts down. As I reloaded, I saw the bazooka flame and the rocket smash through the wooden door and explode inside. Greasy smoke churned out from the small window.

That spooked the Germans by the truck. Three of them ran, trying for the cover behind the building. They didn't get far.

"I'll check the scout car," Niven said, dropping an empty clip and reloading his Sten. "I smelled gas."

"That's the truck," Prentice said. "The Krauts hit the tank. We're lucky it didn't blow. Tires are shot up too."

Kaz and I went to check on the Germans. Not one was left alive. An officer was in the truck cab, but he didn't have any maps. It looked like they were lost, trying to find Peiper's column.

"SS," Kaz said, the disgust in his voice palpable.

Next we checked the building. The explosion and the concussive force hadn't left a pretty picture. The two men had put out a lot of firepower, and I expected to see a machine gun.

"What kind of weapon is this?" Kaz asked, picking up a gun that was still intact. It had a long, curved magazine, the bullets larger than what the Schmeisser submachine gun had. Or my Thompson, for that matter.

"A fully automatic rifle, I'd guess," I said, grabbing a couple of clips. "Better bring it with us. It's sort of like a BAR, only lighter." The Browning Automatic Rifle was a powerful weapon, but it was heavy and unwieldy. This new gun had a nice balanced feel to it. If the Krauts were switching from their bolt-action rifle to an automatic fire version, it would make a helluva difference. Especially if you were on the receiving end.

The scout car started up, and Niven pulled it away from the truck.

"The good news is that our armor held up," Niv said. "The bad news is that it's going to be a crowded ride back."

Prentice made sure the anti-tank gun was destroyed by loading a shell in the breech, elevating the barrel, and dropping a grenade down it. Then he ran like hell. The resulting explosion ignited the gas pooled under the truck, sending acrid smoke billowing skyward.

With the three of us and Prentice's squad of six, it was standing room only. The scout car pushed through the snowy roads, hardly bothered by the load.

"If we run into any Krauts, they're going to be shooting fish in a barrel with all of us crammed in here," one GI griped.

"Oh, do pipe down," Niv said in a loud voice. "Or I won't tell you any stories about mad Hollywood parties."

"First, Smitty, shut up," Prentice said. "Second, what kinda stories?"

"I'm sure you boys know about Greta Garbo, don't you? Marvelous actress, but she only swims in the nude," Niv began. No one complained about the crowded conditions or the Germans for the next twenty minutes.

CHAPTER TWENTY-FIVE

WE CROSSED A road chewed up by tank treads and heavy vehicles. Peiper's column had moved through here less than an hour ago, judging by the churned-up slush just beginning to freeze over. Kaz marked the spot on a map as we headed north through another typical Ardennes village. A narrow, curving road cut through loping fields beneath steep wooded hills. Scattered farmhouses and gray-roofed buildings huddled near a stream. It was a cold and foreboding place to fight a war.

We came to a roadblock a few miles outside the town of Malmedy. Tensions were eased as soon as some of the GIs recognized Prentice and his men, forgoing the need for quizzes about the World Series. A lieutenant from Prentice's outfit ordered his squad to help man the roadblock, and, as they dismounted from the scout car, the main topic of conversation was the massacre. It turned out survivors had already made it back to our lines, and word had spread like wildfire. Red-hot anger and hard determination hung in the air as men arranged themselves in defensive positions.

"Good luck, Sarge," I said to Prentice as we shook hands. "Stay low."

"Only way to go," he said. "See you in the funny papers, Captain."

"Those are good men," Niven said as we drove off. "Jerry will have a rough go of it, I think, especially now."

"Yeah, we have good men," I said. "Now I'd like to see some tanks to go with them. We're a little short of the heavy stuff. If Peiper has turned north, he'll have captured First Army HQ by now."

"He's more focused on finding a way across the Meuse, according to this," Kaz said, patting the satchel. "But if he knew the location of the headquarters, and how weakly it was defended, he could easily have sent a detachment on a raid."

"Look at that," I said as we hit the crest of a hill. Below us, arranged along one side of the road, were stacks of supplies. Canvas-covered crates. Fuel drums covered in camouflage netting. Piles of five-gallon jerry cans, enough to gas up hundreds of tanks. "Let's be glad he didn't come this way."

"Let him head west, I say," proclaimed Niven. "As long as your chaps blow those bridges when he gets there. Otherwise, there'll be hell to pay."

Pulling up next to a wall of jerry cans, we hoisted several on board for Niven's return trip to Holland. There was no one around to wash our windshield, so we left the unguarded roadside supply dump and drove on into Spa where the situation was nowhere as calm as it had been yesterday. Jeeps and motorcycles zigzagged through the streets, and officers wearing helmets hustled in and out of the Hotel Britannique, First Army headquarters. There were so many vehicles out front we had to park several streets away.

The three of us hustled up the steps of the hotel. Kaz carried the leather case, while I held the new German weapon in my grip. Niv unwrapped the scarf from around his face in case we needed to impress anyone.

The lobby was busy as clerks trotted about clutching sheaves of paper while others sat at desks along the wall shouting into telephones. Everyone seemed nervous, especially when they looked our way and saw three grimy fellows toting automatic weapons, and two of them in British uniforms to boot. They must have heard about Germans masquerading as MPs by now, but no one sounded the alarm.

"What do you need, sirs?" asked a noncom carrying a clipboard. He was thickset, cleanly shaved, and his trousers were nicely creased. He clearly thought we'd taken a wrong turn and should be somewhere else. "We don't have any accommodations here if you're traveling through."

"We need to see Colonel Dickson," I said. "Now."

"I'm sure he's busy, but if you wait here, I'll check. Your name?" He wielded his clipboard like a weapon, a pencil stub his trigger.

"Listen, old boy," Niven said, elbowing his way forward and removing his helmet. "It's rather urgent. Tell Monk we have important information, will you?" Niv smiled and brushed back his curly hair. This was where most people probably recognized him and went starstruck.

"Sorry, sir, I'll do my best, but you'll have to wait," the noncom said, turning his attention back to me and asking for my name again before he strolled off to take the staircase upstairs.

"He must prefer the radio to films," Niven said, wincing in disapproval.

We sat, waiting for the sergeant to return. Half an hour later, there was no sign of him. I went to ask one of the clerks manning the telephones where Dickson's office was when a lieutenant walked into the lobby. By the look of his boots and soaked fatigues, he'd been a lot closer to the front than anyone else at the Britannique. He headed for the stairs like he knew the place, so I decided to try my luck with him.

"Lieutenant," I called out. "You know where Colonel Dickson's office is? We need to see him pronto."

"I'm late to report to him right now, Captain," he said. His face was smudged with dirt, and his eyes had a heavy look, like he hadn't slept much lately. "Everybody wants to see Monk, you need to stand in line. Things are a little crazy right now."

"Yeah, we know," I said. "That's why we need to see him."

"It's not only the Germans, Captain. General Hodges is down with the flu. Seems like his chief of staff, General Kean, is running things. It's as confusing as the situation out there," he said, crooking his thumb over his shoulder. Then he noticed the German weapon slung over my shoulder. "Hey, where'd you get that?"

"The same place we got these documents," Kaz said, stepping forward and hoisting the leather satchel. "From dead Germans."

"I know Colonel Dickson," Niven said, standing next to Kaz with shoulders back, his long nose and pencil-thin mustache on full display. "He'll want to see us."

"Come with me," the lieutenant said, passing over Niv's profile as he glanced at the satchel and the automatic rifle. "You just bought yourself an audience."

"I must remember Spa when I want to get away from the adoring crowds," Niven muttered as we followed the lieutenant upstairs.

"Helluva time for General Hodges to get the flu," I said. "It must be pretty bad."

"Can't say. All I know is that he's been holed up in his office since the shooting started yesterday. General Kean just took over," the second louie said. We hit the third-floor landing and he whispered, "There he is."

A stocky, serious-looking general walked across the hall in front of us, his head buried in a report. He opened the door opposite, revealing a glimpse into General Hodges's office. Hodges was slumped at his desk, his head buried in his arms. He looked up as Kean entered, a vacant look on his slack-jawed face.

The door shut, firmly.

It looked more like shock than influenza.

"I don't ask too many questions about generals," the lieutenant said. "Especially with so many of them around."

"Smart man," I said as he opened a door farther down the hall marked G-2. Inside, Colonel Monk Dickson gripped a field telephone and shouted orders as a sergeant standing behind him took notes. "Williams, report," he demanded as soon as he was done. "And who the hell are these people?"

"No German armor, Colonel. False alarm. The boys are jumpy as hell," Lieutenant Williams said. "This British officer says he knows you."

"Niven, by God!" Monk said, rising and extending his hand. "What the hell are you doing here?"

"A long story, but we come bearing gifts," Niv said, introducing Kaz and me. "We picked up these trinkets and thought of you."

"Damn, this is a fine birthday present," Monk said, riffling through the papers. "Can you believe it? I warned everyone from Patton to Bradley about the Germans attacking through the Ardennes, but the damn Germans waited until I went off to Paris to celebrate my birthday."

"We witnessed the massacre at the Baugnez crossroads," Niven said, his voice a low murmur. "Through binoculars, a good distance off. Cold-blooded murder."

"Hell," Monk said. "I guess we shouldn't be surprised at what the SS does, but it still was a damn shock. What's the reaction on the line, Lieutenant?"

"In some strange way it calmed the men down," he said. "They know what the deal is. There's no easy way out, just fight until we win. And I made a point of telling them we need prisoners. But there's not much taste for bringing in Krauts so they can live out the war in a nice, safe POW camp."

"Can't blame the men," Monk said. "The Germans brought it down on their own heads." He then ordered his sergeant and Williams to take the papers to the translators and log every page. He kept the map, spreading it out on his desk.

"We crossed here," Kaz said, showing the mark he'd made, "not long after Peiper's column passed, headed west. From what I could read in the orders, he is to cross the Meuse River and advance upon Antwerp."

"I see," Monk said. "Hitler wants to split the British and American armies. It's an incredible gamble, but in his warped mind he must think the Allies will fall apart if he divides them."

"They can't have enough strength to do that," I said. "Right?"

"It only matters that one madman believes they do," Monk said. "I saw an intelligence report claiming this offensive was the brainchild of Field Marshal von Rundstedt, head of German forces in the west. But I believe it had to be Hitler's. It's crazy, unexpected, delusional, and highly strategic. Hit us hard right when we all believed victory was around the corner."

"And where no sane man would attack in winter," Niv said.

"Right, and with heavy tank forces we didn't think he had. And new weapons like this," Monk said, picking up the automatic rifle, ejecting the clip, and clearing the chamber. "Meet the Sturmgewehr 44. That means assault rifle. It fires an 8mm round, carries thirty bullets in the clip, can be fired in single, semiautomatic, or fully automatic mode, and the muzzle velocity is a third again that of the Schmeisser submachine gun."

"A company armed with these would have the strength of a battalion," Kaz said.

"So, when do we bring our own strength to bear?" I asked.

"We need to protect those bridges on the Meuse at all costs, and we need to keep Peiper away from the fuel depots," Monk said. "I'm trying to get our stuff moved out or wired for demolition, but it's not easy to get a decision made right now. General Hodges is incapacitated, but hell, there's three million gallons of gasoline sitting out in the open right down the road."

"How bad is it everywhere else?" Niven asked, sidestepping what we'd briefly seen of the general and declining to mention we'd helped ourselves to a few of those gallons.

"Monty is safe so far," Monk said, unrolling another map. "We seem to be on the northern edge. South of us, the Germans are trying to encircle Bastogne. That's another town at the center of a road network. It's vital, and word is that Ike is sending in the 101st Airborne to defend it. The Krauts are also pushing hard on our lines all along First Army's front."

"That's quite the bulge," Niven said, tracing his finger around the penetration made since the offensive kicked off.

"I prefer to think of it as a sack," Monk said. "Let's pray we can keep the bastards tied up in it."

"Colonel, I need to contact 21st Army Group about our Golden Arrow wireless unit," Niven said. "They are suddenly closer to the front than they were ever intended to be. I assume they have security?"

"Jeez, Niv, I don't know," Monk said. "I just got back this morning. Hang on." He powered up the field telephone and asked a few questions. He hung up and shook his head. "No one's been sent. I'll organize a platoon to get over there."

"We may need to withdraw them," Niven said. "It wouldn't do for one of His Majesty's finest wireless stations to be overrun by the bloody Hun."

"We need them, Niv," Monk said. "But it does make sense to pull back. It's a British outfit, so it's your bosses' call. They could head for Liège or just north of the Meuse River. Ought to be safe enough, and they can still give us a signals boost."

Niven agreed and went off to the radio room to confirm with Monty's HQ. Monk had coffee and donuts brought in. Good coffee and fresh donuts, one of the benefits of headquarters life.

"What about you?" I asked, savoring the hot joe. "I mean the headquarters and the supply depot?"

"I don't like having our fuel depot dangling like bait for the Germans," Monk said. "I hope Hodges moves it all back. But we're staying put. The general is an old infantryman. Joined as a private before the last war and worked his way up the ranks. He knows how to dig in and hold on. Don't worry."

When I caught a glimpse of the general, he could barely hold on to his desk, much less hold out against German armor. But the Krauts hadn't sniffed around Spa yet, and maybe they'd just pass the Hotel Britannique by.

Besides, Lieutenant Williams was right. Junior officers had no place in the affairs of generals. Except to do their bidding, like so many were doing right now in the ice and snow.

CHAPTER TWENTY-SIX

"LIÈGE IT IS," Niven reported. "The Royal Corps of Signals approved the move, with the caveat that Golden Arrow continue broadcasting until nineteen hundred hours tonight."

"Good. There's a lot of message traffic today," Monk said. "I better get to work. My intelligence report has to be sent out before tonight. Hopefully we'll get those captured documents translated before nineteen hundred, otherwise I'll be calling SHAEF on the telephone and reporting in pig Latin."

"I hope you find something valuable," Niven said. "Happy birthday, old boy."

"You made it memorable," Monk said, returning to his paperwork. "You and the Germans. Oh, by the way, the password for tonight is *Kentucky Derby*. Might keep you out of trouble."

"I wish it were that easy," Niv said. "Cheerio."

"Well, chaps, we could part company here," Niven said once we were downstairs in the lobby. "I'll return to headquarters as soon as I get Golden Arrow situated. I suspect you'll return to SHAEF now that the art theft bit has been sorted?"

"Right, but we need to organize transport," I said. "We can probably scrounge up a jeep, but that can wait until morning. I'd rather make that drive in daylight anyway. Less chance of being shot by our own men or running headlong into Germans."

"We've come this far together," Kaz said. "We may as well visit this marvel of communications with you."

"All right," Niv said with a smile. "A platoon for security will be nice, but you two are grand company, and I'm glad of it."

We hoofed it to the scout car, the biting wind at our backs. A line of civilian vehicles snaked through the town, refugees from the fighting looking for shelter. Not the first time in this war. An old Peugeot sedan ran into the rear end of an even older Berliet truck painted a light green, resulting in little actual damage but a lot of arm waving and cursing. The truck driver checked his bumper and returned to his cab, apparently satisfied.

"Do the locals know something?" I asked. "Are these people coming from the fighting or are they leaving Spa before it gets here?"

"Good question, I shall ask," Kaz said, trotting over to the slow-moving line of vehicles.

"There is likely a good deal of intelligence to be gathered from these people," Niven said as we watched Kaz canvas the occupants of five vehicles. "I wonder if Monk has tried it."

"The automobiles are all coming from the vicinity of Amel, where we know the Germans to be," Kaz said. "Some don't want their sons to be taken for slave labor in Germany, and others are simply afraid. The truck driver works for a moving company and has a delivery. War or no war, he says he must work."

"I'd hate to buy new digs only to find the Krauts moved in next door," I said. "Talk about property values going to hell."

We managed to get around the traffic jam and drove out of Spa, retracing our original route to where we'd spotted the tall Golden Arrow antennas. When was that? Two days ago? It was hard to remember when this had been a relatively peaceful stretch of the line. The road forked and we took the right turn, keeping the seventy-foot masts in view.

"I'd feel better if there was a checkpoint at that fork," Niven said. "Being so close to the headquarters and the wireless unit."

"It is a sign of victory fever," Kaz said. "No one in command imagined the Germans had so much fight left. And what one cannot imagine is difficult to plan for. Perhaps by tomorrow they will be better organized."

Artillery rumbled off in the distance, the sound muted by the rolling, forested hills. Tomorrow might be too late.

We'd lost sight of the masts in the hilly terrain, but eventually the road emptied out into a patch of flat ground. Three tall masts were spaced about fifty yards apart, with heavy cables connecting them to a large truck. Off in another field was a duplicate setup.

"Transmitters and receivers," Niven pointed out. "Best kept apart to avoid interference." He pulled in next to a large stone barn draped with netting where half a dozen trucks were parked. An old farmhouse stood next to it, smoke lazily curling out its chimney.

"No sign of that platoon yet," I said as we got out. The door of the farmhouse opened, and a lieutenant strode our way. Soldiers appeared from the barn and from inside the truck, which I now saw was a very large van with a door and windows.

"We were expecting you, Major Niven," the lieutenant said. "Headquarters said you'd have orders for us."

"Yes," Niven said, halting as soldiers gathered around him. "Hawkins, isn't it? Time to pull up stakes, but not until nineteen hundred hours, so you've time to get ready."

"That's good to know, Major," Lieutenant Hawkins said. "We've been expecting the Germans to pay us a visit, by all the signals traffic. Seems like they're everywhere."

"Only seems like, don't worry," Niv said. "We motored here from St. Vith and arrived safe and sound. Now, your orders are to transmit until nineteen hundred, then be prepared to move out. How long should it take?"

"We've done it in three hours, sir, but in the dark, without lights? Another hour or so," Hawkins said as his men nodded.

"Very well. We'll set a guard around the trucks and get a few hours of sleep, then set out in the morning for Liège," Niven said. "You get cracking, and I'll show these chaps what you do here."

"There was supposed to be a guard platoon here by now," I said.

"We haven't seen a soul, sir," Hawkins said over his shoulder as he trotted off to organize things.

"SNAFU is the order of the day," Kaz said. Situation normal, all fucked up.

"We're getting Golden Arrow on the road just in time," Niven said. "Now I think you should see why this unit is so special." He led us to the first truck, which was really two articulated vans. Metal steps led up to the door, and inside the large compartment was an array of radio equipment and two radio operators. Another man worked a telegraph key, tapping out messages.

"This is the transmitting station," Niven explained. "They relay reports on to London, Paris, or a division in the field. They do remarkable work. Let's leave them to it."

"This is a lot of gear to dismantle," I said, looking at the tall radio masts as we walked to the next station.

"It's designed to be moved rapidly, and the wireless lads are well trained. It will be a bit more difficult in the dark, but we can't have Jerry seeing the place lit up, can we? Now we come to the receiving station. There's actually a bit more to it than previously mentioned."

Inside, electronic equipment was mounted high up on each wall above benches where operators with headsets worked the dials and wrote messages out on notepads.

"They're taking radio messages," I said. "From Phantom and other units?"

"Oh yes, that and more," Niv said, ushering us out. "Let's leave them be; they need quiet."

"They are listening in as well as receiving messages from our own units," Kaz said once we stepped outside.

"Exactly, Baron. Golden Arrow works as advertised, but their side business is intercepting German communications, both encoded and those sent in the clear. That is why they must stay on the air until this evening. We may learn much more about this offensive, especially now that things have not gone according to plan for the Nazis."

"How do you know that?" I asked.

"Because, Billy, nothing ever goes according to plan. It's the nature of things," Niven said. "I wanted you both to know why this unit must not fall into enemy hands."

"If the platoon doesn't show up, we'll need to rotate a guard overnight," I said.

"We should also leave as soon as possible," Kaz said. "The Germans may be sending out patrols looking for the fuel depots."

"I wish we could, Baron," Niven said as we walked to the farmhouse. "But these are heavy tandem trucks. I can't take a chance on them getting into an accident on a dark, icy road. We'll need light, and that means eight o'clock at best."

The wireless section was billeted in a deserted farmhouse. Hawkins said the locals had told him the family was German and had left with the retreating Wehrmacht months ago. This part of Belgium was mostly French with a smattering of German-speaking Belgians, and the latter weren't too popular after lording it over everyone during the occupation. They were probably liking their chances to do it all over again right now.

We settled into the kitchen while the unit's cook heated up beef stew and put out bread and cheese, along with a bottle of Belgian chardonnay, then got to work cooking for the rest of the section. They'd be coming to eat in shifts during the early evening.

The food was good, warm, and plentiful. The war receded for a moment as we sat in the comfortable kitchen, the sensation of eating and drinking with friends overcoming the horror waiting around the next bend.

But as I looked out the window and glanced at my watch, the

implications of fighting in these conditions hit home. It was four o'clock in the afternoon and the sun had already dipped below the western hills. The glass reflected nothing but foreboding shadows. The cook drew the blackout curtains, and we sat in an island of light, surrounded by the looming darkness.

CHAPTER TWENTY-SEVEN

THE EVENING WAS uneventful, save for the clanging of metal as the masts were taken down and stored on racks fitted to the trucks. Niven lent a hand while Kaz and I stood guard with two nervous wireless operators along the main road to their facility. We listened for signs of approaching Germans through the whooshing of pine boughs and rising wind gusts. All we heard was distant artillery, which on the front lines meant that the explosions weren't flinging shrapnel at your foxhole. But from here, it sounded miles away, dull crumps signaling a salvo falling across a dug-in position, a crossroads, or some poor village caught up in the fighting.

At midnight, the new guard detail informed us that the Signals crew had everything packed. Trucks were ready to roll, and weary men were sacked out in the farmhouse or warming their hands around mugs of tea.

"Soon we'll be in Liège, my friends," Niven said as he closed the door, the cold wafting in around him. "A real city, with restaurants and pretty girls, how does that sound?"

"Just fine, Major, unless the Germans have called ahead for reservations," said one of the men, eliciting a ripple of nervous laughter. Niven bantered with them a little longer before settling down on his sleeping bag in the living room.

"Any news before they pulled the plug?" I asked.

"The Germans are attacking Bastogne, but it's holding," Niven said. "The rest of the attack on the southern edge of their advance is making headway. They haven't run out of steam yet."

"And here?" Kaz asked.

"Peiper is still headed west, but hasn't found a way across the river yet," Niven said. "Other reports are rather vague. Nothing from First Army all night, which I find disturbing. If I wasn't so tired and cold, I'd drive back to Spa and see what Monk is up to."

"We'll be passing through there at first light," I said, readying myself for another walk in the snow. "Which is pretty damn soon. We'll ask Monk then."

"Sensible," Niven muttered, and closed his eyes. I made my rounds and soon did the same.

THE COOK WAS up before anyone, brewing tea and whipping up batches of powdered eggs and bacon on the cast-iron stove. As soon as the first group of men were fed, Hawkins sent them out to start the trucks and warm the engines. After Kaz and I ate, we made another reconnaissance as a sliver of light lit the eastern sky. Fog clung to the ground, creating a haze along the tree line that blurred the edges of what little was visible. Snow had fallen during the night, but there were no fresh tracks along the main road. Except for the rumbling of engines, it was quiet. No explosions, near or far.

"Perhaps the offensive has passed us by," Kaz said.

"You think so?" I asked as we walked back.

"No, I was simply trying to keep a positive outlook," he said. "I think it more likely that while the armored elements have already broken through our lines, the infantry following on foot has yet to catch up."

"I like the positive outlook better," I said. But Kaz had a point. The Germans were short on fuel, and a lot of their army depended on foot power and horse-drawn transport. Peiper and the other shock formations probably took the lion's share of fuel allocations, leaving the infantry charged with protecting the flanks to march through the snow. Which meant they could be close, cloaked by darkness and fog.

"No sign of visitors," I called out to Niven as he started up the scout car.

"Good," Niv said, climbing out of the vehicle and rubbing his hands together. "I'll be glad to see the last of this place. I'm keeping up a good front for the lads, but all hell could come down that road any moment now."

"Think there's enough light to leave?" I asked.

"I'm not sure if we should chance it, not with this damned fog," Niven said.

"Which is the greater threat?" Kaz asked. "The chance of an accident or the Germans suddenly appearing? The tracks from the main road leading to this farm are still visible."

"You're right," Niven said. "I can't let them be scooped up. I'll lead the way, but I'll have to risk using headlights. It wouldn't do to lead the trucks into a ravine. Worth the risk, don't you think?" We did. The vehicles were going to make enough noise to announce their presence in any case, so why not use the scout car's headlights?

In twenty minutes, we were on the way, leaving the flat terrain behind and winding along roads hemmed in by hills thick with fog. The headlights might have kept us from running into a ditch, but it was slow going. When the fog began to dissipate, Niven turned off the headlights. With the first rays of the dawning sun, visibility was adequate.

"What's that?" Kaz said as Niven increased his speed slightly.

"Signal we're halting," Niv said, and Kaz and I both stood and gestured to the truck behind us, which had kept a respectable distance. Over the idling of our own engines, the snarl of motors and grinding gears became louder.

"I'd say man the machine gun, but that sounds like the whole

German army," Niven said. "I think there's a road ahead that crosses ours, right around the bend. Maybe they'll miss us."

"I'd guess backing up is out of the question," I said.

"Quite. I'll tell the lads to prepare to burn the trucks," Niven said. "Will you scout ahead and see what we've run into?"

"I'll cover you, Billy," Kaz said, grasping the machine gun. "Be careful."

"Great advice," I said as I got out of the truck. "Gotta remember that one. When vastly outnumbered, be careful."

"Be very careful," Kaz said.

I laughed. It wasn't that funny, but when you think you might have heard your last joke, you give it all you've got. I left the road and worked my way through the pines, snow clumping to the ground as I walked through the heavy-hanging branches. I was too tired to be very careful.

Tires rolling on the snowpack and straining engines told me that the vehicles were crossing our path before I could see anything. If none of them took a look down that side road, we might be okay.

I crawled forward, nearing the road, the noise growing louder. I gently moved a branch, nudging it with the barrel of my Thompson, for one good look at the column.

I laughed again, out loud.

Americans. A convoy, mostly big deuce-and-a-half trucks hauling supplies. Jerry cans, fuel drums, plus lots of wooden crates. Monk had gotten his wish. General Hodges must've ordered the supply depots moved. I climbed out of the trees and walked alongside the trucks, waving to the drivers.

God bless General Motors.

I walked down the side road, waving all clear.

"It's our trucks," I said to Kaz and Niven. "They're moving all the supplies out."

"Best news today," Niven said. "I shall be glad not to have to report the immolation of His Majesty's finest wireless section."

I walked ahead as Niven drove the scout car closer to the intersection, not wanting to spook the truckers with the sudden appearance of an armored vehicle. The sun was now above the tree line, and we had a grand view of the last fifty or so trucks rolling by.

"At least all that fuel will be out of the Germans' grasp," Kaz said.

"As will we, soon enough," Niv said, gunning the engine and crossing the road. "Unless we get caught up in a traffic jam in Spa. Could be more refugee traffic and trucks."

On the outskirts of Spa we did see a few civilian vehicles, but nothing like yesterday. We drove on, the road mostly clear of snow, and took the turn for the Hotel Britannique.

It was a ghost town.

No jeeps or trucks clogged the road. No officers ran in and out of headquarters. Shops along the main street were closed up tight. Signs that designated the hotel as First Army HQ had disappeared.

"What happened since yesterday?" Kaz asked. "Colonel Dickson was certain there would be no retreat."

"Whatever happened, it scared the hell out of the local residents," I said as Niven pulled to a halt in front of the hotel. He sprang from the scout car and told Hawkins in the lead truck to continue to the edge of town and wait for him.

"Unless you hear the machine gun," Niv said. "Then drive like hell. Understood?"

"Yes, sir," Hawkins said. "Best not to dally here. Something must be brewing."

"And it's not tea," Niv said. "If you don't see me in thirty minutes, move out. Stop in the next village and wait ten minutes. If I still don't show, head straight for Liège, and I'll find you there."

"I doubt we'll find anyone at home, much less a jeep to requisition," I said as we watched the column drive past, then turned to enter the hotel.

"They didn't even leave a rear guard," Kaz said. He opened the door, revealing an empty lobby. The radio equipment had been removed, but telephones still sat on desks along the wall. Loose papers were strewn across the floor, a trail of debris left by clerks packing up in a rush. I pushed them around with my boot, picking up one teletype marked *urgent*.

"These are movement orders for the 7th Armored Division," I said. "What the hell is going on?"

"A clever deception?" Niven suggested, then shook his head. "No, Monk would have said something. This is a rushed evacuation."

"Kaz, you look around for any hotel staff. They might know something," I said. "We'll search upstairs."

"They may be in the back preparing for new guests," Kaz said. "Dusting off a portrait of Hitler, perhaps." He went behind reception, merrily ringing the bell on the desk. Niv and I took the stairs, heading to Monk's office. His space was cleaned out, not a piece of paper to be found.

Next was General Hodges's office. The floor was littered with papers, all seemingly innocuous. Supply requisitions, personnel forms, the standard paperwork of any army. Unusual to leave behind, but perhaps understandable in a rush to evacuate. In General Kean's office across the hall, a bulletin board still held memos, forms, and announcements.

"How thoughtful of them to leave a clue," Niven said, tapping one piece of paper. It ordered the requisition of the Hôtel des Bains in Chaudfontaine. "This is only fifteen miles north, on this side of the Meuse River. We'll drive right through on our way to Liège. I'll have to drop in and ask Monk what went on here."

"There's even a map showing the location of the Golden Arrow station," Kaz said, indicating a hand-drawn map showing roadblocks around Spa and the route to the wireless unit. "At least you pulled them out before anybody found this."

"They did depart in a bit of a rush, didn't they?" Niven said.

"Let's finish checking the rooms," I said. "We should pick up any sensitive materials. Looks like we'll stick with you for a few more miles."

"Glad to have you, and I'll be glad to get out of here," Niv said. "An empty hotel is eerie, don't you think?"

"Yeah, I keep expecting to run into people," I said as we checked the next office. It was set up as a conference room, with torn edges of maps still stuck by thumbtacks in the wall. The leather satchel we'd found, minus its contents, had been left on the floor. "At least it's empty."

"We'd best take it anyway," Niven said. "The Germans may recognize it as one of their own. No use tipping our hand, as poor as it is."

A cardboard box was on the floor, and I dumped out the contents. Run-of-the-mill stuff.

Except for the folded map. I opened it, earning a gasp from Niv.

"That's hot stuff," he said. A road map of this area, showing the routes truck convoys were taking to the new supply depots. Also, the two roads First Army headquarters units were being routed on to get to Chaudfontaine, with the Hôtel des Bains clearly noted in the center of town.

"We better see what's waiting for us upstairs," I said. I stuffed the map into the satchel and left it on the door handle. No telling what we'd be carrying downstairs.

The next floor was taken up with what must have been clerk typists and radio operators. The things they left behind were everyday items. Headsets, a box of spare vacuum tubes, even someone's skivvies drying on a line. Not exactly top-secret stuff.

"The upper floor is all bedrooms," Niven said. "I draw the line at rummaging through bedsheets. Let's collect what we've found and move out."

"I'm with you," I said, and we headed for the stairs. I heard a door shut on the second floor and called out to Kaz. "We're up here."

Silence.

"Baron, where are you?" Niven said, projecting his voice down the long hallway. Still no response. I strained to listen for Kaz. That was when I noticed it.

The satchel was gone. I tapped Niv on the arm and pointed. He wrinkled his forehead, then unslung the Sten from around his shoulder.

"Must still be downstairs," he said casually.

"Right," I replied, my Thompson at the ready.

We walked to Hodges's office, and I pushed open the door with the tommy gun. Nothing. Same with Kean's office across the hall. I stood still, listening for footsteps or voices. Were we just jumpy, or was there someone else here? Hotel staff, maybe. The Germans would have been a lot louder, so I didn't think we had that problem. Yet.

I turned to leave and caught sight of the empty spot on the bulletin board.

The requisition for the hotel in Chaudfontaine was gone. It had been right next to the map showing the Golden Arrow unit and other positions surrounding Spa, all now out of date.

"Something's not right," I whispered. Now this hotel was getting really spooky.

We spread out on the wide staircase, each of us hugging a wall.

A shot boomed from below, then another. As I ran down the rest of the stairs, I refrained from calling out to Kaz, not wanting to draw attention to myself, although my heavy boots were doing a good job on that score. The lobby was empty. Niv brushed by and headed for the dining room as I went behind the reception desk.

I pushed aside a black curtain not knowing what was waiting for me, but it was just a small office with a desk and a chair.

Another shot, this one from out back. I arrived in the kitchen at the same moment Niven ran in from the dining room. We made for the door just as a burly man in a leather jacket burst through it.

I noticed three things instantly.

He was the guy with the moving van from yesterday.

He had the satchel slung over his shoulder.

He had a .45 automatic in his hand.

Niv and I fired at the same time, collapsing him in the doorway.

I jumped over the body and found myself in a courtyard. A garage door was swung open and Kaz was walking away from it, helping a young girl, his arm around her shoulder. The girl was sobbing, but unhurt. Kaz held his Webley revolver in his other hand as blood streamed down his temple.

"Are you all right?" I asked.

"I may need to sit down," Kaz said. "As does this brave mademoiselle."

Kaz holstered his pistol, and I took his arm as Niven dragged the corpse out of the doorway. The girl shuddered.

"That is the truck driver from yesterday," Kaz said, a confused look on his face.

"Yeah. You didn't notice?"

"That is not the man who hit me," Kaz said, and he started to sway. I got a good grip on him, and with the girl helping, we kept Kaz upright as she got her tears under control. We sat him down in the office, and Niv cleaned the wound with a wet towel. I was worried about the whack Kaz had taken, but I was even more worried about the guy who hit him.

Who was the second man and what had he taken from the hotel?

CHAPTER TWENTY-EIGHT

"THIS IS YVONNE," Kaz said, wincing as she tended to his head. "She works here as a waitress."

"Hello, Yvonne," Niven said politely. He'd stepped away from his own ministrations when Yvonne fetched a first aid kit from the kitchen and went to work on Kaz. She was about twenty, thin, with dark hair cut short, and a steady hand.

"Bonjour," Yvonne said, gathering herself and getting to work with the bandages.

"Now, Baron, what happened out there?" Niven asked.

"I found Yvonne in the kitchen," Kaz began. "She told me the assistant manager had told her to start cleaning up the place, and then left himself, ostensibly to find the rest of his staff. She was the only one here."

Yvonne spoke to Kaz in gentle tones, patting his arm. Then she applied iodine to the gash just above his hairline. He gasped, then managed his crooked smile as he thanked her.

"Except for the two guys," I said, going through the documents that had been in the satchel. This leather case had seen its fair share of secrets the last few days.

"I only saw one man," Kaz said as Yvonne applied a compress and wrapped a cloth bandage around his head. "In the garage, with the jeep."

"Good lord, they left a jeep behind as well?" Niven asked, leaning against the desk.

"Yes, which is what Yvonne was showing me," Kaz said. "She opened the door and as we stepped inside, I was struck from behind and fell on the hood. A man wearing a gray wool coat grabbed my Sten and pistol and tossed them on the seat. Then he took hold of Yvonne and told us both to be quiet as he watched the hotel. He held a knife to her throat. Fille courageuse." Yvonne smiled at the compliment as she tied off the bandages.

"You are brave," Yvonne said, enunciating the words carefully as she smiled at Kaz.

"Then?" Niven prompted.

"Wait," Kaz said, noticing the satchel. "Billy, what are you doing?"

"First Army staff left a lot of sensitive information behind," I said. "This fellow was sneaking around collecting it while we searched the place. You didn't see him?"

"No, I had quite enough to deal with, thank you," Kaz said, smiling at Yvonne.

"So, what happened?" Niven demanded.

"The gray-coated fellow hit me with the butt of the knife he held at Yvonne's throat," Kaz said. "It occurred to me he didn't want any loud noises to give him away."

"Which is why he didn't shoot. And Yvonne could've screamed if he stabbed you," I said.

"I might have as well," Kaz said. "Anyway, he told us to be quiet and he'd let us go. There was a hint of something in his accent I didn't like. So, I called him a pile of vomit."

"Eh?" Niven said.

"In German," Kaz explained. "*Kotzbrocken.* A nice all-purpose insult. Then I angrily told him I'd lost my blue scarf."

"In German?" I asked, remembering that a blue scarf was the sign of an infiltrator.

"Ich habe meinen blauen Schal verloren," Kaz said. "It caught him off guard. Yvonne as well, but she was quick off the mark.

She twisted away from him, then he gave her a kick. He followed up with a punch to my temple. I believe he still wanted to avoid giving an alarm. Perhaps to give his comrade a chance to escape."

"Where did he go?" Niven asked.

"I wasn't sure," Kaz said. "The blow stunned me. I only saw a blur of gray bolt out of the garage. I grabbed my Webley, staggered outside, and fired two shots into the air, hoping to bring you running. The ground then became topsy-turvy and I found myself face down. Yvonne took my pistol and went after him. She got off one shot as he went running out the rear courtyard."

"That accounts for the three shots we heard," Niven said. "Il est bien fait, Yvonne." She nodded as she packed up the first aid kit.

"Thank you," she said. "I have a little English only. But thank you."

"You are welcome, my dear," Niv said.

"Yvonne does not like the Boche," Kaz said, as he patted her hand. However, it seemed she liked Kaz just fine.

"It's not here," I said. I stuffed the wad of papers back into the satchel after going through them a second time.

"What isn't?" Kaz asked.

"The requisition order for the Hôtel des Bains in Chaudfontaine," I said. "The new First Army HQ. And the German in the gray coat has it."

Kaz quickly spoke to Yvonne, too fast for me to pick up anything except "camion Berliet." I figured he was asking if she'd seen the green Berliet truck our corpse had been driving yesterday.

"She did not see the truck," Kaz said.

"Worst luck," Niven said. "But by now the fellow who got away has already taken it, or another vehicle they had close by."

"Right. This isn't a gang that leaves anything to chance," I said.

"Gang doesn't quite begin to describe them," Kaz said. "German infiltrators allied with the Parisian underworld. I know criminal activity does not stop because of war, but aiding the enemy like this is despicable, even for the Syndicat du Renard."

"Maybe the criminals don't know the whole story," I said. "What if they're being used?"

"How?" Kaz asked, gingerly rubbing his temple.

"Listen, chaps, we don't have a lot of time to sit around and thrash this out," Niven said. "I've got to get my wireless section across the river and operational. I'll get you to First Army and you can inform Monk."

"Or you could inform him," Kaz said, "while Billy and I drive back to Paris and report in. We have a perfectly decent jeep at our disposal."

"We'll split the difference," I said. "It's a good four hours to Paris, and I'd feel better if you had a doctor examine that wound. I don't want to take a chance on you passing out while we're speeding down the road. Have Niv drop you at First Army. Tell Monk what happened, and keep an eye on things there after a doctor sees you. I'll be in touch tonight."

"Do you even need to go to Paris?" Kaz asked. "We could communicate with Colonel Harding by telephone if necessary."

"There's something I want to check out," I said. "Inspector Fayard may be able to help. I'll let you know if it pans out. Now, let's move before Fritz and friends come calling."

Kaz was a bit wobbly as we walked out of the hotel but did manage a bow as he took Yvonne's hand and kissed it. We gave her a box of rations and urged her to stay hidden in case the Germans had questions about the shoot-out in the courtyard. She promised she would, but as she cradled the rations under her arm, I saw the dead man's pistol stuck in her pocket.

"What a delightful young woman," Niven said as she returned to the hotel.

"Even if she didn't recognize you?" Kaz asked with a grin that quickly became a wince.

"Must have been all the excitement," Niven said. "Now, let's see if your jeep needs petrol."

We drove to the rear entrance and into the courtyard. I started the jeep and checked the gauge. It was full, as was the five-gallon jerry can fastened to the rear bumper.

"You won't get lost, will you?" Kaz said as he handed me a map.

"If people are speaking German, does that mean I went the wrong way?" I asked, checking my route. I was heading due west to Remouchamps, where I'd connect with a main road, hopefully avoiding any rampaging panzers.

"It's been a pleasure, Billy," Niven said as we shook hands. "Some of it, anyway."

"Good luck," I said. "Make sure Kaz gets his head checked."

"He should definitely get it checked, having left the wonderful Yvonne behind," Niv said. "If we make it out of here in one piece, and you ever find yourself in Hollywood, look me up, will you?"

I promised I would, the vision of sunshine and palm trees suddenly very appealing. Kaz tossed off a salute, and they clambered into the scout car, heading for Chaudfontaine and First Army HQ. I pulled out, thankful for what little protection the canvas top gave against the weather. I had about 250 miles ahead of me, and the first part of the route was rough going. Narrow two-lane roads barely cleared of snow, with plenty of switchbacks as the elevation increased. But one benefit was that it was north of where Peiper and his bunch were headed.

I hit Remouchamps and the road widened, following the route of a river through a gap in the hills. A roadblock was set up outside of town, manned by MPs and two anti-tank guns dug in on either side of the road. There were a lot of GIs, none of them sporting blue scarves.

An MP sergeant asked me for the password.

"Kentucky," I said, expecting the countersign *Derby* to follow.

"That was yesterday, bub," the MP said. He raised his carbine, aiming it in the general direction of my chest. "What's today's password?"

"Sorry, Sarge, I got that from G-2 at First Army yesterday," I said. "I've been on the move since then."

"What's the trouble, Frosty?" asked a lieutenant. He wore the white-banded MP helmet above suspicious eyes, and he rested his hand on his holster like a gunslinger ready to draw.

"Yesterday's password, sir," Frosty replied, then asked for my papers. He'd either gotten his nickname from the whitish blond hair that stuck out from under his helmet or the dusting of snow on his shoulders. "But I doubt any Kraut could pull off that Boston accent."

I didn't have the right password, but my SHAEF identity card carried a fair bit of weight. More than I had counted on.

"He's okay," a lieutenant said, checking the card Frosty held up for his inspection. "Let him through."

Frosty lowered his weapon and handed the laminated card back to me. "You know about the misspelling, Captain?"

"What misspelling? I asked, studying the card. I didn't see anything wrong with it.

"See here?" the sergeant said, pointing out the line that read: *Not a Pass. For Indentification Purposes Only.*

"They misspelled *identification*," I said. "I never noticed that."

"It's wrong on all the identity cards SHAEF issued," Frosty said. "But the German forgers took it on themselves to correct it. Prussian thoroughness, I guess. Makes it easy to nab 'em. Word is they're Skorzeny's boys, and they're headed to Paris to take out Ike."

"You can't make this stuff up," I said. I wasn't too worried about Uncle Ike. He had rings of security around him, and I was sure it had been beefed up. "Any trouble ahead?"

"Nope, they haven't gotten this far. The road to Paris is clear, Captain. And the password today is *jumping jacks.*"

As I drove through the small town with its gray stone buildings clinging to the riverbank, I thought, *No, they haven't gotten this far.* But I was pretty sure some of them had been here all along.

CHAPTER TWENTY-NINE

AS THE MP said, the road to Paris was clear. Which also meant the road *from* Paris was clear. Everyone was worried, for good reason, about Germans masquerading as GIs. They'd already caused a lot of confusion and some casualties. But there had to be a bigger payoff for all that effort. Niven had said anything Skorzeny was involved with had to have a strategic goal, which meant it needed to tip the scales in some vital way.

Moving signposts wasn't it.

Going after Ike at SHAEF? Yeah, that would fit the bill. I thought about this as I drove through countryside that was flatter than where I'd started. Snow-covered fields edged up to wooded knolls or swift-flowing streams. I slowed as a column of trucks came from the west, hauling men and supplies to the front. These drivers weren't holding back, and I eased over to the edge of the road as far as I dared. The big two-and-a-half-ton trucks didn't leave a lot of room, even for my small jeep. Each vehicle splashed up slush onto my windshield, forcing me to drive even slower as I worked the dashboard lever for the hand-powered wiper.

Traffic eased, with solitary trucks, cars, and jeeps turning on and off the main road, and I could focus again on what the enemy might be planning. But assassinating General Eisenhower? That wouldn't be easy, even if we hadn't found out what was going on with the phony MPs. But now that we knew, every GI who looked even a little suspicious was getting the third degree.

And while it stood to reason that Uncle Ike would be at the Trianon headquarters while the battle was going on, how could Skorzeny be certain of that? The general could have been called to London for a top-level meeting or gone south to the French Riviera for some winter sunshine.

The more I thought about it, the more I doubted it could be pulled off. Even so, the threat of an attack on SHAEF would sow confusion and hamper Uncle Ike's movements. But that lacked the strategic punch Skorzeny was famous for.

As I approached Dinant on the French border, I passed beneath a medieval fortress built atop a steep ledge overlooking the town. Dinant was perched on the banks of the Meuse River, backed up against that granite wall. I spotted the snouts of anti-aircraft guns above and wondered how many wars that citadel had withstood. Then I joined the line of traffic crossing the Meuse on a small stone bridge.

I watched as MPs hustled civilians across without much inspection. Some came from the west bank, but most were looking to put the big river between themselves and the Germans. They were on foot, carrying huge amounts of luggage, or perched on horse-drawn carts. A lucky few had trucks or automobiles stuffed with belongings.

An MP waved through a Berliet truck, like the one we saw in Spa, except older. This one was rusted out and belched smoke. The same MP then checked papers for three GIs in a jeep, taking his time for each one before signaling me to move forward.

I gave the password, *jumping*, and received the countersign, *jacks*. It was the perfect combo, given the trouble Germans had pronouncing the letter *J*.

"I see you're not checking the civilian traffic," I said to the MP as I stuffed my identity card back in my pocket.

"Our orders are to make sure no Germans come through disguised as GIs," he said. "And that's what we're doing. Ain't enough MPs to check all these civilians, Captain. Move along, please."

I moved on. That MP was doing exactly as he was ordered, which is what the army wanted. As I crossed the narrow bridge, a blue van with *plombier* painted on the side passed me in the other lane. What was inside, I wondered, other than pipes and plungers? Weapons? Armed men?

I'd crossed over into France and descended into a wide, open valley, the road taking me toward Reims and then Paris. I settled into the drive, thinking about all those civilian vehicles and if Skorzeny was really gunning for Uncle Ike. Not that I'm a killer commando myself, but I was certain that approach posed too many variables, too many unknowns. On the plus side, everyone around SHAEF knew that Uncle Ike had his private quarters in Field Marshal von Rundstedt's villa out in Saint-Germain-en-Laye, a short drive from Versailles. He'd likely be an easier target there since it wasn't guarded as heavily as SHAEF headquarters. That's where I'd plan the hit, but now that the jig was up, the general would likely not venture far from the Trianon.

So, what was Skorzeny up to? Maybe his Einheit Stielau operation was solely about seizing bridges across the Meuse, and it went to hell when we found out about the phony MPs. Maybe I was overthinking the whole thing.

Which left me with the green Berliet truck in Spa and the dead driver. Not to mention the guy in the gray coat who got away.

Syndicat du Renard men? Did the fact that one spoke German mean he was connected to Einheit Stielau? Or was he simply a deserter who'd swapped one criminal organization for another? Had he known what Kaz's comment about a blue scarf meant, or was he just dumbfounded by his quarry talking about a lost scarf in German?

Finally, in the biggest head-scratcher so far, what was the Syndicat's angle with stolen artwork? We'd assumed that was their primary motive. Were they in the pay of the Germans, doing a side job here and there for them?

I let all that percolate as I headed into Couvin, following the road signs, which seemed to be pointed in the right direction. I found one for Reims and tried to stop thinking about possibilities and unanswered questions, basically because I'd run out of ideas. I stopped outside Couvin to stretch my legs and grabbed a K ration, first opening the tin of pork loaf and eating it with hard biscuits. It stopped my stomach from growling. The chocolate bar was refreshing.

Maybe it was because I wasn't trying to figure things, or maybe it was because I had to take a left turn for Reims, but all of a sudden, I thought of Lefty Sullivan. Lefty was a criminal back in Boston, but a very careful one. He was nicknamed Lefty because he'd lost his left hand in the last war, somewhere around Château-Thierry. I was pretty sure I'd be driving through there after Reims, and I'd have to give a nod to the memory of Lefty's hand, now buried in some farmer's field.

I shivered as the road climbed a forested hill, the wind sending snow swirling over the frozen ground. I passed three trucks pulled to the side of the road, GIs at work changing a tire. I kept a tight grip on the steering wheel as the road became covered in white, nearly disappearing. On the downward slope of the hill, the winds died away, and I was greeted by a view of gray overcast skies and another valley, this one wider than the others. A smudge on the horizon told me Reims was close.

Back to Lefty. He'd come home from the war bitter at the loss of his hand, and word was he'd decided that since life had taken one hand away, he'd grab what he could with the other. My dad had encountered him in his early days, and almost got the goods on him once for robbing a hardware store. According to Dad, that near miss had put the fear of God and the Charles Street Jail into Lefty, and he went quiet for a while.

He used the time to build up a fleet of vehicles. Trucks,

taxicabs, automobiles, and motorcycles, all with stolen or altered license plates. Lefty's name didn't appear on any ownership papers, and he employed only two trusted men, both relatives.

Lefty became a full-service automotive broker for the gangs of Boston. You needed a truck to transport stolen merchandise? Lefty would leave it parked wherever you wanted and give you the key in exchange for cash. Need a car to provide a tommy gun serenade for a business rival? Same deal. The vehicles never had to be returned, and Lefty was careful not to leave any evidence linking him or his clients to whatever deed was undertaken. The gangs liked the arrangement and tolerated Lefty providing his services to competitors and allies alike.

In 1936, in one of life's ironic twists, Lefty died in a car crash. Wasn't even his fault.

Where did this get me? It offered the possibility that the Syndicat was involved with the same sort of service. They'd used a lot of vehicles in my encounters with them. The truck they blew up as a diversion at the cemetery, for starters, then the US Army truck that had intercepted Hansen's shipment, and now the Berliet. There had been no mention of the Syndicat being involved in automotive thefts, which could have been an oversight, or maybe it was because they'd contracted that work out.

Before Kaz and I had left Paris, Salinger had been assigned to investigate leads about stolen trucks. We'd given him the number of the army vehicle the Syndicat had used to ambush Hansen and Pascale, and he was going to find out where it had been stolen. If that had panned out, it might allow us to shake down a few low-level crooks and get some intel.

My money was on Inspector Fayard knowing if there was a Parisian version of Lefty at work providing vehicles to the underworld. That might lead us to who took that green Berliet to Spa, what it carried, and why. Anyway, it was worth a shot.

I wanted to speak to Fayard about another matter as well. Captain Willoughby of SHAEF's Civil Affairs section had told us he was headed to General Bradley's headquarters to brief staff there on cultural sites and possible depositories of looted art. He was also buddies with Henri Grau, the Swiss art dealer who'd made himself useful to Willoughby. I was sure Grau was cultivating Willoughby, who seemed to enjoy being treated to fine dining, to get the jump on other dealers when it came to acquiring works of art.

The location of SHAEF headquarters was well-known. But that wasn't the case for forward HQs like Bradley's or First Army's. Their specific locations were never mentioned in dispatches for security reasons. Willoughby struck me as the kind of guy who liked to brag, especially if his dinner partner was picking up the tab. Had he spouted off about his briefing at Bradley's headquarters in Luxembourg City? Or First Army's in Spa?

I'd heard Grau was headed back to Switzerland, but maybe all the movement at the front had changed his travel plans. Either way, I planned on asking Fayard to check on Grau's movements and what he'd said to his acquaintances. If he'd picked up anything from Willoughby, he might have passed it on inadvertently.

My job would be to confront Willoughby. I didn't know if I'd approach him nicely or come down hard and threatening. At least I had about another hundred miles to think about it.

CHAPTER THIRTY

BONE-TIRED, I PULLED up at the gate to the Palace of Versailles, the ornate gold scrollwork dusted with freshly fallen snow. This time, I wasn't casually waved through. GIs in sandbagged machine gun emplacements kept their weapons trained on my jeep as I went through the identity check.

"Looks okay, Captain," the MP said, handing my identity card back. "Hey, who played center field for the Yankees last season?"

"The Yanks? I don't know. Johnny Lindell, maybe?" I said. "But if you want to ask about the Boston Braves, it was Tommy Holmes."

"That right?" he asked another MP.

"Yeah," his pal said, and I picked up the accent right away. "We didn't go fah, did we, Cap'n?"

"Barely made it out of the cell-ah," I said, and having passed muster, the gates were opened. I drove to the Trianon and climbed out of the Jeep, stretching my tight back before going into the warmth. Up the steps, I was suddenly aware of my appearance. Dirty boots, grimy fatigues, and an unshaven face were pretty much the norm at the front, but here I felt like an interloper. I kicked off as much of the snow and mud as I could before opening the door and traipsing across the polished marble floors.

As soon as I stepped inside, two guards posted by the door blocked my way. I recognized one of them from the more relaxed days of sentry duty, a corporal who'd always been friendly. Now the friendliest thing about him was that his carbine was held at port arms and not pointed at my belly.

"It's Captain Boyle, Corporal," I said. "Just a little worse for wear."

"Identity card," he snapped, shooting a nervous glance at the sergeant standing next to him. I understood. He was under orders to follow an exact procedure. The sergeant tightened his grip on his weapon as I reached inside my coat.

"Easy, boys, we're all on the same side here," I said as I handed over my identity card.

"We got orders," the sergeant said. "One of 'em is checking to make sure people coming in still have their IDs. Doesn't matter if we know 'em."

"Colonel Harding left word you should see him the second you come in, Captain," the corporal said. His sergeant told him to escort me in case anyone got nervous about a Thompson-toting officer in filthy fatigues.

"What's it like up there?" asked the corporal as we took to the stairs.

"Confusing," I said. "Hard to know where the Germans are most of the time. And when you do, there's too many of them. How about here?"

"Nerves are on edge, especially since Skorzeny's men were captured," he said.

"Wait. The phony MPs?" I stopped dead in my tracks.

"Yeah. Three of them got picked up at a crossroads after they gave the wrong password," he said. "Then they admitted their mission was to kidnap Ike. Turned the place into a madhouse is what it did. Everyone's on edge, ready for Skorzeny to kick down the door with a knife in his teeth."

"Well, looks like you've got things under control," I said, giving the corporal a smile and quickly revising my estimate of Skorzeny's intentions as we made for Harding's office. Under control seemed a long way off.

"Boyle!" Harding shouted as I entered his office. Big Mike jumped up from his chair, his grin vanishing and his brow wrinkling.

"Billy, where's Kaz?" he said, clasping my arms.

"He's okay, don't worry," I said. I propped my Thompson against the wall and began to shed layers. "Colonel, did you get our message? Two days ago, I think it was."

"I did," Harding said. "That was one of the first reports to come in of Germans impersonating MPs. Good work. Now sit down, you're exhausted."

I didn't need to be told twice. Harding called for coffee and sandwiches, and that gave me a moment to catch my breath before he peppered me with questions. The first was about Kaz, and the second was along the lines of *Where the hell have you been?*

"Kaz is at First Army headquarters," I said. "In Chaudfontaine, which came as a surprise to us. We went back to Spa this morning and they'd pulled out." I went on to describe Monk Dickson's assurances of the day before that they were staying put, and how we found signs of a rushed evacuation this morning, including sensitive documents and maps left behind.

We were interrupted by an orderly bringing a carafe of coffee and a tray of ham sandwiches. I wrapped my hands around the mug of hot joe and realized how cold I was. A shiver ran through my body, and I struggled to raise the cup without spilling it.

"It sounds slipshod, but they had reports of panzers coming down the road," Harding said. As usual, the brass was hard at work with excuses they wouldn't tolerate from a GI bolting from his foxhole.

"We didn't see any, and we got there after they were way out of sight," I said. "But Peiper's column was close, I know that well enough. We saw the massacre at Baugnez crossroads, right outside Malmedy."

"Damn. How'd you manage that?" Big Mike asked.

"We were headed north, about to cross the route of their line of advance," I said. "We scouted out the column through binoculars and spotted the GIs being hustled into a field. Then the SS opened up. A few guys got away. Not many."

"No, but enough that the news spread across the front," Harding said. I didn't say anything in reply, the vision of our guys being cut down in the white snow playing through my mind as I rubbed my temples.

"There's nothing you could have done," Harding said. "Not at that distance, not against all that armor."

"That's right. You're lucky you didn't run right into them," Big Mike said. Which is exactly how it happened to the GIs in those trucks. "Now, what is Kaz up to at First Army?"

"We came across two Syndicat men at the Hotel Britannique in Spa. We found the HQ empty and tried to gather whatever materials looked sensitive," I said, glad to move on from an image I knew would never leave me. "We realized we weren't alone when we found a bag of the stuff we'd collected gone. We chased the guy down, stopped him before he got out, and recovered what he'd swiped."

"What did he have to say?" Harding asked.

"Well, nothing. It was more of a full stop," I said.

"Deadeye Kaz strikes again?" Big Mike asked.

"No. Kaz was in the garage with Yvonne and the German. I was with David Niven."

"Have some more coffee," Harding said. "You're not making much sense. Who's Yvonne?"

"She's a maid at the hotel," I said.

"The radio message did come from a Major Niven," Big Mike said, shuffling through papers on the table and handing one to Harding. "I didn't think about the name."

"Right," I said. "It's Major David Niven, the actor. I'll explain that later. The important thing is that the guy in the garage got away after he gave Kaz a whack on the head. He got away with a notice left on Monk's bulletin board. The requisition for a hotel in Chaudfontaine."

"Why would the Syndicat care about that?" Big Mike asked. "Are they going to sell the location to the Krauts?"

"Kaz said the guy spoke French with an accent. As they struggled, Kaz yelled at him in German, saying he'd lost his blue scarf. They guy looked shocked, which gave Kaz a chance to get away."

"What's with the blue scarf?" Harding asked.

"It was mentioned in the orders we found in the wreckage of a Kraut personnel carrier," I said. "We brought it to Monk. It mentioned Einheit Stielau and said the phony GIs were wearing blue scarves as a recognition signal."

"That info hasn't gotten to us yet," Harding said. He grabbed the telephone and barked orders for the radio room to contact Monk at First Army and to tell Kaz to get in touch directly.

"How bad is he hurt?" Big Mike asked, his brow wrinkled with worry.

"He was woozy, but he managed to get off a few shots to warn us," I said. "Yvonne bandaged him up, but I thought he needed to be checked out by a doctor instead of spending the afternoon in a freezing jeep, so I had him report to Monk at First Army."

"Why hadn't you contacted us again?" Harding asked, clearly not happy with our silence. Or perhaps that he was only now learning about the blue scarf gag.

"Because Niven's radio went on the fritz. First Army bugged out so we couldn't use theirs. And we were busy helping Niven get the Golden Arrow wireless installation moved out before the Krauts crawled up their ass. Sir."

"Okay, don't blow a gasket, Boyle," he said, which was Harding's version of an apology.

"We also found out about the Klimt drawing," I said. "Not that it's much compared to what's going on now." I took another bite of my ham sandwich, and I could feel the food fueling my tired body.

"It may still be important," Harding said, leaning back into his chair. "Tell us."

I gulped some joe and went over what Peter Seaton and our initial our suspect, Captain Malcolm Rawson, had told us when we'd arrived at Montgomery's headquarters. That Rawson had actually purchased the Klimt in relative innocence from Teddy Dankworth, a Brit who commanded a Phantom patrol currently operating with First Army.

"We hitched a ride with Niven," I said. "He's on Monty's intelligence staff. We found Teddy and his men holding a small village along with an American platoon on the shooting edge of the German offensive. Krewinkel."

"I've seen reports," Harding said. "They held up the German advance in the early hours. Same thing is happening in other small villages. Even a few hours' delay might wreak havoc with the Germans' timetable."

"We brought the order for the platoon to retreat if they were getting surrounded," I said. "Niven wanted the Phantom patrol out to avoid capture, so we withdrew after they started working their way around us. But not before Teddy told us he'd won the Klimt in a card game. Guess who from." I poured myself more coffee and glanced at their expressions. Big Mike was first to get it.

"Jacques Delair," he said. "Which explains why he was killed by the Syndicat. Not for being a snitch, but for stealing from them."

"Bingo," I said. "Teddy and a French liaison officer whom Niven vouched for went looking for a card game and ended up playing faro at the Café Cadet. Delair lost big-time and offered the drawing. Teddy knew the value and snapped it up."

"That's good news," Harding said. "It confirms no Allied officers were involved in deliberate smuggling. I'll ask Captain

Seaton to get a statement from this Dankworth when he returns to Leuven."

"He didn't make it," I said. "We got into a fight on the way back to St. Vith. That's where we found the documents near a burned-out half-track."

"A lot of men didn't make it," Harding said as he shook his head. "Casualties are heavy."

"You think there's any connection between Skorzeny's Einheit Stielau and the Syndicat, Colonel?" Big Mike asked. "It's kind of strange they'd be searching a vacated headquarters."

"We've had no indication of infiltrators dressed as civilians," Harding said. "Although the three Germans we captured said Skorzeny was planning on killing or kidnapping Ike. The general is basically a prisoner in his own office and he's not happy about it. No civilian is going to get within a hundred yards of him without being thoroughly searched, so I doubt they'll go that route."

"Listen, I don't remember if I mentioned it—I'm a little beat— but we saw the Syndicat guy the day before as we drove through Spa. He was in a green moving truck. An old Berliet," I said.

"Maybe there's a stash of stolen artwork in St. Vith," Harding said. "They go to pick it up using a moving truck as cover and decide to see if there's anything worth taking at the hotel. Intelligence is valuable. Nobody accused these guys of being patriots."

"Maybe, but I don't get what they're after," I said. "Things just don't add up. I thought I'd ask Inspector Fayard about any gangs specializing in providing stolen vehicles for other criminals."

"We had this lowlife in Detroit," Big Mike said. "He'd steal cars in Canada and bring them down whenever a gang wanted to pull off a hit. No local connection. Bound to be someone in the same business in Paris. If you weren't about to fall asleep you could come along tonight and ask Fayard."

"What's happening?" I asked.

"Salinger looked into the truck the Syndicat used to ambush

you and Hansen," Harding said. "I'm glad you took the serial number before you let him drive off in it. Turns out it was stolen from the Gare de l'Est rail yard a week ago. Fayard has connections with some of the workers there and came up with a name. He and Salinger are due to meet him tonight at a bar called the Apache Noir. His name is Hugo Paul."

"Can this guy lead us to the Syndicat?" I asked.

"Potentially," Big Mike said. "The good news is Paul is still breathing. Unlike a lot of others who have encountered the Fox."

"The Traction Avant gang," I said, half to myself, remembering that Salinger was going to investigate any links to that bunch. "The Parisian gang named after their favorite getaway car. They came up when all this first started. Maybe they went into the vehicle supply business."

"That's right," Big Mike said. "I don't know how far Salinger got, since he and Fayard were sent to that crime scene at the Belleville garage."

"A garage," I said, wondering at the connection.

"Didn't Fayard tell us one of the dead men was suspected of being with Traction Avant?" Harding asked, shuffling through the papers on his desk. He found a police report and traced his finger along the lines. "Here it is. Roger Dano, suspected in several Traction Avant robberies. I didn't think much of it when we spoke on the telephone. I was more focused on this guy, Alphonse Bussion." Harding jabbed his finger at the page.

"The one involved in the prewar art theft," Big Mike said. "That's who we were most interested in."

"Which makes sense, but we need to factor vehicles into the picture," I said. "With a link to Traction Avant and now the guy Fayard and Salinger are going after tonight, we just might have something."

"I'll fill in Salinger," Big Mike said. "I'm meeting him outside the joint. Then I'll watch the entrance."

"Big Mike would attract too much attention inside," Harding

said. "Better to have him standing guard in case of trouble. Salinger is going in wearing civilian clothes and sticking close to Fayard. His French is decent."

"I'm going," I said, with more determination than actual capability. "I just need to get cleaned up. Any reason a couple of GIs couldn't go in for a drink? I'll take off my bars and Big Mike and I will have a couple of beers. If he's outside, he might never know if there's trouble."

"Makes sense, Sam," Big Mike said.

"You sure about this, Boyle?" Harding asked. "You've been out in the field for two days. You're exhausted, not to mention ripe."

"I'm sure," I said. "I need to check this out. Although I wouldn't mind Big Mike driving me back to the hotel first."

"Can do," Big Mike said after Harding gave him the go-ahead nod.

"Just one thing before I go, Colonel. Could I use your office for a while?" I asked.

"Why?"

"I want to talk to Captain Willoughby from Civil Affairs," I said. "Not in his office. This is more intimidating."

"Even without me in it?" Harding said, a rare smile parting his lips. "Should I even ask?"

"It's a long shot," I said. "Probably nothing, but I need to get him worried."

Harding understood. He made a telephone call to Civil Affairs and ordered Willoughby to his office immediately. Then he left to see if Monk had gotten back to him.

"So, what's the deal, Billy?" Big Mike said as I grabbed my Thompson and made myself comfortable in Harding's chair.

"Bad cop, bad cop," I said. "Let's shake his tree and see what rotten fruit drops."

CHAPTER THIRTY-ONE

I'D SPREAD OUT a copy of *Stars and Stripes* on Harding's desk. I didn't want to get gun oil on his blotter as I cleaned my Thompson. It needed it after the last few days. Plus, it gave me something to do while I spoke to Willoughby. Something unnerving, I hoped.

As I removed the receiver from the stock, there was a knock at the door. Big Mike opened it and Willoughby stepped in, a look of shock on his face.

"Captain Boyle," he said. It was half a greeting and half a question. I probably looked different from the last time he'd seen me. "Where is Colonel Harding?"

"Elsewhere," I said. "Have a seat." Big Mike closed the door behind him, then stood in front of it, arms folded across his chest. Willoughby had no choice but to sit down.

"What is this all about?" he said, one hand gripping an armrest as if he were about to vault out of his seat. "I'm very busy at the moment."

"So am I," I said. I carefully removed the recoil springs and ran a cleaning cloth along the cold steel. "I've been busy. How about you, Captain? Did the briefing for General Bradley go well?"

"That obviously didn't happen, Captain Boyle," he said. "Events got in the way."

"Yeah, they got in my way too. Tell me, Captain Willoughby, how well do you know Henri Grau?"

"What do you mean? He's very knowledgeable, and he's assisted my office several times," Willoughby said. He glanced at the door, nearly invisible behind Big Mike. As his eyes went back to me, I could see him calculating what this was about, and how much he owed to his dinner partner. Not much, it seemed. "Of course, I don't know him personally. Has he done something wrong?"

"Have you seen him in the company of any other foreign nationals?" I asked. I set down the receiver and picked up the barrel. I looked down it, swiveling in the chair until I saw Willoughby's face. "Dirty. Sorry, the barrel is filthy. Not you."

"Is this so important it couldn't wait until you cleaned yourself up?" Willoughby said. Now he was finding his confidence. My question led him to think we just wanted to know about Grau's acquaintances, and the relief was evident in his unclenched jaw.

"A clean weapon is important, Captain," Big Mike said, his voice set to an octave or two lower than normal. "You've heard about the German commandos, haven't you?"

"Of course I have. But Henri Grau is Swiss," he said. "His papers were in order."

"Who said he was a German commando, Captain?" Big Mike said. "Is there anything you're not telling us?"

"No, no," Willoughby said, his neck swiveling between Big Mike and me. "I trust the man, that's all. At least as far as art evaluations. He's been fair in that regard." Now the distancing was in full force.

"Grau is a businessman," I said. I took the cleaning rod and ran a patch of cloth coated in oil up and down the bore. "Not many foreign businessmen have access to SHAEF. Who knows what information he may have passed on. Unwittingly, of course."

"I guess he could have overheard something in the hallway," Willoughby said, with a small shrug of the shoulders. "A snatch of conversation, perhaps."

"Sorry you didn't get to Luxembourg City," I said, changing course to keep him off-balance. "It's supposed to be nice."

"Yes, I was looking forward to visiting the Cathedral of Our Lady," he said. "Undamaged, thank goodness."

"Not so much to see in Spa, is there?" Big Mike chimed in.

"No, not really," Willoughby said. "Some of the mineral spring pavilions are architecturally interesting, but that's all."

"Did you take the waters when you were there?" I asked. I checked the bore. Clean as a whistle this time.

"No, I don't even know if any of the spas are operating," he said. "It was strictly a briefing for the Operations staff, similar to what I would have talked about at General Bradley's headquarters."

"Did Grau have anything to offer on artwork in the area?" Big Mike asked, moving away from the door and facing Willoughby as I reassembled the receiver.

"No, he said he hadn't been there," Willoughby said, his tone tinged with anger. Perhaps the sight of the door handle had given him courage. "Now, are we done?"

"Sorry, I was distracted," I said, rubbing a cloth over the metal, the tang of gun oil lingering in the air. "Grau said he wasn't where?"

"Spa," Willoughby answered, his mouth limp with realization as soon as he said it.

"When you told him you were going to brief First Army staff," I said. "At the Hotel Britannique. In Spa."

"That's information of strategic importance, Captain," Big Mike said, looming even larger over Willoughby.

"When did you tell him?" I asked, attaching the receiver to the stock.

Willoughby sat rigid, sweat breaking out over his temples. He didn't speak.

"Captain, you need to cooperate, and do it now," I said. "If it was an accidental breach of security, tell us about it. It happens all the time, but with this big flap on, we have to follow up every little thing." I tried to make it sound like nothing but a tedious and minor mix-up.

"It must have been two weeks ago, maybe a little more," Willoughby said, his eyes cast down to his hands as he wrung them in his lap. "We were celebrating. Henri had helped us sort through several unidentified paintings and had also made a big sale of his own. It was harmless, really. I mentioned I was leaving in the morning for First Army headquarters, and I had a long drive."

"I bet he asked how long," Big Mike said. He had unfolded his arms, and had his hands stuffed in his pockets. It was an unmilitary look, but a casual one aimed at putting Willoughby at ease.

"No, he said Beaumont wasn't that far," Willoughby said. That's when it fell into place for him. "I told him he was wrong, that I was going to Spa. Four hours or more."

"What else did he say about that?" I asked.

"Nothing, nothing at all," Willoughby said. "We finished our meal, talked about art, that was all."

"Smart," I said. "He didn't press the matter once he had what he wanted."

"He went after it sideways too," Big Mike said. "He got you to correct him and give away the location."

"What's going to happen now?" Willoughby asked. I knew he meant to him, but I was thinking through the broader implications.

"Have you seen Grau recently? You told us he'd gone back to Basel for the holidays," I said.

"He did tell me that, yes. However I saw him coming out of Stephan Narbonne's gallery just two days ago," Willoughby said. "I called out to him, but he didn't hear."

"Did you ask Narbonne about it?" Big Mike said. A quick glance between us summed up what we were thinking. Grau was done with Willoughby at that point. The flatteries and dinner had gotten him what he wanted.

"I did. He said Grau had delayed his trip and had dropped in to invite him for a drink after work," Willoughby said.

"And why were you there?" I asked.

"I'd heard a rumor about a Klimt drawing being recovered," Willoughby said. "One turned up in Rose Valland's hands, seemingly out of nowhere, according to her. I was curious if Narbonne had heard anything about it or any others. He has a lot of connections."

"What'd he tell you?" Big Mike asked.

"Said it was news to him, but he'd like to know who recovered it," Willoughby said. "He collects Klimt and wanted to know if any other pieces are available for legitimate sale."

"And that was the last you saw of either of them?" I asked.

"Narbonne and Grau? Yes. For all I know Grau is back in Switzerland. Can I go, now?"

"One more thing," I said. I waited while I finished reassembling the Thompson and inserted the clip. "Did either man ever ask you about army transport? Or where they could obtain a truck?"

"I'm not in the black market, Captain Boyle, if that's what you're inferring. The only vehicle of theirs I'm familiar with is Henri's prewar Renault," he said. "Now, if you'll excuse me, I have to get back to work."

"Don't leave town," Big Mike said, standing aside for Willoughby to leave.

"That's no way to speak to a superior officer, Sergeant," Willoughby said, trying to regain his authority.

"Thanks for the advice about not speaking out of turn, Captain," Big Mike said, opening the door in a swift movement he made almost threatening. Willoughby wasted no time in departing, and Big Mike let the door slam behind him.

"What do you think of that?" Big Mike asked as he settled himself into the chair.

"He's guilty of having a big mouth," I said. "But I'm curious about Grau still being around. I'd like to ask him what he did with the information about First Army."

"And if it's connected to the Syndicat men you ran into there," Big Mike said. "I think Narbonne asking about the Klimt is interesting. Wouldn't the Fox want to get his hands on it, if only to show that no one can get away with stealing from him?"

"I thought Jacques Delair's corpse would have done that, but it's worth thinking about," I said. "Let's ask Fayard tonight. Maybe he should track down Grau as well and see if he's still in town."

"I'll call him now," Big Mike said. "I ought to let him know about the change of plans, and we might not have the chance to kibitz in the nightclub."

I leaned back in Harding's chair and listened while Big Mike called the Trente-Six, impressed with the bits of French he'd picked up. It didn't sound pretty, but it got him through to Fayard quick enough. I closed my eyes, just to give them a rest, and dreamed of getting myself as clean as my tommy gun.

CHAPTER THIRTY-TWO

"YOU WON'T BELIEVE it," Big Mike said as he hung up the telephone. "Fayard just picked up Narbonne for questioning."

"For what?" I said, shaking myself out of the half sleep that had weighed my eyelids down.

"Trafficking in stolen goods," Big Mike said. "A Citroën U23 truck, to be precise. Formerly a French army vehicle, requisitioned by the Germans, and most recently found in a small warehouse in the Latin Quarter leased by one Stephan Narbonne."

"Now, how did he end up with that?" I asked.

"Apparently it was repainted, and Narbonne says he thought he was purchasing a civilian vehicle," Big Mike said. "He even has a bill of sale, signed by Roger Dano."

"Wait, where have I heard that name before?" I asked, trying to rally the few brain cells that were still on active duty.

"He's one of the stiffs from the garage in Belleville," Big Mike said. "Part of the Traction Avant gang from before the war. Oh, and Fayard said he'd send some men to look for Grau."

"Well, I suppose this all makes sense, but I'm too tired to piece it together," I said. "At least someone is in jail for something. Let's go."

"Yeah, you need to get cleaned up. Apache Noir ain't the swankiest joint around, but I bet they prefer their clientele to smell a little sweeter than you do."

I didn't argue the point. As Big Mike drove to the Hotel Royale, he filled me in on the German offensive, which the honchos at SHAEF were calling the von Rundstedt Offensive, just as Monk had mentioned. The only good news was that Peiper hadn't found a way across the Meuse and was being rebuffed by blown bridges. But other panzer spearheads were still pushing westward with plenty of infantry following on. The weather was still overcast, keeping our airpower from getting to work. The town of Bastogne, where eleven good hard-surface roads intersected, was becoming a critical focal point. The 101st Airborne along with armor and artillery units were digging in there, but they expected to be surrounded before the end of the day. The American forces were badly outnumbered and lacked decent winter-weather gear. The outcome was uncertain. If Bastogne fell, the Germans surrounding it could be cut loose and attack our weakened lines.

"There's no more reserves," Big Mike finished. "Ike is rushing some troops over from England, but it'll be a while. We have to hold, and the skies have to clear."

"No sign of that," I said, looking out at the dark gray sky. At this time of day, the sun was already down, not that it had been visible once today. A thin fog sat along the road, blurring the contours of the dully lit city. The temperature was above freezing, but the damp chill set right into my bones.

At the hotel, I arranged for my dirty clothes and boots to be cleaned. I took a bath, glad that the water was only lukewarm. A hot tub would have put me right to sleep. After shaving, I splashed on aftershave to shock my face awake. I put on clean fatigues, remembering to stuff my captain's bars in a pocket in case I needed to pull rank. On went a shoulder holster with my .38 Special revolver, since a buck private wouldn't go out on the town with an officer's .45 automatic at his side. As I knotted my field scarf and tucked in my wool shirt, I decided I looked like a disheveled, exhausted GI in need of a drink.

Pretty accurate disguise.

"So, what's the skinny on this dive?" I asked as I donned my garrison cap, field jacket, wool scarf, and gloves.

"I drove by today to check it out," Big Mike said as we left. "It's off the rue de la Mare, close to a big park. We'll leave the car there."

"As long as no one steals it," I said. Vehicles were in demand these days.

"You never know," he said. "This joint is named after some old gang and the customers are a rough bunch, according to Fayard. Good jazz band, though."

I'd heard of Les Apaches. Rowdies who'd terrorized the streets of Paris at night around the turn of the century when muggings and worse were commonplace in some neighborhoods. It made me wonder about the crowd we were about to mingle with.

Big Mike left the car near the park where fog hung over the snow. We walked along the rue de la Mare, where restaurants and bars cast a dim light onto the sidewalk. A narrow side street led us to a single light above a sign announcing Apache Noir, with an arrow pointing down to a basement door.

As we descended, the door banged open and two men, arguing loudly as they took the stairs with the teetering agility of practiced drunks, brushed past us as we stood aside. The odor of alcohol and cigarette smoke wafted out after them, followed by the sounds of a steel-string guitar and double bass playing the blues.

Inside, a long bar ran along one wall. Tables were set up in front of the small stage, where a five-man band was hard at work. The rest of the space was crowded, but not with many GIs. In the first thirty seconds, I spotted two exchanges of cash for small white envelopes. If the MPs had known about this joint, it might have been declared off-limits.

Salinger and Fayard were at a table off to the side, deep in conversation with a short, wiry fellow with curly hair. He had high cheekbones and narrow eyes that kept searching the room.

His face and hands were darkly stained , the kind of coloring that comes from working around locomotives, surrounded by soot and oil that never quite comes clean. I nodded to Big Mike, glancing in that direction. That had to be the guy from the rail yard.

"Let's get a drink, pal," Big Mike said, ushering me toward the bar. Booze was necessary protective cover in a place like this. I caught Salinger's eye to let him know we were here, as Big Mike managed to squeeze himself into a place at the bar.

"Deux bières," he said, raising two fingers to the barman. He grinned, proud of his accent. The bartender wasn't impressed. He poured two glasses and slid them clumsily to us, spilling the foam over the side. He stood stock-still until Big Mike tossed some francs onto the galvanized zinc countertop.

"Not many Yanks in here," I said, leaning against the bar and taking a sip. There were eight other GIs, far outnumbered by the locals. There weren't many women either. Those who were here ignored the Americans. Which was unusual, given the quantity of smokes and silk stockings that accompanied soldiers with a two-day pass. It told me who was in charge. The new generation of Apaches.

An argument broke out at a table with three Americans. A tough guy in a worn corduroy coat bumped into a GI's chair and then gestured angrily. "Fichez le camp!" he roared.

"That means *get out*," I said to Big Mike. The bartender came out from behind the counter and confronted the Yanks, crooking his thumb in the direction of the door.

"Looks like he doesn't want their business," Big Mike said. The GIs got up, making a show of saying what a dump the place was, and that the dames were duds. There was some shoving at another table, and within a few minutes, the other Yanks got the message and departed. The band kept playing, a trombone wailing as the khaki-clad customers left.

"I don't like this," I said as I scanned the room.

"The beer or the band?" Big Mike asked.

"They're clearing out the Yanks," I said. "Except for us."

"Billy, I'm the biggest guy in here, and you're with me," he said as the bartender threw his change on the counter. I watched Fayard for any sign that he was aware of trouble. He looked at me, then around the room. Even in the dim, smoky light, I could see the concern on his face as he leaned in to speak with Salinger and their contact.

"They don't want witnesses," I whispered, unsure of how many languages the barman spoke.

"Police!" Fayard shouted, holding up his warrant card as he stood, grabbing the rail yard man by the collar. Chairs were overturned as people moved back in a rush, and the band's tune ground to a halt. A woman screamed as a guy pushed her aside, making for Fayard. Salinger drew his revolver and stood, aiming it dead center at the man's chest. The assailant grinned and drew a knife. I swear I heard him growl, but he didn't make another move.

A commotion arose at the entrance, where two men pushed through the crowd, guns drawn. This wasn't the cavalry. They wore leather jackets with the collars turned up, scarves wrapped around their chins, wool caps pulled down low.

Fayard pushed his prisoner up on the stage, followed by Salinger, as the band bolted. I figured taking him into custody was a spontaneous act, marking him as a wanted man instead of a stool pigeon for the edification of the Apache Noir crowd.

The two leather jackets weren't here for drinks.

They both fired at Fayard, bullets smashing against the back-stage brickwork and ruining the band's snare drum. Big Mike and I were caught in a swirl of arms and bodies trying to run or hide from the sudden onslaught. I couldn't fire without hitting a bystander, although how many of them were innocent was up for discussion.

I crawled on top of the bar, escaping from the swarm, and

pulled my revolver. Just as the first thug put a foot up onto the stage to follow Fayard, I got off a shot and he stumbled forward, falling flat. Big Mike had used his brawn to push through the crowd and grab the second tough from behind, wrapping him in a bear hug and forcing him to the floor, where his forehead hit a beat or two before the guy went limp.

Shots echoed from the rear. While the crowd was momentarily stunned, Big Mike grabbed his guy's gun, and I jumped from the bar. We made it up onto the stage and down a dark hallway before any of the angry local boys had a chance to knife us. I pulled open a door at the end of the corridor, revolver at the ready.

A shot rang out, the muzzle flash illuminating stairs right in front of us. Then came three quick, shrill blasts of a police whistle. I took the steps two at a time, finding Fayard, Salinger, and the Frenchman huddled behind barrels stacked in an alleyway.

"There's someone at the corner," Salinger said, pointing to the side street where we'd entered the nightclub. "He's got us pinned down."

"We can't go back into the bar," Big Mike said, as another shot pinged against the granite wall above us.

"I have officers nearby," Fayard said, and let loose with his whistle. "They'll deal with this fellow."

"Someone talked. Someone who knew we were meeting Hugo Paul here," Salinger said. He spoke calming words to Paul, who was hunched down about as low as he could go.

The basement entryway below us opened, and Big Mike fired a warning shot into the air. The door fell shut, but if anyone down there had a gun, we'd be taking fire from two directions.

Fayard blew the whistle again.

"Inspector, just how far away are your men?" I asked.

"Very far, I fear," he said as he pocketed the whistle and fired two shots at the shooter blocking our path.

Below us, the door creaked open. Big Mike ran down the steps and slammed into it, earning a yowl from the poor sap who'd gotten his hand caught.

"We don't have a lot of time," Big Mike said, his back pressed against the door. Angry voices and pounding fists came from behind it as Big Mike's heels slid forward under the pressing weight.

Paul shouted, cupping his hands around his mouth, his words too rushed for me to make out. Another bullet ricocheted off the cobblestones in front of us. Fayard cursed, and I thought it might be time to say my prayers.

CHAPTER THIRTY-THREE

PAUL CONTINUED YELLING and was rewarded with a shouted response from around the corner. Fayard gripped his pistol in desperation while Salinger looked on in confusion. Big Mike gritted his teeth as the door was battered from the inside. I didn't know what the hell was going on, but I did know Paul didn't look worried, which worried the hell outta me.

Fayard nodded as Paul spoke, and the two of them stood. No one shot at them.

"Come," Fayard said to Big Mike. "Let it go quickly and run!"

Fayard held on to Paul while Salinger and I lined up on either side of the steps, leaving room for Big Mike as we aimed at the door. I gave a nod and Big Mike burst up the stairs, faster than a guy his size had any right to move.

The crowd pressing against the door fell into a tangle, the first few people caught under the heels of others who tried to follow. Maybe they were with the shooters or maybe they were mad about the show being cut short, but we didn't wait to find out. As soon as Big Mike leapt past us, Salinger and I retreated to the corner and whatever salvation awaited us there.

Six men stood around a limp form in the gutter. No gun was in sight, probably pocketed by one of the guys shaking Paul's hand and clapping him on the shoulder.

"What's going on?" Big Mike asked, looking behind him. The

crowd from the stairwell was hanging back, unsure of how far the balance of power had shifted.

"Reinforcements," Salinger said. "Not that we expected it."

"I did not expect any of this, much less the disappearance of my men. They may have been victims of a distraction," Fayard said. "We should leave immediately and finish this discussion at the Trente-Six before more of the Syndicat arrive."

"What about this guy?" Big Mike said, kicking the gunman, who moaned softly. "And there's two more in the club. One knocked out, one shot."

Fayard spoke to the men surrounding Paul. They all had the same look, a thin sheen of oil on their clothes and skin, and black soot in the creases in their faces. Fellow workers from the rail yard. A couple slipped lead pipes up their sleeves while another held a sap dangling from one hand. Fayard's words fell flat as they melted away, each man raising a fist to his forehead in salute to Paul.

"We must leave these creatures," Fayard said in disgust. "We are too exposed here, and I would not count our lives worth much to return to that basement."

Salinger and Fayard took Paul in tow while Big Mike and I hoofed it back to the staff car. Apparently, all the car thieves in Belleville had been at Apache Noir because it was still in one piece.

"You okay?" I asked Big Mike as soon as he got the engine going.

"Yeah, I think so," he said as he pulled away from the curb, his eyes searching the road for threats. "At least now that the good guys showed up. Those were the good guys, right?"

"Tonight they were," I said. "I'm betting they were from Résistance-Fer, the railway workers' underground during the Occupation. Judging by the raised fists, probably a Communist group. That's their antifascist salute."

"So, Paul called in his buddies for backup," Big Mike said.

"And they were there when he called for them," I said, thinking it through. "I wonder if it's such a good idea to go back to the Police Judiciaire?"

"You think there's a bent cop at work here?" Big Mike asked, taking a turn down a thoroughfare. I searched for whatever vehicle might be Fayard's, wishing we'd traveled together.

"Someone wanted Fayard or Paul dead, and they almost got their wish," I said. "Either way, that someone may be inside police headquarters."

"Then let's get there first," Big Mike said, hitting the accelerator and speeding down the road, slowing at an intersection by the Père Lachaise Cemetery, the place where all this began.

"How did we get from artwork hidden in a grave to a shootout in a Parisian dive to having our bacon saved by a bunch of grimy Reds?" I asked. Big Mike knew I was talking to the night and said nothing.

He crossed the Seine at the Pont au Change and drove to the front of the Police Judiciaire. He came to a halt near the entryway to the interior courtyard just as a Citroën cruised through the massive wooden doors a moment before they were pulled shut.

"If Fayard's men weren't drawn away by a distraction, the three of them could be in trouble," I said. "If there was an order, it had to come from within the Trente-Six."

"Well, let's pay the inspector a visit," Big Mike said, and got out of the car. "We might need your captain's bars, Billy."

I pinned them to my collar as I hustled to keep up with him. Inside, an officer sat in the ornate lobby, a telephone on his desk and a sour look pasted on his face along with a graying handlebar mustache. I asked for Inspector Louis Fayard, s'il vous plaît.

He gave out a grunt and took his time having us sign in. We already knew the way to Fayard's office, but I didn't want to make a scene until we needed to. Besides, we were outnumbered by the Parisian cops in their snazzy blue uniforms going about their business, none of them looking like they'd been on a stakeout standing in wet snow. As I surveyed the wide lobby, I saw Commissaire Rochet hustle through the doorway, a couple of officers in tow, and hotfoot it up the stairs.

"Looks like the boss got called in," Big Mike said. "Busy night."

"Maybe he found out about Fayard's detail being pulled," I said in a whisper.

The desk sergeant finally got the okay for us to go up. As we took the staircase, I glanced back and saw him take the telephone from the cradle and work the dial. I spotted a plainclothes cop leaning against the wall across the lobby with a cigarette dangling from his mouth giving us the eye. He stayed put as we started up, but a minute later I heard footsteps behind us on the stone stairs. Instead of going up another floor to Fayard's office, we scooted down a hallway where the sound of clacking typewriters filled the air.

We went into the first office, feigning confusion. A dozen clerks, all women, looked up from their machines. Most smiled, probably glad of a break from typing up badly written police reports from the night shift.

"Perdu," I said, pretty sure that meant lost, and proceeded to give them my best smile while moving into the room and away from the open door. Big Mike did the same as the slap of shoe leather faded away.

"We lost our tail," Big Mike said, peeking into the hallway. Some of the young ladies giggled about "le grand Américain" until an older woman rapped her knuckles on her desk and the typing resumed. Big Mike tipped his hat as we doubled back and headed for the next floor.

Which is where we found the detective who'd been following us, waiting impatiently. He was tall and thin, with a pencil-thin mustache and an even thinner nose that canted sideways, probably broken once or twice.

"Bonsoir, Messieurs," he said, looking up and down the hallway to see if anyone was watching. "Follow me."

"We're here to see Inspector Fayard," I said.

"Yes, but you will not find him in his office," he said. "Suivez-moi."

He didn't pull a gun and walked ahead of us, both good signs, so we followed. We went back down the steps and took a side corridor, ending up at a door marked CONCIERGE.

"The janitor's closet?" Big Mike asked, shooting me a quizzical look. "Better than a cell, I guess."

"I will leave you here," the detective said as he rapped on the door and turned away. We entered. Inside, Fayard and Salinger sat at a small table with Paul, who was writing out a statement. Behind him, shelves held cleaning supplies, typewriters, forms, and the familiar debris of any bureaucracy.

"I am glad you found us," Fayard said. "On the drive here, we decided a certain discretion was required. Old Bouchard at the desk is a trusted friend, as is my colleague who brought you here. No one else knows where we are."

"Paul has been very helpful," Salinger said. "He is making a full statement."

"We have Stephan Narbonne in custody," Fayard said. "We shall interrogate him when we are done here. Also, you asked about Henri Grau. My men also found him at the Hotel Dunkerque, where he has been staying while in Paris. He was very cooperative and is waiting for the questions you have for him. Please, sit."

I grabbed a rickety wooden chair and collapsed into it. The past few days were catching up with me, and I had to work at forming my questions.

"Can you trust Paul?" I asked. At the sound of his name, he glanced at me, then went back to his statement.

"He has no love for the Syndicat du Renard," Salinger said. "They pressured him to join them and set up the theft of two vehicles. When he refused, they threatened his brother, who also works in the rail yard."

"That was a mistake," Fayard said. "The Gestapo couldn't destroy Paul or his men. He was not going to let the Syndicat succeed where the Boche had failed."

"What happened to your men, Inspector?" Big Mike said. He leaned against the wall, wisely staying away from wobbly chairs.

"Called away," he said. "Bouchard is looking into it. A shooting in the park from what we understand. Even so, it should not have happened."

"Listen, I'm glad Paul's backup was there, but one of them could've spilled the beans about the meeting." I saw Fayard's puzzled look disappear as Salinger explained the idiom.

"No. The survivors of Rouge-Fer know how to keep a secret," Fayard said. "I did not know of Paul's plan, but I am certain of their loyalty to each other. They keep their beans to themselves."

"What's Rouge-Fer?" Big Mike asked. Paul had finished his statement and seemed to enjoy watching the back-and-forth.

"Paul explained they were a cell within a cell," Salinger said. "Part of the rail worker's Iron Resistance—Résistance-Fer—but also working as a smaller unit that was known only to them. Red Iron, or Rouge-Fer. They were a tight-knit group and planned their own actions. The Krauts never caught on to them."

"Okay, so what's in the statement?" I asked. Fayard had taken the document and was reviewing each of the three handwritten pages with Paul. They were going line by line, making corrections here and there as they went.

"He has details about the Syndicat trying to muscle in at the rail yard and force the workers to steal trucks, most recently two heavy-duty vehicles," Salinger said. "They have a loading platform where trucks line up to get whatever they're hauling. Wouldn't have been hard for the rail guys to divert a couple."

"More US Army models?" Big Mike asked.

"No, the Syndicat knew precisely what they wanted. Two

Renault AHR five-ton trucks," Salinger said. "Big heavy jobs. The Germans used them, and a lot are now in civilian use."

"Pretty specific," I said. Any US truck would be readily identifiable as an army vehicle. But a French Renault would blend right in. Did the Syndicat want camouflage, or were there simply more of the French five-ton models on the streets of Paris?

"Yeah. Paul doesn't really care much if folks steal from Uncle Sam, but he knew this was different. The Fox only wanted those trucks, and specifically, wanted them empty," Salinger said. I noticed Fayard was questioning something at the end of Paul's statement, slamming his finger down on the page.

"Wait," I said, rubbing my eyes and trying to see all this through a veil of exhaustion. "Paul has seen the Fox? In person?"

"Yes," Salinger said, glancing distractedly at the hushed conversation taking place between Paul and Fayard. "Sorry, we haven't caught you up properly. He has a description. Once we confirm it, we'll have him formally identify Stephan Narbonne, and we can wrap this up."

It was evident something was wrong with Paul's statement. He and Fayard were going over it again, Paul sticking to whatever guns he had.

"The description is not that of Stephan Narbonne, despite the evidence linking him to stolen vehicles," Fayard said, looking up from the statement. "Narbonne is tall and solid with curly hair and a full mustache. Paul describes the Fox as shorter, brown hair, full cheeks, and heavy in the stomach."

"That's Henri Grau," I said. "Exactly."

"I don't get it," Big Mike said. "I thought you had Narbonne dead to rights with that stolen truck."

"So did we," Salinger said. "But the guy who supplied it is dead. Maybe Narbonne's telling the truth. Maybe Grau set him up."

"There's a lot of maybes at work here," I said.

There was one thing that wasn't a maybe, but I didn't say

anything about the Syndicat goon who got away with the document marking the exact location of First Army headquarters. I had to think long and hard about that one. But right now, something else was worrying me, something closer to home.

"Listen, you have both men in custody, so let's start by questioning them," Big Mike said.

"We need to know which one is the Fox," I said. "But it's even more critical to find out how his boys knew to ambush you at Apache Noir."

"They were both here at the time," Fayard said. "Of course, they could have ordered it earlier."

"But *how* did they know?" I said. "You trust Paul and his men. But can you trust your own?"

Fayard leaned back in his chair and let out a sigh.

"The circle of those I trust is very small," he said. "As it was during the Occupation. Once again, we must worry about informers in our midst."

"Informateurs?" Paul asked, picking up on the drift of the conversation. He drew his thumb across his neck in a quick movement. "Pas plus."

No more.

Not a bad solution, but first we needed to confirm who the real Fox was and learn how he pulled the strings that kept us dancing to his tune. Then I'd be all for handing him over to the raised fists of the Rouge-Fer.

CHAPTER THIRTY-FOUR

WE DECIDED TO tackle Stephan Narbonne first. It wasn't that I mistrusted Paul's description of the Fox, but I wanted to push Narbonne about the stolen vehicle. Was he a dupe, or was he an operative of the Syndicat du Renard? The last thing I wanted was to let any of these thugs slip through our hands because we didn't check things out thoroughly.

We headed for the rear staircase. Salinger had left with Paul via a back door to give him a lift home. We made plans to meet at Harding's office at 0700, hopefully after a few hours' sleep.

"Paul said he was nervous about being in the bowels of the Trente-Six, even if he was helping the police," Fayard said as we took the poorly lit stairs to the cellar. "For the first time, I know how he feels."

Fayard spoke to the lone flic on duty in the basement cells. He sat at a small table with a lamp, an overflowing ashtray, a newspaper, and an open book with lines for officers to sign in. Fayard shut the book and leaned in close to whisper to the cop, who nodded his head and grabbed his keys. This was an off-the-record conversation, not an official interrogation.

"Is Grau here as well?" I asked as we walked, our footsteps echoing against the flagstone floor.

"No, he is in an interrogation room," Fayard said. The officer opened the cell door. "Locked and under guard. When he was brought in it was for a simple interview. When we finish speaking with him, we shall adjust his accommodations."

The cell was lit by a single bulb hanging from the ceiling. It cast a yellow glow over the gray stone walls and the sparse furnishings. A cot, a stool, and a wooden table. Not to mention the chipped enamel bucket with a lid that I hoped was tightly secured.

Narbonne sat on the cot, head buried in his hands. He looked up at Fayard, barely registering that Big Mike and I were in the room. Tears streaked down his cheeks, his eyes wide and pleading. I couldn't catch any of what he said in a rapid torrent of words, but I knew fear when I saw it. Fear of something more than sentencing for receiving stolen goods.

"What is it?" I asked Fayard, as soon as Narbonne slowed down enough for me to get the question in.

"He says he is guilty," Fayard said, his shoulders sagging in defeat.

"Of what?" Big Mike asked.

"Of everything. The theft of the vehicle in the garage. The stolen artwork. The ambush tonight, all of it," Fayard said. "We could add a dozen unsolved murders and he would confess to them as well."

"Was he like this when you brought him in?" I asked, gesturing at the broken man before us.

"No," Fayard said. "He was angry and proclaimed his innocence. He showed the bill of sale for the truck, which looked quite legitimate." Narbonne sat motionless, oblivious to our conversation.

"Someone got to him," Big Mike said. "Here, within the last few hours."

I knelt at the side of the cot and placed my hand on Narbonne's arm.

"Monsieur Narbonne? You remember me?" I asked, my voice low and gentle.

"Oui," he said, wiping away the tears welling in his eyes. "Rose Valland, she likes you. And the baron."

"She's une femme formidable," I said. "You helped her identify stolen paintings. Why do you help the Syndicat now?"

"Je suis coupable," Narbonne said, his eyes glued to the wall.

"No, you are not guilty," I said. "We can protect you. The American army can."

"I have a sister," he said. "In Valence."

"The village in southern France, where you lived during the Occupation," I said.

"Oui. Je suis coupable."

"Your sister is alone?" I asked.

"Oui, elle est dans une petite chaumière avec des pommiers. No other people. Comprenez-vous?"

"She is alone in a cottage surrounded by apple trees," Fayard said. "Valence is a very small country village."

"Can you alert the local gendarmes?" I asked as I patted Narbonne's arm and stood.

"Of course," Fayard said, with a mild shrug. I understood the gesture. What chance would the village policeman have against a Syndicat assassin?

"Bring the sister to Paris," Big Mike suggested. "He may change his tune once he sees she's safe."

"It may not be necessary, given Paul's statement," Fayard said. "But I will see to it as soon as we are done here."

"Je suis désolé," I said, my hand on Narbonne's shoulder. As far as I could tell, the guy was set up to be the patsy, or at least manipulated to distract us at a key moment. He murmured that he was sorry too, and I believed him. Grau had put him in a tough spot. Play along or his sister gets whacked.

"Is he safe here?" Big Mike asked as the cell door shut behind us. I barely heard him, thinking about why, specifically, Narbonne had been framed. Was it all a distraction, or was there a deeper play being made? If it was all about distraction, what exactly were they distracting us from?

"Yes," Fayard said as we climbed the stairs. "I will be sure to tell others that he declared his guilt. If there are informers about, the word will get back to the Syndicat. Meanwhile, I will send two trusted officers to Valence to ensure the safety of Narbonne's sister."

"Good. It won't hurt to have two people testifying against Grau," I said. "Especially if the judge isn't a fan of the Reds."

"The men of Résistance-Fer are very popular," Fayard said. "Most people had no idea so many of the railway workers were involved, or at least looked the other way. There is also much sympathy for how they suffered under air attacks from the Allies. They faced death on all sides. But you are right. The prosecutor or the judge may have a political bias against the Communists. We shall not mention Rouge-Fer unless directly asked." That made sense. Being a cell within a cell could protect a member of Rouge-Fer even now.

"How are you going to play it with Grau?" Big Mike asked as we came out into the main lobby. Fayard said he planned to present the statement from Paul identifying Grau as the Fox and see how things went. With the war going on, he had certain emergency powers to keep anyone suspected of collaboration imprisoned. Since the cast of characters in the Syndicat included one SS member for sure, the collaboration angle was his best play.

"First, I need a colleague for an official interrogation," Fayard said. "I must find Inspector Delon, the man who led you to me. Wait here."

We tried to melt into the corner of the room and stay out of sight while Fayard went off. It was late, and most of the arrests had already been made. Old Bouchard sat at his desk on the other side of the lobby, studiously not making eye contact. A few officers went in and out, no one in much of a rush.

Until Commissaire Rochet rushed down the stairs, pulling his coat on as a pair of cops held the door open for him. Bouchard stood at attention, but Rochet ignored him. The commissaire looked over his shoulder as if he might be worried about who was at his back. As he did, his eyes caught mine. His expression deadened, and he stalked out the door, clutching his open coat at the neck. The two cops followed.

"Looks like the boss don't like being called in late at night," Big Mike said.

"It's early in the morning, pal, and I don't like it much myself," I said. I looked at Bouchard, who gave a disapproving shake of his head while I wondered why Rochet needed an escort. He probably had a driver, but two cops as well?

"Why now?" I asked, as I rubbed my eyes in an attempt to stay awake.

"Why now what?" Big Mike asked.

"Exactly," I answered, and it made all the sense in the world to me. It was the now that was important. The distraction was happening now, which meant this was the key moment. The ambush at Apache Noir, Narbonne weeping in his cell, Rochet and his guards, Roger Dano, the dead car thief at the garage in Belleville who'd supposedly sold Narbonne the Citroën truck. The cell within the cell.

"Billy?"

"I'm okay," I told Big Mike, waving my hand in front of my face to ward off any hard questions. I could almost see the big picture, but everything was blurred with a haze of exhaustion and distraction. I needed to let things settle and form into a coherent story. I was almost there, but each time I tried to add things up, nothing held together. "We need to come down hard on Grau. We need more information."

"Better let Fayard take the lead on this, Billy," he said. "It's a French case and he's in charge. We're guests here, remember."

"Right," I said. "It's a French criminal case." I tapped my finger on my lips, as if it were secret code that might unlock what was tumbling around in my head.

Fayard showed up with Inspector Delon in tow. Fayard told

us we could observe but not participate in the interrogation as we headed up one flight and down a hallway.

"Inspector Delon will be taking notes, and I have Paul's statement," Fayard said. "Once I confront Grau with it, we will see how he reacts."

We took a right, a small sign directing us to INTERROGATOIRE. The corridor was a dead end. On one side, windows looked out onto the darkened streets. On the other were six numbered doors.

"Isn't there supposed to be a guard?" I asked.

"He should not have left his post," Fayard said, as he quickened his pace to check the third door.

It opened onto an empty room. Delon checked the others. All unlocked and empty.

"Could he have been moved?" I asked, feeling the bottom falling out of this case.

"I checked thirty minutes ago," Delon said. "He was here, as was the guard."

Fayard let loose with a string of curses I hadn't heard since I booked a trio of French Canadians for drunk and disorderly after they'd busted up a bar in Scollay Square. We followed him as he double-timed it down to Bouchard in the lobby. After a hushed conversation, Bouchard picked up the telephone and made a call. Judging by the expression on Fayard's face, it wasn't good news.

"Commissaire Rochet ordered the release of Henri Grau," Fayard said. "Not ten minutes ago."

"Bâtard," Bouchard growled.

A bastard, yes. But what else was Rochet? And why had he let Grau walk?

CHAPTER THIRTY-FIVE

WE SPLIT UP. Inspector Delon gave Big Mike a lift to the Trianon. The plan was for him to wake up Colonel Harding and brief him on our night out on the town, while Fayard and I made for the Hotel Dunkerque, near the Gare de l'Est train station. It was doubtful that Grau would return there, but the hotel was so close to the train station, I thought maybe he might take a chance, especially if there was anything incriminating in his room.

I took the staff car and followed Fayard, who'd brought along a uniformed cop in case we needed an extra gun. I also hoped he knew where to get a cup of good coffee at this hour. Fayard had also sent a detail to the train station to watch for Grau, but I figured he wouldn't make his getaway by rail. He probably had stolen vehicles stashed around Paris and for all we knew he was miles away, making for the Swiss border. Still, it didn't hurt to cover all the bases.

It was a straight shot up the boulevard de Sébastopol, and in ten minutes, we'd pulled over near a small park. The Hotel Dunkerque was up the block, its sign illuminated by a feeble light.

"We could stand watch, but it may be useless," Fayard said as he exited his automobile. "He is likely gone."

"Agreed," I said, my shoulders hunched against the damp chill. A light drizzle made everything look washed-out, or maybe that was just how my tired eyes saw things. Either way, the cold seeped into my bones and I shivered, clasping my arms around my torso. "It might be worthwhile to station your man in the lobby, in case Grau shows up. Maybe he could get the kitchen to brew up a pot of coffee."

"You have the look of a weary man about you, mon ami," Fayard said as we took the four steps to the main door, which the flic held open for us. "I feel it in my soul as well."

I'd wanted to talk to Fayard about Rochet, but there hadn't been time, and I didn't want to bring it up where anyone could listen in. Dealing with the commissaire was going to be tricky, and right now we had our hands full with Grau and company.

Inside, the air was warm and the carpet soft underfoot. It wasn't a large or fancy joint, but it wasn't a fleabag either. Just the right kind of place for a Swiss businessman to stay while visiting Paris. Or the perfect place to blend in and not be noticed.

Fayard approached the desk and rang the bell. A gray-haired fellow pushed aside a curtain and did his best to muster up a smile that faded as soon as Fayard flashed his warrant card. The clerk gave up Grau's room key without a fuss. Fayard told his officer to stay in the lobby and we took the stairs to room 308. There was a metalwork cage elevator, but it looked like it would make a racket and announce our arrival to the top floor, so we trotted up the stairs, pistols drawn and held low. Best not to surprise a maid and be rewarded with a scream.

On Grau's floor, the carpeting was thinner than in the lobby, and we shuffled along to muffle our footsteps. Fayard held a finger to his lips as he pointed to the other rooms. I got the message. Grau's accomplices might be holed up here as well. We moved to his door and listened. Silence.

Fayard holstered his revolver and grasped the doorknob with one hand and turned the key with the other. The metallic clack of the lock sounded thunderous, and I went inside, crouching low with my gun arm extended, waiting for movement or noise.

The only sound was Fayard shutting the door and fumbling for a light switch.

He found it, and the short hallway was bathed in light. The room was vacant. I darted into the bathroom and saw empty air and a straight-edge razor on the sink.

"He has not returned," Fayard said. "One of the men who picked him up said he had been packing his clothes." The doors of an armoire hung open, and a suitcase was on the bed, folded shirts stacked neatly on top of wool trousers. I picked through the clothing, coming up empty except for a pen and a matchbox in one suit coat. I tossed them on the nightstand and went through that. Not even a Bible.

"I doubt he'd leave any incriminating evidence," I said. "But we should toss the place."

"Toss it?"

"Search it," I clarified. "With little regard for neatness." I emptied the suitcase and cut into the lining with my knife. Nothing hidden away.

"Ah, I understand," Fayard said, and proceeded to lift the mattress and check out the one place people seem to think no one will ever look. Most of the time, if a search turned up something, it was under the mattress. But not in room 308.

Fayard searched the bathroom while I checked the armoire. I felt below the drawer and the back of the polished walnut piece and came up with nothing but a few cobwebs. I moved on to the small writing desk set against the wall opposite the bed. Affixed to the top was a brass mechanical calendar, the kind where you advance the month, day, and year by turning small knobs on either side. It was a nice piece, but the fact that it was secured to the woodwork said something about the hotel's clientele. Worthy of an amenity, but only if it was bolted down. It was the only decorative touch in the room, except for a cheesy painting of the Eiffel Tower.

A map of Paris sat on top of a newspaper on the desk, next to a gooseneck lamp. The folds were worn, showing it had been well used. But Grau hadn't left a single mark on it. Not that I expected he'd leave any obvious clues. I went through the newspaper, page by page, and came up empty.

"Nothing," Fayard said, after his search of the bathroom. I opened the single desk drawer, finding nothing but hotel stationery and a pencil stub. The only other item on the desk was a glass ashtray filled with coins, mostly centimes, with Vichy markings. Probably not the most popular coin these days, but a dime is a dime, in English or French.

Fayard checked the wastepaper basket and came up with a crumpled receipt from the hotel restaurant and an empty matchbox.

"The room must have been cleaned recently," Fayard said, tossing them back into the basket.

"I found a matchbox too," I said, pointing to the nightstand. "But it doesn't look like Grau is a smoker."

"Ah, this is from the Café de la Paix," Fayard said, checking out my find and tossing it to me. "One of the most famous Parisian cafés. It is at the place de l'Opéra, and everyone goes there. Even a cutthroat likes a souvenir."

I studied the colorful art deco design on the matchbox. It was different from the one in the wastepaper basket, which I picked up. This matchbox was dark green, with the image of a golden candlestick and the words *le Chandelier d'Or*.

"Does chandelier mean candlestick?" I asked. I opened the box to make sure nothing was inside.

"It does," Fayard said, leaning in to look at the matchbook. "I have not heard of that café."

"Here's why," I said, after I looked at the back side. "It's on the avenue du Pierre Gaspar. In Spa, Belgium."

"Is that important?" Fayard asked. I filled him in on how we'd encountered a moving van driver in Spa who turned out to be a Syndicat man.

"Perhaps he visited Grau," Fayard said.

"Would've been hard," I said. "We had a run-in and I shot him dead. But it might not have been his first trip. Or Grau went himself."

"So close to the fighting? Why would he?" Fayard asked.

It was a good question, but I didn't want to bandy about a story that included the new location of First Army HQ, even to Fayard. No telling who might end up hearing it. Need to know.

"Probably nothing," I said, and pocketed both matchboxes. "Tell me, what are you going to do about Rochet?"

"What can I do? He is my commissaire, and he may release anyone who has not been charged with a crime. Remember, Grau was only brought in for questioning, not to be arrested."

"Be careful, Louis," I said. "Rochet has been getting in the way of this investigation since it began. He was the one who refused police cooperation at the Père Lachaise Cemetery stakeout. Then, when Jacques Delair was murdered, he was quick off the mark to pin it on Special Agent Salinger. It took Colonel Baril to get Salinger released and put the fear of God into Rochet. His career and reputation are still hanging in the balance over his use of the Milice to put down the La Santé Prison uprising."

"What does all that add up to, mon ami?"

"It adds up to a man who may be looking at losing everything," I said. "His job, his pension, and whatever honor he thinks he has left. It would be worth a small fortune for the Syndicat to have a guy at the top watching out for their interests. Why else would Rochet rush in and out of the Trente-Six in the middle of the night?"

"For now, all I can do is search for Grau without seeming to," Fayard said. "There are enough men I trust to try, at least. Are we done here?"

I glanced at my watch. "Yes. A dead end, I think. I have to meet with Colonel Harding in a few hours. I might as well sack out here since I'm about to fall asleep standing up."

"Keep one eye open in case Grau returns," Fayard said.

"And you watch your back," I said. As soon as he shut the door, I locked it and wedged the straight-back chair under the latch. I flopped down on the bed and grabbed the alarm clock from the nightstand. I wound it, setting it for five thirty, which would give me a few hours' sleep at least.

I turned off the light. I took out my revolver and laid it by my side. The gooseneck lamp was still on, illuminating the brass desk calendar.

21 Décembre 1944.

Almost Christmas, the season of joy. But all I felt was exhausted and troubled. Troubled by the bits and pieces of evidence floating around in my brain. Pieces of a puzzle that didn't fit together. I didn't know if I was missing a piece, or if I had them arranged in the wrong sequence.

Something was off, and then I was.

CHAPTER THIRTY-SIX

I AWOKE BEFORE the alarm, with the missing piece of the puzzle right in front of me. Two pieces, actually. The first dawned on me as soon as my eyes opened. It had been there all along, finally evolving from a nagging irritant into a surefire certainty.

The notion of a cell within a cell, like Rouge-Fer within Résistance-Fer. A clandestine group, hidden within another.

The second was literally right in front of me. The light bulb went on just like the lamplight shining on the brass calendar, clarifying the unalterable fact that today was the twentieth of December, not the twenty-first. I sat up and planted my feet on the floor. The pieces clicked neatly into place as the clock ticked off the seconds, drawing steadily closer to that all-important date.

Grau had been getting ready to leave yesterday, the nineteenth. So why had he set his calendar for December the twenty-first?

Because it was important. It was important to Grau, if that was his real name, since it was the target date for an attack on First Army headquarters. This was what all these distractions were about. The framing of Stephan Narbonne and the attack at the nightclub, especially. If Paul had been killed, it would have worked perfectly, the only witness to Grau's identity dead and buried. But even with Paul alive, we were still left looking at a criminal enterprise. A gang of murderous art thieves.

That's what the Syndicat du Renard was—the larger cell. But within that group, there was a smaller group, a parallel to

Rouge-Fer. They weren't German deserters working for the Fox. They were the enemy. What better camouflage for Nazi soldiers hiding in Paris than the criminal underworld, where deserters from both sides made common cause and formed alliances against the police? The art thefts were cover for their plans, plans that fit in with the Einheit Stielau orders we'd found. Attack headquarters units. First Army HQ would be a critical and high-value target, as it was smack-dab in the center of the German offensive. The Syndicat thug in Spa didn't take the evidence of the new location to sell; he took it to identify the target after General Hodges had suddenly pulled up stakes.

I raced to the sink, splashed cold water on my face, then stopped on my way out to admire the gleaming brass calendar. Grau had been so very careful, but he couldn't resist twirling that knob and showing off the date of the attack he'd been planning, even if it was only to himself.

I bounded down the stairs and out the door, my mind racing faster than my feet. The streets were wet from the night's rain, with patches of fog rising like ghosts. I skirted the Trente-Six on general principals as I drove to Versailles, heading for the Arc de Triomphe and then along the east bank of the Seine until I crossed the Pont Daydé. Traffic was light. It was too late to still be out and too early for anyone sensible to be on the road. There was no hint of sunrise, still hours away.

It was an oddly disjointed feeling to drive through the city in this long night. Darkness had come ages ago and so much had happened. Then I'd awakened as if from a dream, seeing Grau's scheme with crystal clarity. Now all I had to do was explain it to Colonel Harding. He was a sensible sort of guy, which meant he liked things that made sense. Things like proof. All I had was a list of dead bodies, my gut feeling, and a matchbook.

It would have to do.

As I drove down the avenue de Saint-Cloud toward the main gate of Versailles, the sky ahead began to glow white with searchlights. Not pointing to the sky, but playing along the fencing, walls, gardens, and buildings, searching for unauthorized personnel and leaving no shadows for lurking about.

I braked at the gate and showed my identity card, not surprised this time at the weaponry pointed at my chest. I didn't see my buddy from Boston, but thankfully there weren't any questions about the Yankees, and I was finally waved through.

The Trianon was noticeably busy for six o'clock in the morning. I sprinted up the steps to Harding's office and flung open the door.

"Grau is running a German operation," I said, my breath ragged from the run up two flights. I took off my jacket to buy time for my breathing to settle down. Harding and Big Mike were drinking coffee, staring at me over rims of steaming joe.

"What the hell are you talking about, Boyle?" Harding snapped as he set his cup down on his desk.

"It's a cell within a cell," I said. "Just like Rouge-Fer."

Harding looked blank. Big Mike, sitting across the desk, filled him in about Paul's resistance group operating within Résistance-Fer. Harding gestured for me to explain further. The aroma of coffee was beginning to distract me, but I pressed on.

"I was bothered about the setup with Narbonne," I said. "Why did they need him as a patsy, and why now? And why did they try to knock off Paul at Apache Noir?"

"The hit was obvious," Harding said. "If they knew Paul was going to finger Henri Grau."

"Right," I said. "Which means someone within the Police Judiciaire tipped them off. But that's not the important part, at least for right now. They set up Narbonne to distract us, and a good distraction has to be well-timed. I was racking my brain to come up with the key to the timing."

A knock at the door interrupted my speech. It was Salinger, who entered with a bunch of folders in hand. He looked like he'd gotten less sleep than me.

"Sorry to interrupt, but I've been going over the interrogation reports you asked about, Colonel," he said.

"Boyle is in the middle of explaining some theory about Grau," Harding said. "Pull up a chair and see if you can make any sense of it."

"Why the distraction, and why now?" I said, returning to my train of thought before it made an unscheduled stop. "Narbonne was set up with that truck purchase. The guy who sold it to him was a known car thief and was soon killed to ensure his silence."

"Narbonne's confession was as phony as a three-dollar bill," Big Mike said. "He was definitely the patsy."

"Right. He became the object of our attention at just the right time. We connected the dots that Grau had laid out for us," I said. "I only asked Fayard to bring in Grau because I wanted to ask him more about Narbonne, not because he was a suspect. That's the one thing he hadn't counted on, so he had to get himself sprung."

"You think Rochet is in Grau's pocket?" Harding asked.

"Yes," I said, finally giving in and making for the coffee. "Yes, sir. But that's not what's important. This whole thing about trucks and moving art pieces around really has another purpose. I believe Grau is a stay-behind German agent, and some of the men we're thinking of as German deserters are the real thing. Kraut commandos planning an action."

"Explain that one again?" Harding said, finishing his cup of coffee. I took a few slugs of mine.

"It's the perfect cover. The Syndicat is known as a gang that includes deserters from all sides. A German could hide out in the criminal underworld easy enough, especially if everyone else is so afraid of the Syndicat that they don't dare question it."

"So, the whole art theft scheme is a front?" Salinger asked.

"No, that's the beauty of it," I said. "It's a real criminal enterprise. One that brings in plenty of dough and provides a reason for Grau to acquire vehicles as he needs them. The black market and other assorted Parisian crooks might draw the line at working with their former occupiers, but not the infamous and effective Syndicat du Renard. Remember, Paul told us of Grau's latest order. Two big French Renault five-ton trucks."

"For what purpose?" Harding asked. I took a moment to take another swig of coffee.

"To transport men and arms to launch an attack on First Army headquarters tomorrow, December twenty-first," I said.

"Who told you this?" Harding said. He still looked skeptical, but now in a worried sort of way.

"Grau was set to check out of his hotel yesterday, the nineteenth," I said. "He was in the midst of packing when the cops took him in. He'd left his calendar set on the twenty-first of the month."

"His calendar, Billy?" Big Mike asked, his forehead wrinkled in concern. I saw Salinger glance at Harding, the way you do when someone starts spouting nonsense.

"Yes," I said, with more enthusiasm than certainty. What seemed a sure thing when I woke up and saw that date now felt vague and insubstantial, and I knew I was losing my audience. "We did identify a Syndicat man in Spa, driving a moving van. And remember, his partner took the requisition order for the Hôtel des Bains in Chaudfontaine. The new location of First Army HQ. My bet was he was scouting the area when he found Hodges had pulled out."

"Wait," Harding said, holding up his hand. "How did the Syndicat even know First Army was headquartered in Spa?"

"Willoughby in Civil Affairs," I said. "He used Grau as an art consultant, and Grau played him. Willoughby bragged about briefing staff at First Army on cultural artifacts they could expect to find when they push into Germany. Before Willoughby realized it, Grau got him to confirm Spa was where the briefing took place."

Harding frowned and wrote something in his notebook. I

doubted it was anything Captain Willoughby was going to be happy with.

"You're certain the Syndicat man wasn't just committing a crime of opportunity?" Harding asked. "An empty hotel would tempt any crook."

"I'm certain that Grau sent his men to the hotel to reconnoiter it," I said. "After all the shooting, the requisition was the only item missing. Grau has it."

"One piece of paper. A calendar set two days ahead. A secret Resistance cell of Red railroad men," Harding said. "It's all interesting, but does it really add up to a clandestine German commando unit operating in Paris?"

"Don't forget the two vehicles Grau was looking for only a few days ago," I said. "I don't think he has enough stolen art on hand to fill up two five-ton trucks. But men and weapons? That's another story."

"It's thin, Boyle," Harding said. "I can send a warning to Monk at First Army to increase security, but I'm not going to tell them to retreat even further. They need to stay in operation. The situation is getting critical. The Germans nearly have Bastogne encircled. They're still advancing and have gotten across the Ourthe River, heading for the Meuse crossing at Namur. It's not a pretty picture, and I can't disrupt First Army operations over a bunch of suppositions. This is all circumstantial, isn't it?"

It was, but that wasn't anything I wanted to admit. I knew I was right, and the fact that Harding thought things were on a razor's edge only meant that an attack on First Army HQ would be catastrophic. I needed to convince him the threat was real. All I had left was a matchbook.

"I know their rendezvous point," I said. "A bar called le Chandelier d'Or, on the avenue de la Roche in Spa."

"And you know that how?" Harding said, a skeptical frown forming at the corner of his mouth.

"A matchbox in Grau's room," I said, tossing the two I'd found onto Harding's desk. "Either he or someone who visited him has been to Spa."

"Billy, he could have grabbed that anywhere," Big Mike said as he picked up the green matchbox from the joint in Spa. As he studied it, I saw Harding sit bolt upright, his gaze fixed on the other matchbox, the art deco job from the Café de la Paix in Paris.

"Where'd you get that?" he asked, his eyes flicking to Salinger, who took the box and opened it, spilling out the matches and checking the inside.

"In Grau's coat pocket," I said. "In his room, with the Spa matchbox. What's up?" At least now I had Harding's full attention, although I had no idea why.

"We have no reports of any suspicious activity in Spa," Harding said. He snapped up the matchbox from Salinger and held it between two fingers. "But we do have corroborated evidence of a planned rendezvous of German agents in Paris. At the Café de la Paix."

CHAPTER THIRTY-SEVEN

"THAT PROVES IT." I said. "Grau is in on it." I poured myself another cup of coffee with all the satisfaction of a lawyer who's won his case.

"All it proves is that Henri Grau went to the Café de la Paix," Harding said. "So did I, last week. Half the people in this building have been there. It's a famous place. It doesn't prove we're German commandos any more than it proves Grau is one."

"It's worth checking out," I said, trying to muster up a decent argument. I watched Harding drum his fingers on the desktop and knew he was thinking about it.

"Big Mike, get a message coded and sent off to Dulles in Bern," Harding said. "Give him the particulars on Grau and his art gallery in Basel. See if he can confirm he's legit. How's that, Boyle?"

"Fine, Colonel," I said, focusing on the coffee. It was something, but too little too late if I was right. I knew pushing Harding now wouldn't get me anywhere, and I'd have to trust that word would come back quickly. We'd encountered Allen Dulles not long ago, and I knew the head of the Office of Strategic Services in Switzerland was just the guy to look into Grau's identity. If, that is, Dulles wasn't too busy with one of his mistresses.

"Will do, Sam," Big Mike said, tossing a wink my way as he left the office. At least I knew he'd lose no time getting the message out.

"Can you tell me how you know about the Germans using the Café de la Paix as a rendezvous point?" I asked. Harding gave the nod to Salinger, who tapped the stack of files in front of him.

"Reports from CIC agents who interrogated the phony MPs we'd captured," Salinger began. "Several alluded to rumors of other jeep teams headed to Paris to kill Ike and any other high-ranking officers here in the Trianon."

"Rumors?" I said, wondering how their evidence was better than mine.

"Exactly," Salinger replied. "It was a rumor making the rounds at their training camp. But none of them could, or would, reveal anything more specific."

"Until Lieutenant Günther Schulz came along," Harding said.

"He was the leader of a four-man jeep team," Salinger told me. "They tried to get across the Meuse, but they didn't have the password or the right orders. Turns out they were wearing swastika armbands beneath their field jackets, and the jeep was loaded with explosives. Canteens filled with TNT and wired with igniters."

"They didn't have their eyes set on First Army," Harding said. "Schulz admitted their target was SHAEF. It wasn't just a rumor. He said Skorzeny was going to rendezvous with him at the Café de la Paix while his men laid low. They were counting on fifty men to make it to Paris and target Ike either here or at his villa in Saint-Germain-en-Laye. The plan was for them to wear the armbands during the attack."

"CIC has brought in more men to protect the general," Salinger said. "He's agreed to stay here until the danger's past. It's too risky for him to be on the roads."

"We found a colonel who looks a lot like General Eisenhower," Harding said. "He's sleeping in his bed at the villa and making the drive here like normal."

"It sounds like Schulz sang like a canary," I said. "What did his men have to say?"

"Nothing. Which is why they're being court-martialed right now. They'll likely face a firing squad tomorrow," Harding said.

"What's the rush?" By now, my coffee was cold, and I didn't have a good feeling about this. I wasn't hearing any actual evidence, and I got the sense that Skorzeny madness had taken root within SHAEF.

"Ike wants to send a message, especially after the POW massacre by the SS," Harding said. "He wants our men to know we're not sitting back while these Krauts infiltrate our lines. But he's also worried about seeing more of this once we enter Germany."

"So he's sending a message to the Krauts," I said. "Get captured in an American uniform and get shot."

"It's prohibited under the Hague Convention to fight in the uniform of the enemy," Harding said. "A lawyer might argue that infiltrating enemy lines is not fighting, but we're beyond that right now. It's a warning that the gloves are off."

"Schulz said some in the other jeep crews wore their German uniforms under the American clothing, in hopes that they could fight in their own uniform," Salinger said. "His group had only swastika armbands, but even he believed that those wouldn't hold up as a uniform."

"Listen, this legal discussion is fascinating," I said. "But you said you had corroborated evidence. Where is it?"

"We have a German officer in custody," Salinger said. "He's made a statement. That's a lot more than your hunch wrapped around a matchbox. Sorry to say, Billy."

"Is Schulz being court-martialed today?" I asked.

"No, CIC wanted to keep him available in case we have more questions," Salinger said.

"What you're saying is that your evidence comes from a Kraut who spun a yarn that kept him alive for another day," I said. "Otherwise, he'd be tied to a stake tomorrow and shot."

"We know Skorzeny is behind this," Harding said. "Given his

reputation, we must be alert to every possibility and take what Schulz told us seriously."

"Believe me, I agree," I said, rubbing my eyes to keep them open. "Skorzeny is known for making the big play. Rescuing Mussolini and all that. But was this jeepload of jokers up to the standards of an ace commando? No password, bad papers, and explosives crammed in their vehicle? And this wasn't the first bunch picked up, was it? Wasn't the first crew nabbed on the opening day of the offensive? It's amateur hour."

"This might not be Skorzeny's finest moment," Harding said. "Or, maybe the fifty men are already here. We can't take a chance."

"Colonel, I agree with you. Which is why I think we need to take Grau and the chance of an attack on First Army seriously as well," I said. "Tell me, which would have the greatest impact in terms of this German offensive? Killing Ike or an attack that knocks First Army HQ out of the picture? In purely military terms only."

"A crippling attack on First Army would be a disaster in terms of command and control," Harding said, rubbing his chin as he considered the implications. "But an attack on Ike here would be disruptive as well. Although I admit, the battle is being fought by those closer to the front."

"If you were Skorzeny and you'd been ordered to select an army headquarters to attack, which would you chose?" I asked.

Harding stared at the wall map, showing the German advance cutting just south of Spa and Chaudfontaine. "First Army. Strictly for military reasons. The shock value of an attack on SHAEF would be undeniable, but the immediate battlefield impact would be negligible. It might even fire up the men like the massacre at Malmedy did."

Now, the average GI thought the world of Uncle Ike. So did I. If the Krauts got him, the men would feel it. But I really couldn't see a dogface in his foxhole getting broken up over a bunch of senior brass having to shoot it out with Skorzeny's men in a Parisian palace. It was my experience that many generals, when they thought about GIs at the front, considered them to be extras in the war they were waging from the rear, and very comfortable, area. Harding wasn't that type, but I didn't see the percentage in arguing the point, so I nodded my head at that bit of West Point wisdom.

"Why don't we cover all our bases?" I said. "Let me and Big Mike get up to First Army and snoop around the bar in Spa and see what we can find. If you warn Monk, he can increase his security while CIC guards the Trianon here."

"Slow down, Boyle," Harding said, leaning forward in his chair. "Assuming I buy your theory, how did Grau know to plan all this ahead of time? If he and his men are stay-behind agents, it implies this big offensive has been in the works since Paris was liberated last August. Seems a bit of a stretch."

"I'm not sure I have every angle figured, but my bet is Grau did come through Switzerland with his cover story right after the border opened up," I said. "A group of stay-behind agents could have gone into hiding, melding into the criminal under-world. Grau makes contact and starts building his Syndicat du Renard empire. At that point, I doubt anyone knew how this offensive would shape up. But the Germans saw the value of a raid on a rear-area target at some point. When Skorzeny—or whoever it was—planned this operation, they could have easily gotten word to Grau. A coded letter or telephone call from Switzerland. Then it was up to him to locate the headquarters he'd been assigned to attack."

"If the Germans hadn't put together this offensive, it might have been SHAEF," Salinger said. "But with Grau's ruse suc-cessful, it would be tempting for them to pull him in and target the army HQ closest to their thrust."

"Okay," Harding said. "Get up to Chaudfontaine. I'll tell Monk you're coming and to have Lieutenant Kazimierz meet you. I'll give him the basics of your suspicions. See what you can find out and report to me soonest."

"I'll need Big Mike," I said. "I can't stay awake to drive."

"Negative," Harding said. "I need him here to stake out the café along with Salinger and his men. But the good news is you won't have to drive. We have L-4 Sentinels standing by at an airstrip. There's an airfield less than a mile from First Army HQ." His hand reached out for the telephone, and he asked to be connected to air liaison.

"Colonel, isn't that basically a Piper Cub?" I asked. "A tiny little plane? And isn't the weather keeping everything grounded?"

"Yeah, it's the military version of the Piper," Harding said. "Meaning it's painted olive green. Don't worry, the fog is lifting." Someone came on the line, and he gave the order to ready the aircraft. He asked a few questions about weather conditions, then hung up.

"Handy little plane," he said. "You'll be fine. Unless you don't want to make the trip."

"Why wouldn't I?"

"Well, the fog is lifting here. Not yet at Chaudfontaine, but it should by the time you get there," he said. "Cloud cover is still thick and low, but the L-4 can fly beneath it."

"How low, Colonel?"

"You'll have to fly at five hundred feet. Maybe a little lower to pick up landmarks," Harding said as Salinger stood to trace his finger on the map between Paris and Chaudfontaine.

"Colonel, there's hills higher than five hundred feet along that route," he said. "It's crazy."

"Give me a good map and we'll follow the rivers," I said. "Right up the Meuse for the last leg. Piece of cake."

Salinger had been wrong. It wasn't crazy. It was certifiably insane.

CHAPTER THIRTY-EIGHT

"HELL, BILLY, IT don't look like the fog's lifting all that much," Big Mike said as he drove me to the Villacoublay airfield, only a few miles from Versailles. Patches of mist cloaked the low-lying areas along the road, but it was less than what I'd seen a few hours ago.

"Doesn't look so bad," I said. I wiped the condensation from the window of the staff car and craned my neck to look east. I was rewarded with a thin, blurry glow—what passed for predawn light in this long, dark, cloud-shrouded night. "At least I can see the tops of the buildings."

"You sure about this?" Big Mike asked. The road took us up a slight incline and into a wooded section, which was thankfully clear of fog. We came out onto a flat stretch of fenced land with a couple of rotating beacons doing their best to pierce the gloom.

"I'm sure," I said. All I knew was that I wouldn't sit back and let Grau make his move. I wouldn't be able to live with myself if I was right about him and he pulled off this strike. I'm no hero, but I didn't want to spend the rest of my days knowing I could have stopped him. Or tried to.

"Okay, then," Big Mike said. "You got everything you need?"

He'd asked me that a dozen times already. I had my Thompson, a new mackinaw coat, and overshoes. Not to mention a haversack filled with extra ammo and K rations. I'd chowed down on a couple of bacon sandwiches and managed to get my fill of coffee before we left the Trianon. Maybe more than my fill, which could explain why I was so wound up.

"I'll be fine, buddy," I said, as I patted the map I held in my lap. "We'll follow the Oise River east and then scoot along a valley floor until we hit the Meuse. We stay on a northerly course until it hangs a right and brings us to Chaudfontaine. We can cruise at five hundred feet and stay away from hilltops."

"Sounds like a plan," Big Mike said. "But listen to your pilot, okay? He can probably avoid hills a lot more easily than Kraut machine guns."

"Any more words of wisdom to cheer me up?" I asked as Big Mike pulled up at the gate and showed the MP his orders. "Like how the L-4 is basically the same as the balsa-wood gliders we made as kids?"

"Those were fun," Big Mike said as he was waved through. "Especially when you lit the tail on fire before you launched it."

"You're a barrel of laughs today," I said. "Have fun sitting at a café while I'm out risking my neck."

"Won't be that cushy," Big Mike said as he parked near the hangar. "Sam's got me in an upstairs apartment across the street with a pair of binoculars."

"You'll probably be at a higher altitude than me," I said. "Watch out if Grau shows himself. He won't be alone. You better get some sack time before your stakeout."

"Get going," Big Mike said. He extended his hand, and we shook. I thought about saying something, given that I was about to go off in a tiny airplane with no navigation instruments, making for a foggy airfield not far from where panzers roamed.

But I didn't. Our handshake said it all.

Inside the hangar, a room was heated by an ancient wood stove. A corporal sat at a desk, a telephone cupped to his ear and a cigarette dangling from his mouth. He nodded in my direction and tossed a balled-up piece of paper at a lieutenant sleeping in an overstuffed chair.

"What?" the lieutenant said as he sat upright. Then he looked at me. "Oh, you must be the guy from SHAEF. You sure about this?"

"Yeah, I'm the guy," I said. "The captain. And yes, Lieutenant, I am sure."

"You got flight orders, Captain?" asked the corporal as he hung up.

"Here you go," I said, handing him Harding's paperwork.

"Looks legit, Joe," the corporal said, showing him the signature.

"You sure about this, Captain?" asked the lieutenant again.

"You're not the first to ask," I said. "You do much flying in this pea soup?"

"Ha!" the corporal said.

"Given that I don't have a death wish, no. I'm Lieutenant Joe Kiley, by the way. Petey, you got anything new from meteorology?"

"Just got off the horn," Petey said. "Fog is dissipating here. Wind speed is notching up to fifteen miles an hour near Liège, which ought to clear out the fog once you get there. Light drizzle, no icing expected."

"That's good, right? No ice?" I said.

"Yeah, it's terrific," Joe said. "We're not going to be able to see a damn thing, you know. In case you were out to hunt Kraut tanks."

"No, just get me to Chaudfontaine," I said. "You've been there?"

"Captain, I've been to every forward airfield along this front," Joe said. "All by dead reckoning. And I reckon there's a good chance of dead on this trip. You still want to go?"

"I wish you'd stop asking that," I said. "You ready?"

"Yeah, I said my prayers," Joe said. "Come on. See you in the funny papers, Petey."

"Don't worry, Captain," Petey said. "If I thought he wasn't coming back, I'd ask him to pay me the ten bucks he owes me."

I followed Joe out onto the runway. He stopped to check the wind sock above the hangar and then looked to the east. The dull glow had climbed higher, making it easier to see.

"It'll be full light when we get to Chaudfontaine," Joe said, going through his check of the aircraft. "If we get there."

"We follow the river, right?"

"That's fine to start, Captain. The Oise takes us in the right direction. But know what the trouble is with the Meuse? I'll tell you. Germans. Last I heard, they want to get across and they can't. Which means they'll take out their frustrations on us. So, we'll keep the Meuse off to starboard."

"And watch out for hills," I said.

"And treetops," Joe said. "Welcome aboard."

He folded down the door, and I stepped into the rear seat, right behind the pilot's seat. The Perspex windows were wide and high, giving a grand view all around. Joe started the engine and began to taxi toward the runway. He lined up the L-4 at the end, revved the engine, and began the takeoff.

As the plane rumbled down the runway, I saw the twin head-light beams of the staff car at the fence, Big Mike silhouetted against the bright light. I raised my hand as we lifted off, and the solid ground he stood upon had never looked so appealing. I wondered what the hell I'd gotten myself into.

Joe banked the L-4 and headed toward the dawning light, such as it was. We crossed the meandering bends of the Seine at low altitude. The fog was nearly gone, and I was glad to be able to make out buildings and roads. Overhead, it was a solid, dark gray.

"There's the Oise River," Joe said, his voice loud over the sound of the engine as he pointed portside and banked the aircraft. "This is the easy part."

"What's the hard part?" I asked, leaning forward.

"Once we reach Guise, the river thins out," Joe said. "It still follows the course of a valley, but it's tough to spot. We just need to stay with it as long as possible. It vanishes about when we cross the border of Belgium. That's where dead reckoning comes in."

"You were joking about that before, weren't you?"

"I was, Captain. It's simple, really. Once we cross the town of Guise, I know how long it takes at our air speed to reach the Meuse, somewhere between Dinant and Givet. Thirty minutes or so, on an east-northeast line."

"Sounds simple enough," I said, not really thinking that but trying to keep myself upbeat.

"Right. If we have any trouble, I can put this thing down in a field or on a straight stretch of road," Joe said. "As long as the field isn't mined and there's no panzers on the road."

"That's reassuring, in its own way," I said, and decided to stop asking questions. The answers were making me more nervous. I shut my eyes and leaned against the window, wondering if I was tired enough to sleep with the noise of the engine and occasional blast of turbulence.

I was.

I awoke being thrown side to side, then pressed down into my seat as Joe climbed to a higher altitude. I felt the wind shuddering the fabric-covered airframe. Joe's hands gripped the controls as he fought to stay on course.

"Heavy winds," he shouted over the noise. "Stronger than expected. Good news is that the fog will be blown away. Bad news is we might be too."

"Off course, you mean?"

"Yeah. Wind's coming out of the northwest, which means it could push us over the Kraut lines," he said. "I'll get us above it, then see where we are."

The L-4 climbed into the clouds, where the wind lessened. Joe checked his compass reading, and adjusted course. "We should be okay now."

"Where are we?" I asked.

"About to cross the Meuse River," Joe said. "Or already across,

I can't say. I had my hands full. I'm going to drop down in a minute and see if we can pick up a landmark."

"What about the wind?"

"Let's hope it was a stray gust," he said. "We only need a few minutes to pick out a river or town. It's already light and I know this area." I patted Joe on the shoulder, trying to be reassuring as we flew through gray, misty clouds. I was mainly reassuring myself and not doing a great job of it. I looked at the map, but had no idea how far we'd gone off course. I stuffed it in my pocket, trusting to Joe's instincts.

Joe flew in a wide circle, dropping altitude as he went. Wind buffeted the plane, hitting us like a giant backhand. Joe put the nose down and broke out of the cloud cover, holding on to the controls as the L-4 bucked like a wild horse.

He went lower, making for a river straight ahead. We were nearly at treetop level, and it looked like he was using the hills as a windbreak, even if it potentially exposed us to the Germans. A necessary gamble. The plane settled down, and I gave Joe another pat on the back, meaning it this time.

"You found it. The Meuse!"

"That wasn't bad," Joe said. He banked the aircraft, following the course of the river. I checked the altimeter. Three hundred feet. Not much margin for error. As he maneuvered the L-4 along the twists and turns of the river, Joe began to swivel his head, checking the landmarks. He tapped on his compass once, and then again, harder.

"What's wrong?"

"Shit! That's the Amblève River, not the Meuse!" He raised the nose of the L-4 as the wind smacked us again. "I recognize those ruins on the top of that hill. We're coming up on Stoumont."

I wasn't sure which side of the Amblève the Germans were on, or who held Stoumont, but I was glad Joe was making for the cloud cover.

The Germans weren't.

Tracers lit the sky in front of us, and Joe did a diving S-turn to shake the gunner's aim. But he had little room for a dive and had to come up again. He made for a gap between two hills, only to have more machine guns join in. Rounds ripped through one wing, shredding fabric, sending the L-4 into a spin. Joe wrested control of the aircraft, stabilizing it as we neared the gap.

But it meant he had to fly straight, and one last burst of fire hit the side of the plane, splintering one of the wing struts. The wing began to wobble, and the idea of a nice soft farmer's field was suddenly very appealing.

"Will it hold?" I asked. Joe spared a glance and then went back to his white-knuckle flying.

"It should. On this course we can reach the Meuse if I can keep her steady," he said. "It won't be pretty, but we can land. North-northeast will get us close to Spa. No Krauts there, last I heard."

We flew on, low and slow, looking like we'd avoided the worst.

Until the plane began to vibrate. Black smoke gushed from the engine, streaming down the fuselage. The ground looked awfully close.

Then the engine stopped.

It was surprisingly quiet as we dropped.

CHAPTER THIRTY-NINE

I COUGHED. MY eyes stung. The shoulder harness was stretched tight, pinning me in place. I coughed again, inky blackness swirling into my eyes. I reached out, feeling for the pilot's seat in front of me.

No, below me.

Something wasn't right.

I tried to shake Joe's shoulder, but his head flopped to the side.

I fumbled with the harness. I wasn't pinned, I was hanging upside down. I released the buckle and fell against the front seat, trying to call Joe, getting nothing out but a hacking cough. I kicked at the door, which seemed to be in the wrong place. It opened, and I fell out, coming to rest against the shot-up wing.

As I took a breath of air, I heard the crackle.

Fire.

I tried to stand, but it didn't work out. I got up again and held on to the wing, working my way around it. The nose was half buried in a field. The rest of the fuselage had snapped at the wing root, leaving the tail pointing skyward.

At the pilot's door I reached into the billowing smoke to release Joe's harness and pull him out. Before I had him halfway through the door, I knew he was dead. He'd suffered a large gash on his head and a broken neck. Neither was pretty.

I smelled the fuel before I heard the splash. The tanks in the wing had ruptured, and a steady drip was forming a pool on the ground. I dragged Joe away from the wreckage, checking him once again to be sure.

No pulse, no breath, no sign of life.

I fell back as the flames licked at the fuel and the plane exploded in a *whoosh* of smoke and rising red fire. I felt the heat brush against my skin, even as I held my arm across my face. I slowly came to grips with the fact that my Thompson and my haversack were still inside. My helmet too. I was woozy from the crash, and I sat on the cold ground, wondering what to do.

All I could come up with was to fold Joe's hands on his chest and say a quick prayer as I went to grab one of his dog tags. But I stopped myself. The swirling fire could attract anyone. Maybe Americans. Maybe Germans. If the Krauts checked and found a tag gone, they'd know someone else was on the loose. I told Joe I was sorry, and stood, getting my bearings.

Then my Thompson ammo started cooking off, and I simply ran like hell, not wanting to be shot dead by my own bullets.

I caught my breath on a farm lane bordering the field. Hard-packed dirt, not a main road. I hoped that meant it wasn't a main route for the German advance. I really didn't want to bump into any of Peiper's killers out here armed with only my pistol. Across the lane, the land rose to a wooded hilltop.

Which way to go?

I looked for the sun behind the heavy clouds, searching for the east. Which should've been on my right. The clouds were so thick it was hard to tell, but I finally picked out a filtered light that had to be it. I stood with it off my right shoulder. The hill was square in front of me. That was the best compass I could come up with, so I began to climb, aiming to pick out a landmark from the top.

The ascent was harder than I thought. The top seemed to be always out of reach. One ridgeline led to another, the uppermost slippery with snow. Off to my right, which meant east toward the German lines, rolling hills thick with pines blocked my view.

To my left was a cleared area, a logging trail winding down to a small village. No crossroads, so it probably wasn't a military objective. I figured it was still roughly north, and heading down a hill on a cleared road was a lot easier than tramping through these woods.

The logging trail soon joined up with a road leading into the village. An inch of freshly fallen snow made everything look bright, even under the cloudy gloom. I could make out a few rooftops and a steeple nestled in a low-lying area surrounded by towering pines. It was a small farming village, so I prayed there were no Germans holed up there. The best I could hope for was that someone knew where the nearest Americans were. And that the villagers weren't pro-Nazi, waiting for their Kraut pals to return.

I kept to the edge of the road, listening for the sound of voices or distant engines. I was ready to leap into the pines and hide, but it was totally quiet. Perhaps everyone was having lunch. Maybe they'd invite me in. A warm kitchen stove would be just the thing. I was starting to stiffen from the cold and the impact of the crash landing. I ached everywhere, but I was thankful for no broken bones.

At a bend in the road, the first house came into view. A squat whitewashed building with a slate roof set near the road. It stood alone, unlike the others farther on, gathered around the small church. I halted, waiting and listening for any sign of life. A barn sat behind the house, with its wide door open. Somebody at work?

I walked closer. The front door to the house swung open. I stopped, waiting for someone to come out, my hand resting on the butt of my pistol. The wind slammed the door against the house, then whipped it shut in a furious gust.

Something was very wrong.

I drew my .45, spooked by the silence. Where were the people who lived here?

I moved into the trees, making my way closer under the cover of pine boughs dropping clumps of wet snow. There were piles of something in the front yard, covered in snow. Clothing that had been tossed outside? I moved out from the trees as the wind took the door again, banging it against the house.

Startled, I headed for the door to shut the damn thing. Then I saw what was in the yard.

Bodies.

A man, a woman, and a young girl. Snow had formed a shroud over their corpses, each riddled by gunfire. Bullet holes in the stucco of the house behind them were closely grouped, as the family likely was in their last, terrified moments.

I scuffed the ground where I stood, coming up with a handful of shell casings in no time. They were 9mm, the ammo used in the Schmeisser submachine gun.

A patrol from Peiper's group, maybe, or any other German unit that passed through and decided to murder an entire family. But why? And why had the villagers left them here? This had happened before the snow, judging by the casings and the frozen pool of blood beneath their bodies, the white flakes easily swept away.

Not a single footprint marred the scene. The Germans hadn't come back, nor had anyone else. I looked at the girl's face, then tried not to. She was twelve, maybe thirteen. Her eyes were open, frost glittering on her lashes. One arm rested on her mother's.

I holstered my pistol.

I fell to my knees, the cruelty pushing me to the ground. Why? War is horrible enough for those who wage it. Why seek out the innocent to inflict so much pain? I buried my head in my hands and wondered if tears would come.

Nothing.

Buck up, Billy, I told myself. *You've seen worse.*

Yeah, I have, I told myself. Doesn't make it any easier.

I forced myself to get up and search for some sort of clue as to how this happened. And I told myself to stop talking to myself.

Okay, you first, I said. I laughed as I entered the house, not because it was funny but because that's all the emotion I could summon.

Get a grip, Billy.

Inside, the house was a shambles. Looted. Drawers opened; belongings scattered everywhere. Crockery in the kitchen smashed. Not a piece of food left. Bullet holes in the wall by the fireplace, family photographs strewn on the floor. I picked one up and saw the people outside, plus an older son, smiling in better times. A sunny day with a garden behind them.

Wherever the son was, I hoped he didn't come home too soon.

I scooped up an envelope. The address was Ruy, Belgium, which at least told me where I was. I got out my map and searched for the town, finding it west of Malmedy. Not where I expected to be, but not far from Spa. Six miles, tops.

I could hoof it from here, no problem. Then I could get in touch with Kaz in Chaudfontaine and check out le Chandelier d'Or. Simple. As long as I didn't run into trouble in the form of murdering SS bastards.

I went outside and shut the door firmly. It seemed silly, but I hated the idea of that damn door being blown by the wind as the family lay dead in front of it. I decided to do the same with the barn door before I hustled off to the church to see if there was some sort of padre still at his post.

I drew my pistol as I neared the barn, just to be careful. It was dark inside and smelled of moldy hay.

And death.

I blinked, adjusting my eyes to the dark. A German soldier hung from a rope thrown over a rafter. A placard was pinned to his chest. The rope was knotted tightly, and I had to cut through it with my knife. The body landed with a thud, but he was long beyond caring. The scrawl on the placard was too thick with German for me to understand much.

ich wurde gehängt, weil ich zu feige war, das reich zu verteidigen.

I figured *gehängt* meant he was hanged. Something to do with the Reich. I'd heard about the SS rounding up deserters and hanging them on the spot, leaving calling cards like this. I looked at his swollen and disfigured face. As far as I could tell, he was a match to the older brother in the family picture. Tall and dark-haired. Good-looking once upon a time.

A deserter, most likely. He could have been forced to join the Wehrmacht, especially if this was a German-speaking area of Belgium. Whether he'd been a volunteer or a conscript, he'd obviously decided to jump ship. Bad timing on his part, to make for home just as Peiper and his SS were passing by.

I took the noose off his neck, dragged his body out of the barn, and laid it with his parents and sister. I said a prayer, as much of it as I could remember from school, where the nuns had drilled us on it in Latin and English.

Saint Michael, defend us in battle; be our protection against the wickedness and snares of the devil. Thrust into hell Satan and all the evil spirits who prowl about the world seeking the ruin of souls.

Amen.

I couldn't help thinking that the archangel Michael hadn't been quite on his toes when it came to protecting folks around here from evil spirits on the prowl. I turned away, loping to the church, vowing to be his right hand when it came to thrusting Nazis into the pit of hell.

CHAPTER FORTY

AFTER A SHORT jog, I stopped and looked down the road to the church and the four buildings clustered around it. The first thing I noticed was that there were no tracks or footprints in the freshly fallen snow. The second was the pockmarked stucco and brick across the front of each building. The houses, as well as the stout church door, had been sprayed by automatic fire.

At least there were no bodies. Doors and shutters appeared to be locked up tight. No welcoming smoke curled from any of the chimneys. I approached the small church, which was built of red brick with a sharply pointed steeple clad in black slate. I pressed the latch and the door opened with a creak that echoed in the dank interior.

Two candles flickered by the altar. A man rose from the first pew. He had a blanket drawn around his shoulders and wore a heavy coat over his cassock. He shuffled toward me, squinting his eyes behind wire-rimmed glasses.

"Père," I said. "Pourquoi? Les morts." I tried to ask about the dead at the farmhouse, but either my French was lousy, or he was in shock. He looked at me with wide eyes as his hand reached out and touched my arm.

"Américain," he said, patting my arm as if it was news to me.

"Oui. Pourquoi?" I asked again, gesturing with my hand to the village beyond his church door.

"Allemands," he said, and sat heavily in the wooden pew.
Germans.

"Allemands revenir?" I asked, kneeling in the aisle next to him.
I doubted he'd know if the Germans were returning, but it might
save my life if he did.

He shook his head. "Les Américains reviendront-ils?" he asked
and spat out a bitter laugh. He'd seen it all before. In 1940, and
again in 1944 when the village was passed back and forth like a
football. Who knew what 1945 would bring? I tried asking about
the villagers, but the language barrier was too great. Or the trust
wasn't strong enough.

I asked if there were Americans in Spa, as best I could.

"Aujourd'hui ou hier?" Again, he laughed. I think he'd asked
if I meant yesterday or today, and I got his point.

"No Americans?" I asked, pointing in the general direction
of Spa.

"Les Américains sont hors de la route," he said, flicking his
hand in the same direction I had. Americans on the road to Spa
sounded like just the ticket.

"Merci," I said, laying my hand on his shoulder. It didn't register. I left him mumbling a prayer in the cold church as I
wondered if his flock would ever return.

They must have left under threat from the Germans, or as
soon as they heard the vehicles stop to search for the deserter. It
didn't really matter. The villagers fled, a family died, and the priest
prayed. Pretty much sums up how the innocent take it on the
chin when they get caught in the jaws of war.

I hustled up the road, ignoring my aches and weariness as best
I could. I'd have time to rest in Spa once I caught up with the
GIs and got in touch with Kaz. I took in deep breaths of cold air
as I kept up a rapid pace, wondering if the padre had seen an
American patrol or perhaps had heard of a roadblock.

I walked in the middle of the road, having no choice but
to make myself visible. The dogfaces at a checkpoint were

bound to be in a *shoot first* frame of mind, so I didn't want them to spot my slinking movement along the edge of the road. Of course, if I found Krauts instead of Yanks, the joke would be on me.

I froze as I rounded a bend in the road. Ahead, cutting across it, were marks left by a vehicle. Wheel and track marks from the woods, across the road, and into a cleared field. Where these Yanks, or a German patrol?

I soon found my answer.

A jeep, off on the side of the road, with three dead GIs on the ground. The path of the half-track was about fifty yards away, and my guess was a Kraut machine gun had caught the jeep as it came down the road and sent it swerving into the field.

Then I realized what the padre had really told me. He'd use "hors," which meant *off*, I was pretty sure. He was saying the Americans were off the road, not down the road. Dead.

There were a lot of footprints around the bodies. Their coats were open and none of them had gloves, scarves, weapons, or watches. The Germans had looted their bodies, taking anything of value. This had happened after the snow, which told me the Germans were still nosing around, but not in any strength.

All that was left for me were the dog tags. I pocketed the three of them. As I did, I noticed a rifle butt under the jeep, nearly covered in snow. Now I had a carbine. I scrounged through what was left in the jeep and found one extra clip of ammo. All I had to do was make it four more miles on foot.

Which made me think.

I checked out the bullet holes in the jeep. The seats and side panels were shredded, but there were only a couple of hits on the hood. The tires were intact.

Why not try?

I sat in the driver's seat, trying to avoid the sprays of frozen blood. I worked the choke and pressed the starter button. The engine turned over with a small rattle and a puff of black exhaust. Even if I only got a few miles out of her, it sure as hell beat walking.

I gingerly eased around the bodies, gunned the jeep, and regained the road.

I figured I was no more than a mile south of Spa when the rattle turned louder. I made it to the crest of a hill, where the engine conked out. I coasted the rest of the way down, holding tight onto the steering wheel as I pulled off the road.

I recognized the railroad tracks and knew where I was. Not far from the Hotel Britannique. If I didn't spot any GIs with a radio, I knew I could ask Yvonne, our brave waitress from the hotel restaurant, about using a telephone.

I crossed the tracks and took a side street toward the main drag and the hotel. There wasn't a GI in sight, only a handful of civilians, each giving me a wary look as if I was nothing but trouble. I guess they thought their chances of staying intact were better with no soldiers around at all. Even if the locals had been worried about losing the protection of all the GIs around First Army HQ, they had to have breathed a sigh of relief when the Americans decided not to turn Spa into a battleground. It wasn't a major crossroads like Malmedy or Bastogne, so it was unlikely to come under direct attack.

Unlike the Hôtel des Bains in Chaudfontaine, which could expect an indirect attack tomorrow.

I looked around as I walked down the narrow cobblestone street, the brickwork buildings all locked up tight with shutters closed. I couldn't spot le Chandelier d'Or, but I was counting on Yvonne to know where to send me.

The hotel lobby was empty, as was the restaurant. It looked like the offensive had put a crimp into visiting Spa for the waters. I went to the desk to ask for Yvonne, and was surprised when she appeared from the office, dressed not as a waitress but in a dress and sweater.

"Bonjour, Capitaine Boyle!" she said, her face lighting up as she looked behind me. "Le baron, est-il avec vous?"

"Non, le baron is not with me," I said. She hid her disappointment quickly.

"He is fine," I said, "Bien. Do you have a new job?" I gestured to the restaurant and then back to the reception desk.

"Oui, je suis la directrice adjointe," she said. "Assistante to the manager. After he run away." She made a running motion with her fingers across the desk and managed to get the idea across that since she'd stayed on the job, she'd been promoted and now had the position of the bum who'd left her here alone.

"Congratulations, Yvonne. May I, um, utiliser le telephone?"

"But no," Yvonne said, as she lifted up the receiver, listened, then shrugged. "En panne."

"Broken? Un autre? Do you have another telephone?"

"No, Capitaine, it is all telephones broken," Yvonne said. "Morts, all."

"When? Quand?"

"Une heure," she said. "Hour."

"Boche," I said, under my breath.

"They return?"

"No. Not here," I said. "When the telephones work, please call the baron at the Hôtel des Bains in Chaudfontaine. Tell him I am here." I wrote out Kaz's full name and rank, as well as Monk Dickson's.

"Oui, Capitaine," Yvonne said. She held up her hand and closed her eyes, seeming to gather her thoughts. "My father. He goes to Chaudfontaine. With wood, much wood.

Il livre du bois, yes?"

"Your father is delivering lumber to Chaudfontaine? Quand?"

When was within an hour, and he was going to stop at the hotel. Yvonne explained she'd promised him food from the restaurant to eat on the way. I wrote out a note for Kaz, telling him about the downed phone lines, le Chandelier d'Or, and that I was headed straight there.

"I will do it," Yvonne said. "Certainement."

"It is very important," I said.

"Mon père était dans la Résistance," Yvonne said proudly. "A courier. He knows of messages."

"Good. One other thing," I said, as the night and day caught up to me. "I need to sit down."

Yvonne ushered me into the kitchen and sat me at a small table. I leaned my head against the wall and rested my eyes for a moment, which must have turned into minutes, because the next thing I knew she'd set a small pot of coffee in front of me along with a brioche, which was still warm. She stared at me, her forehead wrinkled with worry.

"You are not well, Capitaine?"

"Fatigué," I said, trying to smile. I drank the hot coffee and bit into the brioche. I spent the next few minutes eating, suddenly feeling the hunger that shock had kept at bay.

"Yvonne, do you know le Chandelier d'Or?" I asked, washing down the last of the brioche with another slug of joe. "Where is it?"

"Oui. It is not far. You go there?"

"Yes. I need to find a man." I described Grau as best I could in a mix of French and English. Yvonne had not seen him at the hotel, but promised to keep watch.

"I have mon pistolet," she said. "If the Boche return, I am ready. They take my brother to work in Allemagne. We have not heard from him since. I am ready."

"Faites attention, Yvonne," I said as I stood, hoping she would indeed be careful with her pistol, although I had the feeling she might have handled hardware already if her father was in the Resistance.

"The message to the baron will be delivered," she said. "Now go. Stop them."

CHAPTER FORTY-ONE

I WALKED SOUTH, taking the road I came in on until I hit the avenue de la Roche. No one was out walking the dog, but I saw a few curtains flutter as I walked by, my carbine slung nonchalantly over my shoulder. I tried to look like a GI out for a stroll but given that most soldiers were interested mainly in booze, broads, and soft beds, I didn't think the charade was too convincing.

I crossed the train tracks, this time nearer to the station. The brick buildings here were coated with grime and soot from steam locomotives spewing coal smoke as they passed. It wasn't the ritziest part of town, but the cobblestoned avenue was broad. Wide enough for a large five-ton truck to pass unnoticed.

As if on cue, a Peugeot truck rumbled past. It was one of the smaller jobs, and the open truck bed was empty. The driver, an older gent with a thick mustache, waved energetically. It was nice to be appreciated. He parked in front of a small warehouse just ahead of me, and the double doors swung open to reveal a machine shop. Two men were working at a bench, both of them older, thin, and gray. There weren't a lot of strong young lads about these days. They were either in the army or working as slave labor in Germany. It was a safe bet that these fellows weren't part of the Syndicat.

I knew le Chandelier d'Or was up the road, based on Yvonne's directions, but I decided to try my luck with the driver, who'd gotten out of his vehicle and grinned.

"Où sont les autres Américains?" he asked on his way into the shop. I said there were no others yet, but they'd be back. I was about to tell him I was looking for le Chandelier d'Or, when I glanced over his shoulder and spotted a faded poster of Marshal Pétain, the former head of Vichy France, on the wall above the workbench. If any of these guys were Vichy right-wingers, it might not pay to advertise my destination. So, I wished him a good day and moved on.

I didn't need directions anyway. A minute later, the bar came into view, straight ahead where the road split around it. Two stories, with wide windows on the ground floor and narrow windows above. A couple strolled down the street and entered. Open for business.

Scooting down an alley I took the next street and approached the joint from the rear. I doubted Grau and his men would rendezvous in open daylight, but I figured he might have someone watching, either from the bar or one of the small upstairs windows.

I stepped across the street, trying to keep up my casual gait as I scanned the rear of the building. A short driveway led into an open courtyard, most of which was hidden from view by a brick wall. Another building backed up onto the courtyard, and I walked around to the front. The place was deserted, with flaking paint on the door and windows boarded up. I tried the door. It was locked, but a sharp shove with all my weight behind it took care of that. Wood splintered around the lock, but I was able to shut it.

It was dark inside, but I could make out empty shelves and a counter along one wall. A deserted shop. I made for the back and took the stairs to check out the floor above. The rooms were empty, except for what had been the kitchen, where a table and one wooden chair had been pushed up against the wall. The glass in the single window had been smashed, and the boards nailed across it were doing a good job of keeping out the light but not the cold.

I slammed one board to loosen it. The second time I struck, it moved, and I was able to get my fingers underneath it. I pushed and was rewarded with the wrench of wood and nail separating. I worked it loose, not without a bit more noise, and managed to pull it inside.

Which gave me a perfect view of the Renault AHR five-ton truck in the courtyard below, backed right up to the restaurant's loading dock. That meant at least the driver was here. And that someone at the bar was involved, or at least looking the other way. I drew up the chair and sat, hoping to get some idea of how many of the Syndicat were already here. If the second truck showed up, we'd be in good shape to nab them all tonight. Except that right now, *we* was me.

The back door to the bar opened, and two guys walked along the small loading dock to the back of the truck. They emerged quickly, carrying crates of bottles. They made three trips, then appeared to lock the truck.

What the hell was going on? Was the make and model of this truck a coincidence, and this was just a regular booze run? Or was the liquor a cover, a convenient way to hide weapons and explosives?

Now I wasn't even sure there was anyone from the Syndicat here. My bad guy could have been a wine salesman.

Then I heard footsteps.

I froze, knowing that an old place like this can send creaks echoing in every direction.

The footsteps stopped. Someone else knew that too. My mind went from the Vichy boys up the street to the racket I'd made knocking the plank loose. Or was it the local gendarme checking on the busted door?

I held my breath and remembered the time when a pal and I

broke into an abandoned blacksmith's shop, down near where the train tracks ran by Andrew Square. It had been boarded up for years, and we just wanted to see what was left inside, like any self-respecting ten-year-old kid would. It didn't end well.

We'd pried open a basement window and went in that way. Leaving it open was our first mistake. Heading for the top floor was our second since it left us nowhere to run when the beat cop began stomping around and yelling for us to come down.

I guess I hadn't learned much since then.

The footsteps started up again, slowly and quietly, making for the stairs, at the same moment a motorcycle roared into the courtyard below. I took advantage of its loud exhaust pipes to stand and move to the wall beside the door. I did it in two quick steps, keeping as quiet as my heavy overshoes allowed. Holding my carbine in one hand, I took off my standard-issue GI wool cap and tossed it across the hall, a few feet into the room opposite.

The footsteps neared the top of the stairs. The motorcycle switched off and indistinct voices drifted up from the courtyard, but no one seemed concerned about what was going on in here.

Except for me.

I heard him get to the top of the stairs, the crumbling plaster from the ceiling loud under his heels. Which said to me he was armed. Otherwise, he'd be more careful.

I readied my carbine, not to shoot, but to smack him in the head with the wooden butt. I couldn't risk either of us firing and attracting a crowd. But I had to wait and be sure it was one of Grau's men.

The footsteps drew closer. I heard the faintest sigh of worn leather moving and picked up the odor of a heavy smoker. He was almost here.

His boot scuffed to a stop. He'd seen the khaki-green wool cap. I pivoted and hoisted my carbine, taking in his hulking form just as he began to turn my way. Close-cropped hair. Leather jacket. A calloused hand clutching an automatic pistol.

Not the neighborhood cop.

I slammed him with the wooden butt, going for the bridge of his nose. I hadn't accounted for his height and reflexes, so the blow glanced off his jaw. He staggered back, falling into the doorway and trying to steady himself with his gun hand on the doorframe. That's where I landed my second blow. He dropped the pistol as he yowled, but he still had the presence of mind to pull a knife from his belt. He shook his head, flinging droplets of blood from the gash on his jaw.

Then he grinned as he waved the knife in front of me, stepping back and then forward, trying to throw me off-balance. He looked like a guy who enjoyed a good knife fight, kept his blade sharp, understood his reach exceeded mine, and also knew I didn't dare shoot.

Me, I wasn't much for knife fighting. I knew he'd be on me as soon as his head cleared. I backed out into the hallway, ready to make a dash for the stairs. Given his condition, I might be able to get away.

Unless he was good at throwing that knife. We were too close right now, but if I ran down the hall, I might be giving him the perfect target.

He snarled as he held his injured hand close to his chest and lunged at me. I whacked at the blade with the stock of my carbine but knew that wasn't a move I'd get away with again. It was more of a taunt than an attack.

"German?" I asked, trying to postpone his next move. "SS? Friend of Henri Grau?"

He paused, as if calculating his response. He'd shown recognition at the sound of Grau's name.

The motorcycle started up, that lovely, loud, deep-throated rumble of a bike that needed a new exhaust.

I raised the carbine and shot him in the head.

A blossom of blood appeared over his right eye, which blinked furiously. He stayed up on two feet, the blade still held out before him, for a couple of seconds, then collapsed to his knees and tumbled over.

The motorcycle roared off.

There was no outcry, no stampede to look for a missing comrade. I went to the window and looked. One man, dressed roughly like my dance partner, lounged against wall by the loading dock, smoking a cigarette.

Now all I had to do was figure out my next move. I knew the Syndicat was here, evidenced by the truck, the character in the courtyard, and the corpse in the next room. They might not miss this guy right away, but sooner or later someone was going to wonder where Fritz had gone off to. This would have been a good spot to watch the bar from, but that was no longer in the cards.

I checked Fritz's pulse, just to make sure. Zilch. He was big and mean, tough enough that I didn't want to take any chances. I went through his pockets, finding nothing but a wad of francs, a crumpled pack of Camel cigarettes, and a matchbox from le Chandelier d'Or. Of course. I pocketed the cash, thinking I might end up having a drink on him before this was over.

The absence of any personal items, along with the look of a well-trained soldier, confirmed he was with the Syndicat. I used his knife to cut away the jacket and clothing, revealing his left arm. There it was—the SS blood group tattoo. Type O.

I picked up my wool cap, considered the heft and size of the guy. One of us had to go, and I decided it would be me. It would be a lot easier. But where?

I looked again at the courtyard. The truck was still parked there. The cigarette smoker fieldstripped his butt and checked the doors of the vehicle. He then headed to a door at the far end of the building. Not the door at the loading dock, which I guessed went into the kitchen. He opened it without a key. Maybe it went upstairs, or it might lead directly into the bar.

What better place to hide and keep watch than from within the devil's own lair?

Best wait until dark to try it.

There was only one other place I could hide out until then. Like a bad penny, I was headed back to the Hotel Britannique, hoping Yvonne didn't decide to go with her father to Chaudfontaine. Downstairs, I opened the door to check up and down the street in case there were any surprises in store.

There was one. A bicycle leaning up against the brick wall. Had Fritz bicycled here? Maybe he was on his way to the rendezvous and spotted me breaking in and decided to take care of me himself. I couldn't count on it, but it would explain why no one came looking. They didn't know he was here. I hoped.

One Nazi down, and transportation acquired. I pedaled off, happily, having had enough of walking today.

CHAPTER FORTY-TWO

I LEFT THE bicycle at the back door of the hotel and went in through the kitchen, earning a suspicious glare from a cook, but he quickly went back to his slicing and dicing. I probably didn't look like a guy in the mood for questions.

I went into Yvonne's office behind the desk and heard her apologizing about the telephone to a guest who sounded offended that the war should so severely inconvenience him. As soon as he left, I opened the curtain and called her name.

"Capitaine, no téléphone, comprenez-vous?"

"I understand. Your father? Est-il parti?"

Yvonne said he'd left thirty minutes ago and had promised to go straight to First Army HQ and ask for Kaz. That meant another half hour to go, then who knows how long to convince a sentry to take his message. Some more time for Kaz to organize help. It would take him less than an hour to get here, since Kaz was bound to drive faster in a jeep than Yvonne's father in a truck loaded with lumber.

Of course, that assumed Kaz was sitting and waiting at head-quarters. Chances were good that once we didn't land at the airfield, he'd have gotten a search underway. It's what I would have done. But then, Colonel Harding had said he'd fill Kaz in on my suspicions, which included the Chandelier d'Or rendez-vous.

Trying to figure this all out made my head spin. I asked

Yvonne if there was a bed available where I could sleep for an hour or so. That would give me time to get to the bar by dark and sneak inside.

"Beaucoup," Yvonne said. "Attendez." She held up a finger, telling me to wait, and went to a cupboard behind her desk. She unlocked it and took out a haversack. It looked heavy. "For you. Take, please."

I looked inside. Four fragmentation and two white phosphorus hand grenades.

"Dangereux," Yvonne said, explaining that they had been left behind when the GIs had departed.

"Très dangereux," I said, and followed Yvonne as she took a key and led me upstairs.

She let me into the first room off the landing and left, returning shortly with a bowl of stew, a hunk of bread, and a glass of wine.

"Eat, rest," Yvonne said as she set the tray on a small table.

"Réveille-moi," I said. "One hour, ten minutes."

"D'accord," she said as she shut the door. Ten minutes to eat, an hour to sleep in a soft bed. I was doing a lot better than Fritz.

I DON'T KNOW if it was the food, the sleep, or washing up with warm water, but I felt nearly human, if it was human to be carrying weapons and explosives like these. The white phosphorus grenades, known as Willie Peter, were especially terrifying. Designed to generate smoke to cover infantry movements, the phosphorus charge burned intensely hot and was also used against bunkers and other enclosed spaces where the enemy couldn't get away from the white-hot spray. Effective. Also horrible.

I thanked Yvonne and promised to bring Kaz around for a visit when this was all over. That brought on a smile, which was often the case with Kaz and women. As I walked to the back door, I saw a businessman exiting the lobby, grasping his briefcase as he headed for his next appointment. I felt the weight of the haversack at my side and laughed at the notion of both of us going to work with our tools of the trade in hand. It was ridiculous, but I found myself tickled by the strangest things lately.

I needed a new line of work. Most of the world did too.

I mounted the bicycle and made my way to the bar, avoiding the frontal approach and going around back. It was starting to get dark, and I thought it was safe to check out the building I'd broken into earlier. It would give me a good view of the courtyard and if Fritz was still as I left him, it might mean that his pals hadn't been around. Or didn't want to bother moving him any more than I did. Who knew?

The door was as I left it. I carried the bicycle inside so it wouldn't be spotted. I stood quietly, listening for any sound of movement. Nothing, not from within the building or the courtyard. Going upstairs, I found Fritz stiffening exactly where I left him.

I crossed the hall to the kitchen and peered out through the missing slat.

The truck was gone.

No motorcycle, no tough guy leaning against the wall blowing smoke.

Had they clocked Fritz's disappearance and scattered? Was the Renault out making a pickup of men and weapons? Or had I blown it taking a bit of sack time?

I told myself to calm down and wait. I couldn't have done much anyway when the truck pulled out, except to try to pedal after it and hope to keep up for a few blocks. I pulled up the chair and watched for anything suspicious, hoping to see the second big truck make its appearance.

Half an hour passed, and the light was fading. Fritz wasn't much company, so I decided to try my luck with that back door to the bar. I walked around the brick wall, entered the courtyard, and passed the loading dock. As I did, the door to the kitchen opened and a thin guy wearing an apron dropped a case of empty wine bottles on the loading dock. He gave me a bored look and went back inside without a word. In a few seconds the door banged open again, and he deposited another case on top of the first.

No questions, no calls for help. Hardly the behavior of a Kraut commando, except if he was cleverly disguised as an indifferent dishwasher. I opened the door on the right, revealing a small foyer with stairs leading to the floor above and a hallway to the left that led to the bar, based on the clatter and chatter coming from that direction.

I went upstairs. The hall was narrow and dimly lit. The rooms were all numbered. I don't understand how or why, but sometimes I can sense the threat around me, especially in buildings. It's as if the scent of fear, anger, or maniacal intent works its way into the beams and floorboards allowing me to breathe it in.

I sensed nothing like that here.

The first room I passed was open, the bed stripped and the floor in need of cleaning. I checked it but there weren't any obvious clues lying around. The noises coming from behind the next door told me the couple inside was having too much fun to be planning a commando raid. The next room was unlocked, also in the process of being cleaned. Not a matchbox to be found. I checked the other rooms, finding nothing more suspicious than a gray-haired gent wearing a wedding ring and a smile on his face saying *au revoir* to a mademoiselle as he closed the door behind him.

He winked at me.

The Syndicat was in the wind, but at least someone was enjoying themselves.

I went back downstairs to the bar, sat at a table, and scanned the room. No rough men in leather jackets. A couple at one table was sharing a bottle of wine. Two old fellows sat at the bar drinking rum, the smell of the dark liquor heavy in the air. Four younger men were at a table next to me, drinking beer and playing cards. Aluette, by the looks of how they took tricks. A French game. Their workman's clothes were grimy and their fingernails black. Coal dust from the rail yard was my guess.

I didn't have any idea why the Syndicat pulled out, or if anyone here knew anything about it. But someone had to know something, and I figured the barman was the best guy to start with. He was about forty, with bushy black eyebrows and a jutting jaw.

"Une bière," I said, laying more of Fritz's francs than necessary on the zinc countertop. I slid the money his way. He nodded and began to pour, his eyes steady on the glass. When he was done, he set it in front of me. Not unfriendly, but not exactly welcoming either.

"Les Américains?" he asked, the meaning clear. Are they coming back?

"Oui," I said. "Soon." He didn't get it. I pointed to my watch and said it again.

"Bon," he said, a smile finally creasing his face. Whether he meant good for business or good for the cause of freedom, I couldn't tell.

"Are you the owner?" I asked, using pantomime as I pointed at him and the surroundings. No, he was the manager, I finally understood after some back-and-forth. The owner had left for Liège as soon as the artillery started up. He said his name was Andre, and I introduced myself, glad the language barrier was too great for him to ask what I was doing here.

I didn't see any way to ease the subject into the conversation, so I went full bore ahead and asked about the big Renault truck, le gros camion, that had been out back. That got a response, and at first I thought he was saying it was his, but he was going on about having driven one when he was in the French army. An excellent truck, in his opinion. The guy was a talker, and I quickly realized I could have saved my francs.

I asked if there were two Renaults out back, and he was sure it had been only one. He volunteered that it wasn't their regular driver or truck, but they'd received their expected order of liquor. I said thanks and took my beer to a table by the window to wait for Kaz.

As I sipped the cold beer, I mulled it over. The Syndicat ambushes the regular delivery guy, takes his shipment, and delivers it. The driver finds a reason to hang around for a few hours while the rest of the gang shows up at the prearranged rendezvous. The only thing necessary was for a Syndicat man to know the delivery day. Easy enough, since we'd seen one of the crew in Spa a few days ago.

Those two empty rooms upstairs could have been for Grau and one of his men. Traveling separately and leaving with the truck. The second truck could have been stashed elsewhere, stuffed with weapons and gear. The human cargo went with this one. Somewhere, the two trucks were now together, waiting for the morning.

Maybe. There was nothing else to do until Kaz showed up and had a proper conversation with Andre. So, I drank my beer and looked out the window. A light snow began to fall, glittering white against the lights outside. I thought about Joe, dying in the attempt to get me here. Right now, it looked like it had been for nothing.

Here's to you, Joe.

My glass was empty when I saw a jeep drive down the street, away from the bar. Reconnaissance. Another, this one with a mounted .30 machine gun, parked out front. That got the customers' attention. Which is what it was intended to do.

"Have I come to rescue you, Billy, or have a drink?" Kaz asked. He'd come in the back way, just as I had. He looked around, checking the people in the bar, probably wondering if I was being held prisoner.

"Have a seat and I'll explain," I said, gesturing to my carbine resting against the wall behind me. "The Syndicat has come and gone."

"What happened to you?" Kaz asked. "We waited at the airfield."

"We took fire," I said. "Crashed in a field. The pilot didn't make it. I had to hoof it. How's your head?"

"A few stitches," Kaz said, fingering the bandage under his cap. "Nothing too bothersome."

Colonel Harding had told Kaz of my suspicions about le Chandelier d'Or. I filled him in on my exploration of the building opposite, my encounter with Fritz, and what I'd seen in the courtyard.

"The Kraut who came after me was SS," I said. "Complete with the blood group tattoo."

"Colonel Harding was less than enthusiastic about your theory," Kaz said. "Especially the bit about the calendar being marked for tomorrow. But he did ask Monk Dickson to assist, as you can see." Outside, another jeep filled with GIs pulled up. They got out and looked around, probably wishing they could come in for a drink.

"What do you think?" I asked.

"You did encounter a member of the Syndicat, that is certain," Kaz said. "As for the truck, that Renault model is not uncommon."

"But it wasn't their regular driver or vehicle," I said, explaining what I'd got from the barman. It didn't sound like much. Out on the street, a lieutenant directed his men around to the courtyard. He left one GI on each mounted machine gun and entered the bar. Customers moved back to their seats and clutched their drinks. More Americans might mean a return to normalcy or a brewing battle. Best to drink up while you can.

"Captain Boyle?" asked the second louie. "I've been ordered to assist you in capturing a German agent. It doesn't seem as urgent as it first sounded." He looked at my empty beer glass then back at me.

"We're too late," I said. "There's one dead SS man in the building out back. Give us a few minutes, and we'll figure out our next move."

"Sorry, Captain, my orders don't include waiting around. Colonel Dickson said I was to return immediately to patrolling if there was no sign of this agent. One dead Kraut doesn't count, sorry," the lieutenant said.

"I did not have a chance to tell you, Billy," Kaz said. "Colonel Dickson was even more doubtful than Colonel Harding. The lieutenant and his men must return to searching for Germans masquerading as MPs."

"Another group was just captured near the Meuse, and Monk wants to be sure we find any on our front, especially after they cut all the phone lines around here," the lieutenant explained. "I've got to radio in a report and then head out on patrol."

"Here," I said, and handed him the dog tags from the road outside Ruy. I didn't bother trying to convince him it was the Syndicat cutting off communications around their rendezvous point. I told him about the ambushed GIs, the atrocity in the village, and the crash site where I'd left Joe. "In case you're going in that direction."

"Good as any," the lieutenant said. "Wish I could stay, but my orders were clear."

"We understand," Kaz said, in a way that warned me not to complain. As the lieutenant departed, Kaz explained that Monk had been adamant. If there was nothing at le Chandelier d'Or, the patrol was to head out immediately. "Monk is very concerned about the MPs and hopes to capture a team for interrogation."

"Well, I hope you're staying, and you have wheels," I said.

"Yes, in the courtyard. Did you get any more information from the man at the bar?"

"He doesn't speak English, and I could barely make myself understood," I said. "Maybe you could describe Grau and see if he sounds like one of the guests who just checked out. Not that it matters much at this point."

A few customers had left, perhaps spooked by the firepower on display. Kaz and I went up to the bar, where he ordered a brandy. I peeled off more of Fritz's dough and handed it over. "Tell him it's for scaring off the customers," I said.

Kaz began to chat, in that easygoing way he has, his French way too fast for me to pick up anything. As Andre poured the brandy, I heard Grau's name, and what might have been a description. That got a response.

"Oui, oui, Monsieur Angrand. Charles Angrand," Andre said.

"Of course," Kaz said, taking a sip and turning to me. "Charles Angrand was an Impressionist painter of the last century. Not as well-known as others, but quite influential. Grau must have enjoyed using an artist's name."

"Just like he enjoyed leaving that date on the calendar," I said. I filled Kaz in on the calendar setting back at Grau's hotel. "A secret joke. Ask him if Monsieur Angrand met any others. And did he drive here?"

Kaz drank some more brandy and asked a few more questions. Andre took the long way around answering, but, finally, he stopped, moving off to serve the older gents still maintaining their posts at the bar.

"He did drive by himself," Kaz said. "He arrived in a Citroën Traction Avant. The car of choice for thieves and discriminating drivers."

"What else did he say?"

"Monsieur Angrand, who arrived first, did seem to know another man who arrived yesterday," Kaz said. "They had dinner together. The other gentleman was the quiet type. He signed the register as Jean Moreau. The French cousin of John Smith."

"I bet that means he didn't speak French all that well," I said. "Anything else unusual?"

"I was about to ask if they left together," Kaz said, as Andre returned. He and Kaz chatted for a while, nothing jumping out at me. By the tone of the conversation, I got the impression that Grau had left little impression.

"They left this morning, the other man first. Angrand paid the bill for both rooms, and he departed before lunch," Kaz said. "Before you arrived, I would think."

"Yeah," I said. "Nothing else? Ask him if they talked about anything out of the ordinary. Something that didn't make sense to him."

Kaz shrugged. I could tell he was humoring me, but he pressed Andre, spreading his hands wide as he spoke, as if to emphasize he wanted to hear everything that Grau had said to Andre.

"Nothing," Kaz finally said. "Angrand did not say much to Andre other than the usual. Ordering, paying his bill, that sort of thing."

"Where did they sit when they had dinner?" I asked, desperate not to give up. Kaz sighed and asked Andre, who pointed to the table behind us. It had a good view of the room and didn't put Grau on display in front of a window.

"He must have overheard them," I said. "Did they talk about Chaudfontaine, or the trucks?"

"No," Kaz said after he thanked Andre and let him get on with the other customers. "The only comment Andre remembered was when Grau and his colleague raised their glasses. The toast was made to their favorite color, gold. Andre took it as a compliment."

"Le Chandelier d'Or," I said. "The Golden Chandelier."

"Of course," Kaz said. "Now I suggest we go to Chaudfontaine and convince Colonel Dickson to plan for an attack tomorrow. I am sure we can convince him to divert his patrols and set up roadblocks around the town."

"He really wants to nab one of those Kraut jeep crews, doesn't he?" I said.

"Well, he is an intelligence officer," Kaz said. "It would be a feather in his cap. Also, he was chagrined at having issued warnings about the threat of an enemy offensive only to have it occur the moment he took leave to visit Paris. It did not reflect well upon his reputation."

"Sounds like he's hoping to capture some of Skorzeny's boys to restore it," I said.

"I think so. He has alerted his MPs to the possibility of a raid on headquarters, at least. Guards have been doubled."

"It's not enough," I said. "If those two trucks are filled with men and weapons, they could get within a half mile and move in on foot. The first phony MPs they found were wearing swastika armbands under their jackets. Grau's men could do the same."

"If they have American uniforms," Kaz said, "it would be a golden opportunity."

"Right, let's get to Monk, then," I said. I waved farewell to Andre and glanced at that corner table again. I stood still. "Wait, a golden opportunity, you said?"

"I did," Kaz said. "Why?"

"Gold." Grau had done it again. He had his little inside joke and couldn't resist it. Like the calendar and his pseudonym. "His favorite color."

"Billy?" Kaz asked, his brow wrinkled with worry. "Are you all right?"

"Never better," I said, keeping my voice low. "I know where they are."

CHAPTER FORTY-THREE

"WHAT ARE YOU talking about?" Kaz demanded as we hustled to his jeep in the courtyard. I hadn't wanted to say anything out loud in the bar.

"This was the rendezvous point, right?" I said as I climbed into the passenger seat. Kaz had the canvas top on, but it didn't do a whole lot to keep the cold out. I took out my map and unfolded it. "Once they had everyone collected, they needed a quiet place to wait before the attack was launched. Two trucks crammed with men and weapons might be noticed."

"That makes sense," Kaz said, as he started the jeep. "But how can you know where they've gathered?"

"Do you remember what was on that bulletin board at the Hotel Britannique?" I said. I shined a flashlight on the map, the late-afternoon light fading fast.

"The requisition order for the hotel in Chaudfontaine?" Kaz said. "They took it."

"No, next to it," I said. "The hand-drawn map of roadblocks and emplacements around Spa. It included the location of the Golden Arrow wireless unit. Gold. Grau's favorite color."

"You've come up with this from his toast?" Kaz asked.

"Yes. It fits with his character. He likes these little touches. It's his tell. Plus, it's logical. The site is off the main road, secluded, complete with a farmhouse where they can spend a warm night.

It's northeast of Spa, and they can take the back roads to Chaud-fontaine," I said. "What do you think?"

"I think we should find a working telephone," he said. "Or drive back to First Army and organize a force to take them on."

"You're right about the telephone. Let's get to the Britannique. Yvonne can keep trying to call for us. She asked about you, by the way," I said as I traced the best route back to the Golden Arrow's previous position.

"What about First Army?" Kaz said, as he pulled out of the courtyard, ignoring my comment about Yvonne.

"Well, we could go there, I guess. Engage in debate with Colonel Dickson and see if he'll cooperate. Might take half the night, and Grau might be on the move by then. Or we could take a drive out there ourselves."

"Armed with what?" Kaz asked. "One Sten gun and a carbine? Are you counting on them laughing themselves into surrender?"

"No, I'm counting on this," I said, tapping the haversack at my feet.

"What is in there?"

"Party favors left at the hotel when First Army skedaddled. Yvonne gave them to me. Four fragmentation grenades and two Willie Petes. Did I mention she's the assistant manager now? Very resourceful young lady," I said.

"This should be an interesting night," Kaz said.

Minutes later we were at the hotel. I left Kaz to congratulate Yvonne on her new job and dashed up the stairs, making for the room that had been General Kean's office. The postings on the bulletin board were all still there, including the map. I grabbed it and went downstairs. There were a few people in the lobby, and Yvonne took us back into the office where we could speak in private.

"My father, he is a good courier, oui?" Yvonne said, her eyes sparkling with excitement.

"Most excellent," Kaz said. "Still no telephone?"

"Non. All of Spa, pas de téléphone."

I asked Yvonne to keep trying the telephone to get in touch with Monk. I drew a circle around the Golden Arrow location and wrote a note about Grau and the trucks. Kaz explained the details as I wrote, and Yvonne promised to stay by the telephone all night if need be.

"You go there?" Yvonne asked. "To fight? Seulement vous deux?"

"Yes, only we two," Kaz said. "Perhaps we will just wait and watch. La surveillance."

"Il fait très froid," Yvonne said. "Un moment." She returned quickly with a stack of four US Army wool blankets, more of what had been left behind. Kaz kissed her cheek. I asked if there were any more grenades.

"Non. You need armes? Fusils?"

"You have rifles here?" I asked. She shook her head.

"La Résistance," Yvonne said in a whisper. The Resistance was supposed to have turned in their arms and disbanded under orders from de Gaulle. But this close to the front, some units may have wisely hidden them away in case the Germans returned.

"No, thank you," I said. "This is our fight. It is most important you get this message through to First Army. And your blankets will keep us warm, thank you."

"Faites attention," Yvonne said. She folded the map and placed it in her pocket. I trusted she'd do her best, but she didn't look happy at having her rifles turned down.

It was pitch-black by the time we got back into the jeep. Grasping the map, I navigated by the shaded flashlight, retracing the route we had taken to Spa when we pulled out with the Golden Arrow unit. It seemed like a century ago.

"We need a plan," Kaz said. "You know they are likely to place sentries, just as we did."

"I know," I said. "Take this left. We stood guard at the entrance by the main road, and I expect they'll do the same. So, we just need to find a spot to pull off before the track to the farmhouse and cut across through the woods. We'll look for a place where we can watch the house and try to spot the guards."

"So far, we are spending a freezing night in the woods," Kaz said. "Then what do we do?"

"One white phosphorus grenade for each truck, right under the fuel tank," I said. "That ought to burn brightly. Toss the other grenades, fire off a few rounds, and get back to the jeep. That will leave them on foot and hopefully down several men. How's that sound?"

"It should cripple their plans for an attack," Kaz said. "It's a shame we don't have those jeeps with the mounted machine guns."

"That would be too easy," I said. I was trying to crack wise, but my heart wasn't in it. I knew that we had to do this now, with whatever we had at hand. Otherwise Grau's Syndicat might slip through our fingers once again. If I was right about where they were. I had to be.

"Indeed," Kaz replied. He cut the lights and slowed down. "Easy would be nice once in a while, though."

We turned off the main roadway onto the forested lane we'd taken when we left with the Golden Arrow unit and Niv. We crept along slowly, the way ahead visible only as a white path through the pines. I asked Kaz to stop and hopped out, cupping my flashlight with my hand as I shined it on the snow cover for a few seconds. Tire tracks in the road were being filled in, and there was no way to tell how recent they were. But they did confirm vehicles had been this way.

"Trucks for sure," I said as I draped a blanket over my head, switched the flashlight back on, and studied the map. The farm-house track wasn't on the map, but I recalled that this lane curved away after it. I found the spot.

"We're close," I said, flicking off the light. "Let's find a place to pull off the road."

About fifty yards on, Kaz nudged the jeep into a clear space between two pine trees, far enough in to be well hidden. We got out and I handed Kaz two grenades, keeping the others for myself. We grabbed our weapons and two wool blankets. It might be a long, cold night.

"I figure this angle will bring us in between the farmhouse and the main road," I said, pointing off to our left. "That way we can try to spot guards at both places."

"If we are patient, we should be able to see their sentries being relieved," Kaz said, his blanket over his shoulders. "Only an idiot would spend more than an hour or two out in this weather."

"Right," I said, wondering if the idiot he was referring to was German or a Yank.

We made our way through the forest, pausing often to listen for any movement ahead of us, and to make sure we stayed on course. Our frosted breath rose as we traveled up and down a ravine, huffing and puffing our way across rocks and fallen trees. When I glimpsed a patch of clear white ahead of us, I tapped Kaz on the shoulder, and we knelt to catch our breath. Kaz lifted his head and sniffed the air.

"Wood smoke," he whispered. We were getting nearer.

We moved out, crouching low, careful as we could be in the darkness not to snap a twig underfoot. When the trees thinned out to small growth at the edge of the field, we went prone and tried to make out what was in front of us. The barest glow of a half-moon behind the low cloud cover did little to illuminate the scene.

"Let's get closer," I responded. We crawled slowly through the snow, pulling with our elbows to keep our bodies close to the ground. We halted when we reached a low spot, a depression deep enough to shield our bodies from view. I shrugged the blanket off my shoulders and lay on it, welcoming the barrier against the cold and the dark shape that might blur the contours of my body.

Kaz nudged me and pointed to our right. A dull light glowed, and I could make out the roofline of the farmhouse. Candlelight, probably. Then I saw the sharp rectangular outline of one of the trucks, about thirty yards out from the farmhouse on a nice flat piece of ground.

"The other is probably right behind it," I said to Kaz, keeping my voice low.

"Agreed," he responded. "There's a lot of open ground between us and the trucks. Too far to throw grenades from here. We could be spotted from the farmhouse or by the sentries if we try to get closer."

"Look!" I said, my hand jabbing at the darkness to our left. The faint glow of a cigarette.

"Careless fellows," Kaz said. "They didn't expect anyone would be smart enough to guess their location."

"Thanks," I said, happy at being promoted from idiot. The sentries—I was guessing two—were back from the road junction, hunkered down beneath the branches of a large pine tree, judging by the glow of that cigarette.

"It would be good if we did not have to worry about those sentries," Kaz said.

"I wouldn't have to worry about them if you worked your way closer," I said. "I've got an idea."

I filled Kaz in on my plan. He'd go back into the woods and move along the side of the road, keeping to the trees, and find a spot close to the guards. Grenade-tossing distance would be perfect. I'd begin my belly crawl to the trucks while he was doing that. Instead of throwing WP grenades, my notion was to jam one under a tire, safety lever first, pack it in place with snow, and pull the pin. With the safety lever pressed tight against the tire, it wouldn't spring open and begin the four-second counter to detonation. Until the truck pulled away.

"This sounds horribly familiar," Kaz said, his hand going to the scar on his cheek. He'd lost Daphne back in '42 to a similar explosive device and gained that scar as a constant reminder.

"I'm sorry," I said. "It seems like the surest way to guarantee we get both trucks."

"Very well," he said, after a pause. "But I hope we are not going to wait all night for them to drive off."

"That would be boring," I said. "On my way back here, I'll toss a grenade at the house. That ought to send them running for the trucks."

"Which is my signal to deal with the sentries," Kaz said. "I shall try to be quick."

"Here," I said, giving him another one of my fragmentation grenades. "Three of these oughta do the trick. I'll only need one to rattle their cage. It'll be up to you to stop Grau if he makes a break for it in his Citroën."

"It is not the most brilliant plan," Kaz said, eyeing the distance I'd have to crawl in the open. "You will be in danger if they come out to the trucks for any reason."

"It's our only plan. Besides, I'm only worried about a changing of the guard," I said. "Otherwise, I don't see them leaving the warmth of that farmhouse." I looked at the field. It was rutted and dotted with withered vegetation and several piles of wood that had been cut and left unstacked.

"Use what cover you have," Kaz said. "And make your own." He took his blanket and looped it through the haversack at my side and stuffed one end under my web belt. It covered my legs. Maybe it would make me look like a rock. I left my carbine on the ground. I didn't want it getting in my way as I worked under the truck.

"Meet at the jeep if things go haywire. Faire attention," I said, grasping his shoulder.

"I see I must provide another lesson in French pronunciation," Kaz said. "Tomorrow, perhaps. Au revoir."

He backpedaled out of there. I began to snake my way toward the five-ton trucks.

It was quiet except for the beating of my heart and the rustling of cloth and leather as I dragged myself over the snow. It looked like I had a good fifty yards to go, and my arms were already aching from dragging my body since we left the tree line. It was damn cold plowing through the snow, which thankfully was fluffy. A breeze kicked up and blew the light flakes against my face. I blinked them away, praying that the swirling gusts of snow were good cover.

I kept going, calculating how much time Kaz would need to get into position. He'd be moving stealthily himself, but not as slowly as I was. I figured by the time I got to the trucks, he'd be all set. If he didn't run into trouble on the way.

I'd covered about a third of the ground when I stopped to rest and get my breathing under control. The candlelit window was still visible, but the smoke break in the other direction was over.

A door slammed.

I lowered my head and carefully drew in my gloved hands to shield my face and keep my frosted breath from giving me away. I didn't dare look up, afraid one of them would catch my eye. My dad had drummed his rules of surveillance into me back in Boston. Never look directly at the guy you're watching. Some people are quick to notice eyeballs on them, and it didn't pay to give them a tip-off. He trained me to focus on something off to the side and use my peripheral vision to keep tabs on the quarry.

Right now, I was using a different technique, burying my face in the snow and listening.

Boots scuffed against snow and the frozen ground beneath it. The subtle clink of metal and the creak of leather as a weapon was carried. The low growl of German. Two men, by the sound of their conversation, and they were getting closer.

The wind kicked up, blowing white flakes across me. A welcome feeling, since it meant they'd probably keep their heads down. They muttered some more, probably the usual complaining any soldiers would do about drawing the short straws to pull guard duty in lousy weather.

Ten feet away and closing was my guess. They'd cross in front of me, and if I kept up my act as a rock, all I had to do was worry about the men they were relieving.

The wind whipped up and the blanket fluttered against my legs, moving in way a rock would never do. I thought about easing my hand to my pistol but held back. Kaz might not be ready and there was a good chance one of these guys could let loose with a burst from a Schmeisser before I cleared the holster. I focused on listening to their footfalls, waiting for a sudden stop or turn.

The footsteps faded, a few words of whispered German floating on the wind behind them. I stayed put. If I crawled any farther, the other sentries could easily spot my trail in the snow. I reached behind me and tucked the end of the blanket under my knee. I took off my glove, drew the .45, and pressed every body part deeper into the snow.

It didn't take long for the other two Krauts to make their way back to the farmhouse. Relieved of duty and probably chilled to the bone, their pace was quicker, and I doubted they'd stop to scout for infiltrators. They were almost to me, sounding like they'd followed the footprints of the first two. Then the footsteps stopped.

"Hörst du das?"

"Nein."

From somewhere far off, I heard an engine. It was hard to tell where it came from, the hills and ridges of the Ardennes bouncing echoes in every direction. Then it was gone. It was still early in the evening, and it could have been anyone from an American patrol to a Frenchman heading home late from work. Whatever it really was, the important thing was that it wasn't coming this way.

The Krauts whispered a bit more, apparently coming to the same conclusion. They walked on by, not a care in the world. I planned on changing that.

I holstered my automatic and crawled on, sure that by now
Kaz was in place. If he was, he'd have had a ringside seat for the
two new guys taking up position. All I needed to do was get to
the trucks and place the WP grenades. I brushed against a rock
about the size of my hand and managed to dislodge it. I came
across another and finished the last twenty yards with a rock
grasped in each hand. My plan had been a good one, but it might
need some nudging.

From here I had a better view of the farmhouse. Shadows
passed by windows as the men inside moved about, thinking they
had a few hours of rest before their mission. I got to the first
truck, its high clearance making it easy to move under. The
second truck was parked next to it, not five yards away. Farther
back and closer to the farmhouse was Grau's Citroën. That was
going to be a problem.

But not these trucks. The front wheels were far forward, just
under the high, sloping hood. Which meant that when they
drove off, the grenade was sure to explode underneath the vehicle,
maybe igniting the fuel tank. I scraped away the snow under the
front right tire and carefully pressed one of the Willie Petes into
the space where the tire met the frozen ground, making sure the
safety lever was firmly in place against the tire, with the pin faced
upwards. I tapped it a few times with a rock, wincing at the sound
as well as the notion of banging away at a deadly explosive. It
felt wedged in tight. I left the rock against it and covered everything with snow, leaving just the pin exposed.

I was sweating. This scheme was a lot easier to dream up than
to do.

I slithered out from beneath the truck and pulled myself under
the second one. I looked back and noticed two jerry cans of fuel
strapped on the rear of the side panel. If the fuel tank didn't ignite
right away, those were perfectly positioned.

I got to work, anticipating the fireball of shock that was going
to await Grau and his boys when they drove off. I placed the

grenade, using the rock as I had before. This one was wedged even tighter, the rock pressed hard against it.

Brushing the snow back in place, I took a deep breath and prepared to pull the pin. I pressed one hand against the rock, making sure the safety level was snug and had nowhere to go. Yet. When freed, the lever is flicked away by a spring-loaded mechanism, making a *pling* sort of sound. A sound I did not want to hear.

I grasped the pin and pulled. I slid backward and rolled out from under the truck, the only sound that of the stifled scream in my throat. But no metallic *pling*.

I let out a breath and took a second to assess Grau's vehicle. It was too far away to be caught up in the explosions, and too close to the farmhouse for me to sneak up to it. If I went closer to toss my grenade at it, I'd have too far to go to get back to the woods and my carbine before all hell broke loose. We'd have to deal with Grau when he came out.

I crawled back under the first truck, waiting and listening before I pulled the pin. It was quiet, the wind through the pines whooshing gently overhead. Only one light shone in the farm-house, and no shadows flickered in passing. No one had any idea what was coming.

I laid my gloved hand on the rock covered in snow and made ready to pull the thin metal ring. I applied pressure, grasped the pin, and pulled. I scurried backward and rolled clear of the truck.

Pling.

I scrambled to my feet, fear sending me flying forward in one, two, three great strides before I dove and hit the ground. The explosion was a loud *pop* as the igniter charge went off and released the burning phosphorus at white-hot temperatures. I jumped up and ran as soon as I realized the truck had absorbed the hit from the Willie Peter, which normally would have spread nearly twenty yards in every direction. I don't know what went wrong, but I was glad I'd gotten out quickly.

Two explosions sounded from the road, and I knew Kaz was at work eliminating the sentries. I heard the burst of his Sten gun and skidded to a halt as I felt a burning sensation. I shook off the smoking blanket that still covered my back, pitted in several places with particles of burning phosphorus. Shouts rose from the farmhouse, and I managed to get my grenade in hand and fling it at the door, which by now was wreathed in gray, swirling smoke.

The truck's gas tank went up, engulfing the vehicle in a fireball while the WP ate furiously at the truck bed. Then the gas cans went up, sending flames skyward as fire pooled on the ground. More gunfire came from the road, and I ran for my carbine, knowing the Germans were about to stream out of the farmhouse, armed to the teeth.

I dove to the ground and grabbed the carbine, taking aim at shadowy forms that moved out from the house. They were disciplined, I had to give them that. No shouts, no confused milling of arms. I saw two take up a position on my right, watching for a threat from the woods. I held my fire. I had only two clips and was heavily outgunned. For now.

My next move was to wait.

Theirs was to move the second truck away from the inferno. Since no ammo or explosives had gone off, I figured the first truck had been for transport. The other must be crammed with weapons, and Grau's first priority would be to get it out of here before it became engulfed in flames.

The two men I'd spotted began to fire. Not at me, or at anything I could see. Shadows. Shouted orders came from within the smoke, and I waited, keeping my carbine trained on the two guys I could see clearly.

More gunfire came from the Syndicat men. They weren't firing blindly, I decided. They were laying down fire to keep their invisible opponents pinned. The two men near me fired a few more times, then backed up slowly, moving behind the burning truck.

An engine started. Then another. I readied myself, hoping that Grau's automobile would be right next to the truck when the grenade went off. I spotted a few more soldiers as two men advanced toward the road. By the light of the fire, I could just make out their German camouflage smocks and red swastika armbands. More followed, taking up positions along the path to the road. I counted eight Krauts that I could see, most armed with Schmeissers.

Grau's Citroën Traction Avant made its way on to the scene and pulled to the side of the track. Someone in the car signaled for the truck to move, and I braced for the explosion.

The truck's engine revved, and the driver plowed forward, eager to escape the ambush. The WP grenade had a fuse set for four and a half seconds. In normal circumstances, you wouldn't hit the accelerator and speed off in a five-ton truck, but this was anything but normal.

Which was good news for the driver of the Renault, and horrible news for the Syndicat men surrounding it, ready to trot alongside, weapons at the ready.

The Renault lurched ahead, putting a full truck length between the vehicle and the explosion. This time the bursting effect wasn't tamped down by a heavy truck bed. Shimmering white phosphorus engulfed half a dozen men at least, some lucky enough to die instantly. Others writhed on the ground, screaming, but not for long.

More smoke spread out over the field, and I had no way of knowing how many of them were left. The Krauts didn't know there were only two of us, so I figured to make a run at Grau before they realized it. All I could hope for was that Kaz could stop the truck.

It was like moving through fog. A figure emerged from the smoke asking me something in German, and I answered him in .30 caliber. I picked up his Schmeisser and a couple of clips, continuing on a line that should bring me to Grau. More gunfire came from the road, and I heard the truck downshift. The smoke was slowly rising from the ground, and I thought I saw the truck cab turn and head my way.

Why?

More shouts, very close, and as I turned to see who it was, the front grille of the Citroën bore down on me. I jumped back, letting loose with a few rounds from the carbine just in time to spot a burst of submachine gun fire aimed in my direction. I dropped to the ground, waited for a dark form to come into view, and fired twice.

He staggered back, firing one wild burst. I was out of ammo and loaded my other clip, firing two rounds that sent him to the ground. I ran after Grau's car, which had braked and halted next to the truck. Shots were being fired from the road, and I wondered if the Germans were shooting at their own people in the confusion. Or did Kaz have reinforcements?

It didn't make sense, but nothing in this inferno made sense. The smoke thinned as it was fanned by the wind and the cold updraft, the burning truck lighting the field like a surreal dream. I fired the rest of my clip at the car, tossed the carbine, and advanced with the Schmeisser. I could see six men in camouflage smocks gathered around the truck, which was now backing up to the road. I spotted multiple muzzle flashes from across the way but didn't have a moment to think about it.

I fired a burst through the rear window, then ducked down behind the car. As I did, two more Krauts came at a run from the direction of the farmhouse, making for the truck. I cut them down, then checked inside the car. The driver was dead, the motor still running. Two tires were shot out, but I didn't figure on going that far. I dragged him out of the car, jumped in, and gunned the engine, heading for the stout figure climbing up into the truck's cab, the flat tires making for a shaky ride.

But I had Grau. Finally.

I braked at the last minute and jerked the steering wheel,

slamming the Citroën into the high truck cab just as Grau was stepping into it. He fell back, his legs pinned and his face contorted in pain. He looked straight at me and slammed his fist on the hood, anger now vying with torment. A bullet shattered the windshield, showering me with glass. A Kraut was advancing, pistol drawn, taking aim. I wrenched the car away from the truck and Grau rolled helplessly against the windshield until I braked and sent him flying, into the unwilling arms of his rescuer. Then I accelerated, felt a couple of bumps, and took me and the sturdy Citroën out of the line of fire.

The Fox was dead.

A German machine gun lit up the night. An MG 42 by the sound, mounted in the rear of the truck. Hitler's Buzz Saw, the GIs called it. It was a fearsome beast, firing twenty-five rounds a second. Just the thing to open an attack on First Army headquarters. But now it was being used on Kaz and whoever was with him on the other side of the road. Even if it didn't hit them, the MG 42 would send them scurrying for cover until the Krauts circled around them. I didn't know how many Germans were left, but I did know I had to stop this thing.

I got out of the car and aimed at the driver in the cab. He leaned out of his door and tossed a potato masher grenade my way. I dove back into the car as the grenade bounced off the roof and exploded behind me. I thrust the barrel of my Schmeisser through the shattered window and fired it at the driver, who fell back onto the ground just as he was about to toss another grenade. It exploded right as one of his pals approached, firing at me. Bad timing for him.

The sound of the MG 42 was a constant ripping, tearing noise that shredded trees and shattered frozen ground. I didn't have many options left, so I darted to the truck as bullets zipped around me, not knowing who was shooting at who. I checked the cab and found a sack of grenades on the seat. I grabbed it. Right behind the cab were the two jerry cans of fuel. I took one grenade, stuffed the sack between the jerry cans, unscrewed the grenade's cap, and pulled its detonator cord. I jammed it on top of the sack and ran like hell, diving behind the wrecked Citroën as the grenade exploded.

The MG 42 kept firing. Then the other grenades went off and the fuel cans caught fire, sending flames licking along the side of the truck. Smoke swirled out from the back, the machine gun stopped, and men vaulted from the truck only to be cut down by me as they stumbled on the hard ground.

The vehicle erupted in a violent explosion, blowing the sides off and sending a yellow fireball high into the night sky. The force knocked me flat on my back and burning debris filled the heavens like fireflies on a summer night. I wanted to get up, but it was so nice watching the lights that I just lay there a little longer.

CHAPTER FORTY-FOUR

ARMS LIFTED AND carried me. Fires raged. Ammo cooked off, a constant *pop pop pop* that was no less deadly than the heavy machine gun. Someone called my name, but they seemed so far away, I gave up trying to understand. I opened my eyes and watched the fireflies dance against the clouds. It was freezing cold and burning hot and nothing made sense.

I closed my eyes.

"Billy, wake up," I heard a voice say.

Kaz.

A hand dabbed at my forehead. The white cloth came away red. Yvonne?

"Where am I?" I managed to croak. I was laid out on a chair. Somewhere familiar.

"In the farmhouse," Kaz said. "You stopped them. We all did."

"How?" I couldn't quite form a decent question, but I waved my hand in Yvonne's direction.

"Be quiet for now," Kaz said. "You are concussed from the explosion. But you'll be fine." I had no problem being quiet. I closed my eyes. Or maybe I passed out, it was hard to tell.

"Okay," I said, blinking myself awake. Things seemed clearer than they had before. "How long was I out?"

"An hour," Kaz said as he checked his watch. "How do you feel?"

"Better," I said. "What happened?" Two young men were being bandaged in the living room of the farmhouse, next to a crackling fire. One with a leg wound and the other with his arm in a sling.

"Well, obviously one of the grenades went off prematurely," Kaz said. "You remember that?"

"Yeah, my memory's fine. But fill me in on what I don't know. What's Yvonne doing here? And who are these people?"

"We are Groupe G," Yvonne said, appearing from behind me. She wore a wool jacket with a Sten gun over her shoulder. "Groupe Général de Sabotage de Belgique, at your service."

"Groupe G is one of the most effective resistance groups in Belgium," Kaz said. "Mainly organized by students. I had no idea it was active in Spa. Or that Yvonne was part of it."

"We are everywhere," Yvonne said. "Toujours prêts. Always ready, oui?" Her companions agreed. Yvonne explained these were the only casualties. A few Germans may have escaped, but on foot and with their leader dead, there was little to fear from them.

"Grau? You're sure?" I asked.

"Yes," Kaz said. "I checked. You did a thorough job with the Citroën."

"So, Yvonne, you never got through to First Army?" I asked.

"I did. The telephone came on. I call, but no one will listen to me," she said. "They say I am a provocateur." She made a gesture of hanging up the telephone.

It turned out that the engine I heard was Yvonne's father's truck, carrying ten of the Groupe G fighters. They'd gotten out on the far side of the ridge and climbed down to keep watch. When the first truck went up and Kaz attacked the guards, they joined in and let themselves be known.

"I would not have been able to hold off all of those Germans without their help," Kaz said. "And we might not have survived if you hadn't set fire to that truck. From what I can tell from the remains, they had satchel charges and Panzerfausts in addition to that heavy machine gun."

"That would have been a big surprise at First Army," I said.

"Especially since the Hôtel des Bains in Chaudfontaine has a wide drive leading right up to it," Kaz said. "If they backed up that truck and let loose, it would have been a shooting gallery."

"If everyone's okay, can we get out of here?" I asked. I sat up, felt a little dizzy, but stayed upright.

"The jeep is right outside," Kaz said. "Some of the Groupe G lads brought it around when they went to fetch their truck."

"Allons-y," Yvonne said, and they grabbed their gear. Kaz helped me up and I managed to get to the door without collapsing.

The truck near the farmhouse was nothing but twisted metal and smoking embers. The second truck was still on fire, but just enough to light up the field. Yvonne's comrades were gathering up German arms and loading them into her father's truck.

"We shall not need them," she said as I eased myself into the jeep. "Dieu voulant."

"God willing," Kaz echoed.

"Yvonne!" called out a young woman from near the Citroën, where a group of them had been going through the vehicle. Yvonne hopped on board the jeep and Kaz drove us closer.

"Regardez!" the woman cried out, standing by the open trunk.

Inside were two sets of tubes covered in dark waterproof canvas. Just like the one Big Mike had for transporting the Klimt from England. Two sets of six, each secured by leather straps for carrying, and labeled with the address of Grau's art gallery in Basel, Switzerland.

"Artwork," I said. Kaz shone his flashlight over the tubes, searching for more information and finding none. He unscrewed the top of one tube and carefully withdrew a canvas. Even in the firelit darkness, the colors were spectacular.

"Claude Monet," Kaz said. "One of his water lily paintings."

Yvonne gasped, her hand over her mouth. The others gathered

around, standing silent in the face of such beauty amid this smoldering carnage.

"What will you do?" Yvonne asked as Kaz delicately placed the canvas back in its tube.

"We know just the person to bring this to," he said.

CHAPTER FORTY-FIVE

THE AFFAIR HAD been put together quickly. Rose Valland at the Jeu de Paume had been overjoyed to receive the twelve paintings and got right to work on trying to reunite them with their owners. If they still lived. She'd decided that the best way to do that was to host an exhibition and put them on display, hoping the publicity would draw attention.

Besides the Monet, there was a Vermeer, a Picasso, and a Chagall among others that I had to admit I didn't know. But they were all, in their own way, beautiful. I couldn't stop admiring them, amazed that with all the shooting and the number of bullet holes in that car, none of them had been damaged.

Tonight was the opening of the exhibition, an invitation-only event. Rose Valland was chatting with Colonel Baril, Inspector Fayard, and Harding in the foyer of the museum. Fayard had just filled me in on the fate of Commissaire Marcel Rochet. Baril had gone to see him in his office, and informed Rochet that he was to be arrested in one hour for his crimes in connection with the Syndicat. At that time, his pension would be revoked, and his wife left with nothing but shame.

As Baril waited outside, Rochet committed the first decent act he'd done in a while and put a bullet in his head.

Major Willoughby in Civil Affairs had been demoted and sent home. Probably punishment enough for a sap who was too full of himself to realize he'd been played.

"Billy, I'm headed out," Agent Salinger said, appearing at my side.

"Where to?" I asked.

"Back to the division," he said. "At least up there you know which direction to shoot in. I just came by to say thanks for getting the guy who killed Phil Williamson. Stay safe, willya?" I told him I planned on it. We shook hands and he left without a word. It had been the assassination of his buddy, CIC agent Williamson, that had started this whole affair. Grau had to pay the price for that death, as well as of Corporal Pascale and Joe Kiley. Even Jacques Delair, thief that he was, deserved consideration.

I watched Big Mike drink champagne with Rick Hansen and a bunch of his Monuments pals. This event was for them, officially, but it was also for Kaz's special guests. The young men and women of Groupe G. He'd arranged for them to come down by train and put them up in a hotel.

Yvonne linked her arm in his and they wandered among the paintings, the secret of the resistance unit's involvement strictly between them. The French government might have come down on Groupe G for fighting after the Liberation, which sounded crazy. But that was French politics for you.

Some of Mademoiselle Valland's Parisian friends were in attendance, including Stephan Narbonne, now cleared of any suspicion. When I'd greeted him earlier, he'd said nothing about his phony confession in the jail cell, but he introduced me to his sister, which was more than enough explanation.

I broke out of my reverie to fetch two glasses of champagne from the bar in the foyer. Then I went to find Diana.

Diana Seaton was about to go back on active duty with the Special Operations Executive, and I had pulled a few strings to get her air transport to Paris for this little soiree. Not to mention a couple of days of leave with me.

"Here," I said, handing her a glass as she stood in front of the Monet.

"Thank you, Billy. Where have you been?"

"Watching people. Thinking about the cost of all this," I said.

"Herr Grau certainly had thought about it," she said. "The man was about to make off with a fortune."

"Right. But I'm mainly thinking about those who didn't make it, and what we owe them. We stopped Grau, but the price was terrible."

"How did he even manage to portray himself as a Swiss art dealer?" Diana asked.

"Allen Dulles confirmed that the real Henri Grau died a year ago," I said. "Our fellow, the Fox, took over his identity. It was perfect, since the art gallery was still open, and with so little communication across the border, no one bothered to check his credentials."

"I'm so glad he doesn't have any of this to admire," she said. "It's so serene, isn't it?"

"It has to be," I said. "It had better be damned beautiful. All of it." We stood, staring at the water lilies. Flowers blossomed on lily pads, a promise of renewal. Diana rested her head on my shoulder.

"You're not just talking about the paintings," she said.

I looked at her. She understood. I meant the war, and what it did to so many people. What it did to me.

What it did to us.

When this is over, it damn well better have been worth it. We deserved a world worthy of both the sacrifice of the dead and these exquisite paintings. We deserved a world of love and beauty.

I took Diana by the hand, and in silence we walked out into the cold Paris night.

HISTORICAL NOTE

THIS BOOK BEGINS on the eve of what we now know as the Battle of the Bulge, a titanic offensive launched in great secrecy by over two hundred thousand German troops. They came through the Ardennes, the densely forested area of World War II's Western Front that borders eastern Belgium, Luxembourg, and northeastern France.

At first, the Allies called the attack the Ardennes Offensive or the von Rundstedt Offensive. It was only in early January 1945 that American war correspondent Larry Newman, noting the shape of the fifty-by-seventy-mile-wide salient, coined the now-famous name—the Battle of the Bulge.

Except for a few intelligence officers, no one in the Allied high command had any inkling of an enemy attack. Colonel Monk Dickson of First Army was one of those who predicted the offensive, but as noted in the story, even he took leave in Paris for his birthday and was not present when the attack began. I tried to give some sense of how GIs at the front must have felt as the onslaught erupted, having no idea of what was happening anywhere except directly in front of them.

Casualties were high. First and Third US Armies listed a total of 75,482 casualties (8,407 killed, 46,170 wounded, and 20,905 missing). Estimates of German losses vary, most totaling about 100,000.

The precipitous departure of First Army headquarters from

Spa, and the incapacitation of the commanding general did occur, as reported in the US Army Center of Military History's *A Command Post at War: First Army Headquarters in Europe, 1943–1945*, by David W. Hogan, Jr. That official account stated, "In the rush to evacuate, at least some of the staff left behind working phones, secret papers, and even situation maps."

The Einheit Stielau commando unit was part of the larger Operation Greif, commanded by Otto Skorzeny. His plan was to use American vehicles with Germans in American uniforms to break through the lines and capture bridges across the Meuse River.

That larger operation failed. However, Einheit Stielau succeeded far beyond Skorzeny's expectations, with the forty-four Germans masquerading as American MPs spreading confusion and fear greatly in excess of their numbers. As described, a jeep team was captured on the first day, alerting American forces to the ruse but causing slowdowns at roadblocks as nervous sentries questioned soldiers on baseball, Hollywood stars, and state capitals. One general was detained when he correctly stated that Springfield was the capital of Illinois. The GI interrogating him was certain it was Chicago.

The captured German MPs were also responsible for the fear that Skorzeny was targeting General Eisenhower for assassination or capture. In their training camp, the Einheit Stielau men did not know their target or mission. A rumor sprang up that they were going after Eisenhower. Skorzeny decided not to say anything, thereby adding credence to the rumor. He knew that some of his men were likely to be captured and would talk, if only to brag about their vital mission. That is exactly what happened.

My notion of a stay-behind network of German agents within the Parisian criminal underworld is fictional, but I believe quite in line with the thinking that created Einheit Stielau.

David Niven may seem an unlikely supporting character, but he did serve in the British Army, having trained with the commandos and commanded a Phantom unit. By 1944 he was on British general Montgomery's intelligence staff. Niven did leave Hollywood immediately upon the outbreak of war, disobeying a British embassy directive for English actors to remain and do their bit making films in support of the war effort. At a dinner party in 1940, Winston Churchill singled out Niven, saying: "Young man, you did a fine thing to give up your film career to fight for your country. Mark you, had you not done so it would have been despicable."

By all reports, Niven was levelheaded under fire and in difficult situations. The quips in this book about Errol Flynn and Ginger Rogers are actual quotes made in circumstances similar to those described. But details about his wartime service are sparse, which is how he preferred it.

This is what he had to say on the matter:

> I will, however, tell you just one thing about the war, my first story and my last. I was asked by some American friends to search out the grave of their son near Bastogne. I found it where they told me I would, but it was among 27,000 others, and I told myself that here, Niven, were 27,000 reasons why you should keep your mouth shut after the war.

The Royal Signals Golden Arrow wireless station was a powerful mobile radio and telegraph unit that operated in Italy and northwest Europe, providing top-secret communications for the Allied command.

The GHQ Liaison Regiment—known as Phantom—was a special reconnaissance unit of the British Army. The Phantom patrols were charged with providing information from the front lines directly to higher headquarters. After the British Phantom patrols proved to be highly useful during D-Day, arrangements were made to extend their use within American units.

The Monuments, Fine Arts, and Archives program (MFAA) under the Civil Affairs and Military Government Sections of the Allied armies was created to protect cultural property in war zones. The MFAA was also involved in finding works of art looted by the Nazis and returning them to their rightful owners. In researching these activities, I was struck by how often artwork was abandoned as the Germans retreated through France, and how this may have created all sorts of opportunities for nefarious characters. That is how the notion of trafficking in artwork to fund and cover a Nazi operation came to mind.

Jerome David Salinger served as a Counter Intelligence Corps agent with the 4th Infantry Division. He was at Utah Beach on D-Day and served for the duration of the war, even volunteering to stay on for the postwar denazification program. He had been present at the liberation of a concentration camp and was hospitalized for several weeks with combat fatigue.

Rose Valland was a truly heroic character. As a member of the French Resistance, she kept secret records of artworks plundered by the Germans and saved thousands of priceless objects. She was put in charge of the Jeu de Paume museum, which the Nazis used as a transit point for artwork stolen from museums and private citizens. Based on her underground work, the French Senate later reported that she was directly responsible for the location of sixty thousand looted works of art, with most being returned to France by 1950.

ACKNOWLEDGMENTS

MY WIFE, DEBORAH Mandel, helped shape and improve this story by listening to me read chapters aloud as they were completed. We work through issues of clarity, conciseness, and consistency, sharpening the manuscript in the process. She also provided outstanding support as first reader and editor.

Liza Mandel and Michael Gordon, my beta readers, provided important feedback and spot those pesky typos and errors that eluded detection.

Paula Munier and Gina Panettieri of Talcott Notch Literary Services are terrifically supportive and hardworking guides when it comes to the myriad complexities of the publishing industry. I know they've got my back.

The staff at Soho Press does a fantastic job of bringing Billy Boyle into the world through editing, book design, jacket art, and publicity. But none of this would be the case if not for the cofounder of Soho Press, Laura Hruska, who took a chance on an unknown and unpublished author when she offered me a contract to publish the first two novels in the series. She became my editor, instructing me how to write and edit like a professional. Laura passed away in 2010, but her teachings live on.

I give thanks to booksellers at independent bookstores across the country. Much of the success of this series is due to their extraordinary efforts to match the right book with the right reader. I am indebted to all of you who have read any book in this series, and especially to those of you who have been at Billy's side from the beginning. You're why Billy and his gang are still here, whispering in my ear.